Harps Upon The Willows
The Johnston Family of the Old Northwest

Harps Upon The Willows
The Johnston Family
of the Old Northwest

Marjorie Cahn Brazer

edited by
The Historical Society of Michigan
Ann Arbor, Michigan

All rights reserved. Printed in the United States of America. No part of this book may be reproduced in any manner whatsoever without written permission except in the case of brief quotations embodied in critical articles and reviews. For information address the Historical Society of Michigan, 2117 Washtenaw Avenue, Ann Arbor, MI 48104-4599.

ISBN: 1-880311-02-X

Library of Congress Catalog Card Number: 92-073235

Copyright 1993 by the
Marjorie C. Brazer Trust
Ann Arbor, Michigan

First Edition

Table of Contents

Acknowledgments vii
Introduction ix
Preface xiii
Epigraph xvii

Part One

1. Expectations, Great and Small 1
2. Paddle, Portage, and Posé 19
3. Fateful Island 33
4. Where the Waters Tumble 51
5. Lifestyle 63
6. War 91
7. Aftermath 113
8. Sainte Marie Joins the U.S. 139
9. Generations Arrive and Depart 169

Illustrations

Part Two

10. Of Morals, Rivalries and Village Tempests 205
11. Widening Circles 227
12. Chancery As a Way of Life 249
13. Restlessness 275
14. The Wheel Turns 297
15. Accounts Closed 317
16. Expectations, Lost and Attained 337

Epilogue 353
Endnotes 361
Bibliography 417
Index 425

Acknowledgments

Any publication involves the labor of many, and that was especially true of this book. Marjorie Brazer first contacted the Historical Society of Michigan about publishing *Harps Upon the Willows* a number of years ago, and its completion became her goal as she heroically fought an eventual losing battle with cancer.

We received her manuscript shortly after her death. Completing the publication of a book is difficult; it is doubly so without the author's input, suggestions and assistance. That process was made easier with the assistance of many people, and I want to mention them here.

Ann Fowler, Marj's dear friend, and HSM staff member Deborah Carter Day spent innumerable hours working through the text and putting it into publishable shape. Another of Marj's friends, Joan Blos, also provided insights and suggestions. Elizabeth Jones, an Alma College student, compiled the index. Nancy Marshall, HSM administrative secretary, worked on text editing and preparation as well.

The text, footnotes and bibliography were carefully reviewed by David Armour, deputy superintendent, Mackinac State Historic Parks; Tammy Stone-Gordon, a Michigan State University graduate student; and Florence Surovell, of Alexandria, Virginia. The finished text owes much to their diligence.

Finally, we thank Marj's daughter, Mara, for her support and unflagging dedication to ensuring that her mother's work will be enjoyed and appreciated by so many through this book.

Thomas L. Jones
Historical Society of Michigan

Introduction

The bookstores are full of steamy romances about adventurers who found love and excitement on the frontier of America. Frequently the novel involves a high born Englishman who is captivated by the charms of an Indian beauty. At the conclusion of the story the novelist leaves them to live happily ever after.

Yet, it has often been said that "truth is stranger than fiction" and so it is in the life of the Irishman John Johnston. Leaving his home in northern Ireland he came to America to seek his fortune. After several false starts he became involved in the fur trade which took him to an isolated trading post on the cold and rocky shores of Lake Superior. There he did meet a young Indian maiden who captured his heart and revolutionized his life.

Unlike so many wilderness loves and liaisons the marriage of John Johnston and Oshaw-guscody-way-quay, Woman of the Green Glade, whom he named Susan, lasted a lifetime and created a family of fascinating individuals. Settling in 1792 at Sault Ste. Marie, one of the major crossroads of the upper Great Lakes, the Johnston family left an indelible mark on the history of a vast region.

John Johnston had a literary bent and wrote more than 2,000 lines of poetry plus other descriptions and reports. He also, at great expense, maintained a sizeable library which he used to teach his eight children his religious and cultural values. Susan also was well versed in the oral literature of her Ojibway heritage, and her illustrious father Waub-o-jeeg composed poetry in his native tongue. Within the Johnston family these two traditions merged and enriched each other.

The literary propensity of the family was reinforced by its incorporation of the self-taught scholar Henry R. Schoolcraft who married the daughter, Jane Johnston, in 1823. Henry had wide ranging interest and loved to write. He also was somewhat of a pack rat who threw very little away. Primarily through his efforts many of the manuscripts documenting the Johnston family have survived. These records have made possible the telling of the Johnston story in a depth not possible for most frontier families.

Marjorie Cahn Brazer has made good use of these documents and many others to skillfully weave a tale that will delight and enthrall the reader. Within its pages you will meet a broad cast of fascinating characters, not only the family members, but most people of note who passed through the upper Great Lakes from the 1790's to the 1840's. The author weaves original letters into the text so people speak in their own words.

Life on the frontier swirled with tension and uncertainty, particularly at Sault Ste. Marie which was on the border between Canada and the fledgling United States. Though the Johnstons lived on the American side, John's loyalty was always with the British king. When war broke out in 1812 the family was caught up in the hostilities and lost nearly everything except the house in which they lived. For years to come the family sought to recoup their losses by appeals to governments on both sides of the border.

As American farmers flooded into the Great Lakes region the American government negotiated with the native peoples to sell their lands. Since Susan was Ojibway and all the children were half Indian, the family had a large stake in the treaty settlements. Son-in-law Henry Schoolcraft, a U. S. Indian Agent, sought to protect the best interests of the family and find government jobs for many of his relatives.

Family tensions were not always resolved peaceably, particularly when coupled with the hope of money from a legacy in Ireland. After John Johnston died in 1828, his children feuded and fussed about what they considered their just share of the riches which they hoped would come to them. Most of their hopes were either dashed or squandered by a family that had a difficult time coming to terms with its dual cultural heritage and the pressures of a changing society.

Yet, the family, held together by their common blood and the influence of their remarkable parents, has left a rich legacy for the upper Great Lakes region.

David A. Armour
Deputy Superintendent
Mackinac State Historic Parks

Preface

The American frontier appears in art and story as a barren rangeland, relieved by rocky hillocks and cut by steep-sided canyons, over which desperadoes gallop on horseback to and from brawling, wooden-storefronted and sidewalked towns, while heroes do battle with their Indian enemies. But that is merely the last frontier. The first frontier after independence was the Old Northwest—lush pine and birch forest, laced with rushing rivers, surrounding vast inland seas. There the frontiersmen paddled canoes. And they rarely fought the Indians—they traded and married with them instead.

Fur was the prize on that old frontier, and it attracted its share of lawless, vulgar adventurers. But the Old Northwest was a peculiar frontier in that, from the beginning, it also attracted another kind of man. The Jesuit priests who came to it first were Frenchmen of advanced education and delicate tastes. Anomalies on the frontier, they were eventually driven out, not by the rigors of their difficult lives or the scalping knives of the natives, but by the politics of their own countrymen—they interfered with the fur trade.

Yet the fur trade, too, spawned gentleman adventurers as well as the crude, if lovable, oafs who paddled the canoes and trapped with the Indians. Men who wore broadcloth, lace and periwigs in the salons of Europe or the counting houses of Montreal, who dined to the music of Mozart and quoted Dr. Johnson, also voyaged thousands of miles in a cockle shell canoe, wintered in a bark hut in the howling Northwest, haggled with the unwashed, unlettered natives, and even married them—at least temporarily. To relieve the isolated boredom of those desolate snowbound days and nights they brought their books with them—Swift, Gibbon, Scott, and lesser lights whose popularity was more temporary. After several years in the wild, most of them returned with the fortunes they had made (or without the ones they lost) to the civilized East whence they had come. They left their Indian women and children and settled down in the valley of the St. Lawrence or the Hudson with respectable Anglo-Saxon wives, to manage their enterprises from behind a desk.

One of these did not follow the pattern. He was, to be sure, an educated gentleman of polished tastes, yet he chose to remain in the wilderness—to establish there an outpost of enlightenment and refinement, a miniature Irish country estate in the primeval forest. The place he selected was a strategic one—the Falls of St. Mary, by which Lake Superior empties into the lower Great Lakes. A remarkable procession of people passed by his door during his thirty-five years of residence there—the mighty and the ordinary, the saint and the sinner, the brilliant and the dull. He knew them all and most of them found hospitality at his table. To tell the story of John Johnston is to pull together a thousand diverse threads of Northwest history—of the explorers, the fur traders, the geologists, the government officials, the clergy, the merchants, the soldiers. His residence at Sault Ste. Marie spanned the transition from the raw frontier of the British period and the infancy of the United States to the settlement of a modern midwestern county with all the trappings of civil government, the years 1793 to 1828.

But John Johnston's story is more than the account of a rather remarkable personality, by which the history of a region may be told. The meaning of his life for our time lies in his marriage and the family he founded. There were many white men who married Indian women, but few Indian women possessed the capacities of Susan Johnston. Even fewer were the mixed marriages which endured, and which appeared to combine so successfully the best of two disparate cultures. But did it? The high esteem which John Johnston held for his wife and the cultural traditions of her people was evident from the values and education he transmitted to his children.

And she was able to administer a home in high European style, while retaining the dignity of her own cultural integrity and passing that on to her offspring. But what of those children?

The four boys and four girls were brought up in the mixed heritage of a bilingual household, learning how to fashion moccasins and mocuks, while they read Scott and Burke. They were devout Protestants, but conversant with the ancient lore of the Ojibways. They traveled, dressed fashionably, were literary in their written expression, and were at ease with the highborn, yet they conformed comfortably to the canoe and the campsite, understood the mysteries of nature and shared ideas with their native friends and relations. In short, the environment they were raised in offered the best of both worlds. Did they, then, exemplify the highest promise of a melding of two races and two cultures? The answer, like their parentage, was mixed. In terms of worldly status and achievement the women did, the men did not. The three girls who married, married well into white society, attaining dignified and even important positions. The men never quite made it. For them, the personal conflicts of a bi-racial heritage seemed to impede advancement, even in the relatively fluid society of nineteenth century America.

Unlike the treatises in the Johnston family library, this book makes no attempt to draw moral conclusions or make value judgments. What really conditioned and motivated the personalities in the story can only be inferred from their letters and from what others said about them. The bi-racial heritage both enriched their lives and imposed a hurdle which only a few could jump. Whatever their individual destinies, the Johnstons as a family, were one of the most unusual to stamp the American frontier.

Marjorie Cahn Brazer

Epigraph

By the rivers of Babylon,
There we sat down, yea, we wept,
When we remembered Zion.
We hanged our harps
Upon the willows in the midst thereof,
For there they that carried us away captive required of us a song,
And they that wasted us required of us mirth, saying,
"Sing us one of the songs of Zion."
How shall we sing the Lord's song
In a strange land?
If I forget thee, O Jerusalem,
Let my right hand forget her cunning,
If I do not remember thee,
Let my tongue cleave to the roof of my mouth,
If I prefer not Jerusalem above my chief and joy.

Psalm 137

They tell me, the men with a white-white face
Belong to a purer, nobler race;
But why, if they do, and it may be so,
Do their tongues cry, "yes"—and their actions, "no"?

They tell me, that white is a heavenly hue,
And it may be so, but the sky is blue;
And the first men—as our old men say,
Had earth-brown skins, and were made of clay.

Ojibway Song

Expectations, Great and Small

PART I

Chapter One

Expectations, Great and Small

During the latter part of August the southerly breeze moving up New York Bay from the ocean first crosses the low marshes and sand banks of the Jersey shore. There it heats up from the land, bringing the dog days of summer to the island city. But it is a fair wind for a sailing vessel passing through the Narrows to her landfall. And so it was for the *Clara* on the 24th of August, 1790. No Lady of Liberty stretching her arm of welcome to the young man stationed expectantly at the rail existed then, nor did the spires of a glass and concrete fairyland rising from the soft haze of a summer sunset. But to his intent gaze as the ship swung around Governor's Island "the city, like a splendid amphitheater, burst upon the view [and he] was absolutely transported with pleasure and delight."[1]

Eager though he was to step ashore and begin his new life after almost two months at sea, John Johnston slept on board one more night so that in the morning "I might put my foot on American ground the day of my birth; having just attained my 28th year."[2] He would use the quiet hours while the ship rode to her moorings in the North River to reflect on where he had been and what he had done during the first 28 years of his life, even if he could not truly imagine where the future was taking him. The stocky, red-headed young Irishman, with high forehead and bright blue eyes,[3] was a thoughtful person, with an unshakable Presbyterian faith in the good will of Providence.

Like so many other young men of his generation, who were carrying the torch of empire to the far Occident and the distant Orient, he came of good family, not exactly of the aristocracy, but with some excellent connections thereto. Although he could barely remember his father, he knew something of his ancestors for several generations. The first John Johnston of record originated in Scotland, from which he emigrated after clan warfare culminated in the massacre at Glencoe in 1692. However pretentious or otherwise his connections may have been in Scotland, once in England he married into the eminently genteel house of Leathes, of Bury St. Edmonds, Suffolk. His son, William, grandfather to the voyaging John, established the Irish branch of the family after he acquired one estate in County Antrim and another in County Down. In 1733 he sold the latter to raise capital for a rather novel venture for a gentleman of his day. Moving his family to Belfast, he undertook to construct and manage a water supply system for that city; he would be known henceforth as "Pipewater Johnston."

The Earl of Donnegal owned the city of Belfast and most of its surrounding countryside, and no one could undertake such an enterprise except at his pleasure. Accordingly, the Earl granted a 41-year lease to William Johnston for "all rivers, waters, brooks, wells and water streams adjacent and continuous to the Town of Belfast," except what he had already granted to mill operator George McCartney, for an annual rental of 21 shillings. So long as the Donnegals obtained their water without charge, they were pleased to encourage the venture by exacting only a nominal rent.[4] Pipewater Johnston laid an elaborate network of wooden conduits from the wells south of town to a large number of houses, but despite the encouragement of the Lords of the Manor the project was never a financial success.[5] As early as 1753 Johnston offered it to anybody who would accept it for a period of not less than seven years. No takers appeared at that time, but in 1762 James Hall sublet the works and assumed its management.[6]

By this time old Pipewater had passed on, leaving five sons and four daughters. Three of the girls married well, and all of the boys entered military careers after receiving a good education, one as a chaplain, and three attaining lieutenant-colonel rank before they died. John's father, William, the second youngest son, was the only one to enter the Navy, serving as a midshipman at Louisburg in Nova Scotia in 1759. At the conclusion of the Seven Years' War, however, he resigned his commission and won the appointment of surveyor of Port Rush near Coleraine on the northern coast of Ireland. He had by then a wife, Elizabeth McNeil of Coulreshkan (Wheatland in English), a daughter, Jane, and son John, born August 25, 1762.

Grandfather Pipewater's Antrim County estate had passed to older sons, but William received as a marriage portion his bride's interest in the McNeil family estate of Craige, at the apex of a triangle formed by Port Rush and Coleraine. Here John grew up with his brother and three sisters—Eliza, William, and Charlotte were born later—in the beautiful, rolling countryside of the Antrim coast, just three miles from the fabulous basaltic formations of the Giant's Causeway.

At the age of seven, like all proper young gentleman, his family sent him off to boarding school in Coleraine. He would not see his father again. One day that fall William rode out to visit a friend across the River Bush. Returning home later than he expected to, he found the tide had come in where he usually forded the river. Rather than go two miles out of his way to the bridge, he swam his horse across and caught a cold, which developed into pneumonia. He lingered for a couple of months, then died at the age of 43, leaving his widow and five children in difficult financial circumstances.

Elizabeth McNeil Johnston's major source of income was the modest rents from Craige; the half interest in the unprofitable waterworks, to which she fell heir, yielded little. But she found an unexpected and invaluable helpmeet in her late husband's unmarried sister, Nancy, who came to live at Craige, contribute her income, and assist Elizabeth in the rearing of the five children.

Although Elizabeth was anxious that her older son receive as good a start in life as she could give him, financial constraints forced her to withdraw him from school after three years. And none too soon, in the opinion of Nancy Johnston, a woman of some intellect. Examining her nephew upon his return home from school, she was horrified to discover that he had learned neither Latin nor English grammatically and could barely write at all. "So much for an Irish Latin school," John later recalled, "and that too kept by an Episcopalian clergyman!"[7]

Now, at age ten, life assumed a pattern for John that he was old enough to remember in later years. His mother and aunt hired a tutor to teach him writing and arithmetic, but his devoted aunt took upon herself his instruction in English grammar as well as ancient and modern history. In her firm, yet kindly, way she introduced all the children, but most especially John, to the magic world of fine literature. Every day after tea the ladies and young girls sat with their handiwork, while John, and later William, read aloud from the classics of prose, verse, drama and history. This might go on for two or three hours. Elizabeth and Nancy took care to avoid monotony by appropriate interruptions to point out the subtleties or beauty of particular passages and engage the children in discussion of the vices and virtues of history's characters. One tragic episode marred the tranquility of those childhood years at Craige—the death from smallpox of John's adored baby sister, Charlotte, at the age of seven. He never afterward could speak of her without emotion catching his voice.

But childhood passes inevitably to adolescence, and with that transition John Johnston found the need to break away from the cloying influence of a house full of females. The servants, the peasant boys round about, and the "low characters" of the town were all willing to help a young lad sow his wild oats. John took to spending most of his time "coursing with greyhounds, shooting, fishing . . . and still more debasing gratifications."[8] This was preferable to the stuffy atmosphere of Reverend Robert Sturrock's Academy of White Park, only a mile from home, where he declined the opportunity to study along with his respectable neighborhood friends—boys like Edmund McNaughton, who would become M.P. from Antrim and a Lord of the Treasury; his brother, Francis, who would later be knighted; and Robert Stuart, who would become known to history as Lord Castlereagh. And John Johnston—what and who would he become?

His patrimony, for better or for worse, lay in Belfast, in those subterranean jointed pipes of hollowed elm tree trunks. There his mother sent him in 1779 at age 17 to take his place in the world as manager of the water works. Perhaps he could restore something of the family fortunes and make a responsible man of himself at the same time. Perhaps she worried too much about his character. John rose to the challenge and did, in fact, improve the operation of the works, or at least its financial management. But the wild oats were still there, and with money in his pocket and leisure time on his hands the big city offered a much more interesting theater of operations than had the village of Coleraine.

In his later reminiscences he was teasingly nonspecific, but often alluded to a foolish life of wasted youth over the next decade. What dark and dastardly deeds did he wish to forget? While he was learning the effective business management demonstrated in his later career, was he also gambling? Drinking heavily? Duelling? Chasing whores, ostensibly respectable or not? And why did this young man, whose romantic and domestic inclinations would also be revealed later, not marry during these years? Because of some hopeless, tragic love affair, or because the life of a roue´ did not include marriage? He never explained, but only declared that it was the love of reading, so firmly implanted by his devoted aunt, that saved him from complete dissipation. No doubt he also began to develop his own penchant for self expression in verse, but no Johnston literary fragment remains from that period.

Nor did the ten years he lived and worked in Belfast damage the religious faith that had been inculcated since childhood. Indeed, his trust in God grew and flourished, as experience weakened his faith in men—especially "noble" men. Grandfather had been able to obtain only a lease for the water works because the then Lord Donnegal was insane, and his trustees were not empowered to make outright grants. But, according to family history, "the next heir pledged himself and family at a public dinner given by the town to my grandfather, that the works should be granted in perpetuity as soon as the circumstances of the [Donnegal] family would admit of it. But this word of honor, so publicly plighted was afterward shamefully broken."[9] The Earl had renewed the first lease early, at about the time of the sub-lease to Hall, but the second one was due to expire by the early 1790s. When John approached the present Earl, while his Lordship was on a visit to his Irish estates during the latter 1780s, he not only failed to obtain fulfillment of the promise but the Earl denied renewal of the lease as well.

John attributed this renege to artifice and pressure brought to bear on the weak Earl by the corporation of Belfast, which hoped to increase its wealth and influence by acquiring the works. This is not likely the case, however. In addition to the water works' erratic record of profitability over the years, its product had deteriorated drastically. Families who could afford it bought their drinking water from casks delivered by cart from springs that yielded a purer supply than the wells and natural water courses used by Pipewater's system. Even the Charitable Society of Belfast got into the business, as a means of raising money for its philanthropy. And so successful was it that when the Johnston's lease did expire, his lordship granted responsibility for supplying the town with water not to the Belfast Corporation, but to the Charitable Society. Under an arrangement unique in the history of the British Isles, Belfast's water came to be supplied and managed by the "welfare department." That was not so illogical at the time as it sounds today, for the rich could buy their water from casks, while the poor were obliged to suffer the inconveniences and risks of the public supply.[10] Apparently, John got out just in time. In September, 1790, after his arrival in the New World, the *Belfast News-Letter* carried the following comment:

> There are few even of the most insignificant villages as ill supplied with water as Belfast: a town where this great necessity of life is equally scarce and bad—and its conveyance through the

different streets imperfect, and the pipes in general decayed and rotten. The health and comfort of so populous a place are objects of such importance that it is the duty of every inhabitant frequently to point out the abuse.[11]

When John's advance application for a renewal of the lease failed, he faced a crisis. Career opportunities were scarce in Ireland for impecunious' young men with limited connections of influence. After much thought he decided to join the growing procession of his contemporaries who were forsaking Ireland for the promise of fortune beyond the sea. First, however, he launched his younger brother, William, financing his passage to New York for apprenticeship to a merchant. By the fall of 1789 John was ready to take steps on his own behalf, beginning with Lord McCartney's visit to his castle at Lisanore near Craige. His Lordship had been a schoolmate of John's Johnston uncles, and Aunt Nancy supplied John with a letter of introduction. Explaining his business disappointments in Ireland, John expressed a wish to try his luck in India, from which Lord McCartney had recently returned.

In as kindly a way as possible, his Lordship explained that "he had not advanced himself in the world without being under obligations to many friends, whose services it was his first duty to repay;"[12] at the moment 26 such persons were waiting in line. If John was determined to go to India, nevertheless, the Earl would do what he could, but he could not promise much. He then went on to point out that one heard a great deal about people who returned from India with large fortunes, but very little about "the hundreds who fell victims to the climate, and the excesses into which young men were liable to be led in such a voluptuous country."[13] If they did not return broken, they died young.

John was convinced. How about Canada? Could Lord McCartney give him a letter to Lord Dorchester, another classmate and currently Governor General there? Not only would his Lordship be glad to write such a letter, although he was not intimately acquainted with Lord Dorchester, but he would obtain letters from two of the

Governor General's closest friends, Lord Liverpool and Brook Watson, with whom Lord McCartney was well acquainted. With these valuable references, Canada it would be.

The next step was to unload the moribund lease and obtain enough cash to reach Canada and tide him over until he began to earn an income again. Lord Donnegal authorized his agent for Belfast, Mr. Alexander, to negotiate and to give John £400 on the unexpired portion of the lease, with the remaining value to be paid later to his family. Apparently Lord Donnegal never did this. But with the girls married and William and John off in North America, his mother could live in reasonable comfort on the income from Craige. John was able to embark on the *Clara* in June of 1790 with his mind at ease so far as his family was concerned, and with little regret at leaving the scene of his mysteriously unspecified "follies and misfortunes."[14] He would no longer look back. Although the future was uncertain, and he would undoubtedly feel strange in a raw, new land, he would put his trust in the Almighty and look ahead with optimism.

The voyage turned out to be a pleasant one, after initial days of utter misery. Although John had grown up near the sea, he had never sailed upon it, and for those awful first two days he lay limp on the cabin floor. Then he suddenly felt ravenously hungry, ordered a beefsteak and porter, and never afterward suffered *mal de mer*. Shipboard life settled into the customary routine, including much eating and drinking among the four men who messed at Captain Collins' table, two of whom were old friends of John's and the third a Scotsman from Edinburgh. In fact, they enjoyed such liberal rations of wine, porter and spirits that John sent as a gift to the steerage passengers the large hamper of wine, spruce beer, oranges and lemons one of his friends had sent him for *bon voyage*.

Adventures occurred as well. The ship had barely left Belfast when a British naval officer detained her for several hours off Carickfergus, while his men searched for escaped sailors. Despite the captain's protestations that he was harboring no one, it appeared that the officer might detain the ship all night until she lost her fair wind and tide. John took it upon himself to draft a letter to his friend, the Marquis of Devonshire, which he read aloud and prepared to send ashore by someone who had decided to leave the ship. Whether this eloquent complaint to a high place persuaded "the man of brief authority,"[15] or whether a snack and a pint of half-and-half mellowed him, he shortly thereafter took his departure with civil wishes for the *Clara's* safe passage.

And safe it was until a 60-gun ship of war appeared off the Azores and began to follow. First it displayed a Spanish flag, then hoisted the French colors. The captain concluded that it was, in fact, Algerian, and altered course to sail before the wind while the ship fired at them from the rear. Fortunately, the *Clara* was a light vessel that sailed well, and overnight she managed to outdistance the "enemy," which finally abandoned the chase. One of the passengers, a Reverend Lindsay from Scotland, offensively rebuked Captain Collins for his cowardice in running away and refused to accept the captain's courteous explanation that his first responsibility lay to the safety of his passengers and the interests of the ship's owners. John was delighted when the Reverend Mr. Lindsay got his comeuppance some time later and could still chuckle at the episode 40 years afterward.

While crossing the Gulf Stream the ship was overtaken by a heavy gale, with mountainous seas. During the night the cabin windows were stove in, and two or three feet of water sloshed around on the floor. Trunks and boxes broke from their moorings, and the occupants of the lower berths were likewise afloat with all the mess.

> Some were praying aloud, others confessing their sins, others screaming from fear and pain, whilst escaping from drowning in their berths. Amongst the latter sufferers was . . . Mrs. Lindsay. . . . Whilst sprawling on the floor she was struck in the head by an iron bound trunk, which laid it open for about three inches. When candles came down, the dead lights lashed in, the scene exhibited such a mixture of frightful and ludicrous as fairly

surpassed description; poor Mrs. Lindsay, who at best might have passed for one of the witches in Macbeth, now looked a perfect Hecate; her matted locks dripping with gore, and her vulgar unmeaning countenance distorted into a most unearthly grin. No one pitied her or her fanatic husband.[16]

After this the passage was uneventful, and the birthday disembarkation at New York brought John a joyful reunion with his brother. William was now in a mercantile partnership with Samuel Hill, brother to a friend of John's. They were doing quite well, and later on the partnership would move to Albany. John spent a happy week in New York, staying at the Water Street home of the Sadlers, who were distant relations to his mother. The people he met in this rustic capital city were kind and surprisingly urbane. At Trinity Church on Sunday he saw President Washington in a nearby pew and regretted that he would not be staying in town long enough for the opportunity offered to meet him. But the sloop, *Hibernia*, in which John had booked passage, was ready to sail for Albany; a long trip still lay ahead of him.

It is quite likely that the two brothers never saw one another again. No record of a second visit exists before William's untimely death in Santo Domingo, while on a voyage to the Caribbean. Nor is it known just when this sad event occurred, but along with news of his passing, John learned that the larcenous captain of William's ship had simply appropriated his trunk, his papers, and his money.[17]

Three days up the majestic Hudson River, stopping frequently to take on and discharge passengers, brought the sloop to Albany, where John took a room at Lewis's Hotel, the best in town. Four or five days elapsed before he was able to arrange the next leg of his journey. Civilization and its conveniences were receding. How different he found the country from anything he had known. He had his first brush with wilderness conditions the day an afternoon stroll took him as far as a mile from his lodgings. Suddenly five or six armed men emerged from the woods, startling in their uncouth appearance.

They were friendly enough, however, and warned John, whom they recognized as a stranger, about wandering so far from the city unarmed. They were stalking a pack of wolves which had attacked a man on horseback at the very spot on which they were standing; the speed of his horse was the only thing that saved him. John hurried back to town.

Having made the acquaintance of a Mr. Bedient, of Boston, who was also on his way to Montreal, John joined him in hiring a wagon to take them to Fort Edward on the Hudson River. The countryside was partially cultivated until they came to the outpost of Saratoga, "where the scenery was dark and gloomy, and the roads most intolerably bad, being made of round logs laid beside each other, forming causeways often for miles. These roads I was informed were made by General Burgoyne in his ill-conducted, and consequently ill-fated expedition." Looking at the battleground John felt the pain and humiliation of his defeated countrymen, which he was forced to conceal, "as no one would have sympathized with me."[18] This loyalty to the British Crown would cast a long shadow over his life in the years to come. But ultimately, in a letter of remembrance written almost 40 years later, he would be able to say of the United States, "How different are my present ideas on the subject, when pride and prejudice no longer blind my eyes, and I can trace the hand of Omnipotence, battling the efforts of tyrannic power to strangle the infant Hercules, who is destined to give law to the western world!"[19]

From Fort Edward the travellers hired a *bateau* to take them down Lake George. On this beautiful trip they stopped at the only house then on the lake, where John met an American hunter for the first time. The man had just returned from three months in the woods, and at first sight John thought him to be an Indian, so strange was his dress. Cooper's description of Leather Stocking suited him exactly, as John later recalled. It was a style and manner to which he would grow intimately accustomed.

The trip required a day's layover at the inn at Ticonderoga before another boat could be hired to take them the length of Lake Champlain in a three-day sail to

St. Jean, Quebec, on the Richelieu River. One stopover on the way occasioned the only contrast with the old country that appears in Johnston's memoir of this trip. "We passed the first night at a blacksmith and farmer's, where we had everything clean and comfortable, the contrast between their mode of living and the beings we call farmers in the north of Ireland was painfully striking."[20] The two men arrived at St. Jean after the commandant had gone to bed and had to spend an hour in the guardhouse before permission was granted for them to seek an inn. When they finally met Lieutenant Boyd the next day, he turned out to be an acquaintance from home, the first of many John would encounter on this distant continent. They spent the day together before John's departure in a *calash* which drove him to LePrarie.

From there he hired a canoe to take him across the St. Lawrence River to Montreal, but the canoeman landed first at a small island, where he disappeared into the woods. After about an hour John became suspicious and went looking for him. Finding the man skulking aimlessly about, John was convinced that he was planning to rob his passenger. He forced the sullen suspect back to the canoe and to get underway by "swearing that if he did not take me to the mainland I would split him to the teeth with my paddle."[21] The threat worked, but still John took no chances. When they landed he made the lout march ahead where he could be watched, burdened by the luggage on his shoulder to prevent any surprise moves. Thus occurred his grand entrance into Canada's second city.

O'Sullivan's Coffee House doubled as a hotel in those days, and John was glad to settle down for a few days after more than two weeks of constant travel by numerous conveyances. His trip was still not ended, as he had another 160 miles to go to Quebec, but a few days rest allowed him to recover from the devastation of his enormous crop of mosquito bites. His enjoyment of the frontier city of Montreal was further enhanced the next evening when yet another old friend from home walked into O'Sullivan's coffee room.

Andrew Todd was looking well and talked with enthusiasm about his business activities here in the provinces. His Uncle Isaac had been one of the many English merchants in Montreal after the conquest of 1761 and had early invested in the fur trade, soon joining forces with the McGill brothers. The firm of Todd, McGill had been sending goods to the Indian Country west of the Great Lakes and bringing back furs for 15 years now and had grown rich in the process. Andrew, as a partner, was on the way to personal wealth, too, although he did not easily attain his rewards. The life of a fur trader was hard, and more failed at it than succeeded.

When John outlined his plans and hopes for a government appointment or a business opportunity in Quebec through the good offices of Lord Dorchester, Andrew expressed skepticism. He wished his friend well, but suggested that in the event his expectations did not materialize John should return to Montreal for the winter. Then, in the spring, Andrew would take him west to Michilimackinac, where he might try his luck and skill at the fur trade that was the foundation of Canada's existence.

They parted on this note, although John had no intention of taking up Andrew's offer. He left in *a calash* which departed for Quebec a few days later. The last three-day lap of his journey was in certain hilarious particulars the most memorable. His single traveling companion was M. Labadie, the King's courier, whose mission obliged them to travel continuously, day and night, without rest in a bed or a change of clothing. But in no way were they deprived of culinary refreshment. "My friend Monsieur Labadie weighed nearly 300 pounds and was determined that neither bad roads nor the most jolting vehicle in the world, should cause the least diminution of his *en bon point*."[22] In a word, he ate continuously and often shared with John, who had the frequent pleasure of paying for their "slight repasts" when they stopped at some roadside house of supply.

Quebec quite fascinated John. He had never before been in a fortified town, and once settled in at Frank's Hotel, he took rambling walks along the Plains of

Abraham and the high walls, which gave a magnificent vista of the river and the rolling land stretching north and south to the mountains. His strong sense of history peopled his imagination with the actors of the crucial battle that took place there 30 years before. One of them would come to have a unique influence in his life, although he could not possibly foresee it then. Perhaps it was preoccupation with the scene, perhaps it was his unmilitary nature, despite his several uncles, that explained his failure to respond one evening when a sentinel called him to halt and show his pass. Not until the soldier raised his musket did John realize he had better return promptly to his hotel.

Very early the next morning Mr. Franks came agitatedly to his room to wake him with the news that the town major was below waiting to take Mr. Johnston to the commandant. Apparently the sentinel had reported John's suspicious foray of the evening before to headquarters. John blandly asked Mr. Franks to tell the major that he would be pleased to accompany him in a couple of hours, after he had dressed and breakfasted. With that Franks, in his distress, was certain that his cool guest must be a spy. Nevertheless, he had taken a liking to the amiable young man and offered to facilitate his escape. It took John a while to convince his host that he only wanted breakfast, not a disguise. When the obliging town major returned, they went off together to see Colonel England and get the whole matter straightened out. In his usual outgoing fashion, even in these circumstances, John made a friend of the commanding officer, who invited him to breakfast next morning.

His visit with the Governor General was considerably less satisfactory. Lord Dorchester received him warmly and inquired after John's uncles. But after the usual small talk about common acquaintances, his Lordship broke the news that he had just been recalled to London and that General Sir Alured Clarke had come to take his place as Governor General. Regretfully, he was in no position to offer any kind of government post. Having come so many thousands of miles on his quest, John's disappointment must have shown conspicuously in his face. The kindly Dorchester came up with another idea. The merchants of the city might be interested in a scheme to import goods directly from Ireland. If John wished to draw up a proposal along those lines, his Lordship would arrange for a presentation. Its acceptance might lead to a mercantile appointment.

John went back to his hotel and spent the next several days working on the project. As promised, Lord Dorchester invited him to dine at the castle along with the leading merchants of the city. The gentlemen were enthusiastic about the proposition, but in the general discussion that followed John's exposition, the captains of commerce concluded that they could not afford to jeopardize their connections in London, despite the lower cost of a direct Irish trade that John had demonstrated. Another expectation dashed to the ground. John returned dejectedly to the hotel and relieved the depression of his feelings with his pen, in an ode:

> To Hope
>
> Hope, deceiver of my soul,
> Who with lures, from day to day,—
> Hast permitted years to roll
> Almost unperceived away.
> Now no longer try thine art,
> Fools alone thy power shall own,—
> Who, with simple, vacant heart,
> Dream of bliss to mortals known.
> Every effort have I try'd
> All that reason could suggest,
> Cruel? Cease then to deride
> One by fortune still unblest.
> Ah! Yet stay, for when thou'rt gone,—
> Where shall sorrow lay her head?
> Where, but on the chilling stone
> That marks the long-forgotten dead.[23]

His somber mood eventually gave way to an optimistic one, however, as he still had Andrew Todd's fortuitous offer to fall back on. He would return to Montreal.

When he told Lord Dorchester of his intentions, the solicitous Governor General urged him to stay in Quebec. He, himself, would be there with his family until spring, and he would introduce John to the Bishop of Canada, with whom he might spend the winter studying French. Then if anything suitable turned up, his Lordship would do all he could to see that John got the appointment. It was a considerate offer, but too uncertain for a man of limited means who must find a way to earn his living, and soon.

Before John left for Montreal a few days later, Mr. Motz, Lord Dorchester's private secretary, came to say, in the most delicate manner he could, that his lordship had authorized him to offer Mr. Johnston whatever amount of money he might need to tide him over the winter. John was deeply touched by this offer, but as he had long ago adopted the policy never to assume a financial obligation he might find difficult to repay, he assured Mr. Motz that he had quite sufficient funds at the moment. He would be grateful, however, for a letter of introduction to Sir John Johnson, Commissioner of Indian Affairs in North America. He had come to admire him and his father, Sir William Johnson, Indian Commissioner for New York before the rebellion, through what he had read about them.

The secretary delivered the requested letter promptly that evening, and John departed next morning in the gloom of November snows. Arriving back in Montreal, he got in touch with Andrew, who was as warm and ebullient as ever. He introduced John to his friends among the military officers and gentlemen of trade. And through the letter of introduction from Lord Dorchester John established a lifelong friendship with Sir John Johnson and his family. In fact, the two men of almost identical name felt such an immediate rapport that Sir John urged him to live with their family over the winter. But John felt no greater ease in accepting a large obligation of hospitality than he did of money. Although he would attend the debut of Sir John's daughter and other social events in the city over the ensuing months, he found modest lodgings at the home of an M. Vienne at

Varennes, about 15 miles below Montreal on the other side of the river.

Why this sociable man chose to remove himself so far from the city remains another of the puzzles posed by the earlier years of John Johnston's life. Was he trying to economize? Would cheap lodgings in Montreal embarrass his pride in a way that removal to the country would avoid? Had he come to the conclusion, after ten years in a large town, that a rural setting really suited him best? Or did he avoid city life, even in the unsophisticated outpost of Montreal, because he was striving to change his "dissipated" habits? Whatever his reasons, he settled in at Varennes for the winter to study French, read, and reflect on himself and his future.

That future he had pursued for so long eluded him still. He had come a quarter round the globe to launch a new life, bringing little in his meager baggage. What he possessed of value was in his head and in his heart—in a mind with the wisdom to learn from life's experience, in a spirit humbled but not damaged by past adversities, with a pride and dignity that allowed subservience to no man, but with a modesty and humility born of true reverence for God. His immutable faith was a personal matter between him and his God that required no church. It protected him and rendered his spirit independent of the frailties and venality of other men, yet free to love his fellow human beings. Nor was he without faults of his own. He tended to self-righteousness, was often harsh in his judgments of others' behavior. And he was ultraconservative in his views, resistant to new ideas. He was also a man of refined tastes, though without pretense. He was a modest man, but not weak. He was an intellectual man, but not a snob.

What did the Will of Providence, in which he placed all his trust, have in store for him? He doubtless never recognized the true nature of his destiny—that it was the will of Providence that this man should bring to the rude wilderness of the frontier the gentle light of learning, of graciousness, of an unpretentious piety that saw no superior and inferior among the races of God's children, but only better or worse in the characters of individual men and women, of a love that could unite the primitive with the sophisticated and culminate in a group of offspring to represent the best of both. His would not be an "important" life in the world of large affairs. Indeed, he never wanted such a life, although through his friendships with important men who deeply respected him he might have striven for it. Rather his existence would touch lightly, yet in profound ways, the people of all kinds who came within his orbit—the mighty and the ordinary, the saint and the sinner, the brilliant and the dull—leave them a little happier, perhaps a little worthier, for having known him, and cast the shadow of a good man after he was gone.

Chapter Two
Paddle, Portage and Posé

The riverbank at Lachine presented a scene of orderly chaos when John arrived to take his place in a Todd, McGill canoe bound for the upper country in May of 1791. He had observed much that was new to him during the past nine months. But what he witnessed now and for the ensuing weeks was a process unique in the world—found only on the intricate river and lake system of northern North America. Here a vast, lucrative, commercial empire, for which men had already fought several wars and would fight yet another, was built upon the fragile invention of a primitive people—the birch bark canoe.

The remarkable craft he would travel in was about 35 feet long and five feet wide, fashioned from the carefully peeled rind of the white birch tree. Strips of bark, a mere quarter of an inch thick, sewn together with the tough stringy roots of the red spruce over a framing of white cedar strips, were waterproofed at the seams with pine resin. A series of four-inch boards, suspended from the gunwales, served as seats for the six paddlers, called *milieux* (middlemen). The *gouvernail* (steersman) would stand in the stern with his long sweep throughout the journey. The *avant* at the bow occupied a seat to himself, where he had plenty of elbowroom to exercise his extraordinary skill in manipulating the very long red cedar paddle that would guide and steady the vessel through as many of the rapids as could be safely run.

Makers of some of the canoes painted and decorated them with a picture on the high prow or stern. They painted all of the paddle blades bright red and placed creative markings of black and green on them to express the artistry of their owners, for the Canadian voyageur was proud of his profession and its tools.[1] He had been bred to his occupation for generations, as a new kind of trade system evolved in accord with the geographic and political conditions the white man encountered in the wilds of North America. On his several visits to Montreal during the previous winter, John had learned something of this system, inaugurated by the French 100 years earlier, elaborated and refined by the English during the last 25.

Heart and symbol of the trade was the beaver. That intelligent, engineering animal had, since the beginning of memory, yielded both food and clothing to the Indian tribes of the vast north country. The tail was most delectable to eat, and the pelt, taken in winter, trimmed and sewn with moose sinew into robes worn with the fur side against the body, kept man, woman and child so warm that they needed no other garment. After 15 to 18 months the coarser guard hair wore off, leaving the thick, soft down to enfold the body in luxurious comfort and warmth. The first white men to journey up the St. Lawrence River from beyond the sea admired these garments and traded them for the knives and awls that would make fashioning the clothing so much easier.[2] The natives were delighted; they had struck a bargain.

As for the worn furs, they were sent back across the ocean to clothe the natives on the other side. Over the years the message was returned that the fur of the beaver, with its microscopic barbs, was uniquely suited to the manufacture of felt. Who is to say whether the beaver arrived first or fashion led the way? The fact remains that within a few years enormous hats of beaver felt became the indispensable badge of all ladies and gentlemen of rank and all persons with pretensions thereto. And so the North American fur trade was born. The hatmakers of Europe clamored for beaver, especially the highest quality peltry from which the active bodies of the North American Indians had abraded the rough guard hair. The French settlers, carrying the *Fleur de Lis* of empire to Quebec and the wilderness outpost of Montreal, eagerly traded the clothes right off the Indians' backs.[3]

In return for their furs the North American natives acquired the marvelous metal tools of the white man—kettles, knives, hatchets, awls, fire-steels and, most important of all, the miraculous musket. Never had their lives been easier. With firearms, the hunt seemed hardly a contest any longer; food was much more accessible. The steel and flint made fire for cooking and warmth in one tenth the time of the old stick method. Knives dressed meat and skins with amazing speed. In a brass kettle, food seemed to cook almost instantaneously and could be kept hot indefinitely. If all these miracles could be wrought with just the hide of a beaver, then the pale French should have all the beaver they might want, both the worn clothing and the freshly trapped animals. Everybody would get rich.

But growing wealth and rivalry for the lucrative trade also added fuel to the fires of traditional Indian hostilities. The richest fur-bearing lands lay around the Great Lakes, 500 to 1,000 miles west of the French settlements on the St. Lawrence. The Ojibways from Lake Superior paddled their birch bark canoes the longest distance to bring the peltry down; while the Ottawas, Hurons, and Iroquois in between, who were farming and trading rather than hunting tribes, all fought each other for the carrying trade of the less sophisticated inland peoples. Continuous inter-tribal warfare, combined with the casual Indian attitude toward time and acquisition, made total reliance upon native cartage too risky for the French traders. Even the relatively civilized Ottawas might or might not come down every year, and the size of the cargo could vary greatly. For the merchant who held a large inventory of European trade goods ordered from France a year in advance, and who could not afford to send the ship back across the ocean half empty, regularity of the trade was essential to a decent profit. One solution was to send traders into the interior to winter with the Indians, see that they trapped diligently, make certain that they brought their skins to Montreal each year, and keep the peace that would make it all possible.[4]

This innovation seemed to improve matters at first. But it soon became apparent that transient traders who camped in the winter, now with this band now with that, and then returned to the St. Lawrence with their Indians, were not sufficiently influential to stabilize the trade. Warfare continued to cause serious interruptions. Then another difficulty arose. In their eagerness to supply the insatiable demands of the European market and thereby acquire more goods and brandy for themselves, the Indians over-trapped. They took every animal they could find, young and old—lynx, marten, muskrat, and fisher, as well as beaver. Lakes and streams that had so recently teemed with animal life became barren. The hunters must move on—beyond the shores of the Great Lakes—to find new lands and waterways where the fur-bearing animals, especially the beaver, were still plentiful. But from this high northwest country, *le pays en haut*, the Indians' lengthening journey to the French settlements on the St. Lawrence became less profitable. It occupied too large a part of the year.

It was in response to these two problems—intertribal warfare and the lengthening trade routes—that the unique logistics of the fur trade developed into a system that would endure, unchanged in its essentials, for the next 150 years. Men established permanent trading posts, though they might be no more elaborate than a 20- by 30-foot bark house, at strategic locations, usually portages, around and beyond the Great Lakes. Here a trader, a *bourgeois*, arrived in late summer with one or two canoes of trade goods, manned by Canadian *engagés—voyageurs*, who for many years seemed to be inexhaustibly supplied by the village of Trois Rivieres on the St. Lawrence. Here, in the fall, the traders extended to the tribesmen and women the goods they needed for the winter, on credit. A voyageur might be dispatched with a group of families as they fanned out into the woods to hunt, to keep them honest about returning by spring with their payments in furs. When the ice broke up in early summer, the Canadians loaded the canoes with furs and paddled to market. The Indians remained in their own territory to attend to their summer food needs and such wars as the trader-diplomat was unable to prevent.[5]

By the 1730s and '40s the traders no longer conveyed the furs to Montreal in one trip. The bourgeois and their voyageurs from the Northwest brought them, via Le Grand Portage from west of Lake Superior and via the Kaministiquia and Nipigon Rivers from north of that lake through St. Marys River to the great fortified depot at Michilimackinac, where Lakes Michigan and Huron come together. Here the traders from the southwestern posts— the region between Lake Michigan and the Mississippi River—brought their peltry as well, via La Baye (Green Bay). Then a different brigade, manned by different crews, carried the entire output across Lake Huron, up the French River and down the Ottawa to Montreal. Along with the furs they carried the traders' orders for next year's merchandise and supplies, which they would bring up the following summer. Meanwhile, the *hivernants*, the wintering bourgeois and voyageurs, loaded the trade goods and supplies that the Montreal canoes had just brought, supplemented by Ottawa-raised corn from the fields along Lake Michigan's shores and Ojibway-caught whitefish from St. Marys River, and headed back to their winter posts for another year.[6]

This was the system found in 1760 by the first Englishmen to appear on the Great Lakes after the Conquest. And they simply took it over, including the French personnel. A number of French and English bourgeois formed two-man partnerships, a mutually advantageous arrangement. It assured the French traders access to goods which the law now required to be obtained in Britain, and the Englishmen were safer and more acceptable to the suspicious, if not openly hostile, Indians, who continued for years to believe that Onontio, their French father, would return to drive out the hated English. And the canoemen, the voyageurs, would continue to be French or French-Indian through all the years that the trade endured on the Great Lakes.[7]

Isaac Todd and James McGill had supplied Francois Le Blanc with trade goods to the *pays en haut* around Lake Winnipeg as early as 1765.[8] In the ensuing years each of them wintered at least once in the Northwest beyond Lake Superior, but during the '70s and '80s their business became more extensively engaged to the southwest of Michilimackinac, beyond Lake Michigan. It was during this period, 1765 to 1780, that most two-man partnerships came to divide the labor in such a way that a Michilimackinac- or Montreal-based member imported and prepared the outfits of trade goods and provisions, hired the voyageurs to transport them to the interior, and marketed the peltry brought down the following year, while the wintering partner undertook the long journey into the interior, built the outposts and made the actual exchanges with the Indians of goods for fur.[9]

In 1779 the two-man partnerships began to join together into larger, though loosely organized, associations, to reduce cutthroat competition and to realize some economies in joint purchase of goods and marketing of furs. The largest of these went by the name North West Company and based its field operations at Grand Portage at the western end of Lake Superior. Todd, McGill had been a party to the original North West agreement of 1779 and the renewal in 1781. But when the war with the American colonies ended, they found themselves in disagreement with Simon McTavish and Joseph Frobisher, the leaders of the group, about the implications of American independence for the fur trade. Todd and McGill firmly believed that American settlement would never extend as far as their primary trading grounds between Lake Michigan and the Mississippi River, even if the peace treaty did grant them nominal jurisdiction over it. McTavish and Frobisher, on the other hand, were convinced that prudence directed them to withdraw their activities from that region and concentrate on the legally British Northwest, beyond Lake Superior.

Consequently, Todd, McGill did not participate in the renewal of the North West Company agreement in 1783, but in 1785 formed their own Michilimackinac Company, locating their distribution depot on the island that bore that name.[10] Their prediction proved accurate, at least at the time. Although the 1783 Treaty of Paris had drawn the boundary between the United States and British North America through St. Marys River and the middle of Lake Superior, all of the nominally American territory south and west of that line was still, in 1790, entirely controlled by the British. So effective was British law, currency, commerce and military presence that the Englishmen's recent war and peace had made no difference whatever to the fur trade. And so it would remain for years to come.

Meanwhile, the trade had grown large enough that many partnerships added an intermediate layer of personnel between themselves and the canoeman. The clerk was also called a bourgeois, but he was an employee on salary. He might, nevertheless, aspire to partnership, especially in the great North West Company, which specifically provided for advancement after seven years of satisfactory service. Partners generally wintered at the larger outposts, perhaps with a clerk or two in attendance, while senior clerks took charge of the smaller posts.[11]

The long voyage, the most salient characteristic of the fur trade, began at Lachine. The men deposited 6,000 pounds in 90-pound packs, or *pièces*, on long poles laid in the bottom of the canoe in such a way as to distribute the weight evenly. They placed the 40 pounds of personal gear allowed to each voyageur under his seat. On top of the cargo they arranged the supplies needed for the trip, including an oilcloth for protecting the cargo or hoisting as a sail on the large lakes, a huge bailing sponge, 60 yards of rope for towing up rapids and, if any bourgeois passengers came along, a tent and table appointments for their comfort.[12]

When the canoes were ready to begin the journey, the men paused in their work for a last blessing by the priest at the Church of Ste. Anne. None of them would know that grace again for months, and for some, wintering in the West, it would be years. As each departed the church he dropped a coin in the box for good luck on the voyage. Then they pushed the canoes into midstream and the long, arduous upward passage began.

The passengers were comfortable enough in low chairs amidships, although confinement for 15 hours in an unfamiliar position might result in agonizing cramps to an inexperienced anatomy. John must have marveled, however, at the stamina of the voyageurs. They hardly shifted their bodies and legs during all those hours, while their powerful arms maintained a pace of 40 strokes a minute to the rhythm of hundreds of songs they would sing through the miles—and all of this on two meager meals a day. The distances covered in the 50-minute hours the men paddled were measured by the pipes they enjoyed at rest for the remaining ten. Thus a "pipe" equalled about four miles.[13]

Strength and endurance were two universal characteristics of the voyageur, whose costume presented an interesting cultural mix—white man's clothing above the waist, Indian dress beneath. He typically wore a cotton shirt over his loin cloth, tied round with a gay sash, from which he suspended his beaded tobacco pouch. His thighs were bare, deerskin leggings encased his legs and moccasins protected his feet. The presence of a blue cloak over his shoulders might be dictated by the weather, but his red worsted cap (adorned with the coveted feather if he were an initiated Northwester) was perched permanently on his head of tousled black hair. To tolerate the vicissitudes of his dangerous life, the voyageur usually displayed a sense of humor to moderate his quick temper and readiness to fisticuffs. He also tended to be lighthearted and carefree to the point of irresponsibility, save where his craft and his calling were concerned. And mixed incongruously with his crude and rough qualities was a gallantry and an exaggerated code of courtesy that set him apart from all other laboring men.[14]

Where the river narrowed there was a sudden lightness of the canoe as eight men leapt from it while it was still under the momentum of the last paddle stroke and jolted John from his thoughts. They then laid hold of the gunwales simultaneously and brought it to a gentle stop in midstream. They had arrived at one of the 36 tortuous portages between Lachine and the Great Lakes. It was time to unload all the meticulously stowed cargo. The sturdy voyageurs took the passengers and the goods ashore upon their backs. They did not expect a bourgeois, a gentleman trader, to suffer wet feet and trousers merely because a fragile birch bark canoe must not touch bottom with anything in it.

Once the cargo was ashore each man grabbed the two "ears" at the top of two 90-pound packs and hoisted them onto his back, to be held in place by a strap passed over his forehead. Under this load he trekked through thick brush, climbed steep hills of bare rock, or sloshed through mosquito-ridden swamps to overcome a barrier that nature had placed in the way of the fur trade. After a third- to a half-mile they put down the packs while the men ran back for another load, which they deposited in like manner. They repeated this process until all the packs and canoes had been brought up to the first stopping place, and they kept as close as possible for security against Indian raids. Then, after a smoke, the men started again to the next place where they put down their burdens. In this way they measured the whole portage in "put downs" or *posés*, as the voyageurs called them.[15]

For every portage on the route *a décharge* occurred—a place where the rapids were less powerful, and only a part of the lading and crew needed to be unloaded, while the men "lined" the canoe up the rapids, guiding it with long ropes and setting poles, and often becoming thoroughly soaked as they labored through the icy water. At many of the portages and décharges they saw one or more rough crosses pounded into the earth, or propped up against a pile of rocks. Thus someone had marked the grave of a voyageur who had stumbled under a cruel load and snapped his neck in a fall on granite, or one who died on the spot of a strangulated hernia, or who drowned in the swift river when he slipped while lining a canoe, or one whose heart simply stopped in mid-carry. The men never failed to murmur a prayer for one of the fallen as they passed his marker.[16]

Every night they unloaded the canoes again before they could be pulled up on shore and turned over as a rude sleeping shelter for the men, tortured from sunset to sunrise by mosquitoes and black flies. John and Andrew slept in a tent with netting that gave them a little protection from those tiny, vicious beasts of the north woods. But as the tent poles were the same as those used to support the cargo in the bottom of the canoe, the two bourgeois had to be out of bed promptly or they might find the tent pulled down around their ears while the men stood around and roared at the joke.

They wasted little time preparing food. When the brigade stopped for the night they suspended a 10-gallon pot of water over the fire, into which they threw each crew member's daily ration of one quart of dried peas, to be boiled all night with a couple of pounds of pork. [Pork was available only on the voyage to and from Montreal, not in the interior beyond the Great Lakes. The voyageurs who paddled that part of the trade route were, therefore, known as *mangeurs du lard* or pork eaters]. This meal stayed hot in the canoe during a first light passage of *trois pipes* before a brief stop for breakfast. The leftovers they would reheat for supper over the evening fire, while they prepared tomorrow's brew. Such was the fare of the sturdy voyageurs; the bourgeois enjoyed a different and more delicate diet especially prepared for them. And the important partners of the great trading companies were served on china with fresh linen spread on a folding table.[17]

In this routine, the brigade slowly crept up the Ottawa River to its junction with the Mattawa, then up that winding stream to the height of land dividing the watersheds of the Ottawa Valley and the Great Lakes. A pair of navigable beaver ponds eased the labor of carrying across the divide to a tiny creek, which led to the insignificant La Vase River, which in turn flowed into Lake Nipissing.[18] For a few hours the canoemen enjoyed an unobstructed passage of about 40 miles across the lake before descending the turbulent, boulder-strewn French River to the broad expanse of Georgian Bay and Lake Huron. Now all they had to worry about were storms and adverse winds. An inside passage through part of Georgian Bay and the protection of the Manitoulin Islands, which stretch across the top of Lake Huron, helped. Nevertheless, the men followed the ancient custom of propitiating the wind, affectionately known to them as *La Vieille*, whenever they entered one of the Great Lakes. A bit of tobacco thrown overboard and the soothing chant, "Souffle, souffle, La Vieille," was a precaution no sensible man failed to take.[19]

During the journey John gave himself over to enjoying the wild and beautiful scenery. Although they might pass Indian encampments along the way they saw no farm or village the entire distance to disturb the majesty of the primeval wilderness. For him the only detriment to the experience was the hordes of voracious mosquitoes. "I, who had nothing else to do but defend myself from them the best way I could, was left a perfect spectacle of deformity, my eyes near closed up, and my mouth distorted in a most frightful manner."[20]

Once out of the North Channel and past the mouth of St. Marys River, the shores of Lake Huron are low and uniformly wooded. The beauty of the passage then derives from the emerald waters of the lake itself. But as the lake narrows at the Straits of Mackinac, dividing what are today the upper and lower peninsulas of Michigan, a high island rises from its depths unlike all its neighbors, Michilimackinac, the Great Turtle, which is indeed shaped much like one. Its terraced limestone bluffs reveal lake levels that existed in earlier geological times, and the fantastic rock formations of the island display the mighty power of wave action. This magnificent island, the Ottawas and Ojibways firmly believed, was the dwelling place of the gods and for them such a sacred place was only for use as a summer resort.

But the white man was not so intimidated by the work of the Almighty, and he built thereon a permanent village. It was dominated by the whitewashed, limestone fort perched on the bluff overlooking the harbor, accessible by a long, sweeping flight of steps from the lakeshore. Built by the British garrison in the early 1780s, when they moved from the original French fort on the mainland south shore of the Straits, it remains today virtually unchanged from when John Johnston first saw it as he approached from the lake. The officers lived on the military post, but clustered at its foot were the log and shingle homes and warehouses of the fur traders who made the village their permanent residence.

The summer had not yet begun, and John spent a pleasant few weeks roaming the woods, where wildflowers burst into profusion in early spring, marvelling at the limestone formations such as those dubbed Sugar Loaf and Arch Rock and Devil's Kitchen, and indulging his favorite pastime of reading. Consistent with his experience since crossing the ocean, the commanding officer of the garrison, Captain Charleton, turned out to be an acquaintance from home. They had a good time reminiscing, although it made John homesick to contrast this meeting with their first one at his mother's home, when

Charleton had commanded a detachment guarding a shipwreck less than half a mile from Craige.

Then, abruptly, the gentle tranquility of the island village was entirely shattered. The traders arrived from the interior posts—canoe after canoe of singing voyageurs, with their bourgeois as anxious as they to reach this single outpost of civilization and sociability. They converged on the island to exchange their furs with the Montreal partners for new goods and provisions for another winter inland. But they were here for another purpose as well. Rest and recreation in that day meant that

> riot and revelry, festivity and song, swept all descriptions down its heady current with scarcely a single exception. The excuse pleaded by the traders is their many fatigues, risks and privations during the winter, and often an entire seclusion from all society, so that when they again meet at Mackinac, where they are sure to see their Montreal friends, and an ample supply of wines, spirits, etc., etc., they think themselves entitled to make up for what they call lost time, by making the most of the short interval that elapses between the sale of their furs, and their repurchase of goods for a new adventure. The chief traders and Montreal merchants keep open table for their friends and dependents, and vie with each other in hospitality to strangers. But the excess of which their indulgence is carried, seldom ends without a quarrel, when old grudges are opened up, and language made use of that would disgrace a Wapping tavern, and the finale a boxing match, as brutal and ferocious as any exhibited in ancient times by the Centaurs and Lapythe.[21]

But somehow the work as well got done. They unloaded and stored the furs, parceled out the bales of trade goods in appropriate quantity for each winter trading post, packaged and distributed provisions of food and tools, repaired canoes or supplied new ones for the return trips. For the year just ended they settled accounts. The tally of furs against last summer's stock of trade goods usually yielded a good profit, but no one would know precisely how much for another year, until they delivered the peltry to England and sold it in next winter's London market. The company paid the clerks and canoemen their wages, but the latter rarely saw much of the cash; it promptly went to settle their accounts of purchase or allowance from the "company store." Then one day in late July it was all over. The roistering ended, the brigades shoved off one by one—the Montreal canoes heading back with their precious cargo of fur, most of the inland brigades fanning out around the shores of Lake Michigan, and a few canoes headed up St. Marys River for Lake Superior. Quiet settled over the village for another 11 months.

Several firms operated from Mackinac Island, but Todd, McGill was the largest, supplying independent traders as well as their own clerks. It was under the former arrangement that Andrew supplied an outfit to John. With one canoe packed with trade goods, five voyageurs, and the courage to carry him into the formidable unknown, he started out for Lake Superior about the middle of August, 1791. From here on John would encounter no more old friends, and few, if any, white men at all to render aid if needed.

Chapter Three

Fateful Island

Lake Superior, the largest inland lake in the world, John Johnston learned, discharged its 32,000 square miles of water through a half-mile wide narrows in St. Marys River with no little commotion. At the place known as *Ba-we-ting* to the Ojibways, *le Sault de Ste. Marie* to the French, and St. Mary's Falls to the English, the river roared and foamed and frothed in a rapids plunging 20 feet in one mile. But the rushing waters no longer inspire the awe felt by observers in his day. Modern hydroelectric power has reduced the mighty rapids to a short stretch of dancing wavelets, whose roar is barely a whisper and whose spray subsides before it can rise.

Like every other traveler who bucked the current almost 60 miles from Lake Huron, John disembarked to walk the portage around the rapids, past a few traders' cabins and Indian lodges, before the party launched into the widening stretch of river that led to the lonely vastness of Lake Superior. Passing such wonders as the Grand Sable Dunes and the Pictured Rocks, the little vessel traversed more than 300 miles to its destination at La Pointe, largest island in the group now known as the Apostle Islands, and directly across Chequamegon Bay from the mainland Indian village. On this first passage, the palpable power of the lake and its magnificent vistas inspired John, and for the rest of his life its beauty and majesty would enthrall him. It moved him to fill ten or twelve pages of his journal with "reflections, remarks and some poetical effusions."[1]

High winds kept the party encamped for days at a time as they struggled westward mile by mile, and it was late in September before they arrived at the wooded island. With little time to get ready for the severe winter, fishing and house building began immediately. The log houses, one for John and one for the men, were doubtless typical of such fur-trading outposts—20 by 30 feet, with a log frame bed in one corner, a stone fireplace and log walls chinked with clay, a rough table and chairs, pegs for clothing, and a corner cupboard made of boards for storage.[2]

Two of the men spent their time fishing for the supply that would keep them all alive during the winter. They caught the trout, whitefish and pike and hung them up by their tails on willow branches, and during the cold autumn nights the fish froze solid by morning.[3] While the men worked at these jobs, John distributed trade goods on credit to the neighboring Indians, who then moved out into the woods in small family groups to hunt the fur-bearers. That done, he turned, with his men, to the business of cutting fire wood. Although he was new at the business, things did seem to be going well.

Then, on November 17, disaster struck. His men absconded with his canoe and nets for fishing, his axes and other tools, and, worst of all, almost his entire supply of frozen fish. One teenage boy remained who, fortunately, knew a little of the Ottawa language and could make himself understood with the local Ojibway Indians. John suspected that a pair of Canadians trading nearby had conspired with his men to desert, so he knew he could expect no assistance from that quarter. He, a soft-handed country gentleman, an urbane litterateur, accustomed to the salon and the counting house, was virtually alone, without proper equipment, in an alien, lethal winter wilderness. He almost despaired, though his later recollection would be softened by understatement. "I sat down rather in bad spirits to ruminate on my situation, and at length it struck me that my case, in many particulars, had a resemblance to that of Robinson Crusoe, and I got up determined to follow his example by making every exertion in my power to ameliorate it."[4]

First he improvised new axes, then he and the boy set out to chop as much wood as they could possibly lay up. Warmth in the northern winter was the first priority.

By the second day of their effort John's hands were covered with blisters, but he worked until his axe handle became too slippery from his own blood. Then he divided the labor; the boy would do all the cutting and he would do all the hauling. Exhaustion from hard work induced sound sleep and left little time for bitter reflection on his misfortunes. In two weeks they had six cords laid up. They wouldn't freeze, and as soon as the bay did they could fish once more, through the ice, with hooks and lines. They wouldn't starve, either. Calling forth a resourcefulness he hardly knew he possessed, ingenuity overcame inexperience and the neophyte learned how to winter in the north woods. John Johnston felt sure he would be all right.

Perhaps if he had known something of the history of La Pointe he would have been less optimistic. It was an island dogged by misfortune. How badly was for generations a closely guarded secret of the Indians who shunned the place. But during the mid-19th century, a part-Indian descendent of one of the early settlers managed to pry the story out of the old chiefs from whom he gathered the material for his *History of the Ojibway Nation*, first published in 1852.[5]

Linguistically a part of the Algonquin group, the Ojibway nation originated on the eastern seacoast, according to their tradition. Why they began to move westward has been forgotten, but migrate they did, fighting the Iroquois all the way until they arrived at Ba-we-ting, the Sault de Ste. Marie. There they lived in peace for many years, but gradually the nation separated into two groups as people continued to move west—one along the north shore of Lake Superior and the other along the south side, first to Grand Island, then L'Anse-Keweenaw, and finally to Chequamegon Bay. Now they were out of reach of their ancient enemies, the Iroquois, but had new nations to fight in the Foxes and Dakota Sioux. The Ojibway leaders decided to build a central fortified village and concluded that the safest place to do this was on an island. The one chosen was called *Mon-ing-win-a-kaun-ing*—place of the golden-breasted woodpecker—later to be called La Pointe, and later still, Madeline. The year is calculated by Ojibway reckoning to have been 1490.[6]

They built the village on the side of the island that faced the mainland, with gardens for corn and pumpkins, although the people lived mainly by fishing. And, for the most part, they were safe. On one occasion a large party of Foxes came down the Ontonagan River to attack the village. They landed their small, inland canoes on the island in the dark of night and at dawn next day waylaid four young women on their way to cut wood. Carrying their victims with them, they retreated in their canoes under cover of a dense fog. Jubilant about the successful sneak raid, the kidnappers foolishly yelled back a whoop of scorn to the Ojibway village and began to sing a scalping song as they paddled away in the fog. The Ojibway warriors immediately launched their large, fast lake canoes and followed the sound of the singing until the Fox canoes were opposite a steep, rocky coast where they could not land. Then the Ojibways attacked, easily overturning the small, inland canoes and killing every last man as he struggled in the water. That was the only recorded naval battle of the Ojibways, and it was a gratifying victory.[7]

The Ojibways of Chequamegon Bay lived well for some three generations. They were deeply religious and the rites of Me-da-we, the sacred medicine, flourished. In the center of the village stood a big teepee where they conducted the ceremonies. As time passed and the medicine men grew ever more powerful they seemed to become possessed by an evil spirit. From this ensued the long-secret disgrace.

The priests learned how to use very subtle poisons. If anyone offended them in the least way, even unintentionally, he died suddenly and mysteriously. Then, after they buried him, his murderers secretly disinterred his body and presented it as a midnight feast for the man's relatives. If anyone, man or woman, guessed what he was eating or refused to partake, he or she became the next victim. In this way the people developed a taste for human flesh and the medicine men so terrorized them, they dared not refuse even their children for sacrifice. At the same time the medicine men successfully promoted the belief that they, themselves, were invulnerable to death.

Eventually, according to tradition, the numbers of victims became so large that their souls began to wander and to wail in the night. This was more than the surviving inhabitants could bear. In panic, they fled the island to the last man, woman, and child, and scattered into the forests or back to older villages. There they gradually recovered their sanity, gave up the eating of human flesh, and never afterward allowed the medicine men to become so powerful. But neither did they return to the place where this demonaic evil had occurred.[8]

This was the state of affairs when the first white visitors of record reached Chequamegon Bay. Médard Chouart, Sieur des Groseilliers, and his young brother-in-law, Pierre Radisson, came up from Trois Rivieres in the summer of 1660 to see what the Lake Superior region had to offer in the way of beaver. Establishing their headquarters on the mainland shore, they made friends of the Indians in the neighboring villages and visited many of the bands around the western end of the lake, as far as Nipigon on the north shore. The following spring they led a flotilla of canoes down the St. Lawrence, thereby reestablishing the connection between the Ojibways and the French settlements below that had been broken up over the past decade of Iroquois warfare.[9]

Chouart and Radisson never again saw Lake Superior, but the most unusual explorer-adventurers of all history, the Black Gowns of the Society of Jesus, did. First came Father Réne Ménard, returning with the fleet Chouart and Radisson had led down. He gave the place its Christian name—La Pointe du Saint Esprit—to honor his Lord and to signify the long, curving arc of land, thrusting out from the shore to enfold the island-studded bay. But poor Father Ménard's mission survived only a while. He died a lonely death in who knows what agony when his cruel and indifferent "parishioners"[10] deserted him in the forest the following spring. Many years later his breviary and cassock turned up in a Sioux village far to the west.[11]

Father Claude Allouez (1665-1669) and Father Jacques Marquette (1669-1670) were somewhat more successful. But as the villages around the bay began to lose population in the manner of nomadic encampments,

Marquette decided to remove his mission to a more strategic location. He established St. Ignace on the north side of the Straits of Mackinac. So much for the faith at La Pointe du Saint Esprit. Another mission would not exist there for 160 years.

But the traders continued to build and occupy posts from time to time. More often than not they chose the large island, just two miles off shore, as a site for their trading posts, giving it the shortened and secularized name La Pointe. This location, distant yet accessible from the Indian villages, and surrounded by a "moat," was considered safer than a site on the mainland might be. But apparently the curse of the island persisted.

Some time during the decade before the British Conquest the proprietor of the stockaded post left his clerk, Joseph, in charge for the winter. Joseph had his wife and two small children with him and one Canadian canoeman. Unfortunately for the health of this small society, the Canadian developed a passion for the wife. By early spring the man could contain himself no longer. Such Indians as dared to live on the island near the post were away sugaring on the mainland, and when Joseph was off duck hunting one morning, the voyageur entered his master's cabin to force himself on the young mother. Threatening to tell her husband, she grasped at a hunting spear with which to defend herself, and in the brief struggle the powerful Canadian wrested it from her and rammed her through.

Terrified at what he had done, the voyageur hid behind the stockade gate. As soon as his master walked through it, the Canadian shot him in the back. By this time the six-year old girl had set up such a howl of terror that her life lasted only another few minutes. The desperate man spared the toddler, of whom he was fond, but not for long. After three days the child continued to cry so much for his parents that he, too, was done away with. He threw all the bodies into a shallow grave, and then the man sought to flee the site of carnal horror he had created. But the ice was at its worst stage in the spring breakup—he could neither walk on it nor paddle through it—and he had to turn back after two attempts, barely escaping with his life.

When the Indians returned, the guilty man, who had by now composed himself, explained that the clerk and his family had started over the ice by dog team to visit them at the sugar camps. Since they had not arrived, they must have drowned. The natives looked in vain for the bodies along the shore of the island and the mainland. But when the proprietor returned, he grew suspicious at the confused story elicited by his questions. Then he noticed blood stains on the walls of the cabin. As he walked around the compound he poked his sword into a pile of odorous rubbish. The rapidly decomposing bodies were soon revealed; the murderer could no longer deny his guilt.

Two versions of the villain's ultimate fate exist—both equally appropriate. One relates that he escaped on his way down to trial at Montreal and hid among the Huron Indians, adopting their dress, customs, and language. Once, at a war dance, when everyone was "striking the red stake" as a sign that he had an exploit of which to boast, the man got carried away and told his story. The warriors were so horrified by the tale of base deception and cowardice that one of them arose before the story was completed, exclaimed "Dog!," and cleaved the man's skull with a tomahawk.

The other version states that they paroled the murderer on the way to trial so that he could fight the English on the St. Lawrence, and that it was at a dance near Sault Ste. Marie that he boasted of his crimes. The Indians then invited him to a feast. As he started to partake of the food along with the others, the chief told him that when he stopped eating he would be killed. The Canadian ate and ate until he could stuff himself no more—he had no choice but to die. The Indians boiled his body, as though he was a prisoner of war, but the young men refused to eat any of it because, they said, he was worse than a bad dog.[12]

By the time John Johnston arrived at La Pointe in the fall of 1791, 40 or 50 years after the last grisly episode, native families were drifting back to the island to be near the traders stationed there. During the winter most of them left to penetrate the interior along the

Chippewa and St. Croix Rivers of present-day Wisconsin, in search of fur-bearing animals. But one old man was too far along in years to travel so far. He hunted nearby and returned to the island just as the ice in the bay closed in hard. John watched as his unscrupulous neighbor traders observed the Indian approach, hurried to the shore to help him beach his canoe, and took possession of the eight or ten beavers he had brought in. In return, they kept him and his two wives plied with liquor for a few days, then abruptly cut off the supply of both alcohol and food. It mattered little to them if the old folks starved.

Some time later the poor old man came to John for help, explaining that his wives could not reach a cache of wild rice they had some distance away on the mainland because the weather was too bad. John Johnston was no fool, but he was a compassionate man and agreed to share what little he had with these destitute people, who had been so pathetically bilked of their one marketable resource. He could not then know how that humane decision would determine the future course of his life. But his irrepressible curiosity did induce him to talk with the old man in their mutually broken French and sign language. Perhaps he learned the man's story now, perhaps later. At any rate he found out enough during that winter to know that this pathetic individual known as Ma-mong-e-se-da had once been a man of singular importance and stature, worthy of the respect which John accorded him.

Ma-mong-e-se-da's birth resulted from one of the odd anomalies often characteristic of intermittent warfare. During the early years of the 18th century the Ojibways, growing in numbers and strength, continued to search out new hunting lands on which to trap the ever-receding, overkilled beaver. As they fanned out both south and west of their Lake Superior homeland, conflict with the Dakota Sioux became more frequent and violent. Little likelihood of a compromise existed, since the lifeblood of both tribes was the hunt and, as game and fur became scarcer under the long arm of white influence, the territorial needs of each group became larger and larger. A final settlement could come only when one nation completely routed the other. The Ojibways must push the Dakotas across the Mississippi, or the Dakotas must drive the Ojibways back into Lake Superior. In the meantime they fought—mostly seasonal spring and summer battles. By unspoken understanding in the winter they devoted their time entirely to the demanding and uncertain labor of finding food. But occasional interludes of truce occurred.

During one of these a young Ojibway woman of the La Pointe band married an important Dakota chief. When warfare began again a few years later, safety required her to return to her own people. But she must give up to her husband the two infant sons she had borne him. At about this time, a young man of the Ojibway Reindeer Clan, noted for his success as a hunter, moved from Pigeon River on the western lakeshore to Chequamegon Bay on the south. He married the divorced young woman, and in time she bore him a son, whom they named Ma-mong-e-se-da. Like his father he became a famous hunter, almost legendary in the fearless manner in which he stalked the richest territory of the Dakotas. And he, too, would sire a legendary son.[13]

In the telling of one favorite tale, a strong band of Dakota warriors fired on his camp at a time when only a few men but many women and children were in camp. When the warriors wounded one of his men Ma-mong-e-se-da marched out of the compound, calling loudly in the Dakota tongue to inquire if the great chief, Wabasha, was present. At that, the firing stopped, and from the woods emerged a regal figure, clothed for war with full headdress of eagle plumes.

Ma-mong-e-se-da then identified himself as the brother of his enemy, invited Wabasha and his warriors to interrupt hostilities and dine with him in his lodge. Wabasha gracefully accepted, but in offering his hospitality Ma-mong-e-se-da had failed to reckon with the fierce patriotism of Waub-o-jeeg, his five-year old son. As the tall Wabasha stooped to enter the lodge, the child, unnoticed near the door, brought his toy war club down on the head of his enemy uncle with all the force he could manage. Straightening up in astonishment, the great chief identified his assailant, and with a hearty laugh scooped the boy up in his arms. He predicted a noble future for him as a worthy adversary of the uncle's own sons. For, although the two half-brothers might call an afternoon's truce to become acquainted, the conflict between the Ojibways and the Dakota Sioux was too fundamental to conclude in any way short of total victory.[14]

Some years after this episode Ma-mong-e-se-da found himself engaged in a totally different kind of war. Word came up the lakes to the village on Chequamegon Bay that Onontio, the great French father of the Ojibways, needed their help to fight the hated, cold-hearted English. Ma-mong-e-se-da, by this time the undisputed leader of the Lake Superior Ojibways, gathered his warriors and joined the forces recruited by Charles Langlade and Louis le Gardeur, Sieur de Reptentigny, for the 1,000-mile journey to Quebec. Fighting beside the Marquis de Montcalm on the Plains of Abraham where John Johnston had so recently strolled, the war chief was amazed to observe first hand the tactics of European-style warfare. Ever afterward, the Ojibway word for English would be *Shaug-un-aush*, "appearing from the clouds," in grim tribute to the brilliance of General Wolfe's appearance from a totally unexpected direction.[15]

For many years the Indians of the West simply refused to believe that the Conquest was permanent. After all, the French king had many times promised to be their father forever. A chief named Pontiac was so firmly convinced that a demonstration of Indian arms would induce the French to resume war that he executed a series of brilliant victories in the capture of every western fort, except Detroit, in the summer of 1763. But all was in vain, and the Ojibways of Lake Superior were among the first to accept the distasteful truth.

By the year of Pontiac's uprising they were in desperate want of European goods. After 100 years of trading with the French, the Indians had become utterly dependent upon the white man's firearms, ammunition, metal tools and kettles, and, unfortunately, his *"eau de vie."* Years of wartime privation had reduced them pitiably. Once more Ma-mong-e-se-da set out for the St. Lawrence Valley. This time he went only as far as Fort Niagara on Lake Ontario to meet with the English Indian Commissioner, Sir William Johnson, and ask for a trader to be sent to his needy people. This man, father of John's lately acquired Montreal friend, Sir John Johnson, was one of the few Englishmen to win the love and confidence of the Indians. During that bitter winter of 1792 Ma-mong-e-se-da proudly showed John the silver gorget Sir William had given him almost 30 years before. At his death a few months later, the precious heirloom passed to his son, Waub-o-jeeg, White Fisher, chief of the La Pointe Ojibways. From Waub-o-jeeg it later passed on to a younger brother, Ca-mu-dwa. But the winter that Ca-mu-dwa and his entire family starved to death near the Brule River, the treasured throat ornament was lost forever.[16]

Although neighboring traders were unscrupulous in their treatment of Ma-mong-e-se-da, John met one man there who was honorable. John realized that he had sold his stock of rum too cheaply during the fall and winter trading, and by early spring was out of it, although he had other goods left. He was pondering what to do—whether to return to Mackinac early with the furs and leftover goods, or whether to stay in hope that the bands yet to come in would trade with him even if he was out of rum—when a voyageur brought a stranger up to his post. A visitor was always welcome, whether trading partner or competitor, for winter was a long and lonely time and most days were passed huddled in isolation before the cabin fire, unless absolute necessity required one to be out of doors chopping wood or fishing through the ice. The new arrival, Jean Baptiste Perrault, of a prestigious Quebec family, turned out to be another independent who was also supplied by Todd, McGill. He had been trading in the west for almost a decade, most of that time in the country between Lake Superior and the headwaters of the Mississippi River.[17] As they got acquainted over a glass of whiskey, John explained his predicament.

Perrault had rum left over, pointing out that he traded it very carefully, not only for high profit but to allow less of it down the throat of any one Indian. John, in the open, generous way that marked his style, invited Perrault to remain at La Pointe to sell his rum; his judgment and trust in the man's honesty were soon validated. Jean Baptiste sold out his rum at a higher price in furs than John had been extracting, but when the Indians asked him for goods as well, he responded, "For goods, trade with your trader. I am not allowed to do that."[18]

When the ice broke up in the spring of 1792 and the hunters returned from the inland camps, John met this Waub-o-jeeg who, like his father, was a famous man. His reputation had been assured after his brilliant victory at the battle of St. Croix Falls, about 1770. Fulfilling the prophesy of Wabasha, this second son of Ma-mong-e-seda was then, at 23, already a warrior of renown. But he was much more than that; he was a man of thoughtfulness and sensitivity. He would grow into a great civil leader as well as war chief. And he was eloquent, accomplished in the literature of his people:

> Where are my foes? say, warriors, where?
>   No forest is so black,
> That it can hide from my quick eye,
>   The vestige of their track:
> There is no lake so boundless,
>   No path where man may go,
> Can shield them from my sharp pursuit,
>   Or save them from my blow.
> The winds that whisper in the trees,
>   The clouds that spot the sky,
> Impart a soft intelligence,
>   To show me where they lie,
> The very birds that sail the air,
>   And scream as on they go,
> Give me clue my course to tread,
>   And lead me to the foe.[19]

Warfare with the Foxes was an old story, but the Ojibways believed that after some recent battles the insolent tribe had moved permanently to the Mississippi River region. Now they were again invading Ojibway hunting lands in their former territory of the upper St. Croix River area and made an alliance with the Dakota Sioux for the expedition. Waub-o-jeeg and his older brother mustered 300 Ojibway warriors (very large for an Indian army) from the Sault de Ste. Marie, Grand Island,

L'Anse-Keweenaw and Grand Portage, as well as Chequamegon Bay.

When the moment arrived for the impatient young soldiers to embark from La Pointe, their spirits had already been raised to fever pitch. The night before they had stripped off all unnecessary and cumbersome clothing, greased their bodies for silence and swiftness, painted themselves in the war colors of vermillion, black and white, and for hours sung the songs and danced the dances that told of the valor of their people and the justness of their cause. Then, at first light, they launched 100 canoes, filling the bay in front of the village.

Several days of westward paddling—along the red sandstone lakeshore to the Bois Brule River, up that stream to the portage to the St. Croix, and down the St. Croix as it broadened in its course toward confluence with the Mississippi—had brought no contact with the enemy. As they approached the great falls of the St. Croix, with its narrow portage that could easily become a trap, they sent scouts ahead. Quickly they reported back to the camp of waiting Ojibways at the head of the falls. A great army of Foxes was landing at the foot of the falls and with them were the Dakota Sioux. Here is where the battle would be joined.

The young novices, boys on their first war party, jumped into the water to wash off the black paint that denoted their inferior station. Now they would join their elders in putting on the vermillion of war, and the seasoned warriors who had earned the right to do so placed eagles' plumes in their headdresses to signify numbers of enemies slain. Waub-o-jeeg, an acclaimed orator, held the silent attention of the throng arrayed on the narrow strip of ground between the forest and the river. Their spirits fine-tuned for glorious battle, he urged them to their utmost exertion and called upon the Master of Life to grant them strength, victory and honor. At the conclusion of his prayer, the released warriors poured down the narrow portage trail to meet the enemy.

The Foxes, too, had earlier sent their scouts to reconnoiter. Numerous as the Ojibways were, the Foxes mustered even more men and, to achieve the greatest measure of glory, they requested their Dakota allies to refrain from the battle, which they were certain would be short. The Dakotas obligingly sat down on the sidelines and lit their pipes. The two war parties met in a reverberating clash almost exactly in the middle of the portage. For the observers, the battle was a confused one fought at very close range, for little room existed to maneuver on the neck of barren rock, cut by several deep ravines, between the forest and the falls. The nature of the terrain determined that this would be a battle to the death for the Foxes. Waub-o-jeeg had wisely posted sentries throughout the woods beyond the portage in case the enemy should decide to retreat that way. For both sides escape by water was impossible; no place to launch canoes was available beyond firing range of the enemy, and directly below them lay the deadly rapids.

Musketry at such close quarters left many wounded, dying and dead warriors on both sides, but by noon the Foxes were beginning to retreat before the superior firepower of the Ojibways. At this time they welcomed their Dakota allies into the battle and the tide turned. As the day wore on, Ojibway ammunition began to give out, and slowly the Foxes and Dakota Sioux forced the warriors from Lake Superior back toward their waiting canoes. Waub-o-jeeg was brave, but he was not a fool. What benefit to the Ojibways to win, if the enemy killed all their strongest warriors? The enemy would return the next year, and the Ojibways would be defenseless. Too many of their outstanding men had already gone down. Among them was Waub-o-jeeg's older brother; now he was in full command. Although he was wounded in the chest and losing blood himself, his judgment was clear. Prudence dictated retreat if the battle could not be decisively won. Waub-o-jeeg reluctantly gave the order.

But the Master of Life had heard his prayer. Sixty fresh warriors from the Sandy Lake band suddenly appeared, paddling furiously down the river. Without wasting a moment they leaped ashore into the fight, bringing a new supply of precious ammunition and allowing the battle-weary Ojibways time to regroup. The moment of decision had arrived. Fighting evenly at first, the combined Foxes and Sioux gradually began to give ground, then fell back more quickly, and at last their accelerating retreat became a rout. Fleeing before the fury of the Ojibways, who had found new strength with victory so close at hand, the defeated warriors were slaughtered by the score as they tried to escape in their canoes or were broken upon the rocks as they fell and jumped into the rapids. Never again would the Fox nation pose a threat or an annoyance to the Ojibways.[20]

The story of this heroic battle and magnificent victory spread quickly through the forest lands surrounding the Great Lakes, and it would be told through many generations. Waub-o-jeeg was now one of the most celebrated military leaders of his time. Once the wound to his flesh healed, he expressed the wound to his heart in sorrow for his fallen brother and friends and determination to avenge their loss.

> On that day when our heroes lay low—lay low
> On that day when our heroes lay low.
> I fought by their side, and thought ere I died,
> Just vengeance to take on the foe,
> Just vengeance to take on the foe.
>
> On that day when our chieftains lay dead—
>   lay dead,
> On that day when our chieftains lay dead,
> I fought hand to hand, at the head of my band,
> And here, on my breast, have I bled,
> And here, on my breast, have I bled.
>
> Our chiefs shall return no more—no more,
> Our chiefs shall return no more.
> Nor their brothers of war, who can show scar
> for scar,
> Like women their fates shall deplore,
> Like women their fates shall deplore.
>
> Five winters in hunting we'll spend—
>   we'll spend,
> Five winters in hunting we'll spend,
> Till our youth, grown to men, we'll to war
>   lead again,

And our days, like our fathers, we'll end,
And our days, like our fathers, we'll end.[21]

It was doubtless their mutual love of language and poetry that drew John to visit often at Waub-o-jeeg's lodge after the chief returned from the hunt in the early spring of 1792. On Waub-o-jeeg's part, gratitude for the new trader's humane treatment of his father would prompt the early civilities. But gradually an interesting friendship developed within the bounds of formality required by the Ojibway code. And John found another attraction in the 60-foot lodge of the wealthy Waub-o-jeeg, who was reported to take a handsome $350 in furs each year. He had married rather later than most men, to keep his time and attention focused on his military and magisterial duties during the prime years of his early 20's. His first wife had been an older woman, a widow, by whom he had two sons. He had then chosen a young girl of 14, who presented him with a daughter,[22] who on this first meeting with John Johnston, had just passed her own 14th year.[23]

What went on in the mind and heart of John Johnston as he sat before the fire of Waub-o-jeeg's lodge that spring? His autobiographical letters, written in the last year of his life, end abruptly with Ma-mong-e-se-da showing him the gorget from Sir William Johnson, just prior to Waub-o-jeeg's return to La Pointe. And in no other preserved letters or documents did he speak further of his youth. When and why did he decide—suddenly, it seems—to transform what had begun as a temporary venture in the fur trade into a permanent way of life, vastly different from anything he had heretofore known or contemplated?

That it was a hard life he well knew from his experience of the winter. That it was a beautiful, inspiring country in which to live he also had come to know and appreciate. For a man who revered the wonder and magnificence of nature, perhaps this was enough. Perhaps, too, he had had enough of disillusionment at the hands of sophisticated men of the world. Maybe it was the opportunity to operate independently of other men's caprice that attracted him, although on an elemental level, men can be more dependent upon one another in the wild than in the city. Perhaps the uncomplicated, if difficult, life of a fur trader in a setting that brought one so close to God offered rewards of peace and contentment well worth the price of worldly position. In any event, it is quite evident that something occurred in John Johnston's life and thought during his very first year in the wilderness that touched a desire or a need which had lain dormant and unknown to him for 30 years. Judging by the kind of life he ultimately made for himself, his decision is not so surprising. What is puzzling is that he reached it so quickly.

It is not likely that he suffered love at first sight for Waub-o-jeeg's daughter. By all accounts she was not a beautiful woman, although she was known by the beautiful name of *Oshaw-guscody-way-quay*, Woman of the Green Glade. If beauty did not captivate him, surely he could not have had any real acquaintance with her personality and mentality, given the steep language barrier then standing between them. Only her quiet grace and dignity and her low, musical voice could have been apparent to him.[24] What, then, made this 30-year-old bachelor, who had spent all his years save the last one in a genteel, urban setting, who had surely met many attractive women, yet never married, who had taken a canoe load of trade goods to the god-forsaken wilderness only for want of something better to turn to, suddenly ask Waub-o-jeeg for his 14-year-old daughter's hand in marriage?

It remains an interesting question, and one that almost became moot. Waub-o-jeeg refused. Experience had taught him well the ways of the white man. Much as he might like this literary young redhead, such a one from a wealthy and indulgent society would likely linger only briefly with a woman of the forest and would certainly never take her back with him into his world. John pleaded his cause as eloquently as he could, making it clear that he recognized and respected Oshaw-guscody-way-quay's aristocratic lineage, and that his intentions toward her were exactly what they would be to a respectable woman of his own nation. But Waub-o-jeeg remained adamant, bending only so far as to suggest that

John return to Montreal for a while to see whether the white women there might not put this girl out of mind. If not, then he might return for further discussions, but the protective father would make no promises.[25]

And the girl? What were her thoughts and preferences? Was she resigned to a fate revealed to her the previous year during her initiation into womanhood? Like all Ojibway adolescents, she had gone off alone into the forest to build herself a small teepee of saplings and cedar boughs. There she had dwelt in solitude and fasting for ten days, tasting only the water her grandmother brought, to communicate with the guardian spirit who would mediate between her and the Master of Life. The first few days not much happened. She had difficulty concentrating on spiritual thoughts while her stomach clamored for food. But gradually she forgot her hunger, and her mind drifted off into a reverie between sleep and wakefulness. She lost all track of time; how much she slept and dreamed or when she hallucinated in wakefulness she would never know. But when her destiny was revealed to her by her spirit, she recognized it—the face and figure of a white man.[26]

Perhaps because of this she watched John's fur-laden canoe as the oarsman paddled it eastward across Lake Superior with certainty that he would return. Did she await that event in fearful knowledge of how white men treated Indian women? Did she even find this man, barely as tall as she, at all attractive?[27] Or were his red hair and blue eyes grotesque to her taste? Her feelings, too, are unrecorded. Only the years would tell.

Chapter Four
Where the Waters Tumble

Montreal must have looked like a very different place to the returned voyager from the western wilderness than it did to the new arrival from the cities of the Old World. The shift in perspective no doubt transformed its appearance from a crude frontier town on the one occasion to a center of luxury and sophistication on the other. Nevertheless, its attractions were not sufficient to detain John Johnston longer than necessary to transact his business. He exchanged his furs at the warehouse of Todd, McGill for a credit to his account against the supply of goods he had taken to Lake Superior the previous fall. The precise amount of his profit could not be determined until the following spring when the returns of the winter sale in London would come back across the sea. Meanwhile, the quantity and quality of his pelts were a matter of record, while Todd, McGill supplied him with another outfit of trade goods and provisions for the 1792-93 trading season.

After settling in at his post on the island John returned to the lodge of Waub-o-jeeg to claim his bride. The women of Montreal had not deflected him from his intentions, although his charm and eligibility had undoubtedly aroused their interest. All things considered and reconsidered, he was still certain that marriage to Oshaw-guscody-way-quay was right for him. So much so that he brought back for her a ring to seal the betrothal. Fashioned of blue and white enamel, surrounded with seed pearls and centered with a lock of his own hair under glass, it remains to this day in the possession of their great-great-great granddaughter, Claire Ewing.

Waub-o-jeeg, however, imposed one more condition before he gave his final consent. The marriage was to be solemnized according to the white man's ritual as soon as possible.[1] John readily promised, although the opportunity to keep his word would not occur until 1821. At that time his wife took the easily pronounced Christian name of Susan that John had doubtless been using all along.

Johnston and Waub-o-jeeg might come to agreement, but that did not guarantee that the marriage would succeed. One problem occurred with which they both failed to reckon. The bride was terrified—so terrified, in fact, that after being carried to the nuptial home she wrapped herself tightly into her blanket and curled up in a corner of the cabin. She would have absolutely nothing to do with her new husband. John, with infinite patience, tried every device he could think of to reassure her and gently persuade her out of her corner, but nothing would induce the frightened girl even to look at him. At the end of ten days of stalemate she ran away, and after fasting alone in the woods for four more, took refuge in her grandfather's lodge. Ma-mong-e-se-da was unable to persuade her to return to her husband before her father came back; he feared what the consequences might be.

Sure enough, Waub-o-jeeg, away on a hunt, dreamed of his daughter's improper behavior and hurried home in a two day march. As she might have expected, his cold fury at her ignoble disregard for sacred promises was not to be assuaged by any arguments she might present, if, indeed, she dared to present any at all. With a beating now and threats to cut off her ears if she repeated her performance, the irate father marched his rebellious child back to her husband, bearing gifts and apology.[2]

Gradually John's capacity for patience and tenderness overcame her fear and shyness, and the marriage began to blossom into a devoted union that would endure for 36 years. Even if it did not start that way, it surely became a love affair, so carefully did John consider Susan's needs and wishes in every decision he subsequently made. She, in turn, adapted herself and the habits of her upbringing to his way of life in an unceasing effort to make him comfortable and happy. It was a marriage of unabashed mutual affection, respect, and accommodation. And most assuredly it was a partnership. Susan Johnston was a wise and clever woman. In a way that was distinctive from both cultures, and almost unique to the Johnstons, she came to be her husband's helpmeet in business as well as domesticity.

Shortly after the marriage John faced a critical decision—the location of their permanent home. He had begun to recognize his need to create around himself an enclave of civilization, even in the midst of wild beauty. Only in this way could he secure the best of the two worlds he loved. He must find a congenial place in which to build a comfortable dwelling and raise a family. But his business was also location-sensitive. If he was to prosper in trade, he and his goods must be accessible to the Indians in the fall when they extended credits, and he must station himself in a place they would be certain to return in the spring with furs that would pay their debts. La Pointe was certainly a good candidate. Trading posts had existed there for over a hundred years; it was a beautiful and fertile island; it was close to Susan's family and friends. Why did they not select it, then? Perhaps it was too close to his wife's family to suit John's hopes, just beginning to be formulated, of recreating a bit of genteel Ulster in the wilds. Perhaps it was also too far from the one tiny outpost of European grace at Michilimackinac.

For whatever reasons, John, with Susan's reluctant consent, chose to set up shop and house at the single most strategic location in all the Northwest—the Sault de Ste. Marie.[3] Here, where the immensity of Lake Superior funneled into a turbulent cataract one mile in length by a half-mile in width, any and every passer-by must pause in transit to and from the vast interior. Whether Indian or white man, trader or missionary, soldier or sightseer, he must disembark from the vessel which carried him across the lakes and walk himself and all his baggage along the timeworn path around the rapids. Scenically, the flat, sandy St. Marys River shore was not so beautiful as the Apostle Islands, although the high hills back of the north shore provided a lovely, if distant, vista to residents of the south side on which lay the portage. To John they must have been reminiscent of the mountains of Antrim bounding the horizon of his childhood home on the River Bush. And the Falls of St. Mary were only 80 miles by water from Michilimackinac, where a small knot of congenial gentlemen resided, and where they stored enormous quantities of trade goods and provisions for distribution.

Finally, the site offered a unique market attraction. The tumultuous rapids were literally choked spring and fall with the choicest specimens of the most delectable freshwater fish in the world. Natives congregated there from great distances just for the whitefish catch—risking their lives as they rode the rapids from a standing balance on the gunwales of a canoe and deftly scooping their prey into a long-handled net. Precisely at the trading season John's customers would be flocking on his doorstep. Later on, as he prospered, he could hire clerks and send them into the interior regions to reach an even wider market. He willingly sacrificed scenery in the immediate environs of his home for these locational advantages.

Nor would John and Susan live there in isolation as at La Pointe. The Sault de Ste. Marie was on its way to becoming a village. Jean Baptiste Cadotte had been there for 40 years and Jean Baptiste Nolin for 12. Just last year John Sayer, a North West Company partner, had established himself on the other (north) side of the river and was building facilities that would bring in more families. All of these men were married to Indian women, who might provide friendship for Susan, while John would be able to enjoy the company of other white men in residence at St. Mary's and Mackinac or just passing along the portage. Jean Baptiste Barthe, who had traded at the Sault since the mid-70's, had recently returned to Detroit. John would fill the trading void left by his departure.

The strategic importance of the Sault had been recognized as soon as men discovered it, about 150 years before John Johnston's arrival. The visit of Fathers Isaac Jogues and Charles Raymbault to the Saulteur Indians, as they called the local residents then, was the first recorded mention of the place, but unlettered *coureurs de bois* had undoubtedly been there before them. As an outpost of the white man, its history began with the mission established by Father Louis Nicolas in 1667.[4] And a few years later, in June of 1671, it was the scene of an impressive spectacle in which François Daumont, Sieur de St. Lusson, took formal possession in the name of King Louis XIV of all of North America west of the St. Lawrence River.

Preparation for this important event had been carefully executed. Early in the spring Nicholas Perrot, seasoned fur trader engaged as aide to St. Lusson, sent parties of Indians to visit the tribes north of the Great Lakes and urge them to send their chiefs to a great council that would be held at the Sault de Ste. Marie. He impressed upon them the unprecedented importance of the occasion and the necessity for all the tribes to be represented. Then he, himself, went to La Baye to summon the chiefs who lived south and west of the lakes. Thus from every direction the customary annual congregation at the Sault for the spring whitefish run was augmented by the presence of additional tribes and dignitaries from farther afield.[5] It was probably the largest assemblage that traditional meeting ground had ever hosted. Not only did the natives number in the thousands from 14 different nations, but a large number of French traders came as well, and all the Jesuit missionaries came in from their scattered posts for the occasion.

June 4, 1671 dawned bright and cool. Wind blew smoke from hundreds of lodge fires gently into the pale blue sky from the bustling encampments on the flat plain by the river. The French, in as full dress as individually and collectively they could muster, formed a procession to the top of a breezy knoll overlooking the churning rapids of Ste. Marie. The chiefs of the 14 tribes, dressed in deerskins intricately and elaborately worked in colorful feathers, beads, and porcupine quills, also assembled on the rise, with all their people ranged in solemn witness on the ground below.

The proceedings began when Father Claude Dablon, Superior of the Ottawa Mission, blessed a large wooden cross "with all the ceremonies of the Church."

God took precedence over even the Sun King. As they raised the cross upright into the post hole prepared for it, the assembled French, clergy and laity, sang the *Vexilla*. Then they raised the escutcheon of France, the *Fleur de Lis*, on a cedar pole even higher than the cross, to show that Louis would protect the Church of God. While they sang the *Exaudiat*, Father Dablon offered another prayer, for the person of his sovereign. Whereupon the Sieur de St. Lusson assumed the center of the stage to declare with solemn and awesome dignity that henceforth and forevermore all the lands and waters from this place east to the St. Lawrence River, north to the Northern Sea, west as far as man could know, and south to the Southern Sea were the possession of the mighty King Louis of France. "*Vive le Roi! Vive le Roi!* " the Frenchmen shouted to the accompaniment of a volley of musketry.

  Eyes glowing and heads nodding, the assembled natives expressed their approval of this ceremonial display. Then the upraised arms of the Black Gown, Father Claude Allouez, brought silence to the crowd while he, in fluent and sonorous Ottawa, explained to them the significance of what they had just observed, astounding his hearers with his eloquent description of the wealth and power of the Sun King Louis. St. Lusson may have found the Jesuit's performance a hard one to follow, but he, too, outdid himself in commending to the Indians the protection of the great monarch and unification of all these lands under his rule in return for their unswerving allegiance to him. Round a great lighted bonfire, the Frenchmen closed the ceremonies with a glorious *Te Deum*.[6]

  The French staged this elaborate pageant to serve a very practical political purpose. A year and a half previously an event had taken place in London that profoundly disturbed M. Colbert, Minister of Finance to King Louis, and to M. Talon, Intendent of New France, as well as to all those Frenchmen on both sides of the Atlantic who were getting rich on the fur trade. A special sale had been held to market the first enormous shipload of top quality peltry that had come out of North America by a new route—Hudson's Bay. The two rogues from Trois Rivieres, Médard Chouart and Pierre Radisson, unable to convince French authorities of the merit of a trade route via Hudson's Bay, had sold the idea to the British. Those canny gentlemen set up a Company of Adventurers of England trading into Hudson's Bay to negotiate an end run around the virtual French monopoly. And the Dutch from Fort Orange (Albany) in the Hudson Valley were also getting bolder in their incursions into French territory. But trade depended on peace among and with the Indians. If the French could secure their firm allegiance, they could control the supplies of peltry at the source. One ceremony would not, of course, guarantee the trade, but it would and did establish an important precedent in all future dealings with the natives (including justification for Pontiac's rebellion) and also served notice on the other European powers that France meant to secure her vast claims in North America.

Eighty years later they had to establish their claim all over again. Only now the English were firmly established on Hudson's Bay and, having taken over the Dutch trade, were competing much more strenuously from Albany and Oswego.[7] The French presence in the fortified village of Michilimackinac on the south side of the Straits kept the region south and west of Lake Michigan under effective control. But the Indians from the more lucrative fur breeding areas north and west of Lake Superior flouted and abused the French traders among them, then either paddled north to Hudson's Bay or bypassed Michilimackinac to carry their peltry to the English on Lake Ontario. In both places they received better goods at lower prices.

What was wanted was a second fortified village at a location as strategic for the Northwest as Michilimackinac was for the Southwest. This would keep the "French" Indians at home where they belonged and facilitate peace-keeping among the natives as well.[8] The site of the old Mission of Ste. Marie du Sault, abandoned since 1689, was ideal for the purpose. The Indians still came there to fish, and they had to portage their peltry to go down the lakes.

Louis le Gardeur, Sieur de Repentigny, was chosen by the governor of New France, Marquis de la Jonquiere, to establish the new fort in 1750. He was a seasoned officer from an illustrious Quebec family. Moreover, he was familiar with the area, having served under his brother's command at Michilimackinac. But as Jonquiere had no money with which to pursue the enterprise, he devised a clever scheme to finance it. In return for establishing and supplying a garrison at the Sault, the French government granted to Louis Le Gardeur a half-interest in the largest seigneury in New France—18 miles of frontage along the Riviere de Ste. Marie, extending 18 miles inland. His silent partner was Louis de Bonne, Sieur de Miselle, Jonquiere's nephew and captain of his guard. Of course at this moment in time all that land was worth virtually nothing, nor was there any reason to believe it would ever be of any use for agriculture. The government expected de Repentigny to derive his future fortune from what passed through the seigneury and its monopoly position at the rapids, not what he could raise on it.

But the King was suspicious of fur traders and their honesty in rendering Caesar his due. To induce him to approve the concession and grant the estate, the traders had to play down trade in favor of colonial interests. The Custom of Paris required that to hold the seigneury the land must be continuously occupied by de Repentigny or his tenants. But they made no explicit requirement as to the number of tenants or the nature of the improvements they must make. A token peasant settlement would, in fact, satisfy the conditions of the grant; its military and commercial aspects were far more important.

The enterprise paid off in the very first year. In the spring of 1751 de Repentigny carried with him to Quebec over 400 packs of made beaver, each pack weighing 90 pounds. The token "peasant" he left behind at the new post was Jean Baptiste Cadotte, a voyageur from Trois Rivieres. During the first winter he had had time to build only one house, on the south bank of the river just below the rapids. The old mission had probably stood in about the same place; nearby was the hill from which St. Lusson had declared the sovereignty of France. By the time de Repentigny returned in September, Cadotte had two more log houses built and was starting to cut pickets for the stockade. It was a crude beginning, but from now on there would always be a settlement at the Sault de Ste. Marie.[9]

But a seigneury? That was a matter for some doubt. And it would, in fact, remain in doubt until 1867. Just a decade after the King had granted it, the fortunes of war and diplomacy snatched the estate from de Repentigny's hands. He could have kept it. The 1763 Treaty of Paris, which sealed the British conquest of North America, confirmed security of property to all Frenchmen in the colony. But the British law required a *quid pro quo* of those holding the title of seigneur—an oath of homage and fidelity to His Britannic Majesty. For those declining to take the oath, His Majesty permitted the disposal of their property through sale to a British subject without prejudice, prior to their emigration from Canada and within a period of 18 months from the effective date of the treaty. Governor General Murray encouraged de Repentigny to stay, but "an oath of fidelity to the new master . . . was too hard for my heart."[10] He sold his other seigneuries on the St. Lawrence and sailed "home" to the France from which his great-grandfather had emigrated 130 years before. As for the seigneury in the wilderness, de Repentigny did nothing with it; he simply walked away. And his partner, de Bonne, was dead, killed at the battle of Sillery. The legal status of the Seigneury de Ste. Marie hung in limbo.

But its "tenant" did not. Solid, canny, and capable Jean Baptiste Cadotte stayed right on at the post, planting and reaping his field of corn and caring for the livestock he had brought in several years before. He continued the semblance of a farm at the Sault for several years, but Jean Baptiste, like all others of his kind, engaged mainly in the fur trade. In 1765 he formed a partnership with Alexander Henry, one of the first three English traders to arrive on the scene after the Conquest.[11] Together they prospered during more than a decade of wintering around the shores of Lake Superior and inland as far northwest as the Churchill and the Saskatchewan Rivers. In 1776 Henry retired to Montreal to concentrate on the mercantile end of the trade, while Cadotte continued to operate from Sault Ste. Marie as an independent. He never noticed the ringing of a bell in far-off Philadelphia that summer. In fact, the ensuing five years of war for the independence of His Majesty's rebellious colonies caused barely a ripple on Lake Superior beyond the inconvenience of delays in the shipping of provisions from the lower lakes.

Nor did the 1783 Treaty of Paris make any difference at all in the lives of the inhabitants of the Great Lakes, although in negotiations the shrewd Benjamin Franklin and his fellow commissioners, John Adams and John Jay, nearly won all of Canada as a 14th state. They did not quite pull that off, but they did manage to push the British territorial claims northward from the Ohio River to the middle of the Great Lakes. Twenty-five years later John Johnston could still deplore the settlement that "has wantonly given away several thousand leagues of the richest fur country to which the Americans had no more right than they had to the Province of Bengal."[12] Not that it mattered at the time. It would be 13 years before the Long Knives, as the Indians called the Americans,[13] arrived to take possession of their Northwest Territory, and almost 20 after that until they could hold onto it.

In the meanwhile, the resilient Jean Baptiste Cadotte carried on as he always had—under the French or the British or the American flag—tending his "farm" in summer, trading with the Indians in winter, and raising his half-breed sons to bourgeois status by sending them to be educated in Montreal. That shrewd old man knew how to take advantage of each turn of fate and nationality, having been plucked from the plebian ranks of the voyageurs by his French commander and having entered the bourgeoisie of the fur trade with his English partner. By the time the Americans arrived, he was well past 70 and retired—the grand old man of the Sault.

Some day John Johnston would succeed to Cadotte's position as the man who had lived long enough by the rapids to see dramatic changes in the country and its society. Now, in the summer of 1793, John built his first proper house at the foot of the falls, on 40 acres with 300 feet of river frontage, near the old fort of de Repentigny.[14] After he had given out his credits to the

Indians in the fall, he and his young wife settled in to await the birth of their first child.

Chapter Five

Lifestyle

In some respects the Paris Treaty of 1783 obtained for the United States little more than the right to struggle for existence free of a shooting war. A decade later the new nation was still commercially hamstrung by British power, nowhere more evident than in the Northwest, where the nominal change in authority was barely noticeable. In 1794 Chief Justice John Jay went to England to negotiate another treaty. Hopefully it would eliminate the restrictions on American trade that the British lion continued to impose—on the fisheries of the Northeast, on the West Indies trade of the middle Atlantic cities, and on the fur trade of the Northwest frontier. The last theater represented his major success. Britain and the U. S. guaranteed freedom of passage for nationals of both countries along the boundary waterways, and Britain promised that "His Majesty will withdraw all His Troops and Garrisons from all Posts and Places within the Boundary Lines assigned by the Treaty of Peace to the United States. . . . on or before the first Day of June One thousand seven hundred and ninety six."[1]

This time His Majesty kept his promise. Along with the other western military posts Britain turned Fort Mackinac and an American garrison over to Lt. Henry Burbeck, a little late, on September first.[2] The British troops removed to a new installation at the southwest corner of St. Joseph Island on the international boundary of St. Marys River, an abrupt comedown from the handsome facilities on Mackinac Island. Fort St. Joseph never became much more than a crude outpost, with a scruffy little settlement nearby that contrasted sadly with the picturesque Michilimackinac.[3] Officers, their ladies, and their troops would continue over the years to seek sociability and entertainment at the beautiful island in the Straits, about forty miles to the southwest.

The change in garrison personnel at Mackinac in 1796 exerted no further influence over the residents at Sault Ste. Marie than the nominal change in flags had done in 1783. Montreal remained the Mother City, from which goods flowed and to which they carried peltry; they continued to reckon the fur trade in pounds sterling, although they still contracted the wages of the voyageurs in French *livres*; and the fortunes flowing from the Northwest continued to accumulate in the vaults of Montreal Scotsmen and their London agents, all loyal subjects of His Majesty. Article Two of Jay's treaty stipulated that

> All Settlers and Traders . . . shall continue to enjoy, unmolested, all their property of every kind. . . . such of them as shall continue to reside within the said Boundary Lines shall not be compelled to become Citizens of the United States, or to take any Oath of Allegiance to the government thereof, but they shall be at full liberty to do so, if they think proper, and they shall make and declare their Election within one year after the Evacuation aforesaid. And all persons who shall continue there after the expiration of the said year, without having declared their intention of remaining subjects of His Britannick [sic] Majesty, shall be considered as having elected to become Citizens of the United States.[4]

John Johnston undoubtedly never read Article Two, but it would come to have a profound effect on his life and those of his children. He certainly made no move either to become an American citizen or to declare formally his continued allegiance to the Crown. He simply minded his own business, extended hospitality to all of good will who came his way, and retained his commercial independence through scrupulous avoidance of contractual entanglements with partners or fur trading companies. Why was he so passionate about this independence? Had he been so bitterly disillusioned by his experience at the waterworks in Belfast that he overreacted in determination never again to entrust his fortunes to the vagaries of another man's behavior? Certainly the conduct of the organized fur barons displayed a ruthlessness and rapacity that he found abhorrent. He often expressed that view with sufficient emphasis to induce William McGillivray to reply on one occasion, "Why Johnston, you are much better suited for a preacher, than a fur trader."[5] Yet the same tycoons whose tactics he deplored were his personal friends, and so long as he avoided participation in their trading associations they remained so. His ambivalence toward them reflected his ambivalence toward his own activities in the fur trade—hatred of the meanness it evoked, which he strove personally to avoid, yet fondness for the individuals engaged in it as human beings. He saw the cosmic drama of good and evil played eloquently on this wilderness stage and was paradoxically caught by his own irrevocable choice in bondage to a business he fundamentally despised.

Although he did not accept invitations to join, John, like everyone else on Lake Superior, lived in the shadow of the North West Company. It had originated in 1779 as a loose association among the pioneers who opened the rich fur-bearing network of lakes and rivers that stretched for thousands of miles beyond the farthest extremity of Lake Superior—to the Rocky Mountains and the Arctic Ocean. By 1793, when the Johnstons settled at Sault Ste. Marie, the North West Company commanded scores of posts throughout their 2,000-mile domain; in time 125 or more would extend over twice that distance.[6]

The logistics of supply for this far-flung empire came together at the elaborate depot the company built at Grand Portage, a beautiful, sheltered bay near the Lake Superior mouth of the twisted Pigeon River. Here the 4,000 to 6,000-pound lading of the 36-foot *canots du maitres*, which came from Montreal, was transshipped to *canots du nord* of 20 to 25 feet, which could be handled on the difficult portages and tortured waterways of the interior. The *canots du nord* accommodated a payload in trade goods of only 2,000 pounds, however, for they also had to carry food for the long voyage inland, which might last up to two months, plus every last tool, tobacco plug, rifle bullet, and account book, every fabricated item of any kind that would be needed at an interior post for the coming year. Once arrived at their destination, the men lived (or starved) off the land and what they brought with them.

At the place where all this loading, unloading and reloading occurred, where they stored goods, provisions and furs to await the process, where they built and repaired canoes going either way, and where the partners met annually to settle accounts and lay their plans for the future, the trappings of a village grew up. In mid-July, when all the personnel congregated, 1,200 men encamped round the compound and 100 bourgeois sat down to dine at one sitting in the Great Hall.[7]

Only one element of supply was not accommodated at Grand Portage. The North West Company operated a smaller depot for a different purpose a couple of hundred miles inland at Lac La Pluie. Winterers at many of the interior posts, especially those in the remote mountain, arctic and sub-arctic locations, could not rely upon local fish and game for food. But a clever invention of the plains Indians, pemmican (preserved buffalo meat), combined with the birch-bark canoe of the forest Indians formed the lifeline of that distant trade. Enormous nutritional value compressed into a small packet of food, easily transported by canoe in summer or by backpack during winter snowshoe travel, pemmican was indispensable to the success of the North West Company. At a string of posts through the prairie country of the South Saskatchewan and Red River Valleys of present day Manitoba and North Dakota, the natives traded pemmican in the same way they traded peltry elsewhere. The traders extended credits to the Indian hunters and their women, who pounded the buffalo meat and mixed it with grease into the life-sustaining foodstuff that remained well preserved for months. They then carried the precious cargo to Lac La Pluie, where they waited to load it on the upbound canoes for the return trip to the interior.[8]

The elaborate detail of fur trading operations in the inhospitable and distant regions of the *pays en haut* required a commensurate organization at the center if it was to be profitable. It was this logistic necessity that promoted the growth of the North West Company and its eventual absorption of virtually every two-man partnership and small company trading in that region. Competition could be, and often was, devastating in the circumstances of the fur trade because it was conducted on the level of human life.

Wintering bourgeois from competing firms literally faced each other in stockaded posts built at a strategic portage or, more likely, on a lake where the ice fishing was abundant. In the fall each used every deceitful device he could think of to secure the loyalty and the promise of furs from the local Indian bands and families. Usually this involved plying them with as much liquor as feasible, thereby hastening the destruction of Indian lives. But many of the Indians were shrewd enough to play their suppliers off against each other by taking credits from several traders against the same future furs. Then the traders spied on one another all winter and spring to make certain that one man's Indians did not bring their peltry to another man's house. If a bourgeois thought that had happened, he and his men marched into the offender's post to try and take the furs by force. In the ensuing armed violence the lives of one or more voyageurs would be forfeit—often it was a clerk, occasionally a partner.

By a peculiar code of the trade, however, opponents who might engage in armed combat over a pack of furs, never failed to share such provisions as they had with a starving competitor whose fishing had gone sour. Lonely opponents needed each other just for human contact. During periods of truce they took tea in each other's houses and exchanged their worn books and magazines—until the next band of Indians came along. Then the tug of war resumed with no holds barred, including kidnapping and imprisonment of whole native families until they extracted the furs.[9]

Combination, then, into a single company, made

sense both from the profit standpoint—through economies in joint purchase, shipping, and marketing, and centralized administration—and in terms of the decency of human life. Enormous profits were possible in the fur trade, but the long three- to four-year trading cycle (from the ordering of English goods to ultimate sale of the furs), combined with the hazards of nature, made the potential losses as great. Sharing the risks offered a strong inducement to association, but the independents of the fur trade were willing to give up only so much of their individual authority and responsibility. No matter how large, rich, and administratively complex the North West Company grew, it remained organizationally the simple partnership they formed at the start.[10]

In effect, each man put in the value of a year's outfit of trade goods every fall, and when the peltry came down the following summer, they settled accounts and distributed profits at the annual meeting at Grand Portage. This arrangement turned out to be both the company's strength and its weakness. A large measure of independence within the organization might be necessary to keep the contentious and individualistic partners affiliated. On the other hand, as an organization, it lacked the stable capital resources and continuity needed to meet the threat that inevitably came from a larger and more dangerous rival—the joint stock, limited liability Hudson's Bay Company.[11] Nevertheless, during its halcyon 40 years the North West Company served its members admirably, made scores of men wealthy, and unrolled the map of a continent as the partners continued to explore ever farther north and west.

John Johnston's operations, and those of other independents, reproduced in miniature the logistical procedures of the North West Company. These smaller outfits traded inland from the south shore of Lake Superior, where the Company's interests were minimal. Their depots were at Mackinac and Sault Ste. Marie, their outposts at places like Grand Island, L'Ance-Keweenaw, La Pointe, and Fond du Lac.[12] From these locations, usually the site of an Ojibway summer village, and from the Sault itself, John's growing staff of clerks and voyageurs followed the Indians to their winter hunting grounds up the rivers—the Tequamenon, the Two Hearted, the Carp, the Laughing Whitefish, the Ontonagan, the Montreal, the Brule. Because the distances from supply sources were much shorter, and the climate somewhat milder, the independents did not require pemmican. While this factor simplified their administrative problems, they, unlike the North Westers, did suffer the hazards of competition.

Nevertheless, John prospered. Whether he was able to do so without resort to the tactics he deplored among his competitors is hard to say. He had the reputation of an honorable man. And he had superb connections among the Indians, which may have enabled him to keep aloof from the vicious methods of other traders. His obvious respect for his wife's people and the esteem inherited by the daughter of the great Waub-o-jeeg, which she fully justified in her own right as she matured from a frightened girl to a self-possessed woman, were probably enough to keep John's regular customers loyal. But another element, subtle and too rarely perceived, also existed.

The North American Indian had no concept of private property. To him it was preposterous that one man or a group of men could say, "I own, exclusively, this piece of God's earth and all the animals and plants that dwell upon it." Nor could they comprehend the corollary which states, "This house and the food and clothing within it are mine, and you may come in and get some of it only if I give you permission and you give me a *quid pro quo* in return." For the Indian no "mine" and "thine" existed, only "ours" by grace of the Master of Life. The majority of white men, even those who interacted all their lives with the Indians, never understood this. And, therefore, they never understood why the Indians continued to "steal," to "poach" in violation of "treaties," and to return to "beg" for more provisions after they had been "paid."

But John Johnston did understand. Just as he knew that he could walk into any Indian lodge, uninvited, and partake of the food it contained on an equal basis with the family, he knew they expected him to open his house and share his food with them if they were in need. Just as he knew that the Indians brought him fur mainly because he wanted it, he knew also that they expected him to give them the things they asked for simply because they wanted them. The notion that this amount of peltry equalled that amount of tobacco was the white man's invention. Let him play with these equations; the Indian had more important things to do. Consequently, the Indian never kept track of the "accounts." If he came to the white trader because he needed something and the trader told him his "credit" was used up and he had to give more fur to "buy" it, the Indian accommodated him, though he considered it foolishness. If he had no more peltry to give, he accepted whatever the trader let him have in exchange for a "debt" in a ledger and thought no more of it.

When the white men wanted their land as well as their furs, the Indians had no way of reckoning how much this forest or that stream was "worth" in terms of horns of gunpowder or iron pots or lengths of calico. If it pleased the government treaty negotiator to write on a piece of paper that it was "worth" so much, what difference did that make to the change of the seasons or the yield of the hunt? But when the traders occasionally denied the negotiated quantity of goods that was to be annually disbursed to the Indians, because the government had paid the Indians' "debts" to the traders, the Indians looked perplexedly at the "statement of accounts" neatly prepared for them and failed to understand. And when they were told later on that the government had already "paid them for" their land even though they (the Indians) had used up the ammunition, worn out the pots, and used all the calico, they had no way to argue because they had not kept count. They knew only that they were hungry and naked, and that the fur was gone and so, apparently, was their land. Gradually the Indians came to realize that they had lost a game they had been playing under the "wrong" set of rules. But by then it was too late.

Most of the traders and certainly the government agents never intended to cheat the Indians. They truly believed they were fair and honest because they kept such careful track of all the transactions. They could no more comprehend the Indian's unconsciousness of the sanctity of property and contracts than the Indian could comprehend the white man's lack of appreciation for the communality of mankind. In short, few Indians and whites ever really spoke *with* each other. They talked *at* each other, and neither understood.

John Johnston came closer than most. He gave his Indians what they needed, and if sometimes they did not bring enough fur to "pay" for it all at the going rate, he rarely carried the debt over on his books. When whites criticized Indian morals, he defended them, and on one occasion was reported to have "poured forth a torrent of eloquent, but vituperative satire against the fashionable follies of the civilized world."[13] The natives' good will toward this man, who understood their ways and did not try to impose the white man's accounting upon their lives, brought him enough furs and enough profit for him to live as comfortably as he wished. What more could he ask?

Little doubt exists that Susan had much to do with both John's understanding of the native society and his success in business. Described as "a woman of excellent judgment and good sense,"[14] she, like he, had the mental capacity to appreciate and relate functionally to a world view different from her own. Together they bridged the gap between their cultures, each learning from the other as they evolved a strong and viable cultural compromise of their own. Susan understood the white trader's methods, so she was able to work out with her husband on the one hand, and with her clansmen on the other, the trust and the understanding that permitted a mutually beneficial relationship.

No Indian, save one who might be drunk or abusive, ever came to the Johnston's home who was not welcome to enter, whose moderate requests for provision or assistance were not honored, and who was not treated with kindness and respect. Most especially did they find at that house an unusual gift of great value—medical aid. John dispensed generously without hint of "payment" or "credit" his stock of amelioratives and restoratives, expensive and otherwise. If a case puzzled him he pored over the medical books in his library until he found a plausible diagnosis.[15] He undoubtedly made some prescriptive mistakes, but for 30 years John Johnston was physician and pharmacist to a wide community—without fee.

In this fashion John was able to live according to his creed of honor and Christian belief, avoiding the avaricious excesses of his commercial rivals, and prospering while he did so. In 1794 he built a substantial two-story log house, part of which stands today. This was no ordinary "log cabin" for he had it constructed in the traditional Quebec chamfered method. Rounded logs were tapered at the ends to be mortised into slots cut into the upright end posts, with plaster applied between the logs for weatherproofing.[16] As improvements were made, milled door and window frames were sent up from the cities below. Into this house he gradually placed furnishings brought over by ship from England and Ireland and laboriously hauled to the wilderness piece by piece and barrel by barrel—polished mahogany, snowy linen, delicate crystal, translucent china, gleaming silver.[17] Most precious cargo of all was the accumulation of books that over the years grew into a library estimated by one visitor at a thousand volumes.[18] Gradually, by the Falls of St. Mary, the county seat of a genteel Irish squire took shape. Adjacent to the house was a compound of out-buildings for the storage of goods and provisions, the stabling of cattle and horses, and the quartering of clerks and canoemen when they were in port, rather a miniature Michilimackinac or Grand Portage without the unseemly "riot and revelry." Beyond lay truck gardens and fields that fed the family and completed the facilities of a country estate.[19]

It was from this setting that the renowned Johnston hospitality emanated. They greeted native visitors to the house and discussed their affairs in a room set aside for the purpose, with a special entrance just outside John's office. Either he or Susan might talk with these callers and meet their requests. (They usually did come with requests.) European or Europeanized gentlemen they entertained rather differently for, understanding though he was, John Johnston was enough of an aristocrat to differentiate the status of his visitors. Few gentlemen, and virtually no Europeanized ladies, resided at St. Marys in the early years, but a continual parade of travelers came passing through on their way to and from Lake

Superior. And most of them, whether personages or merely persons, Mr. Johnston cordially invited to dine with him at the accustomed hour of four o'clock.[20] Susan's role was as important on these occasions as it was in hosting the Indians who called, but it was much less conspicuous.

She carefully prepared the foods to be served, usually assisted by a young native servant girl—game in the North American style, puddings and pies to the English taste, fresh vegetables of international appeal, and that *specialite du pays*, the magnificent whitefish. She saw to it that the native servant properly laid out the linen, silver and crystal on the table in the fashion John had taught her and that she filled the wine and whiskey decanters on the sideboard. Then Susan remained quietly and efficiently in the background, while the gentlemen dined and talked of business and absent friends. Unobtrusive though she might be in her habitual black calico dress, ornamented perhaps by a brooch her husband had given her, and underpinned with beaded Indian leggins and moccasins, Susan's capable and dignified presence was palpable in the household, and no visitor or correspondent ever failed to pay her their respects. She understood the English or French in which they addressed her, but she responded only in her native Ojibway.[21]

The most regular guests at the Johnston table were the partners of the North West Company, who passed through the Sault on their way to and from the annual meeting at Grand Portage. Simon McTavish, a shrewd and audacious, though dandified, little Scotsman, was the guiding genius of the company from its inception. He, with his partner Joseph Frobisher, who had been among the earliest to open the Northwest trade, ran the company from Montreal. But Simon never failed to attend the annual meeting at Grand Portage to put out the brush fires constantly arising among the wintering partners and see that all ran smoothly at the fur gathering end. One of the significant sources of discontent was Simon's tendency to nepotism. An inexhaustible supply of McTavish nephews existed in the County of Inverness, and Simon brought most of them over to join the North

West Company. He groomed his favorite, William McGillivray, to succeed him eventually as general superintendent of the company.[22] Will served nine years in the *pays en haut*, "retiring" to Montreal and partnership in McTavish, Frobisher the year John settled at the Sault. But he, too, returned every July for the annual meeting.

The arrogant and cunning Simon McTavish was not a man to John's taste, but the more genial and candid William McGillivray and the intellectual Roderick McKenzie became his friends. McKenzie was cousin to North West partner Alexander Mackenzie, who discovered the Mackenzie River in 1789, following it to the Arctic Ocean, and who in 1792 was the first white man to cross the continent by land to the Pacific Ocean. For these exploits the King knighted him a few years later, but his cousin was the unsung hero of those glorious adventures. The modest, gentle, Rory, as he was known to his friends, hated the frozen isolated life of the Northwest. Yet he remained years longer than Company service required, at the farthest outpost of Fort Chipewyan on Great Slave Lake, minding the store so that his cousin Alexander could achieve fame and reward. Only his books, laboriously hauled up every year, made that life tolerable.[23] His library was so large and distinguished that Fort Chipewyan was known as the Athens of the Northwest.[24] He and John Johnston had much in common.

While John enjoyed these men and numerous others for their urbane conversation and worldly interests, they shared another area of common experience that must have evoked John Johnston's pain and disapproval. All of them had taken Indian wives; William McGillivray's was even named Susan.[25] But each of the North Westers left his *sauvagesse* in the *pays en haut* where she originated when he "retired" to Montreal. Later they married young English, French, or Scottish women. Although men like Will provided well for their halfbreed children, several of whom grew up to become senior clerks (never partners) in the North West Company, desertion of a young family was an act John Johnston could never have brought himself to. His family was uncommonly precious to him, and every decision he made was motivated by their welfare. When away from them, he never failed to close a letter to one of his children with "Kiss your dear Mother and all the children for me and may our Father and our God guide, guard and help you all."[26]

The children had begun to appear promptly. Lewis Saurin was born October 16, 1793,[27] named for the most illustrious of the Johnston connections, the Archdeacon of Derry, father to John's Uncle William Saurin (his father's sister's husband), who was Vicar of Belfast. The archdeacon was one of the more notable Huguenot clergymen to emigrate from France after revocation of the Edict of Nantes.[28] Lewis, unfortunately, would not live up to his name. Rather it was George (*Kah-men-tay-ha* in Ojibway),[29] who came into the world April 10, 1796,[30] who would grow up to become his father's aide and confidante. A first daughter was born January 31, 1800.[31] Jane (*O-bahm-we-wa-ge-she-ge-quay*, The Sound Which the Stars Make Rushing Through the Sky),[32] named for John's much loved older sister, was to become the adored companion of his intellect from the time her own mental and literary abilities showed up at an early age. Eliza (*Wah-ba-mung-o-quay*, Woman of the Morning Star)[33] 1802,[34] and Charlotte (*O-gen-a-bug-o-quay*, Woman of the Wild Rose)[35] March 1, 1806.[36] Each of John's beloved sisters now had a namesake.

It is unlikely that John ever wintered in the wilderness away from his family at Sault Ste. Marie, but the intimate knowledge of the geography of Lake Superior revealed in the one essay he wrote for publication, indicates that he made frequent spring-to-fall trips to his subordinate posts along the lakeshore. While his men paddled the canoe he was able to indulge his deep love of the manifold beauties of that incomparable inland sea. For him it represented the ultimate expression of the glory of God. He wrote of a little island he named Contemplation, that it had the power of

> filling his mind with a pleasing melancholy and a desire for quiet sequestration, where every worldly care and every mean passion should be lulled to rest, and the heart left at full liberty to examine

itself, develop each complicated fold, wash out each stain with a repentant tear, and finally become worthy of holding converse with nature, approach the Celestial Portals and, though at an infinite distance, be permitted a glimpse of its Almighty Sovereign, but [sic] our Father and God.[37]

Whether John's own canoes voyaged in the opposite direction, down to Montreal, is not certain. By the turn of the century the number of merchant sailing ships carrying goods, especially heavy equipment and supplies, to Mackinac and Sault Ste. Marie from Detroit and Buffalo had risen substantially. On the Canadian side of the border as well, men used sailing vessels for transport from Lachine to York (modern Toronto) where they transshipped goods by river, lake and wagon road to Georgian Bay,[38] and again loaded them on ships for the voyage to Sault Ste. Marie. John, like the North West Company, undoubtedly brought up much of his merchandise, certainly the heavy furniture he imported, by either or both of these lake routes. But the furs customarily went down to Montreal by canoe. John's operation was hardly large enough to warrant a brigade, but given his cordial relations with the North West partners, it is entirely possible that he contracted for cargo space in their canoes or sent a canoe or two of his own in convoy with them. Like the cattle on a later frontier, he clearly identified his canoes and his packs with his mark: <II>[39]

David David, John's agent, received the peltry at the other end; John had transferred his account to David David from Todd, McGill some time after he settled at the Sault. This change of agent was consistent with his policy of avoiding involvement with the large fur trading organizations. David's father, Lazarus David, had come to Canada in the wake of Wolf's army around 1760, and when he died in 1776 he was the first Jew to be buried in consecrated ground in the city of Montreal. Son David became prominent in Montreal business affairs as a founder and director of the Bank of Montreal and a charter member of the Montreal Board of Trade.[40] Correspondence reveals that a warm relationship prevailed between Johnston and David for 30 years or more until Johnston's death.

How often John himself went down to Montreal is uncertain, but he was definitely there during the winter of 1807-1808. On December 19, 1807, Joseph Frobisher, secretary of the Beaver Club, recorded that "Mr. John Johnston of St. Marys was proposed as a Member by Mr. R. Mackenzie [sic]. Ordered to be balloted for at our next meeting." And on February 2, 1808 "Agreeable to the Resolve at our last Meeting Mr. John Johnston was balloted for & was unanimously elected Member of this Club."[41] It was a club unique in all the world to which he had the honor of admission.

Nineteen seasoned bourgeois had organized the Beaver Club in the winter of 1785, its membership limited exclusively to comrades who had wintered in the *pays en haut*. Offering no lofty purpose, no elaborate regulations or rituals, it provided an excuse for its members to get together over hearty food and heady liquor and reminisce about a way of life that only those who had lived it could share. Illness or absence from the city were the only acceptable excuses for failure to attend the (usually) semi-monthly dinner meetings at Dillon's Hotel.

These meetings soon fell into a pattern. They rendered with feeling five toasts to launch the evening: To the Mother of All Saints; to His Britannic Majesty; To the Fur Trade in All Its Branches; to Voyageurs, Wives and Children; and to Absent Members. Then came the feast during which platter followed platter of roast beaver, pemmican, sturgeon, wild rice, bear meat and venison, with bottles of madeira, port, brandy and gin. By the end of the evening the 40 or 50 members in attendance, barely able to sit, let alone stand, ranged themselves on the floor in paired rows. Then with walking stick, umbrella, or whatever suitable article each could find, they paddled their way through memories of glory, as they belted out the lusty songs of the voyageurs.[42]

John attended several meetings of the Beaver Club that winter. On March 26 he took his turn as Cork, his duties presumably relating to the disbursement of the liquid refreshments. He also engaged in more serious matters with his friend Roderick McKenzie. Rory had long planned to write a definitive history of the fur trade, which would include descriptive material about the Northwest and its posts, and the customs of the Indians as well as the white traders. He solicited contributions from all the bourgeois, partners and clerks whom he thought might cooperate, and many did send in essays and notes. He particularly urged his literary friend, John Johnston, to contribute.[43]

Although John enjoyed writing both prose and poetry, he had neither the inclination nor the patience to correct and polish his work; he wrote for his own pleasure with no thought of publication. Rory McKenzie's request, therefore, required rather more care, and it took John a long time to get around to complying with it. He made the effort, however, and in July of 1807 he had sent down a first installment in the care of Duncan McGillivray, with a covering note of apology:

> I know not how to apologize for my breach of promise with respect to my little manuscript. To say I had positively forgotten it would not be truth; the fact is, on reflecting upon the crude and undigested state in which it now stands, I dreaded its meeting the eye of a person whose correctness and superior knowledge of the subject I am sensible of. But when I reflect that that person has honoured me with the name of friend, I no longer hesitate to submit to his inspection the beginning of a work which perhaps may never be finished, and which I fear will only be a proof of my vanity and weakness.[44]

Whether John, himself, delivered the rest of the manuscript when he went down to Montreal in the fall, or sent it at a later time is not known. McKenzie never completed his ambitious work anyway, and the notes and manuscripts simply gathered dust until his son-in-law, L. R. Masson, published them in his two volume *Le Bourgeois de la Compagnie du Nord-Oest*, in 1889. Then John Johnston's "An Account of Lake Superior" finally saw the light of day.

The account is a graphic description of the south

coast of Lake Superior—its contours, vegetation, soil and rock formations. He apparently drew the line, however, at his friend's request for Indian lore. John had begun to collect some of the traditions and legends from the earliest days of his acquaintance with Waub-o-jeeg, but after his father-in-law died of tuberculosis in the summer of 1793, he was unable to find another reliable source. He might painstakingly record a fable or a custom or a tradition explained to him by one person, and some time thereafter discover it completely refuted by another "authority." The uncertainties of oral transmission of culture explained the problem in part, but John realized, too, that many of the most important Ojibway traditions were secret to the members of the tribe, and some of the contradictions probably resulted from deliberate efforts at obfuscation. He finally gave up the project in disgust and even destroyed all his notes.[45] His wife, whom he certainly trusted not to deceive him, was apparently not sufficiently knowledgeable about these traditions to clarify matters for him. Nevertheless, through her he did become proficient enough in the Ojibway language to translate her father's poetry in the appropriate mood and meter.

Although his happiness and the force of his energies focused on his family, John Johnston was a gregarious man who relished socializing with his peers. The settlement at St. Marys was still too small to offer much scope, and the North West partners paid only the briefest of visits. Michilimackinac continued to hold the center of the social stage, and it was there, and among the officers at Fort St. Joseph, that John found several satisfying friendships. The combination of gentleman traders from Sault Ste. Marie and Mackinac and officers from the two military posts created an international community of interesting diversity—French, British, American, Catholic, Protestant, autocratic, democratic, military, commercial. Among the women was the additional leavening of Indian blood. The full-blooded Indian wives were less likely to attend the teas and balls than the more Europeanized half-breed wives. But the latter played virtually the same role as the English, French and American women from the East, whom they certainly outnumbered.

During the summer, visitors from the cities "below" and from other posts along the Northwest frontier augmented this resident society. Among them in the year 1808 were John Campbell, United States Indian Agent at Prairie du Chien, and Redford Crawford, a British trader operating on the Mississippi. The cause of a quarrel that occurred between these two at Mackinac is obscure. According to John Johnston it was "trifling."[46] John Askin, Jr. thought it was precipitated "over the bottle."[47] For whatever reason, and despite John's best efforts to prevent it, the two men insisted upon meeting one August morning in a duel at Detour near the mouth of the St. Marys River. Duelling was illegal, so they could not engage under the nose of the commandant at Mackinac, but why they chose a ground 35 miles away is a mystery. John acted as Campbell's second and reported to Hoffman that "tho' I shall ever regret that the accommodation agreed to between you and I [sic] did not take place I must declare that it is impossible any thing of the kind could have been conducted with more candour and honour when the Parties met. This I am induced to in justice to myself and the two other Gentlemen concerned, who, I make no doubt will ever deplore the fatal issue of so trifling a quarrel."[48] John Campbell died of his wounds a couple of days later at Fort St. Joseph.

The unfortunate man knew he was done for when he fell, and in the boat crossing the river from the fatal spot to the fort, he asked John to handle the arrangement of his affairs, particularly to send a Mr. Frank Dease back to Prairie du Chien to help Campbell's young son through a difficult winter. With even greater pathos he asked John to take his little daughter, Nancy, who was with him at the time. The warm-hearted Johnston readily agreed that "if the Executors of the estate will permit I shall adopt her as my own."[49] Nancy Campbell lived in the Johnston household for a number of years,[50] probably until she was grown, but no record shows what ultimately became of her.

She must have found an enthusiastic welcome among the growing family of Johnston girls. Four of them now made a large enough group for games, although Charlotte was still too little to be good for much. But the three older ones helped to fill the schoolroom void left by Lewis and George, who were sent to Montreal for their advanced schooling. Winter was the time for education. After John had given out the credits and dispatched his clerks and voyageurs to their posts near the hunting camps, John could devote himself to the children. Each shipment of goods from Montreal included important additions to his library and, in addition to instructing his charges in the three Rs, he continued the custom in which he had grown up. Every evening, as the family sat before the fire, he and the children took turns reading aloud from the classics of literature, history, biography, and religion. The day then closed, as it opened every morning, with all the household assembled in the parlor for prayers and the reading of a psalm.[51] A loving and kindly teacher, John could be stern and uncompromising in the inculcation of moral principles. On one of his trips to Montreal he sent a message to the younger ones through a letter to George: "many pretty and good things . . . shall be given to those that will merit them but if I hear of any impropriety of conduct my lasting displeasure will be the consequence."[52] His admonition to Jane was of a more intellectual cast

> The improvement of your mind is dearer to me, than every other accomplishment. External manners are soon acquired, but if instruction is neglected in youth, it can never be regained. Your being sequestered from the world at present, is therefore, a blessing from providence as you have now the time and means of storing your mind with good and religious ideas, that in a future day will be of more use in directing your conduct and preserving you from the snares of a base and wicked world, than the greatest fortune could possibly do. I hope you will be able to keep your word respecting the improvement of your dear little sisters.[53]

John might teach his children to read and write well in the English language; he might show them enough mathematics for daily use and bookkeeping; and he could surely impart to them a strong sense of history and a loving intimacy with the great works of literature. But there was a level beyond which his instruction could not go. His own training in Latin had been so weak that he could offer little to his children in this important discipline. Nor was his French strong enough to teach them the grammar and syntax that would make them literate in that language, which they spoke as fluently as the English of their father and the Ojibway of their mother. The children undoubtedly learned much of their French from the illiterate Canadian canoemen, and John took care to import books in that language, as well as English, so that they would learn the classic forms in addition to the *patois* of the voyageurs. All of his efforts did not satisfy his standards, however, and when the children approached adolescence he sent them away to school.

Lewis and George had gone to Montreal, but Jane's education was a different story. Almost as soon as she appeared in the world John's mother wrote that it was her wish to bring the child to Ireland for her education when she was old enough. Elizabeth Johnston must have yearned for the growing family of grandchildren so many thousands of miles away whom she would never see. Her two daughters lived near enough to her but, though both were married, neither was blessed with children. They made a lonely family circle of adults. A little girl in the house again would bring light to an old woman's declining years. Sadly, Elizabeth declined too soon. She died in 1804 before her hope to at least see one of her grandchildren was realized. But her daughter, Jane, the child's namesake, took up the project. She and her husband, John Moore, a retired naval officer, would warmly welcome little Jane at their home in Wexford, and see to it that she received a proper gentlewoman's education.[54]

Jane early showed an intellectual promise that excited and delighted her father. She was a delicate little creature, with serious dark eyes, who relished all that her father had to teach her. She worshipped him and he adored her. When she was nine years old they set out together to cross the sea—his first visit home in almost 20 years. What mixed feelings he must have had about the contrast between the free spirit of the wilderness in which he now lived and the staid traditionalism of the highly cultivated milieu in which he had grown up. Culture shock mingled with emotion at the reunion with family and old friends.

For the doting father, what a charming experience it was to watch a nine-year old's face and listen to the wonder in her voice as she observed and commented on her first long journey—canoe passage across Lake Huron and down the French River-Ottawa route to Montreal; a visit with friends in the city, which doubtless seemed enormous and densely congested to eyes that had never beheld an aggregation larger than the village on Mackinac Island; passage for weeks on end in a sailing ship far larger than any of the schooners that called at the Sault; the landing at Cork; the jolting stagecoach trip by way of Dublin to visit friends; and, finally, arrival at the Moore's lovely home in Wexford. How good, then, to rest in one place. Jane, in fact, had not stood well the rigors of the trip and she was more pale and frail than usual by the time they arrived at her destination. For John the pleasure of reunion with his sisters was marred only by the absence of his mother.

Leaving Jane in the loving care of her aunt, he spent the fall and winter traveling about Ireland making personal calls and tending to business. Foremost on his agenda was the situation at Craige. Indeed, it was Craige's need for his personal attention that had motivated the long and expensive journey from Canada. He had maintained close correspondence with his brothers-in-law, John Moore and Henry Kearney, who looked after the management of the estate as best they could, but neither lived near it and John was, after all, the heir. He did not want to sell the place. He had long held a hope that some day he might return to live there. Or, if not he, then perhaps one of his children. After examining the records and making necessary decisions about Craige's future, he appointed John McLoughlin to collect the rents and look after the property.[55] Then he left for Belfast, feeling easier in his mind about the beloved estate.

There he visited with friends of his youth as well as relatives. His first cousin, William Saurin, had been appointed Attorney-General for Ireland in 1807, after a distinguished eight years as member of parliament. His new position was the most powerful in Ireland and Saurin would serve ably for 15 years.[56] The reunion was pleasurable for both men, and Saurin was clearly impressed with John's story of success in the adverse wilderness. He invited him to a good position with the government, if he wished to return to Ireland. Here it was, at last—confrontation with a prospect that until now had been little more than a fantasy of long winter evenings. As his children grew older and his financial position stronger, he had thought more and more often about the possibility of returning to his native land. Now a concrete job offer impelled what was probably an irrevocable decision. He was strongly tempted to accept.

The congenial atmosphere of Irish gentility had enveloped John with comfortable familiarity within hours of his arrival home. He had never enjoyed the haggling of the fur trade. And surely return offered superior advantages to the education and achievement of his children. Then he thought of Susan—going quietly and efficiently about her tasks in the whitewashed log house by St. Marys Falls, instructing and comforting the five children there, secure and serene in her world and oblivious to the urbanity of modern Belfast. Perhaps he understood then how much he truly loved her. She had, to his delight, become a most capable chatelaine, presiding over a home and a dining room as gracious as any, despite its rusticity. But though she might accommodate much of European culture at St. Marys, he knew she could never successfully uproot herself from the primeval setting to which generations had bred her and adapt to the artificiality of a modern European city.[57] He could not bear the prospect of seeing her wither in longing for the fishing in the icy, deep lake and the spring sugaring in the virgin maple woods, though she would never reveal the pain of removal from the touch of the Master of Life. No, he knew for certain that the long held prospect of returning to Ireland had been only a dream. All that was dearest to him lay on the willow-draped riverside almost four thousand miles away. That was where he truly belonged now. With mixed emotions he declined Saurin's offer.

From Belfast John went to London. There he called on his old school friend and neighbor, now Member of Parliament for Antrim, Sir Edmund McNaughton. Through him he arranged commissions for his sons—in the Navy for Lewis and the Army for George. (No evidence exists to show that George ever took up his commission, but Lewis saw active service.) He also arranged with a Mr. Black of the British Bible and Foreign Missionary Society to bring the light of revealed religion to the backwoods of the Sault through establishment of a mission there. The box of Bibles they shipped from London arrived intact, but the missionary himself later concluded that Quebec and Montreal were quite wild enough for him; he refused to proceed farther west.[58]

It was probably either Sir Edmund or William Saurin who offered the opportunity for presentation to the King. John declined because, according to family tradition, he saw no advantage to him in his remote location, and such an occasion in his life would serve only the purpose of flattering his vanity.[59]

While in London he undoubtedly involved himself in the activities of the fur market, and he probably renewed acquaintance with many old North West Company friends, who had retired to Britain in preference to Montreal. In fact, so many of them were in London that the group supported a kind of branch chapter of the Beaver Club, known as the Canada Club. When they got together, their dinners and drinking bouts followed closely the ritual of the Montreal gatherings.[60] Much talk occurred that winter of 1810 about a new and strange set of developments in the fur trade.

Rivalry between the North West Company and Hudson's Bay Company had been heating up for several years, as the former tightened its monopoly and expanded ever westward and northward. For a hundred years the Hudson's Bay Company had stayed close to the shores of its frozen sea, but during the past 35 years it had responded to the competition of the North Westers by establishing a growing number of substantial posts inland. The two firms clashed at many places throughout the Northwest. But as the lines of communication for the Montreal company became stretched and attenuated, their costs rose and it became increasingly difficult to compete effectively with the London company.[61] The strategic advantage of Hudson's Bay itself was more painfully apparent with every passing year. Simon McTavish had recognized this as long ago as 1790, when he tried unsuccessfully to break the London monopoly and obtain legal right of access. In 1805 Will's brother, Duncan McGillivray, had offered the Hudson's Bay Company £2,000 per year for rental of transit rights. Now Alexander Mackenzie was trying a different scheme, to gain control through acquisition of shares. He estimated that £30,000 worth would be enough to gain membership on the governing committee.[62]

Mackenzie did not dare go into the market openly to buy shares; anything available would disappear in a minute. He decided to operate through Thomas Douglas, Earl of Selkirk. Selkirk would make the actual purchases with North West Company funds. But something happened. Lord Selkirk, it seemed, was more active in the market on his own behalf than he was for the North West interests. He had recently married Jean Wedderburn Colville, whose family had a large interest in the monopoly firm, and his loyalties were deeply divided. Not surprisingly, it was his Canadian associates who lost out.[63] Another impasse for the North Westers.

But Selkirk had a different motive for buying control of Hudson's Bay shares in his own name. It was explained by the peculiar circumstances of his personal life. He had become Fifth Earl of Selkirk at the age of 38 quite by tragic accident—his six older brothers had all died, two in infancy and four as adults. Never having expected to inherit the title, Douglas had devoted himself to intellectual pursuits. In his university student days he became concerned with the problems of the poor, and he was convinced that the only solution for them was emigration. When he found himself in command of a personal fortune he made up his mind to put his theoretical solutions into action. That purpose had unswervingly directed his life for the past ten years, and Canada provided the means to its achievement.

He had some years back established a colony on Prince Edward Island for Scottish highlanders who lost their land through enclosures. Gratified by the success of that venture His Lordship looked about for land on Lake Huron. He decided upon a location at St. Marys Falls, but in 1805 Simon McTavish and William McGillivray adroitly blocked his purchase on the north side of the river.[64] Selkirk had to settle for another place farther south on the Canadian side of the lake, but that colony never quite took hold.[65] Now a splendid opportunity for a third and even more ambitious colony had come his way.

The Red River Valley lay deep in the heart of Rupert's Land, the 1,486,000-square-mile empire that King Charles II had granted outright to the Governor and Company of Adventurers of England Trading into Hudson's Bay. Lord Selkirk's careful research told him that this was a fertile valley wherein to settle his Scottish emigrants. His large purchases of Hudson's Bay shares, combined with his brother-in-law Andrew Colville's seat on the Committee, assured him of the control necessary to reorganize the company and create an agricultural colony in Rupert's Land.[66]

But the Red River, which rises in present day Minnesota and flows to Lake Winnipeg, thence by devious routes to Hudson's Bay, lay athwart another empire—the domain by pre-emption, if not by law, of the North West Company. In fact, the river and its valley not only lay within the North West field of operations, it provided the company's most indispensable life line—the pemmican route from the buffalo prairies to the frozen north. Control of this valley by the rival company was an ugly enough prospect, but an agricultural settlement that would drive off the buffalo and the fur bearers portended disaster. Selkirk had dealt a double blow to the North Westers—foreclosure on the possibility of passage through Hudson's Bay and invasion of their own carefully nurtured territory.[67] Anxious as they were over the latter outcome, they had no legal recourse. Technically the land was part of the Hudson's Bay Company charter and the Montrealers were mere squatters. Their only real hope lay in the failure of the colony—not unlikely, given the brutal winters and the vast distance from support from the motherland. They decided to bide their time.

Meanwhile Lord Selkirk, in his energetic and efficient, if fussy manner, proceeded with detailed arrangements from his London base. His agents were in Scotland, recruiting the first contingent of colonists for departure in the summer of 1811. As yet, however, he had not found just the right man to manage the enterprise as Governor of Rupert's Land. To John Johnston's utter astonishment, on brief acquaintance, Lord Selkirk offered the post to him. It did not take John long to turn him down, however politely, for three good reasons. To begin with, John worried enough about the education of his children in a place as distant at Sault Ste. Marie; to take them to an even more remote wilderness would be utter folly. Also, he had carefully avoided embroilment in all fur trading rivalries up to now; he was not about to get himself involved in a contest between giants that might ultimately become a death struggle. Finally, the project would probably fail. The Red River Valley was doubtless fertile as Lord Selkirk said it was, and he was probably right, too, that its produce could nourish the traders while the sons of the colony provided a labor pool for them. But John knew, as did every other participant in the trade, from partner to voyageur to Indian hunter, that farms and wild animals could not survive side by side. The meat and the fur would desert the valley. But before that happened the tough engagés of the North West Company, with their local Indian and Métis (half-breed) allies, would probably destroy the colonists, if starvation did not. John Johnston wanted no part of such an ill-starred adventure.

By April of 1810, John was anxious to leave London. He missed his family and had come to realize that the wild scenes of the upper Great Lakes were dearer to him than he knew. He was, in a word, homesick. So, too, was little Jane. The chill dampness of the climate and the gloom of a childless household, plunged into mourning after the death of its master from apoplexy that winter, depressed the child both physically and spiritually. She longed for home and family. Her father, who was probably having second thoughts about leaving his beloved daughter, was delighted to take her back with him.

But it was not so easy to get home. Pickpockets had robbed John once while he was living in London, and robbers again stole his money, jewelry and papers on the way to Liverpool. Then delays and uncertainties in transatlantic passage, aggravated by war in Europe, followed by the hazards of cross-continental travel in North America, contrived to keep them in transit until late November. They just beat the ice to a joyful family reunion.[68]

Chapter Six

War

By the third week in June the low, tidal country around the District of Columbia is already warming up to the steamy sultriness it endures all summer. John Jacob Astor did not urge his horse any faster along the road to Washington than a comfortable trot. Whatever thoughts he may have been indulging as he rode were abruptly interrupted by a horseman galloping toward him from the capital city. The man reined up breathless with his ride and his news—President Madison had that day declared war on Great Britain.[1]   Astor doubtless received the information with an outward blandness that was characteristic. But inwardly he must have smiled with satisfaction to be among the first to know, and his thoughts whirred and clicked with precision as he continued on his way at a brisker pace. This long-anticipated war would come to the Upper Great Lakes country—John Jacob Astor would be sure to send it there.

It was only in the last few years that Astor had extended himself directly to that part of the world but, as was his custom, once involved he was thorough. He had organized his American Fur Company in 1808, with a post at Mackinac to trade directly with the Indians between the Great Lakes and the Mississippi River. Prior to that time he had been content to import top grade northern peltry for the United States market from the North West Company.[2] Then problems arising from the deterioration of international relations made it advisable for him to enter the northern trade directly. His encroachment at Mackinac aroused the enmity of Montreal-based traders there. But they were in an awkward position for retaliating, operating imperiously as they did in a foreign country, to the exclusion of its own nationals and in ways that were not always entirely legal, like nonpayment of duties on trade goods. Nevertheless, Astor preferred commercial diplomacy to commercial war, especially if it enabled him to circumvent Jefferson's Non-Importation Act and obtain the British trade goods he needed. He had gotten together with his old friend, William McGillivray, to make a deal.

In 1804 McGillivray had become chief partner in McTavish, Frobisher (later reorganized as McTavish, McGillivrays) after Simon McTavish's sudden death at age 54. He continued Simon's policy of negotiating a division of the fur country between the North West Company in securely British territory and the Michilimackinac Company in disputable American territory, an allotment that they reaffirmed by formal agreement between the two groups in 1806.[3] But in 1811 McGillivray saw a way to obtain a share in the lucrative southwest trade without jeopardizing the security of the North West Company. Despite the politically explosive times, he joined with United States citizen John Jacob Astor in a new South West Company, whereby the trade would be supplied in equal proportions by the Montreal-controlled Michilimackinac Company (now including McTavish, McGillivrays) importing from England via Quebec and the American Fur Company importing from New York. The North West Company was protected because the new firm was not to operate beyond the territorial limits of the United States. The *quid pro quo* was delivery to the South West Company of those North West posts which lay within the United States east of the Mississippi River. West of that divide, to the Pacific Ocean, all territory was open for conquest.[4] William McGillivray and John Jacob Astor—the canny Scotsman and the shrewd German— were a fair match for one another. They cooperated with a healthy skepticism, each in full knowledge that the other would sell him down the river when it suited his interests to do so. Nor had McGillivray ever underestimated the problems created for him by American jurisdiction in areas vital to his interests. Indeed, he had been taking steps to extricate himself and his company for more than ten years. Three critical places existed in which he had foreseen that the United States would eventually crowd him: the customary lake shipping route from Montreal; the depot at Grand Portage; and the buffalo-pemmican prairies. He tackled the first one first.

By the mid-1790s, when the Jay Treaty took effect on the upper lakes, the traders shipped much of the heavy equipment and supplies used by the North West Company by sailing vessel from Lachine to Sault Ste. Marie by way of the St. Lawrence to Kingston; it then crossed Lake Ontario to the Niagara portage, went over that isthmus for placement on another ship to cross Lake Erie, crossed the Detroit River and Lake St. Clair to the St. Clair River to Lake Huron, and finally it sailed up St. Marys River to the Sault. Although light winds often made it difficult to fight the current in the connecting rivers, this transport system was far cheaper for heavy goods than the Ottawa-French River canoe route. But once the American military controlled it, it became too risky for Montreal merchants. The Company therefore invested in improvements to an alternative all-Canadian route—the Yonge Street portage from York (later Toronto) on Lake Ontario to Lake Simcoe, thence by barge and canoe from Lake Simcoe to the Nottawasaga River to Georgian Bay. Transfer here to a sailing vessel carried the cargo through the Canadian waters of Georgian Bay and the North Channel of Lake Huron to St. Marys River and Sault Ste. Marie.[5]

There, in 1797, the North Westers began construction of a canal and lock on the north side of the river. It was the most ambitious engineering project in the Northwest. The canal was almost 3,000 feet long and led to a 38-foot timber-lined lock with a lift of nine feet. A planked trough, 300 feet long and 8 1/2 feet wide, conducted water from the canal to the lock for filling. Finally, along the entire length of these structures a roadway was cut, 45 foot wide, as well as a 12-foot wide log towpath for the oxen that pulled the boats through the canal.[6] The builders took several seasons to do the construction, but all was ready in time for sending up the outfits of 1799 to Grand Portage. To complement this structure, they greatly enlarged the Sault with storehouses, a saw mill, and facilities for a larger staff.[7] The British side of the river began to take on the appearance of a village like the American side. And the shipyard built earlier at Pointe aux Pins, nine miles upstream, continued to turn out sailing vessels like the *Otter*, the *Athabasca*, and the *Invincible* to carry North West goods from the Sault to Grand Portage.

The great depot at the western end of Lake Superior represented the second major trouble spot for the North Westers in their relations with the United States. Passage along the nearby boundary waterway was ostensibly free for citizens of both nations. But the first United States Customs Agent, sent to Mackinac in 1797, made it clear that he intended to enforce not only the tariff, but all the petty regulations designed to harass the Montreal merchants, such as the requirement that liquor be carried in large casks, when only small kegs could be accommodated in the inland canoes and on the difficult portages of the *pays en haut*.[8] Yet it was not entirely clear that the U.S. customs agent, in fact, had jurisdiction at Grand Portage.

The Paris Treaty of 1783 had drawn the boundary to pass "through Lake Superior northward of the isles Royal and Philipeaux, to the Long Lake, thence through the middle of said Long Lake, and the water communication between it and the Lake of the Woods. . . "[9] But the negotiators in their powdered wigs and satin knee breeches had never seen Lake Superior or its water connections to the west. And the map they chose to rely on was not altogether reliable. "Isle Philipeaux," if it ever existed had apparently sunk beneath the waves, and the "said Long Lake" was nowhere to be found. And to which "water communication" did the treaty refer? The Saint Louis River from Fond du Lac, present day Duluth (some of the British knew enough to prefer that)? The old unused French route up the Kaministiquia River (perhaps Dog Lake on this route was what the Americans had in mind for Long Lake; it was to their advantage)? Or the Pigeon River just north of the Grand Portage which would have been a compromise, but no significant lake, long or otherwise, showed up there before Lac la Pluie, to which all through-routes led? The boundary would not be finally settled until 1842. In the meanwhile the North West Company found itself in an untenable position at Grand Portage. Legal niceties notwithstanding, common understanding placed the boundary on the Pigeon River.

But where could they go? Individuals had undertaken explorations for an alternative route from the lake to the interior intermittently since the 1780s, but they had found no feasible track. Then in 1798 Roderick McKenzie had a stroke of luck. On his way inland from the annual meeting he fell into conversation with a family of Indians at the height of land above Grand Portage. They described another all-water route to Lake Superior and promised to meet him in the spring to show it to him. His informants failure to show up at the appointed rendezvous confirmed McKenzie's skepticism, but his curiosity was also aroused. Consequently, he decided to try and find the route himself, on the basis of what the family of Indians told him the previous fall. He and his men had a very difficult time, but good fortune held when they found another Indian guide along the way. Sure enough, an alternative route from Lac la Pluie via a series of rivers, lakes and portages to the mouth of the Kaministiquia River, the River Difficult of Entrance, on Lake Superior did in fact exist. The McKenzie party had rediscovered the ancient and abandoned route found originally by de la Noue in 1717. And it was indisputably in British territory. The Kaministiquia River, enfolded by the splendor of Thunder Bay, lay 50 miles northeast of Pigeon River. The annual meeting of 1799 voted to establish Fort Kaministiquia, renamed Fort William in 1807 to honor General Superintendent McGillivray. In time, the size and amenities of the new post would outshine Grand Portage.[10]

The third American threat, to the buffalo-pemmican prairies, was more remote. The United States acquired this vast territory in the Louisiana Purchase of 1803, but American settlement was a long way off. (Settlement by impoverished Scotsmen, under Lord Selkirk's scheme, on the other hand, was a clear and present danger to North West prairie operations.) Nevertheless, President Jefferson had recognized the conflict of interest there, as shrewdly as William McGillivray, when he sent Meriweather Lewis and William Clark not only to explore the Missouri River, but to secure the loyalty of the Plains Indians to the United States and to American fur traders. Without a military presence in the early years of the century, their diplomacy had little long-range effect, however. The North West Company's destiny there would be decided by internal British conflict rather than by confrontation with the United States.

By 1802, when the North West Company had removed the Grand Portage depot, they housed themselves entirely in British Canada, at Kaministiquia, at Sault Ste. Marie, and at a substation they had built near the fort on St. Joseph Island to serve the trade north of Lake Huron. The company bought the first two locations directly from the Indians, but on St. Joseph the government was the purchaser of a big piece of the island for 1,200 pounds sterling. The government would dole out payment to the natives over the years as "presents" in an annual summer gathering at the fort.[11] The company, in turn, bought its land from the government. Other traders, including John Johnston, also established facilities near Fort St. Joseph, but the British island never truly rivaled Mackinac Island as a trade center.

Contemplating the state of affairs at the junction of the three Great Lakes on that June 18, 1812, John Jacob Astor continued on his way to Washington. His thoughts moved first to the large supplies of British trade goods his South West Company already had stored at St. Joseph and the valuable peltry that would be coming into Mackinac in the next few weeks. Citizenship and patriotism were trivialities where money was concerned. His property on the upper lakes would be safer in British hands than American. His relationships lay with the established Canadian merchants, not the Americans struggling for a toehold. The moment he arrived in the capital city he dispatched messengers to the Great Lakes. They beat the British Government in reaching Major General Isaac Brock, lieutenant-governor of Upper Canada, at his post on Lake Ontario, and on July 8 they found Astor's agent, Toussaint Pothier, at St. Joseph Island. Pothier brought the news immediately to the commandant, Captain Charles Roberts, who had the same day received orders to prepare for an attack on Michilimackinac.¹²

Roberts was a resourceful man, although heretofore he apparently had not been a highly successful one. After long service in India, he was assigned in 1811 to Fort St. Joseph, one of the dreariest installations in British North America. His 40 enlisted men were a sullen, unkempt lot, who considered they had been banished to Siberia and who often vacillated between mutiny and desertion. As an example of their miserable life at the isolated, badly constructed, never-quite-completed post, the last supply ship failed to make it through before ice closed navigation in Roberts' first year of command. The men faced a lethal winter without overcoats; their last issue of 1807 had long since worn out. Roberts' ingenuity surfaced when he requisitioned from trader John Askin, Jr. a supply of three and a half-point blankets (identified today as Hudson's Bay blankets) and set the Indian women round the post to making overcoats out of them for the garrison. Thus was born the "mackinaw coat."[13] Now, with the declaration of war, Roberts' resourcefulness was tested again. He recognized the advantage he enjoyed from Astor's timely dispatch of the message to Pothier. The American commander at Fort Mackinac had probably not yet received the news. If Roberts could attack before an American courier arrived, surprise would enable his 40 lackluster soldiers and four officers to overcome the much larger Mackinac garrison. But he had more than his own command to rely on. The British high command had foreseen the imminence of war months earlier, and General Brock had arranged for trader Robert Dickson to bring a force of about 150 Sioux, Winnebago, and Menominee Indians from west of Lake Michigan to Fort St. Joseph. They arrived about this time. So did Redford Crawford with 140 Canadians. In addition, three half-breed sons of three prominent trader fathers—Michel Cadotte, Jr., John Askin, Jr., and Charles Langlade, Jr.—quickly organized 300 of their Ojibway and Ottawa kinsmen. Pothier, himself, rounded up a substantial contingent of South West Company voyageurs as they came in with the furs and opened the South West Company store houses to supply the expedition. Roberts' dispatches to his superiors referred to John Johnston as "the Gentleman at the Sault of St. Mary's."[14] The Squire of the Northwest was by then clearly distinguished from the ordinary run of bourgeois in that locale. With his voyageurs and Indian relations he, too, joined the force gathering at Fort St. Joseph.

Then, when the preparations were falling neatly into place, orders came to "suspend hostilities."[15] Roberts was deterred only momentarily. He kept on preparing and on July 15 his perseverance was rewarded. Just when he feared he could hold his assorted and restless Indian allies no longer, the hoped-for letter came from Brock. It said, in effect, "use your own judgment." Roberts acted. He commandeered the North West Company schooner, *Caledonia*, as a troop transport. Using this, his only sailing vessel, as flagship Roberts sailed out of St. Joseph harbor at 10:00 a.m., July 16, 1812, trailed by his improbable invasion fleet of assorted canoes and bateaux.

In one of them sat John Johnston, loyal subject of His Britannic Majesty, who had volunteered without hesitation when the request came up the river. Had he no qualms of conscience, no slight sense of doubt about the honor of his position? He had lived in the United States since his second year in North America. Although he had sworn no oaths he was technically an American. His children were born citizens. Was it right to take up arms against the country in which he had lived and prospered for 20 years? To say that he committed treason would be an overstatement. He had never renounced his British citizenship, nor sworn allegiance to the United States. Indeed, when five years previously Captain Durham, American commander at Fort Mackinac, had proposed at a public dinner a commission for him as justice of the peace for Sault Ste. Marie, John had signified his gratitude for the honor, but declined on the specific ground "that he was born a british [sic] subject and would die one." He went on to say that "so long as I remain within the limits of your territory, I will be amenable to your laws, but so soon as a Sword is drawn between the two countries. . . if I should not be able to walk, I will creep on all fours to have a shot at you."[16]

Nevertheless, under the Jay Treaty his continued residency was considered tantamount to adherence to the United States. If his behavior was not traitorous, it could easily be considered dishonorable, despite his passionate declaration of 1807. Yet dishonor was antithetical to every other aspect of John Johnston's personality and to the entire record of his life. How, then, can his decision to join Roberts' attack on Fort Mackinac be explained?

First, it must be viewed in the context of the time and place in which he lived. The War of 1812 has been called the Second War for Independence. In many respects the title is apt. Until that war was fought the United States of America was not taken very seriously by the world powers, especially Great Britain. On the Great Lakes frontier the United States government was considered more of a nuisance than an authority. The "citizens" it inherited from the First War for Independence were almost all British in their allegiance, not to say French in their culture. In fact, virtually no "Americans" lived on the upper Great Lakes. It is not really surprising, then, that most of the residents in the area remained loyal to the Britain from which they derived their livelihood and, in effect, considered the American garrison an army of occupation. They had few qualms about ridding themselves of it.

For John Johnston an additional justification existed. Insofar as he considered politics at all, his views were very conservative. He was intensely loyal to the Crown and to the noblest traditions of British parliamentary authority. If he had lived in one of the rebellious colonies prior to 1776 he undoubtedly would have been a United Empire Loyalist and, as such, would likely have emigrated to Canada. Arriving in the United States long after the Revolution he was still a United Empire Loyalist in spirit. The recollection, penned years later, of his feelings when he visited Fort Ticonderoga and other places connected with the revolutionary struggle testifies to the strength of his Loyalist position. He truly believed the colonies should not have revolted, even if they had been independent for 15 years before his arrival. It was a mistake—one that could still be corrected.

In short, the tenor of the time and place, his own principles of political conservatism and economic self-interest all dictated, without even a suggestion to him of dishonor, the second most momentous decision of his life. The first one, to settle in the wilderness and marry Susan, had generated glowing success. What would this one bring?

While the invasion fleet was moving slowly across the blue expanse of Lake Huron in the full brightness of midsummer sunshine, Lieutenant Porter Hanks, in command at Fort Mackinac, worried. He had first become uneasy when he noticed that relatively few Indians were assembling in the village for the summer trading. His intelligence told him that a larger number than usual was congregating at St. Joseph Island. His suspicions aroused, and aware that war might be imminent, he requested a resident trader, Michael Dousman, to visit St. Joseph and report back to him whatever was going on there. Dousman's canoe was intercepted by the *Caledonia* on the night of the 16th just off Goose Island, about 15 miles east of Mackinac. Under questioning by Roberts, Dousman revealed that the Mackinac garrison was weaker than had been believed, that only 61 men were billeted there. More important, he confirmed that Hanks did not know that a state of war existed. Dousman was cooperative. Like most of the other local residents, he was no more loyal to the American government than to the British, probably less so. If not intercepted he doubtless would have completed his mission for Hanks. On the other hand, a British takeover at Mackinac would cause him little distress.

But an anxiety shared by both parties to the conflict concerned the consequences of wartime Indian alliances. Few white military leaders on either side harbored illusions about the degree to which they actually controlled native warriors once they were led to battle. The Indians believed in total war, against civilian and soldier alike. The native irregulars greatly outnumbered Roberts' British troops and French voyageurs. The Indians would not understand the commander's limited military objective—to capture the fort—and he might not be able to prevent them from inflicting murder and pillage on the civilians of the town. As one solution to the dilemma, Roberts released Dousman so that he could return immediately to Mackinac Island and warn the townspeople that the invasion would take place next day. This would give them time to get out of the way of marauding Indians. Dousman gave his word that he would not contact Hanks, or anyone else at the fort, that he would speak only to civilians.

Roberts' trust was justified. Dousman used the remainder of the dark night to rouse the citizenry and quietly lead those who wished refuge to his own stone-walled distillery. The flotilla, approaching the Straits of Mackinac from the east, carefully avoided the narrow passage upon which the village and its harbor faced, backed up by the heavy guns of Fort Mackinac. Instead, they took a long northerly detour through St. Martin's Bay, to come around the back of the island and anchor off the northwest shore, unseen and unsuspected.

It was three o'clock in the morning when five hundred men came stealthily ashore on the narrow strip of gravel beach between the forest and the lake, at the place known forever after as British Landing. Captain Roberts allowed the exhausted paddlers and oarsmen a few hours of sleep. At dawn only the birds broke the stillness of the sacred island. Silently the invasion force moved through the tall forest of pine and birch, southeasterly toward the fort. They soon found themselves toiling upward, as the sun grew hotter, taking turns dragging one of the two unwieldy cannon they had brought with them. The ground rose more steeply as they neared the center of the heavily wooded island. It was almost mid-morning before they reached the apex. And there, below them as they emerged into a clearing, lay the handsome fortress of Mackinac, unsuspecting and serene—impregnable from the sea, naked and vulnerable to the forest. Roberts' soldiers placed their six-pounder carefully, with its muzzle ominously focused on the parade ground.

At this very moment the post surgeon, who lived in the village, was in Lieutenant Hanks' office, informing him of Dousman's warning to the populace. The astonished Hanks looked out of his window and upward to the malevolent gun above his head. Surrounding the gun was a group of menacing armed figures, clothed in everything from loin-cloth and vermillion grease to red coats and leather boots. Striding down the hillside to the parade ground was a small detachment of British soldiers carrying a white flag of truce. Hanks did not deliberate long. Outnumbered and outmaneuvered he had no choice but to surrender.[17] Thus ended the most nonviolent military encounter in American history.

Meanwhile, John Johnston had been left at the rear, in charge of the fleet and the few civilian prisoners taken by advance British scouts. Among these was Otis Durham, brother of the former commandant, who had been trading on Lake Superior in association with Johnston. When word of war came to the Sault, John pledged his protection to Durham if the latter would accede to the status of prisoner of war, rather than risk a perilous solo journey to Mackinac. Protection of the prisoners against the vengeful mode of Indian warfare was not easy. But John, along with Askin, Langlade, and Cadotte, used his influence with the native chiefs to restrain their warriors from the usual depredations among prisoners and villagers alike.[18] Perhaps the pacific behavior of the white enemies was contagious. At any rate, Captain Roberts was able to report to General Brock that the situation "demands the greatest praise for all those who conducted the Indians that although these peoples [sic] minds were much heated, yet as soon as they heard the Capitulation was signed they all returned to their Canoes, and not one drop either of mans or animals [sic] Blood was spilt, till I gave an order for a certain number of Bullocks to be purchased for them."[19] The grateful villagers came out from hiding to find their homes and shops intact, and their gardens and livestock thriving peacefully in the sun.

Tragically, the nonviolence of the Mackinac encounter was not repeated elsewhere. When news of war reached other tribes around the lakes they attacked American posts ferociously. Virtually the entire garrison of Fort Dearborn (Chicago) was slaughtered while it was evacuating to Fort Wayne. The latter, too, fell, and then Detroit.[20] Only 12 days after his arrival in Detroit, on parole from Mackinac, the ill-fated Lieutenant Hanks lost his life to a British cannonball.[21]

Once Mackinac fell, the clangor of war was reduced on the upper lakes to a remote echo. With the British firmly in control, the peltry went down safely to Montreal. Most of the new season's supply of trade goods had arrived before hostilities began, though some shortages were already showing up. Nevertheless, the outfits of 1812 went out much as usual, and the winter passed quietly. In 1813, it was another story. The war was heating up, and the western trade began seriously to feel the effects. In recent years John Johnston had been buying some of his provisions from the North West Company, shipped to Sault Ste. Marie on the lake route. But the Navy had commandeered virtually all the trading vessels, including the North West schooner *Nancy*, which normally carried much of the cargo between Georgian Bay and the Sault. That summer little came up from Montreal, and John's clerks went into the interior very thinly supplied. His outfit totaled $19,200 of capital, distributed by his clerks at seven outposts: L'Anse-Keweenaw, Lac du Flambeau, Lac Court Oreille, Follavoine, Chippewa River, La Pointe, and Fond du Lac.[22]

John worried about what shortages would do to his relatively small operation and went down to Montreal in August, probably by express canoe. The voyage took nine days, with the furs expected later.[23] He would spend the third winter in six years away from his family, but he felt it imperative to arrange personally for next year's outfit. A second season of inadequate provision would mean serious trouble for him. The Indians had learned enough of white men's ways to withhold the fur if the trade goods were not forthcoming—the natives extended no credit. Nevertheless, from Montreal the prospects for the fur sale looked good, and through his old friend and agent, David David, John secured a better stock than he might have if he had relied upon correspondence. He planned to bring the goods up by canoe as early in the spring as the ice breakup allowed. In this wartime year the old French-Ottawa route was virtually the only means of transport available. Meanwhile, he enjoyed the company of his friends, who invited him to "dine out almost every day" from his lodgings with Dr.

Munro, where he paid £8 a month and "furnish my own liquor."[24]

Nor was it easy to send letters back and forth, even in peacetime. Sault Ste. Marie lay in Indian Country, beyond the pale of civil government in Canada, in fact beyond Canada itself, and well beyond the reach of any kind of postal service. One entrusted letters to a ship captain or to a friend or acquaintance about to make the journey in either direction, addressing the folded, sealed pages to one's relative "at St. Mary's," or if written to a roving fur trader "wherever he may be found." They transmitted packages and gifts in the same way. The absence of government also created some legal inconveniences in the growing settlements of the Indian Country, and John returned in the spring of 1814 with a commission appointing him "Civil Magistrate and Justice of the Peace, for any of the Indian Territories a part of America not within the limits of either the Provinces of Lower or Upper Canada"—a rather odd appointment for a resident of United States territory.[25]

In John's absence Susan was, of course, the final authority at the Sault. When he was away he also relied heavily on his chief clerk, John Holiday, who was with him many years, and 17-year-old George was now beginning to take on more responsibility. His father confided to him some of his plans, corresponded with him from Montreal about business matters, and sent him along with Holiday to L'Arbre Croche on Lake Michigan to buy provisions.[26] Holiday took charge of the post at L'Anse during the winter trading season, leaving George the man of the house at the Sault.[27] John missed his family dreadfully during the long winter away from them, writing George that the newest baby, William (*Mien-gum*, The Wolf[28]) born October 18, 1811,[29] "is ever in my thoughts and tears from me many a sigh."[30] But he had much more reason to worry over his first born, Lewis, serving on H.M.S. *Lady Prevost*, in Lake Erie.[31]

First, Lewis's general incompetence was not only a disappointment, but a source of anxiety. Somehow the boy must be helped to make his way in the world. John went to his prominent friend, Sir John Johnson, for an introduction to Sir George Prevost, commander-in-chief of

His Majesty's forces in North America, so that he could "speak for poor Lewis"[32] in an attempt at least to hold his job for him. The year before John had barely obtained the intercession of Major General Isaac Brock, who recognized that Lieutenant Johnston "may not be very efficient but then consider the claims of his family."[33] Now, apparently, he was again in trouble with the authorities. But an additional reason existed for concern about Lewis. Britannia's rule of the Great Lakes' waves was about to be challenged by an audacious young American naval officer, Oliver Hazard Perry.

By most accounts the War of 1812 was shamefully mismanaged from Washington. Only England's preoccupation with Napoleon saved the fledgling republic from military destruction. Indeed, John in his letters from Montreal mentioned casually that the American army was on Lake Champlain—no one was very excited about that—while he went on at length about the Duke of Wellington's stunning victory in Spain.[34] The United States had virtually no navy on the Great Lakes until Captain Perry teamed up with a talented boat builder, Ebenezer Crosby, at Erie, Pennsylvania, where they put together a fleet of two brigs and three gunboats during the winter of 1812-13.[35]

The British were fully aware of what was happening, and Major General Henry Proctor, commander at Amherstberg, yearned to attack before the American fleet could be launched. But his chief naval officer, Captain Barclay, had only a couple of dozen experienced sailors to man the whole fleet, including the newly launched *Detroit.* Army personnel could not be expected to maneuver sailing ships in battle. Proctor pleaded for naval reinforcements all summer, but by the time they arrived it was too late.[36]

On August 4, 1813 the new American fleet sailed out of Erie harbor, but various maneuvers and vagaries of the weather precluded serious action until September. Perry's first tentative probings at the British Lake Erie fleet, anchored off its Amherstberg headquarters and shipyard near the mouth of the Detroit River, were inconclusive and may have lulled some of the British officers (though not Proctor) to underestimate Perry and his squadron. Certainly John Johnston seemed little worried about his son when he wrote on September 17 that the news contained "nothing of importance from the Lakes."[37] Word of what had happened on Lake Erie September 10 had not yet reached Montreal.

The American squadron, augmented by four more little ships, had stationed itself at Put-in-Bay, a picturesque and protected harbor among the Lake Erie Islands, just off Ohio's Sandusky peninsula. For various reasons, despite the shortage of able seamen, Proctor decided to take advantage of favorable wind and weather. The British fleet sailed out of Amherstberg to punish the insolent Americans then putting out of Put-in-Bay. The lines were formed by 10:00 a.m., ship matched for ship like a well-ordered football lineup: the American flagship, *Lawrence*, opposite the brand new British flagship, *Detroit*; the American *Caledonia* next, opposite the British *Hunter*; the *Niagara* opposite the *Queen Charlotte*; the British *Chippewa* covered by both *Ariel* and *Scorpion*; and the American *Somers*, *Porcupine*, *Tigris* and *Tripp* ranged before the *Lady Prevost* and the *Little Belt*. Nine smaller American vessels against six larger British ships of war. They jockeyed for position for more than an hour before the *Detroit* opened the engagement with her cannon. In the battle that followed Perry's boldness may well have been the Americans' most effective weapon. He came in so close to fire effectively at his enemy that his ship was virtually shot out from under him, and in the midst of the smoke, cannonballs and uproar he transferred himself, his command and his flag from the *Lawrence* to the *Niagara*.

That episode marked the turning point. Once aboard the second ship, he moved his smaller more maneuverable vessels in for the kill, taking both the *Detroit* and the *Queen Charlotte* at almost the same time. Surrender of the entire British squadron came at about four o'clock in the afternoon. Four hours of blistering exchange had cost the British 41 killed and 94 wounded; the Americans lost 27 to immediate death and 96 were left wounded. Most of the American losses occurred on the two ships Perry personally commanded, but they did not figure in his famous report to General William Henry

Harrison: "We have met the enemy and they are ours; two ships; two brigs; one schooner and one sloop."

Next day one of those touching acts of gallantry, which often footnote the hideous annals of war, occurred. The remnants of both fleets returned to Put-in-Bay, where they were to bury the fallen. The British and the Americans accorded full military honors to the heroes of both navies. In the mournful and strangely fraternal procession, they alternated the bodies of Englishmen and Americans as they carried them to their common resting ground and consecrated it in a common service.[38]

Lewis Johnston was among the more fortunate who escaped serious injury. He was wounded in one arm, however, by which circumstance he was sent to the American base at Erie. There he made the acquaintance of a young American physician, Usher Parsons, who had been the surgeon on Perry's flagship, *Lawrence*, and who subsequently penned a vivid account of the battle. Over 40 years later Doctor Parsons would chance to pass through Sault Ste. Marie and meet George Johnston. By then Lewis was long dead, but George, who inherited his father's strong family sentiment, later wrote to Parsons requesting an account of his friendship with Lewis. The doctor responded, in part:

> The wounded officers of both squadrons were brought to Erie and . . . boarded at a hotel kept by Judge Bell. I had daily interviews with them and enjoyed their society very much, particularly Midshipman Johnsons, [sic] who I learned was from the Saut Ste Maries [sic] and was able to give me particular accounts of that region and of the Indian customs, character and condition (though I did not once suspect at the time, that he belonged to that race) and I therefore sought interviews with him more than with the other officers. His slowness of speech I referred to his education in french, [sic] which I supposed to be his vernacular tongue . . . his correct behaviour candor, plain good sense and unpretending manners, had in a high degree won my friendship and esteem.[39]

Although the government later paroled Lewis and he did not see action again, the Battle of Lake Erie ultimately had an entirely different impact on the Johnston family. Perry's victory at sea enabled General Harrison to retake Detroit by land and to pursue the British Army into its own territory of Upper Canada. The next military objective was Fort Mackinac, but with winter coming on that assault had to be postponed until the summer of 1814. Everyone on both sides knew it was inevitable.

July 1, 1814 five vessels of the Lake Erie squadron sailed north from Detroit under Perry's successor, Captain Arthur Sinclair. Twenty-two-year-old Lieutenant-Colonel George Croghan commanded the troops carried on board.[40] Although the taking of Mackinac was the expedition's ultimate objective, the fleet called first at St. Joseph Island.[41] They had removed the garrison from there two years previously, but the North West Company depot remained an important supply post, both military and commercial. In the view of American military intelligence little distinguished the North West Company from the British Government in this part of the world; and American military intelligence was correct. The British navy on the upper lakes consisted of the North West fleet; British officers distributed North West goods and provisions to keep their Indian allies loyal, and the company had formed its own military brigade to fight in the St. Lawrence Valley. Crippling of the North West Company through capture of its trade goods and its peltry was an appropriate military objective.

But in mid-July the depot at St. Joseph was all but deserted. The annual meeting was in progress 350 miles to the northwest at Fort William, and only a skeleton staff was in residence at the island in St. Marys River. Nor was much stored there. The trade goods had already gone up to Lake Superior and, by a two-day squeak, the 47-canoe brigade, carrying over a million dollars in furs and 135 armed voyageurs, had slipped by into the North Channel on its way down the French and Ottawa to Montreal.[42] Sinclair and Croghan could not find the prize they were seeking at St. Joseph, but perhaps it was still at Sault Ste. Marie. To prevent further use of the post, they put to the torch the buildings on St. Joseph, and the

Americans sent Major Andrew Holmes upriver with a small detachment to raid the Company's facilities at Sault Ste. Marie. Holmes arrived at the North West post there July 23. He found part of what he was looking for—not furs, but guns, ammunition, building tools and supplies, as well as stores of food and clothing. What he did not confiscate he fired, including the sawmill, which went up like a matchbox. By another stroke of luck the North West schooner, *Mink*, lay at the wharf loaded with flour. She was scuttled and the painstakingly constructed lock and canal were blown up. While they had effectively decommissioned the North West Company facilities at the Sault, Holmes found no person of authority in residence here either, only minor clerks. Determined to be thorough, he pursued another target intelligence had suggested to him. Mr. Johnston resided on the American side of the river, but he was reputed to be an agent of the North West Company and the British Government, who also stored munitions and supplies for the Indian allies of the British. Holmes dispatched to him the following peremptory note: "I require you to report yourself to me tomorrow morning at six a.m., and to bring with you an inventory of Goods & property in your possession belonging to the North West Company. I am ordered to respect private property; but if I discover that you have secreted any thing whatever, it will be my duty to destroy your houses & furniture, & to take you prisoner to Michilimackinac."[43]

But the "Mr. Johnston" he so arrogantly addressed was not there to receive the note. Eighteen-year-old George was the one who responded promptly in his father's name. It was an awesome responsibility for a boy with little experience in the world to try and dissuade an emotionally charged military officer from plundering his father's hard-won fortune. Fear and anxiety may well have hampered George's inherited facility with words. He was totally unsuccessful against an adversary convinced that he was dealing not merely with a British agent, but with an American traitor. Holmes left George a prisoner under guard in the rooms he had appropriated on the Canadian side and crossed the river with his men to the Johnston property. Helplessly, John Holiday, who had not yet left for his winter post at L'Anse, escorted the officer through the warehouses bulging with the supply of goods and provisions John had so laboriously negotiated for in Montreal the previous winter. No military supplies were found, no evidence that the Johnstons were agents of either the North West Company or the British Government, as George had tried so desperately to establish. Nevertheless, Holmes confiscated the contents of all the storerooms, rifled and vandalized the office, and burned the buildings, sparing only the Johnston's own residence. He and his men then returned down the river, permitting George to come home to the devastation they had wrought.

Grieving for his failure to prevent the catastrophe, George sent word to his mother that it was safe to come back. The day Holmes had arrived on the Canadian side false information had come to her that Iroquois allies of the Americans were coming up by land. Susan had hastily bundled five children—Eliza, Charlotte, William, Nancy Campbell, and infant Anna Maria (*O-mis-ka-hug-o-way*, Woman of the Red Leaf)[44] who was born March 27, 1814,[45] —into a canoe and retreated with them to the relative safety of Lake Superior, where they could stay at the lodge of her brother, Waishkey, on the bay that now bears his name. Eloquent as she was in Indian diplomacy, it was unlikely that she could have been any more successful with Holmes than her son.[46]

In many respects Holmes' behavior was justified. Johnston may not have been storing military supplies, but where was he? He was at Mackinac, about to assist in the defense as he had in the attack two years before. He may not have been in the paid employ of the government or the North West Company, but he could hardly deny being an enemy of the United States. That the United States should so deal with him was not inappropriate.

Some disagreement occurred in the record as to just why John Johnston was at Mackinac Island at this time. One version asserts that while Holmes was sailing up St. Marys River on the east side of Sugar Island, Johnston with a force of voyageurs and tribesmen was paddling down the west side of the island to bolster the garrison at Fort Mackinac. That story seems highly unlikely, for the simple reason that he had Jane with him at the island.[47] Surely if he had been headed for danger and war when he left home, he would not have taken his adored 14-year-old daughter. It is much more plausible to conclude that John had gone to Mackinac in the course of his business, perhaps in pursuit of his continuing wartime effort to obtain more winter supplies for his men and was trapped there by military events. But he did volunteer to help in the island's defense, and Lieutenant-Colonel Robert McDouall, who had taken over command from Captain Roberts that spring, short on officers, appointed him a captain of militia.[48] Fortunately, he was spared the shedding of blood.

When Holmes left the Sault on July 24, he rejoined the fleet at the mouth of St. Marys River for the movement westward to attack Mackinac. This was the very military circumstance Fort Mackinac had been designed for—siege from the sea. The defenders enjoyed a double advantage from the height of their fortification. The guns of the attack warships could not be raised high enough to bombard the fortress, while the land-based artillery could pin down the ships with heavy fire. The fleet took shelter behind Bois Blanc Island, effectively held there by the firing from the fort whenever it ventured out. Then fog closed in the Straits of Mackinac for a whole week. Gunplay ceased. When the fog lifted the American fleet was no longer before the impregnable fortress. McDouall was not surprised. He was prepared for the Americans' next move—a naive attempt to repeat the strategy the British had employed so effectively two years before.

Perhaps it had occurred to Colonel Croghan that the British would fortify the height of land from which they, themselves, had captured the fort in 1812. But given the problems of frontal attack, he had little choice but to disembark his troops at British Landing for an assault on the rear. They landed on the morning of August 4 and began to hack their way through the dense woods as far as what is now the Wawashkamo Golf Course. All along the way, Indian snipers McDouall had placed among the trees harassed them, and once on the plain, they were clear targets. Major Andrew Holmes was the first to fall.

When it became clear that his troops would not be able to rush the fort through the murderous musket fire that was dropping them at a rapid rate, Croghan called retreat. The American soldiers had not even passed beyond the line of the woods to engage directly the defending British troops.[49] Fort Mackinac and the island it protected would remain British yet another year until a group of men around a table in far-off Ghent should decide that it be restored to the United States. In memory of the event Fort George would be renamed Fort Holmes.

Three of the American ships sailed for Detroit, carrying the wounded. *Tigress* and *Scorpion* were left to patrol the upper lakes. For a while the presence of these ships prevented John and Jane from safely returning home. John was desperate for news of his family. He heard something of the destruction that took place at the Sault, but he was still unaware of the enormity of the damage and its significance for his future. He viewed it as a "robbery" as soon as he could ascertain the amount of the loss. He did not say in his letter home to George, sent by an Indian traveler from Mackinac, just who he expected would compensate him. He was much more pre-occupied by the "misery of silence concerning you all under which Jane and I have labored for 16 days. . . . Oh why have you not sent Mr. Drew or Waishkey to deliver me from the torment of suspense."[50] His suspense was relieved a few days later when he returned to Sault Ste. Marie, to find his wife and children safe and well—and his future in ruins.

Chapter Seven

Aftermath

After rounding the bend in St. Marys River at the narrows between Sugar Island and the mainland, the little settlement came into view half a mile beyond. From the water it did not look very different from the scene John had left a few weeks before. Only when his canoe drew closer to the landing stage could he glimpse what had happened there.

In his anguish George had been unable to write his father of the desolation Holmes had wrought. Now the vacant shelves and charred frames of the storehouses stood as a grotesque mockery of what had been. The shambles of John's office desk and cabinets defied him to calculate the precise measure of his loss. But this much was obvious—it was far worse than he had expected.

Better Holmes had stolen his personal possessions than the trade goods that sustained his livelihood. Without goods this month he would receive no furs next spring, and without furs next spring he would be unable to discharge the debts for trade goods shipped to him last month in good faith. Even more devastating, with no furs next spring he would be unable to finance a new outfit for the following year, hold his posts against stiff competition and restore, bit by bit, his capital and fortune. Until this moment John Johnston had been a prosperous man, but like all his colleagues, his wealth consisted mainly of merchandise in hand and the delicate cycle of faith and credit that was the Canadian fur trade. Now the goods were gone and the cycle broken. It would be hard to re-establish.

Yet re-establish he would try. At age 52, after 22 years of strenuous and distasteful work, he would, as always, place his trust in God to allow him the means to repair his fortune. Sadly he scraped together what he could to send his "poor starving people . . . into the Lake [Superior] with a few blankets, and a little ammunition, instead of ample equipments [sic]." For the family, only one barrel of flour was left and what little could still be gained from the harvest; the potato crop had failed from early frost. "Thus it is the will of God that we should be reduced from plenty to a scarcity of every necessary of life; but his holy will [sic] be done. We must not repine, let us rather reflect on all his mercies with love and gratitude, and...bear our present distress, which he [sic] can soon change again to plenty . . . ."[1] But he did not rely exclusively upon God and his voyageurs. John, himself, took steps to repair the damage. First was the possibility of compensation. In the course of discussions about the parole of American prisoners following the cease fire at Mackinac, Commodore Sinclair had assured Colonel McDouall of "the instructions of my government as . . . to individuals and their property, both of which will be held sacred." Referring specifically to the episode at Sault Ste. Marie, he went on to say that he had an inventory of all the confiscated property placed aboard his ships by Major Holmes, and that if it was adjudged to be private property "the strictest justice shall be done to the individual."[2] John believed at this time that he would be compensated by the United States Government. But restitution might be a long time in coming, certainly not until after the war. It would not take care of next season's needs, nor hold his business together in the meantime. For that he had no choice but another trip to Montreal.

During the long, still hours, wrapped in fur robes against the cold wind and rain of an autumn canoe passage, John had plenty of time to reflect on his position and to struggle against the twinges of bitterness that intruded. Barely three years ago he had faced up to his distaste for the fur trade, calculated his assets, and concluded that another year or two would provide the wherewithal to retire comfortably, if modestly, to Montreal. There his children could benefit from a superior education; he could enjoy the association of his social and intellectual equals; and his wife would find acceptance, if not the prestige she enjoyed at the Sault, amid natural forest and river surroundings in a suburban location.[3] The declaration of war a few months later had caused him to postpone his plan. The catastrophe of July 23, 1814 demolished it.

The welcome of old friends relieved somewhat the miseries of that winter of 1814-15 in Montreal. He missed his family dreadfully; "they are never an instant out of my mind so much so that I dream of them every night."[4] The effect of wartime inflation on his expenses gave him further cause for worry. David David, with his customary reliability, had sent off all the furs to England, except the martens, which could command a better price on this side of the Atlantic. It was comforting, as well, to know that he could rely on Susan's good judgment at home. She wrote David even before John arrived that she had sent all their men and canoes into the field, as provisions were so low at the Sault that they could do as well or better living off the land.[5]

Goods were scarcer than ever in Montreal, but John obtained what he could and arranged to ship them by the first canoe in the spring, despite the expectation of American harassment on the lakes. News of the cease fire in December removed that anxiety, but John was as dismayed as all his friends by the terms of the Treaty of Ghent. Although the British had won most of the military victories, the treaty restored the status quo ante, and the boundary remained precisely (and disputably) where it had been placed in the Treaty of Paris. John's position was as anomalous as ever.

Furthermore, the likelihood of recompense from the American Government receded with the terms of the treaty. Although he had always made his loyalties perfectly clear, he foresaw the American government might construe his behavior as traitorous and deny his right to its declared respect of private property. Compensation from the British Government, as a reward for his military assistance, appeared a likelier prospect. Accordingly, he visited Sir George Prevost, with whom he enjoyed cordial relations, and Sir George forwarded the statement of

John's losses to the colonial secretary, Lord Bathurst. The estimate ran to £5,811 12 6, and included the following among scores of other items that illustrate the scope of his merchandising:[6]

    2 batteaux, newly repaired
    70 pairs men's, women's & children's fine shoes
    76 pairs fine worsted and cotton hose
    20 men's fine hats
    5 dozen capots
    93 cotton and calico shirts
    12 kegs assorted paints, oils, etc.
    2 cases iron tools, e.g., spades, scythes, adzes, frying pans
    174 blankets
    600 cod hooks
    106 pounds net thread and twine
    87 fishing lines
    5,000 gun flints
    13 kegs gunpowder
    125 pounds worsted
    144 yards white cotton cloth
    30 dozen mirrors
    14 rolls assorted ribbons
    18 dozen knives
    Over 50 kegs, barrels, bottles of wine, spirits, brandy
    36 pounds coffee
    80 pounds refined sugar
    1 keg rice
    1 large feather bed and 5 pillows
    10 large copper kettles
    Hams, tongues, corned beef, hogs, etc.
    Corn, flour, peas for Canadians
    20 damask table cloths
    12-15 Irish linen sheets
    Crystal inkstand

In addition to losses incurred at Sault Ste. Marie, the Americans had destroyed two of his buildings on St. Joseph Island: a one-and-a half-storey house, 30 by 40 feet, nearly finished, and a 30 by 25 feet store. They had also destroyed 26 new window sashes there, and when the British scuttled the schooner *Nancy* in the Nottawasaga River to avoid capture by the Americans, he lost 50 bags of flour and 50 bags of white Russia sheeting (used for tents) carried on consignment.[7] While he had the ear of the commander-in-chief, John took the opportunity to plead the cause of his irresponsible first born son. The Americans had given Lewis parole from captivity, and he was living at home, but soon military orders would place him under Colonel McDouall at Mackinac, or elsewhere when the fort changed hands. Sir George assured John that he would do for Lewis whatever Colonel McDouall might recommend. "Therefore my dear son," wrote the patient and ever hopeful father, "pay the strictest attention to his orders and strive to gain his esteem."[8]

The frivolity of social life in a rapidly growing city was exaggerated by wartime privations and inflation, and John found it "oppressive" to observe that "real happiness is sacrificed to external appearance, and the gentler virtues of the heart and solid improvement of the mind is sunk in a vortex of vanity and folly, or at least so far thrown into the back ground, as to appear more a shadow, than the only real and solid good we can possess."[9] But the Beaver Club was different. Here the sincere, unaffected camaraderie of men who understood each other's sufferings as well as their joys comforted the lonely visitor. John attended every meeting, taking his turn as Cork on January 14, Vice-President on January 28, and President on February 11.[10] For the first gathering after his arrival, November 19, he expressed his pleasure in poetic tribute that began:

> Ye wanderers o'er Canada's wide domain,
> What pleasure here to meet you once again!
> Here, to recount the toils and perils past,
> Perils and toils still longer doom'd to last.

And concluded:

> Soon, then, as this portentous storm is o'er,
> And peace our traffic shall again restore,
> Be it our constant effort to improve
> The Indian's comforts, and secure his love.
> And may the *Beaver Club* from year to year
> In peace renew its social meetings here.[11]

The Beaver Club might continue to meet regularly after peace was restored, but the northwest fur trade would never be the same again. Two recent arrivals on the scene were about to effect the transformation, one purposefully, the other inadvertently.

John Jacob Astor never did anything inadvertently. He had laid his strategy carefully before and during the war, and at its conclusion he effectively supplanted the North West Company south of the international boundary. The South West Company he and McGillivray had formed was totally absorbed into the American Fur Company.[12] From this base the organization continued to grow and expand across the continent until it became a virtual monopoly in the United States. Fur meant Astor. As for small traders like John Johnston, Astor embarked upon a gradual process of co-option.[13]

John was not unaware of Astor's tactics and objectives. But at a time when he was so short of capital that he could barely keep his organization together, when prices continued to rise with renewed warfare in Europe, and when his legal status in the territory was in some doubt, the advantages of association with a power like Astor forced him to set aside his commitment to independence—provided he could be associated, not swallowed. Accordingly, with the outfit of 1816 he became Astor's agent at the posts on the south shore of Lake Superior. He was not an employee of the company, merely a subcontractor or co-partner, and the arrangement gave him the breathing space he so desperately needed.[14]

When Fort Mackinac changed hands for the last time in 1815, the British Government faced a dilemma. Just where would the international boundary fall when the two countries finally interpreted the Treaty of 1783? How would the line be drawn through the waterway that connected Lake Huron and Lake Superior? As they looked at the map, St. Joseph Island, where the garrison had been stationed previously, appeared to fall into United States territory. They decided, therefore, to build a new post on Drummond Island, which, as one of the Manitoulins, appeared to be on the British side. As it happened they guessed wrong, but in the meantime the usual kind of trading community grew up around the new Fort Drummond.

Fort Drummond was not well built nor adequately financed, but the military presence there established the island as the place for annual distribution of presents to the Indians.[15] This ensured a large gathering of natives, to the commercial benefit of the traders both as suppliers to the government of the goods to be distributed and as dealers in additional wares the Indians might purchase. Accordingly, a number of merchants, like John's good friend Dr. David Mitchell, moved their operations to the island in 1815.[16]

John Johnston, along with the others, built a storehouse there, managed mainly by his second son. George, tall, sturdy, and large featured, resembled his mother's family, but he shared his father's refined tastes in clothes, literature, manners, and lifestyle. Proud to be his father's aide and confidante, he displayed during these years the steadiness and dependability inherited from both his parents. He supplied the government fort with items like hay from the Sault, while conducting the Indian trade.[17] The Johnston relationship with Astor was kept entirely separate from operations at Drummond.

George's presence on Drummond Island served another useful purpose. Lewis was stationed there, and George might be a steadying influence on his older brother's wild ways. John could transmit good advice to both his boys—"Wisdom and grace, when we strive to merit [God's] protection, friends and fortune, at least as much of the latter as he [sic] sees most fitting for us, are sure to follow"—and "your mamma [could send] you three pairs of shoes."[18]

Just as Astor was reorganizing the trade on the American side, the instrument of fundamental change on the British side was Thomas Douglas, Earl of Selkirk. It was not his Lordship's intention to alter the structure of the northwest fur trade. His only desire was to relieve the suffering of the poor Scottish Highlanders. If his singleness of purpose inconvenienced the "Pedlars from Montreal," as he scathingly referred to the North West Company, so be it. The Red River settlement *would*, by force of his will, be established and perpetuated. The first settlers had gone out in 1811, as planned, with a new boatload following each summer.[19]

After John Johnston declined the job, Selkirk recruited Miles MacDonnell to direct the affairs of the little settlement established on the site of modern Winnipeg and called Assiniboia. Despite the cruel hardships of the prairie winter, scarcity of game, and enmity of most of the Indians and Métis (halfbreeds), they constructed a fort and stockaded village, planted fields, and even brought in a small harvest after a couple of years. Then, in 1814, MacDonnell rashly flouted Selkirk's instructions that the settlement live quietly and mind its own business. He confiscated the cargo of a North West Company pemmican brigade on its way down the Red River to Lac La Pluie.[20]

Until then the North Westers were content with a policy of malign neglect. Although they had rescued the first contingent of settlers from impending starvation, they were confident that the settlement would soon die of its own impracticability, assisted by native hostility. But direct interference with the Company's business in the name of a self-appointed regional authority was intolerable. The Company's annual meeting of 1814 voted retaliation.[21] At this time the boundaries of Canada were still defined by the outlines of Upper and Lower Canada, later to become Ontario and Quebec, respectively. The land beyond the St. Lawrence Valley and Lake Ontario was Indian territory and, as such, beyond the reach of provincial laws and courts. Yet the Canada Jurisdiction Act did permit those who sought justice under British law to present themselves and the accused at bench and bar in York or Montreal or Quebec. And from time to time respected persons authorized by affidavit acted as official magistrates in those remote regions. In 1814 the government appointed John Johnston civil magistrate and justice of the peace for Indian Territories.[22]

In the spring of 1815 North Wester Duncan Cameron appeared at the colony's Fort Douglas with a warrant for the arrest of Miles MacDonnell and Sherriff Spenser, who were packed off to Canada to stand trial. Then Cameron offered the settlers free transportation to farms in Upper Canada. Many were happy to escape the nightmare in which they had been trapped; some were too suspicious to accept but, sensing trouble ahead, fled to Lake Winnipeg. A few stubbornly remained to defend their rights and the hard labor they had already invested in breaking the soil. Later a band of Métis set the torch to Fort Douglas, although they made no attempt to harm the colonists.

When Colin Robertson, Selkirk's agent, arrived from Montreal later in the summer he reinvigorated the settlement and rebuilt the fort to receive another contingent of 80 settlers under a new governor, Robert Semple. Selkirk's second choice for govenor was probably worse than the first. This man announced himself as Governor-in-Chief not only of Assiniboia, but of all Rupert's Land.[23] Such arrogance was dangerous in the Northwest.

Meanwhile, the Earl had arrived in Montreal to clarify the disquieting reports that came only once a year by fur ship from York Factory and to find out for himself exactly what was going on. Discussions with the North West people over the winter moved from cool to belligerent. In Selkirk's view the arrogant "pedlars" not only refused to acknowledge the supremacy of the Hudson's Bay Company charter and recognize that they were trespassers on a Crown land grant, but they had the temerity, the brutality, to arouse the Indians to exert illegal force in ejecting colonists from land that was rightfully given to them.

McGillivray denied the allegations of violence, pointing out how the proprietor at nearby Fort Gibralter had assisted the first settlers, how the Company's generosity had been repaid by larceny of its vital pemmican shipments, and that the colonists were invading the ancient hunting lands of the Indians. Certainly the North Westers would never take such suicidal action as to incite

Indians to warfare. He told Selkirk what Johnston had tried to convey to him six years earlier; farmers and the fur trade were mutually incompatible.[24] Selkirk, believing his colonists in great danger, requested armed protection from the government, but Governor Sir Gordon Drummond concluded that this was a private, commercial contest and denied him troops. His Lordship was, however, granted a commission as justice of the peace for Upper Canada, to give him an official status that could be extended to the Indian country beyond. Selkirk, not readily deflected, determined to go to his beleaguered colonists when navigation opened in the spring, and advise them that he would bring his own private army to protect them—recruited from a wartime Swiss mercenary regiment just being disbanded.[25]

While his Lordship struggled against his adversaries in Montreal, a new act in the drama was opening in Assiniboia. On the basis of the threatening letters and documents found in an intercepted North West Company canoe, Governor Semple seized Fort Gibraltar and arrested its proprietor. The fiery Duncan Cameron exploded with every epithet in his colorful vocabulary, but following prudent North West policy made no effort to resist. In the same way, they took over Fort Pembina, upriver. Semple then destroyed Fort Gibraltar—and thereby lit the match to the tinderbox.

For the Métis of the Red River Valley the North West Company, with its huge demand for pemmican, was the vital link to European goods; the land swarming with buffalo was their ancestral heritage. This hated colony, led by these hateful men, was destroying both. In June of 1816, one Cuthbert Grant headed a party of 20 or 30 carrying pemmican to Lake Winnipeg. On the 19th they struck off on a short cut across a big bend in the Assiniboine at its confluence with the Red River near the site of Fort Gibraltar, that brought them out in back of Fort Douglas.

Governor Semple got word of the approaching group. Knowing Grant's reputation and the inflamed state of the Métis, he led 30 men out of the fort to a nearby plain. If trouble was to occur, he would go to meet it, keeping the settlers out of harm's way. As the two groups warily approached one another near a little wood characterized by seven venerable oak trees, François Boucher broke out of the Métis ranks and rode toward the colonists, shouting curses. Semple strode up and grabbed the bridle of the man's horse, matching threat for threat. Before anyone knew quite what happened, the angry words were summed up in a gunshot, and Robert Semple lay wounded on the ground. That was the signal for general firing. When the smoke of the "Battle of Seven Oaks" had cleared, one Métis and 20 colonists lay dead. Grant, more prudent if no less angry than his compatriots, had tried to move the wounded Semple out of the line of fire, but one of the others finished him off before Grant could get to him.[26] This half-breed son of one of the earliest North West partners then took command of Fort Douglas in the name of the North West Company. One hundred and thirty settlers now declared themselves ready to accept the Company's standing offer of sanctuary in Canada.[27]

John Johnston first heard of these tragic events in a letter William McGillivray wrote to him on July 18 from Fort William. "The story will be told in a thousand ways that . . . the N.W. Co. . . . destroyed the colony," he predicted lugubriously.[28] McGillivray knew that Selkirk was on his way up from Montreal, as yet in ignorance of the affair, and he knew that Selkirk held Johnston in high regard. He therefore requested his old friend to speak with Selkirk on behalf of the North West partners, using his disinterest and his eloquence to placate the volatile philanthropist and lay a foundation for settlement. It was a ticklish assignment, and John doubted his presumed influence, but he would never shirk a request to act as peacemaker.

When his Lordship reached the Sault, John welcomed him at the handsome stone house trader Charles Oakes Ermatinger had built two years before on the north side of the river. The unpleasant task of breaking the news therefore fell to Ermatinger and his visiting friend, Johnston.[29] Selkirk took the intelligence quietly, but John was troubled by the smoldering fury he could detect beneath the calm surface. The Earl was much more tense than he had been last time they met in London, and he looked thin and drawn, in poor health, both physical and mental. John's doubts that he could accomplish much as a mediator were confirmed. Selkirk was both stubborn and overwrought, an explosive combination. He would never give in, and neither would the North West partners, whose very lives were the northwest fur trade.

But Selkirk retained his confidence in Johnston's wisdom and integrity. Despite his acknowledged friendship with McGillivray, Selkirk requested him to accept deputization as justice of the peace, and in that capacity accompany His Lordship to Fort William to represent the law on Lake Superior. John said nothing about the appointment he had received two years earlier, which might still be valid. Rather he declined any official status, while offering to help in any informal way that he could. He agreed to go with Selkirk to Fort William as a mediator and exert every effort to bring him and McGillivray together to work out their differences, but he did not wish to be placed in the position of rendering judgments. Ermatinger, likewise, refused to be deputized.[30] Reluctantly, Selkirk accepted John's compromise, and the brigade set off at the end of July, 1816.

A week later Selkirk staged his grand entrance to Thunder Bay, arranging the canoes in a military formation with his private army dressed in full regalia, flags flying, to sail flamboyantly past the watching North Westers at Fort William. John's hopes sank lower. His canoe dropped out of the flotilla at the fort, while Selkirk and his men went a mile or two up the Kaministiquia River to camp on the opposite side. John planned to arrange a meeting between the antagonists for the next day, but he never had a chance to bring it off.

Early the following morning, two soldiers arrived from Selkirk's camp with a warrant for the arrest of the Honorable William McGillivray. The charges—treason, conspiracy, and accessory to murder. The men had orders to bring the prisoner back to camp with them. Determined not to give his Lordship any legal excuses to bring additional charges until he had a chance to play the whole thing out in the law courts of Canada, McGillivray went without resistance. Two of his partners, Dr. John McLoughlin and Kenneth McKenzie, voluntarily accompanied him. They would try once more to reason with Selkirk.

But as the day wore on and they did not return, John became more and more worried. By afternoon Selkirk's intentions were clear. A substantial detachment of his soldiers came into view on the river, and before the gates of the fort could be closed against them, they disembarked and took command. They arrested the remaining partners and placed all of the property and papers of the North West Company under heavy guard. John Johnston and his voyageurs took a hasty departure before they could be caught in the net; word must be sent back promptly to the Canadian authorities.

What followed at Fort William was, in the eyes of the North Westers, a demoniacal proceeding. Selkirk moved into the fortified depot with his army, confiscated papers, files, furs, and provisions, and settled in for a winter's perusal of all the Company's private affairs, from which he would construct the legal case he intended to bring upon his return to Canada. He dispatched the entire company of North Westers to Montreal in three badly overladen canoes. Almost within sight of St. Mary's a sudden Lake Superior storm overtook them, and nine men were lost in the roiling frenzy of Whitefish Bay.[31]

In the end nobody won the contest. Two and one half years later the upshot of long and costly litigation was dismissal of most of the charges and countercharges, conviction for murder against one of the mercenaries, and a £2,000 judgment against the Earl of Selkirk. He had already sunk £100,000 into the colony, and returned to England broken in health and spirit.[32]

But for the Montreal fur barons the consequences were far more sinister. Another five years of warfare between the great North West Company and the mighty Hudson's Bay Company would be fought on the rivers and in the forests of the *pays en haut*, in the law courts of Canada, and in the counting houses of London. By 1821 the North West Company was no more. It was swallowed up by the power of a rival Royal Charter, by the disruption of its extended trade lines while the opposition monopolized the shortest route, and by the massive force of the Bank of England on the side of the enemy.

The demise of the North West Company transformed the Canadian fur trade. It was no longer directed by adventuring proprietors, who knew every aspect of its operation, from the habits of the beaver to the color of beads and the weave of cloth the Indian women liked best. Sons would no longer follow with pride in the traces of their fathers, as the North Westers had done. From now on, salaried employees of a remote and impersonal directorate, who knew only columns of cold figures in a ledger, would operate the trade.

With departure of the North Westers, the transporters would abandon the old Canadian lake and river canoe routes for the icy waters of sub-Arctic seas. For Americans, the Great Lakes fur trade would thrive for another 15 years, but they would carry the cargoes by Mackinac boat and sailing vessel. No more would Lake Superior see huge brigades of birch bark canoes flashing past to the rollicking tune of an ancient French chantey. No more would a thousand men, with their women and children, congregate at a great depot to make the forest ring with dance and gaiety. The voyageur—that unique breed which stood pridefully apart in dress, custom, and language from both his employers above and his clients below—would gradually die out. Washington Irving penned the epitaph: "The feudal state of Fort William is at an end, its council chamber is silent and desolate, its banquet-hall no longer echoes to the auld-world ditty."[33]

In the late summer of 1816 all this was but dimly foreseen. John Johnston still had a fur trade to pursue, better supplied this year than last, thanks to John Jacob Astor. Nevertheless, another wearisome trip to Montreal was in the offing. Again he left a newborn infant behind, John McDouall[34] (*Wau-be-quon*), the last of the Johnston offspring, born October 12, 1816.[35] He traveled down the lakes with Will McGillivray after the sad events at Fort William and Whitefish Bay, his first journey by the Georgian Bay route to York. He waited there for over a month to see Governor Gore and to board the one and only downbound ship, delayed until "Emperor" McGillivray presented his case against Selkirk to the authorities.[36] John's meeting with the governor general was quite satisfactory, as Gore promised to forward the account of the 1814 losses, with memorials to the ministry. Perhaps another important name appended to his pleadings in London would move officialdom a little faster.

His wait for the ship was somewhat less than pleasant, as he and McGillivray had a disagreeable argument. Apparently McGillivray upbraided Johnston for a letter he wrote to the Hudson's Bay people and expressed some dissatisfaction with John's conduct as mediator. "You see how hard it is to steer between parties," he wrote to George, "no matter how just our motives may be, the least error subjects us to blame, however I pray to God to enable me to always act with rectitude."[37] But the two old friends made up before traveling the rest of the way to Montreal together. And the following spring McGillivray penned his and his Company's official thanks with recognition that

> Success does not always follow our best exertions. I most willingly give you credit for your intentions and the only circumstance to be regretted is that you were not sufficiently aware of the designing character of the man with whom you had to deal. . . . It is not the intention of the agents to fix any just estimate of the time you sacrificed in your trip to Ft. Wm by a pecuniary consideration adequate thereto. I am therefore to request your acceptance of Fifty Guineas for which I inclose a [draft] payable at sight.[38]

John relieved the loneliness of a winter in Montreal away from his family, in the usual way, partaking of the conviviality provided by the Beaver Club. And this year John had the satisfaction of seeing his good friend, David David, along with a Mr. Franks, elected to membership after nomination by Alexander Mackenzie.[39] The haughty anti-Semitism of the Old World did not entirely permeate the New. But the warmth of the club could not keep out the chill of news from Washington that Congress had passed a bill excluding all British subjects from the Indian trade in the United States (although Canadian canoe men were explicitly exempt)[40]—another blow that seemed to be aimed directly at John Johnston, the principal trader on the American side of Lake Superior. "What is to come of us in future god [sic] alone knows. I fear there is no other alternative, but to become American citizens or to abandon the trade and country, which without a proper knowledge of any other business, and what is worse, without a Capital is next to an impossibility. May the Almighty counsel and direct us. We have no other friend."[41]

Although Congress could pass such a law at the behest of John Jacob Astor, enforcing it was another matter. American troops re-occupied Fort Mackinac, but civil law had not yet reached the upper lakes. For a while, at least, John could go on as he had. Nevertheless he took the precaution of forming John Johnston and Company when he returned home in the spring of 1817.[42] And Company meant George, whose citizenship was his birthright. George was also becoming more intimately involved in his father's affairs, representing the firm in most of its dealings with Ramsey Crooks, American Fur Company partner and Astor's agent in the Northwest. A cordial relationship grew up between the two men. George spent the winter of 1818-19 in Montreal, and Crooks expressed genuine disappointment when he altered his plans for continuing on to New York in favor of returning home. "Your father gave me reason to hope I should have had the pleasure of your company here this season; [to show you] this part of the world."[43]

But dealings with Ramsey Crooks did not generate the kind of easy friendship John had with David David. John was troubled by Crooks' policies and methods. He wrote to George in Montreal, "Mr. Crooks writes me that he is anxious to know my determination for this Years Order, surely a moments reflection on the terms of the Invoice he forwarded me in direct opposition to my agreement should lead him to conclude all further business between the Fur Co and me must forever cease."[44] The association, which had always made him uneasy, was about to fall apart, although the Johnston sons would in the future move in and out of Astor's orbit. That made the citizenship issue even more critical.

During the winter of 1819, John wrote to the

governor of Michigan Territory, Lewis Cass, to ask "if from my length of residence in this country I might have liberty to send into the interior. I received his answer . . . in which he mentions that unless I choose to become a citizen under Jays Treaty I could not have the liberty of trading beyond the established Posts, therefore to this Post I shall restrict myself unless the Almighty in Mercy enables me to quit their Territories forever."[45] Neither of those alternatives could be seriously entertained, of course; he could afford neither to leave the territory, nor to restrict himself to trading at the Sault. George's legal status was pivotal to their business.

But that was not a sure thing either. John, swallowing his pride, sent George to Mackinac to take an oath of allegiance before Colonel George Boyd, the first Indian Agent, but feared that Boyd might refuse to accept it. In that case all John could do was bluster. "Inform him," he wrote George, "that I shall go to Washington . . . , where I have several matters of business to transact and I shall then ascertain whether I am the only Man in this country who is to be persecuted whilst every other of every character and description are allowed all the protection and facility they require."[46] Not until 1821 would they be able to rest easy about George's citizenship, when Governor Cass personally intervened and wrote to Boyd that "George was born upon our side of the line. . . . he cannot be divested of his character as an American Citizen. I am very anxious that you should extend to him the same privileges as to other persons, and sure I am that it will not be abused."[47]

Meanwhile, despite the difficulties with the American Fur Company, business began to recoup, and John's interests broadened out a bit. In the fall of 1817 David David got him in on the ground floor of the new Bank of Montreal that David was forming with other merchants, with an investment of £500 in ten shares.[48] A new kind of enterprise was developing at the Sault—commercial fishing—and John participated on a modest scale. His men took only 90 barrels of fish in the fall of 1818, but "a Mr. Smight from Detroit . . . made a hundred barrels in a fortnight . . . Mr Nolin who followed his instructions took 1200 fine fish at a draught of his line. . . .

Mr. Steward [Adam Stewart] the Collector [of Customs] wishes to join me in carrying on the fishing."[49] International animosities waned rapidly on the frontier where the community was still so small that citizens of both countries formed a single society. John had also resumed his old friendships at Mackinac. In October he proudly took his daughters, Jane and Charlotte, to visit Captain and Mrs. Pierce (the captain's brother would become America's president several decades later) while he attended a grand ball. By then he had also restored the buildings and grounds of his demesne.[50] As normal daily life resumed, the prospect of compensation for the 1814 losses seemed only to recede. John realized once more that he could not rely upon the good offices of other men, but must carry his appeal directly, by his own presence, to the responsible authorities in London. In the fall of 1819 he went down to Montreal by the lake route to escort Eliza and Charlotte to a school in Sandwich (present day Windsor) and leave William to pursue his studies at Cornwall on the St. Lawrence River, before taking passage to England.[51]

At the suggestion of his brother-in-law, Henry Kearney,[52] John addressed a petition to the Duke of Richmond, relating the pertinent incidents of his history and reporting that the accounts sent to Lord Bathurst by the late Sir George Prevost and Lieutenant Governor Gore had been, in turn, transmitted to the Treasury Board. Nor did he neglect to petition directly the Lords Commissioners of His Majesty's Treasury. And in supporting evidence of his patriotism he submitted a letter, dated 27 December 1819, from Lieutenant-Colonel Robert McDouall, describing his appointment of Johnston as a Captain who ably assisted in the defense of Fort Mackinac and opining that John's great misfortune would probably not have occurred had he not been absent from his premises in his Majesty's service.[53] Despite the friendships that he still enjoyed in high places, John could only wait and wait and wait.

When the long anticipated response finally came, it carried the distressing intelligence that the "humble petitioner" had been too late! But the letter from Lord Bathurst offered a cube of sugar.

> With reference to Lt. Gove Gore's dispatch . . . and other strong testimony in his favour, their Lordships are of opinion [sic] that it would be hard to exclude him from receiving those benefits to which he might have been entitled if his claims had been preferred in due time, and I have therefore to desire that Mr. Johnston may be placed on the same footing with persons who forwarded a statement of their loses *(sic)* while the commission was sitting.[54]

In other words, they granted John the special privilege of remaining in the queue. Disgusted by the indignity of dancing attendance on great men, John left London in midwinter to journey to Edinburgh and thence to Ireland. The latter visit was not entirely social. In fact, it provided a reason for the voyage from home of equal importance with the petitions submitted in London. John's beloved Craige represented his largest single asset, and at this low state of his fortunes, just when his family required the largest outlays for education, the time had come to part with it.

All through the years in America, John had corresponded regularly with his two sisters and their husbands and stayed in touch with other relations as well. They all kept him informed about conditions at "home." The idea of repairing his fortunes through the sale of Craige occurred to him when he realized within a couple of years of the 1814 disaster that compensation would be a long time coming. Advice from his worldly cousin, Irish Attorney-General William Saurin, and other business connections in Belfast suggested that he should be able to obtain a good price for the property, in excess of £3,500. That figure, a little more than half his estimated losses, would inject badly needed capital into his enterprises, and get him out from under John Jacob Astor. In letters exchanged during the winter and spring of 1817 with another cousin, John McNeil of Ballycastle, McNeil hinted at his interest in purchasing the property, but he placed a much lower value on it, less than £2,500. By March of 1819, however, McNeil was making a firm offer of £3,000, "as I had every desire to keep the property in the family, I was willing to stretch a point,"[55] and John's sister, Eliza, and her husband Henry Kearney, were urging him to accept it.[56]

Some final bargaining after his arrival in Ireland in the winter of 1820 secured the sale at £3,250.[57] In addition, the deed of transfer incorporated the text of a much earlier document. In December of 1789, when John was arranging his affairs before emigrating to Canada, he was concerned about the financial future of his two then unmarried sisters. In the event of his mother's death he would automatically inherit the estate under British laws of primogeniture. He therefore executed a Deed of Release, which settled on each of his sisters a £400 interest in the estate. Even if they sold or mortgaged it, they and their husbands, if they married, were to receive throughout their lifetimes the current rate of interest on £400, payable from the revenue of the estate. After their deaths, the income would continue to their issue, but if either had no children the £400 principal would revert to the estate.[58]

At the time John sold Craige to John McNeil, his sisters had been long married but would clearly leave no issue. Nevertheless, despite his own difficult circumstances, he did not hesitate to continue the arrangement—for the widow Jane, a fearful, hypochondriacal woman, who had apparently been left fairly well off, and for impecunious Eliza, whose fussy, ineffective husband, Reverend Henry Kearney, made a meager living in the hamlet of Kilgobbin near Dublin. With incorporation of the deed of release into the bill of sale, the £800 was undoubtedly deducted from the purchase price, leaving John with a net yield from the sale of £2,450. When Jane died the next year her £400 reverted to the estate and then rightfully back to John. Once more, however, he gallantly ordered that it be left in the estate with the interest paid to Eliza to augment her income.[59] When John made all these arrangements everything seemed perfectly clear. But his carelessness about keeping papers and records, and his inclination to rely upon his own spoken word and that of men he trusted, would result in 20 years of acrimonious argument and litigation after his death, not to be settled until almost mid-century.

When John sailed from Ireland in the summer of 1820 he mused on the stark contrast with his first departure almost 30 years before. Then he had been young and full of hope as he exchanged home for a strange, unknown land. Now, at 58, he was becoming elderly and his hope was badly bruised, but he was *going* home. He would never see Ireland again. The open, rolling fields of Craige, marked off by their neat stone fences against the backdrop of the Antrim Hills, belonged to somebody else now. His children would never claim that patrimony. He doubted then that his sister Jane, whom he had often urged to resettle with him in the warmth of family life, would live much longer.[60] She had become a sickly old woman. Nor would he and Eliza enjoy their declining years together. Henry could never earn his livelihood in the New World, nor would its atmosphere suit either of these hothouse plants. Sorrowfully, he put the world of his childhood and youth forever behind him.

But his future was bright with the promise of his adored children. The little ones kept him young—Baby John McDouall, "John Bull," as his father liked to call him, not yet four, was as full of amusing surprises as his seven older brothers and sisters. Anna Maria, at six, was the sprightliest child he had ever known. The older ones marked too quickly the passing years. Dear, delicate, intellectual Jane was now 20 and of marriageable age. Quiet, enigmatic Eliza, at 18, grew more like her mother each day. Charlotte, though only 14, was the beauty of the family.

With the joy of them came pain as well. It was likely too late for 27-year-old Lewis ever to grow up. Affable, irresponsible, and alcoholic, he was the despair of his father's heart. Now assigned to the Indian Department at Drummond Island, he held onto his army appointment only by dint of John's influential contacts and their respect for the gentleman-trader. It was George to whom John confided his admonitions concerning Lewis, in the hope that the brother might have more influence than the father:

I hope Lewis is striving to oeconomize [sic] and abandon those habits that have for some time past been leading him fast to the utter destruction of soul, body, and character. May the Almighty in Mercy open his eyes and give him grace to repent and strength to reform before it is too late . . . I should write to Lewis were it not for his having deceived me by continuing his base connection with that abandoned woman, and his unblushing falsehood which makes me fear he has lost all sense of shame.[61]

John was coming to rely upon George in personal matters as well as business, especially during his too-frequent long absences. "You my dear son are doubly called upon both by your precept and example to give no excuse to those under your charge for inattention to their learning or any species of laxity or misconduct, let alone the least appearance of vice . . . [we] cant expect God's help in our time of trouble if we dont strive to deserve it."[62]

Now, as John stepped off the ship in Montreal good old reliable George, age 24, was there to meet him. A problem had arisen with William that George did not feel competent to handle; Papa must see to it. The child was almost nine years old and still virtually illiterate. The school in Cornwall had been an utter failure. Another must be found, and George had brought the boy along with him so that his father could take care of the matter then and there. William was a strange, moody little lad, and John worried about him sometimes, but if money could obtain a good education, the boy would have it. He found that Mr. Parkins' school in Chambly was expensive enough to have a good reputation. Unfortunately, money did not guarantee a good education, and despite several years' attendance, William learned little.[63] He apparently missed out on the family gift for literary expression, and for many years his cumbersome letters were a torture of misspelled, ambiguous communiqués. Then, when he was about 25 or 30, either he suddenly discovered his heritage, or he found a good editor; his letters vastly improved.

After a blessedly quiet winter at home with his

family, improvement in John's financial position began to show up from the injection of capital from the sale of Craige. Furthermore, by the spring of 1821, David was writing him optimistically about the prices of fur and how well he expected to do for him on the invoice that included 57 black bears, 47 cub bears, 840 martens (sable), 40 otters, 23 fishers, 118 minks, and assorted others, including 340 "D & S." [64]

At the same time prosecution of the war damage claim had come to a complete standstill. It was as though the Lords of the Treasury had swallowed Lord Bathurst's recommendation that they entertain Mr. Johnston's claim and thought no more about it. In the summer of 1822 John wrote Robert Peel once more, and received a courteous reply enclosing the response to his private inquiry of Mr. Wilmot. Another turn of the merry-go-round.

> Sir P. Maitland has recently been instructed to appoint a new commission to renew the proceedings of the former board in hopes that some arrangement may be made for compensating the numerous claimants, and as due notice will be given, Mr. Johnston will of course forward to the commission all the proofs he posseses in support of his claims. Under these circumstances I am sure you will at once perceive how impossible it is for Lord Bathurst to interfere in Mr. Johnston's particular case.[65]

But "due notice" was not given to Mr. Johnston. He just happened to read in a York newspaper that found its way to Sault Ste. Marie about the convening of the Board of Claims at York by Sir Peregrine Maitland, Lieutenant Governor of Upper Canada, in the fall of 1823. He wrote immediately to Maitland. Was he too late again? Or were the papers he had earlier sent presented to the Board? Was his presence required?[66]

He was too late for 1823, of course, but the board sat again in the summer of 1824, and they permitted him to appear then. He brought with him the time-worn summation of his losses at the Sault, St. Joseph Island, and on the Nottawasaga River. This affidavit was further bolstered by new depositions from John Holiday and George Johnston, sworn before Justice of the Peace David Mitchell at Drummond Island on July 1, 1824. Each testified as to his presence and the role he played in the events, the value of goods and property seized and destroyed, and the absence of the owner of said property because he was "serving as a Captain in a corps of His Majesty's Volunteer Militia at the Post of Michilimackinac."[67] By now the total value claimed, including ten years of interest at six percent, amounted to £9,809 0 4. On August 6, 1824 the Board handed down its ruling:

1. For losses sustained at St. Joseph Island £145 of the claim for £178

2. "That had the principal losses which the claimant sustained in the Territory of the United States occurred within the Province the Board would have awarded a further sum of £3875," of the claim for £5811 12 6

3. For the cargo of flour destroyed in the schooner *Nancy*, [£138 18 1] the general rule applied that claims for losses for goods in transit are disallowed

4. "That the 3 items of charge for 10 & 12 years interest on the several amounts [£3680 9 9] the Board considers to be wholly inadmissable"[68]

Out of a total claim of £9,809 a provisional award was made of £4,020. But the wording of Item 2 assured that the bulk of it would never be paid. The final decision of his Majesty's Government was a denial of responsibility for war losses sustained on foreign soil, even though at that time His Majesty ruled the said territory in fact and by conquest, and the claimant was a commissioned officer in His Majesty's service. Perhaps they paid the £145 allowance. If so, it was eclipsed by frustration of a decade's hope for justice.

That ruling effectively put the period to John

Johnston's business life. By the 1824 season he was 62 years old and semi-retired. Let the young ones carry on. He would live modestly, trading only at the Sault itself, among old clients, and devoting his remaining years to his family and books. His long-time clerk and associate, John Holiday, had moved on to the American Fur Company—still a friend. The struggle to recoup was over; the struggle to build he would leave to others.

But their experience would bear little resemblance to his, for in the difficult decade just past, the fur trade had been transformed. The men who had opened the continent were gone. And with them the unique style they had created. John Johnston's friends among the fur peerage of Montreal no longer crossed his threshold. Now he formed his friendships among men of a different nation.

Chapter Eight

Sault Ste. Marie Joins the United States

While John Johnston was pursuing his ten-year quest for justice, the settlement of Sault Ste. Marie grew up with his children. Within six months of the signing of the Treaty of Ghent, the United States Government made the second appearance in its 32-year dominion. This time the republic's representatives came in peace, although they were a military delegation. Samuel Abbott, a trader from Mackinac Island, escorted General Brown and his party up St. Marys River in three yawls, to arrive on a bright morning in June of 1815. While they were setting up their camp by the riverside John, recently returned from Montreal, strolled over with George to greet the party. The pain they had suffered at the hands of American troops was still raw, but John's natural affability, his thankful acceptance of peace, and his accustomed position as Squire of Sault Ste. Marie combined to evoke a spontaneous welcome and offer of hospitality. He invited the group to tea.

If John Johnston could readily get on with the business of peace, the Indians of the region were not so amenable. They continued to cherish their hostility to the Long Knives, as their grandfathers had continued loyal to the French long after the British Conquest. At this moment an exceptionally large congregation of natives was at the Sault for the spring whitefish run, and John's neighbor, old Jean Baptiste Nolin, came in excitedly to report the warning he had received from a friendly Indian woman. The Indians, assembled in secret council, planned to attack the Americans after they pitched their tents that night. John offered his guests shelter in his own house, but General Brown declined. The party had come in peace and friendship to visit Lake Superior. Wishing to display neither fear nor belligerence, it was barely armed.

At that intelligence John insisted on loaning the group guns and ammunition. In addition, he sent George, John Holiday, and several of his Canadians to keep watch between the camp of the Americans and the Indian lodges. As he had hoped, nothing happened. Nevertheless, over breakfast at his home next morning, he persuaded Brown that it was too soon to visit Lake Superior.[1] The United States Government should give the local folk a little more time to accept the idea that they now lived in American territory, in fact, as well as in law. Come back again next year.

So they did—this time in the person of General Alexander Macomb, commander at Detroit, with a party of several officers and the recently appointed collector of customs at Mackinac, Adam Stewart. John offered the customary hospitality of his house, which General Macomb was happy to accept. The time seemed auspicious for the General to extend his journey into Lake Superior, and John supplied not only a canoe but his best voyageurs and most able chief canoeman, Le Clair, to assist the expedition. While the men carried the canoe around the rapids, the gentlemen walked the well-worn portage road, tranquil in the warm sunlight of an early July day. The next time John walked this road only a few weeks later, it would lead him to his fruitless mission as mediator at Fort William. But now he waved a confident farewell to his guests as they embarked on the journey to introduce the United States officially to the natives and resident traders of Lake Superior.

But the right time still had not come. The party, American colors flying, arrived at its first stop, the large Indian encampment at Point aux Pins, a few miles beyond the head of the portage. Just as the men jumped into the water to ease the frail canoe ashore, a rabble of drunken Indians spilled out of the lodges brandishing guns and clubs. In their stumbling progress toward the canoe, one, less drunk than the others, took aim at the General. Fortunately, his gun jammed, giving Le Clair the essential moment to wrest it from him and knock him flat with the butt end. The coxswain and his men wasted no time in pushing the canoe off shore and leaping back into it for a swift paddle back to the Sault.[2] Only disaster could ensue, to Americans and Indians alike, from the kind of confrontation they had just escaped. The authorities of Michigan Territory were determined that a peaceful, if not a cordial, relationship be established from the outset with the Indians of the upper lakes. Macomb, like Brown, returned to Detroit, mission unaccomplished.

The next attempt to send a government expedition into Lake Superior would not occur for another four years. Meanwhile, American administration of the region was firmly established at Mackinac Island. In addition to the military garrison at the fort, and the assignment of Adam Stewart as collector of customs, the government established an Indian Agency there, directed by George Boyd. Whereas the French had operated in concert with the Indians, and the British had cultivated a formal business relation, the Americans adopted a paternalistic policy in the early years of the Republic. Recognizing both the threat that westward settlement posed to the Indian way of life, and the degrading dependency on white supplies and alcohol that had become the Indian's lot, the government made a genuine effort to gain their trust and eventual allegiance by dealing fairly with them in trade, while at the same time protecting them from unscrupulous merchants.

The government factory system, first introduced in the south about 1796, was established in the Northwest Territory in 1802.[3] The factory was actually a store, run by a presidentially-appointed Indian agent, where the natives could purchase merchandise at lower, fixed prices than the traders charged. They paid, of course, in furs. The store traded no liquor. But the policy was ambivalent from the start, for the government also empowered the agents to issue trading licenses. Thus the government authorized its own competition. Furthermore, the wares offered at government factories were inferior to the privately supplied goods, and the proscription against liquor did little to attract thirsty customers. Finally, the factory system violated the tenets of Indian culture by refusing the ceremonial amenity of gift-giving as a prelude to the conduct of business. For all these reasons, the system was a dismal failure, although it limped along on the books until 1822.[4]

The Indian Agency office itself, however, continued for several decades as the instrument for regulating trade, implementing the welfare policy of the time, and laying the groundwork for treaty negotiations. Regulations demanded strict licensing of all traders, a passport for each canoe, a careful count of kegs and packages before embarkation, and prohibition of all liquor in excess of one keg per canoe (presumably for the traders and canoemen, not the Indians) unless allowed by special permit. In an effort to protect the natives' livelihood, the government allowed no white person to engage in trapping or hunting (except for his own food.)[5]

John Johnston had no problem complying with the rules designed to protect Indians. But with John Holiday now working for the American Fur Company, he must take care to send only American clerks to the few posts he maintained beyond the Sault itself. In 1822, for example, he took on a young man from Cleveland, named Youngs Morgan, who was trying his hand at the fur trade. Johnston licensed Morgan for Lake Vermillion, beyond the west end of Lake Superior, and he ended the season with 81 skins of beaver, 32 bear, 58 otter, 1,370 muskrat, 148 marten, 72 mink, 12 lynx, 3 fox, one racoon and one badger. When he returned to Sault Ste. Marie and John cast up the accounts, Morgan's share came to $144.66, paid in the form of a draft on David David. When no one would cash the draft, even on the Canadian side, John gave him $28 in currency and two notes for $58.33, payable in October. With this nest egg, Morgan concluded his fur trading career and returned to Ohio to farm.[6]

As more Americans appeared on the upper Great Lakes frontier, and John got to know them better, his earlier antipathy to the United States began to abate. Like most people, he had focused on his small part of the world and its affairs. Prior to the War of 1812, these associations had all been British. What he knew of the United States he learned through newspapers, doubtless from a British point of view, and he did not like what he read, particularly American expansionism that threatened the fur trade. But by the end of the second decade of the 19th century, Sault Ste. Marie was on its way to becoming a real village, an American village, and with its growth, he modified his views far enough to see nobility in the American experiment. Encounters with American men of affairs, whom he respected, reinforced the transition, and by the close of his life, he was as loyal as any citizen.

Furthermore, the focus of his social life gradually shifted from British to American, especially after 1821 when his old North West Company friends no longer passed through the Sault. By 1817 his social visits to Mackinac Island resumed their pre-war pattern. Now he had his daughters to escort to the balls and fêtes and introduce to "society" there. Jane was his especial pride and joy—as delicately formed as she was fragile in health, she charmed everyone with her refined manners and intelligent conversation conducted in the high, tremulous voice then fashionable. Eliza seemed less comfortable with the formalities of "society," and she went less often with her father. Charlotte, on the other hand, although still a little girl, captivated all the ladies and gentlemen with her beauty and sparkle.[7]

The next official party bound for Lake Superior arrived at the Sault in June of 1820 while John was still in Ireland. This expedition was highly organized. After the state of Ohio was carved out of the Northwest Territory in 1803, the remainder was renamed Michigan Territory. Territorial government came under the jurisdiction of the War Department, as did the conduct of Indian affairs, which was something of a hybrid between foreign relations and warfare, with a modicum of welfare thrown in. An Ohio lawyer and war hero, General Lewis Cass, was appointed governor in 1814. Cass was an able administrator, a man of large ideas and broad vision. He obtained authorization from Secretary of War John Calhoun to mount an expedition to Lake Superior that would not only establish the United States presence and make treaties with the Indians, but would also survey the natural features of this vast, scientifically unknown region—its geology, topography, and botany.

Captain David B. Douglass, Professor of Mathematics at West Point, was appointed topographer, assisted by Charles C. Trowbridge, a recent 20-year-old arrival in Detroit who would become a successful banker there, and Alexander Chase (brother to statesman Salmon P. Chase), who was also in charge of the commissary. Mineralogist for the expedition was Henry Rowe Schoolcraft. Dr. Alexander Wolcott, Jr. was the medical officer, and a young Detroit lawyer, later to become a judge and governor, successively, of Wisconsin and Utah Territories, James Duane Doty, was appointed official journalist. Cass's able secretary, Major Robert A. Forsyth, completed the team. Cass, himself, took responsibility for ethnographic observation of the Indians they would meet, and each member of the group was to record his biological and climatological observations. In addition, a troop of soldiers, commanded by Lieutenant Aeneas Mackay, nine Indians, and two interpreters accompanied the party. Altogether, 43 people, including 12 voyageurs, set off from Detroit in three 30-foot canoes on May 24, 1820.[8]

After picking up an additional troop of soldiers at Mackinac three weeks later, the expedition arrived at Sault Ste. Marie June 14. George Johnston was fully prepared by training and predilection to play his father's customary role. With a taste for fine clothes, and the tall, well-built body to carry them off, he greeted General Cass at the landing impeccably attired in the best broadcloth and linen. Offering the traditional Johnston hospitality in the polished phrases of a country gentleman, he was impressive indeed. The professional members of the group were delighted by the grace and comfort of the whitewashed house, set in its gardens back from the river, where Jane received them along with her brother.

"The son & daughter of Col. Johnston," Doty recorded, "were very polite to the party. They are well educated and accomplished." After explaining the absence of the master of the house, "his family received us with marked urbanity & hospitality, & invited the gentlemen . . . to take all our meals with them. Everything at this mansion was done with ceremonious attention to the highest rules of English social life; Miss Jane, the eldest daughter, who received her education in Ireland, presiding."[9] As for Susan, Trowbridge observed in his journal that she was "not very comely in her person . . . yet extremely easy and polite in her manners."[10] The little ones, apparently, were kept out of the way.

One of the important objectives of the expedition was cession of a parcel of land from the Indians for establishment of a military post at Sault Ste. Marie. Accordingly, a council was arranged for June 16, to be held in a big tent General Cass had brought for such purposes. In one sense the timing was propitious because an unusually large assemblage of Indians was at the Sault. On the other hand, the reason so many were there was a potentially dangerous one—they were passing through to Drummond Island for their annual presents from the British Government. British generosity in "paying" for treaty land and perquisites through an annual distribution of goods (a policy the Americans had not yet regularized) offered an additional incentive to loyalty, over and above the weight of tradition. It made George Johnston uneasy as he took his place with the Cass party at the General's invitation to participate.

The chiefs filed in and seated themselves in a semicircle on the ground before the white group. Cass then ordered an interpreter to bring in a quantity of tobacco and place it on the ground within the circle. In the ensuing discussion Cass explained his purpose in calling the council, pointing out that under the 1795 Treaty of Greenville the United States Government was already entitled to the four-mile-square area he wanted for construction of a military post. Moreover, although the land had already been purchased twice— once by the French and once by the English—he was prepared to pay for it again to facilitate the transaction.

After Cass's speech the chiefs conferred among themselves. They were sharply divided in their views. The Treaty of Greenville meant absolutely nothing to any of them. It had been signed at some far-off place by chiefs they did not know. But some of them did recognize that land at the Sault had belonged to the white man for many generations. They made a counter-proposal that the old French lines be set as a boundary, provided that the land not be occupied by a military garrison. This condition was unacceptable to Cass, who declared that the question of a garrison was unarguable.

During the entire proceeding one of the younger chiefs, Sassaba, had been standing by the door, dressed in British military regalia. He was a leader of the young radical faction, whose hatred of the Americans was implacable and who were determined to resist further encroachments on their land, whether paid for or not. He had been growing more impatient by the minute. When he saw one of the older chiefs pick up a plug of the tobacco and begin to cut it with his knife, Sassaba strode to the circle, kicked aside the presents, shouted "How dare you accept of tobacco thrown on the ground as bones to dogs,"[11] and strode from the tent. That ended the conference.

A short time later a British flag was seen fluttering over the Indian camp situated only a few hundred yards from the American. Now it was Lewis Cass's turn to be enraged. But he carefully controlled his anger under a cold manner. Accompanied only by his interpreter, William Riley, he marched, unarmed, across the ravine and through the Indian encampment to Sassaba's lodge. Without hesitation he pulled down the flag. He then told Sassaba in stern tones that he would not suffer the indignity of a foreign flag raised in anger on American territory, and that if such an insult were repeated he would open fire. Then he quietly turned his back and returned to his own tent.

Cass had judged well. No matter how hostile, the Indians greatly admired bravery, and they would not attack a man who came unarmed into their camp. But his threat caused a near panic. [Running toward the canoes] "the lamentations of the screaming women & the bawling children set the dogs howling & the river side became a perfect scene of confusion."[12] Within ten minutes women, children and baggage were all crossing the river, leaving behind the warriors and their weapons. The Americans doubled the guard at their camp as nightfall settled uneasily on the watchful, waiting population.

But for some the night was a busy time. When George reported the events of the day to his mother, she commissioned him to go to the older, more responsible chiefs and bring them to her at the house. This he did. During the course of the secret meeting, from which they excluded the young hotheads, Susan labored to persuade the chiefs to her own position in the matter. Susan Johnston was above all a realist. Although she and John had been loyal British subjects through the war period, they now accepted their status as Americans without rancor. The time for armed resistance was long past, she told the chiefs. Firm peace treaties had been made between the English-speaking nations, and the British Government would no longer help them to fight the Long Knives. Moreover, this man, Cass, would not be intimidated. It was possible, if difficult, for the two cultures to live side by side so long as they were willing to settle their differences in a spirit of compromise. She pleaded with them to prevent Sassaba from a rash and inevitably disastrous attack. She counseled a prudent policy of peace.

At length, after much debate, she won her points. It was very late when the lamps were finally put out at the Johnston house. As they returned to their camp, the chiefs met Sassaba and his followers moving down the portage road, armed and painted for war. Shingabawossin, whose name meant Image Stone, but who was known as The Orator, used all his gifts as spokesman for the peace faction, backed up by the determination of his group to resist Sassaba's passage. Despite Sassaba's threatening movements, Shingabawossin kept on talking and eventually persuaded the band to return to their camp.

Sassaba remained hostile and troublesome all the rest of his life, but next day the other chiefs, through George as their go-between, sent apologies to General Cass. George and Susan offered their premises as neutral ground for a renewed council, and on June 16, 1820 both parties signed the treaty of Sault Ste. Marie in the Johnston house. The Indians ceded 16 square miles to the United States Government in return for a stipulated quantity of merchandise and the right of the Indians to fish in the rapids of St. Marys River forever.[13] (Later the Sault locks would be built right through the point of land from which they launched their fishing canoes.)

At the conclusion of the council, George sent for two bottles of wine to celebrate its outcome. Lewis Cass, even as his own star rose over the years almost to the Presidency of the United States, never forgot his debt to the Johnston mother and son. It was gratitude for George's critical assistance in negotiating the treaty that prompted the important letter regarding his right to citizenship. "I feel much interest for this family," he wrote. "While necotiating [sic] with the Chippewas last year for a cession at the Sault, the family zealously aided me, and without their assistance I could not have effected the object. I was even then apprehensive that the exertions would be injurious to them and would embroil them with the Indians and the British government. I am now satisfied, that this effect has been produced, and I should deeply regret having had any agency in a transaction calculated to injure them."[14] But perhaps the governor was too apprehensive. The Johnstons never recorded any heightened hostility to them from the Indians or the British as a result of their assistance to him.

Once they concluded the treaty, the voyage into and through Lake Superior was peaceable. The group carefully observed and noted all the natural phenomena they passed, the Pictured Rocks exciting aesthetic admiration as well. Where the red mud of the Ontonagan River lays a fan-shaped swath on the blue of the lake, they turned aside for a journey upriver. Rumors of an immense boulder of pure copper had circulated for centuries, and Cass was determined to verify or disprove its existence. But copper was sacred to the Ojibways, and only after much argument and many refusals, did one man reluctantly agree to guide them over the rough course of the upper Ontonagan. The difficult journey was rewarded, however, when their own eyes confirmed the existence of the incredible four-ton mass of almost pure float copper, scarred by centuries of chipping by fire and stone tools.[15] Schoolcraft collected his specimens, as would countless tourists after him before the Ontonagan Rock was removed to the Smithsonian Institution in the 1840s.

An additional scientific objective of the expedition was location of the source of the Mississippi River. At the western end of Lake Superior the flotilla passed up the St. Louis River to the Sauvanne Portage, then through a series of northern Minnesota lakes and streams to Lac Cedar Rouge, which they renamed Cass Lake. Recognizing that they had not yet attained the source of the Mississippi, Cass nevertheless found it necessary to turn back because the season was getting on and the river beyond was too shallow for their equipment. They descended the Mississippi to Prairie du Chien, then ascended the Wisconsin and Fox River route to Green Bay. There the party divided, one group going on to Mackinac, another to Chicago and by horseback back to Detroit. Altogether, this first large-scale American scientific expedition traveled 4,200 miles in 123 days.[16]

The major scientific report was expected to come from the pen of David Douglass, the senior scientist of the group. He was also charged to draw the definitive map eagerly awaited by government officials and citizens alike. But on his return to West Point, they appointed him chairman of mathematics, and his new responsibilities prevented him from getting to it immediately.[17] Later he moved to a professorship at New York University and then became President of Kenyon College. As his academic duties and reputation rose, he pushed the map and report of the 1820 expedition further into the recesses of his pending file, much to the disappointment of Lewis Cass and many others. In the end, he produced neither.

But for Douglass, an additional disincentive to do the work may have existed. Henry Schoolcraft had stolen the march. Having no employment obligations at all on his return, Schoolcraft wrote and submitted his report to the government promptly. Then he went further and published the findings for public consumption in *The American Journal of Science*, despite the prior understanding among Cass, Douglass and Schoolcraft that the public report be a joint effort. But important as the Cass expedition and his publications about it were to Schoolcraft's reputation, they were not the most significant outcome of his participation. It was his contact with the Johnston family at Sault Ste. Marie that would profoundly influence the remainder of his life—and he theirs.

Henry Rowe Schoolcraft was born March 28, 1793 in Albany County, New York, somewhere in the middle of the 13 children of Lawrence and Margaret Rowe Schoolcraft. His father was a glassmaker, and the family moved around a bit before settling finally at Vernon, New York when Henry was 16. His intellectual inclinations were evident from an early age, directed to languages, poetry, mineralogy, and painting in water color, all of which he pursued all his life. Although he prepared for Union College he never attended, but went to work for his father in 1809. By the time war broke out in 1812, Henry was an expert glassmaker, and in 1813 he was engaged to supervise a factory at Salisbury, Vermont. His two years there were happy ones, during which he read avidly, taught himself Hebrew and German, and was able to obtain the only formal higher education he ever had; he studied natural science with Professor Hall at nearby Middlebury College.[18] Although it never seemed to bother him or his admirers, the minimal extent of his formal training and the hazards of undirected self-education would become painfully evident in the unorganized and diffuse character of his later work and publications.

He was very well paid at Salisbury—at $1800 he received the highest salary in the state, the president of Middlebury being paid $1100 and the governor $800—and in 1815 he invested some of it in a new glass factory at Keene, New Hampshire. But the wartime boom was over. The domestic glass market collapsed as cheap European imports flooded once more into the United States. Henry hung on for two years at Keene, but business was so slow he had time to write a book on vitreology. Unable even to find a job, he went home to his parents' place to live for a year on his savings and use the time to continue his studies in geology and mineralogy.

In 1818, when those savings had dwindled to about $60, he decided, like so many others of his generation, to make a trip to the West.[19] His journey began near home at the headwaters of the Allegheny River, when navigation opened in March. In the course of the next year and a half of frugal living, occasional jaunts on foot or by water, odd jobs, and continuous geological observation, his travels took him down the Ohio River Valley to the Mississippi (with extended stops at Pittsburgh, Cincinnati, and Louisville), then upstream to Herculaneum and St. Louis, by land to Potosi, where he spent three months examining minutely the lead mine district, a winter in the wilds of the Ozarks, returning down the Arkansas River in a log canoe, then by steamer to New Orleans, and passage in the brig *Arethusa* to New York. He had made a 6,000-mile circuit of the Union in the interest of science, and even while quarantined on Staten Island during the yellow fever season, he studied its geology.[20]

Earnest, serious, ambitious, and voracious in his curiosity, Henry had met some important people on this trip, had developed some useful ideas, and had hit upon the means for making his way in the world. He perceived that his access to fame and fortune lay with the United States Government and that its doors would be opened by the important people he could cultivate.

When he arrived in New York City he began to lay the groundwork for his future. Taking up lodgings at 71 Courtland Street in August of 1819, he arrayed the large mineral collection he had acquired and invited leading men of science to come and view it. They were sufficiently impressed that he was shortly elected to membership in the Lyceum of Natural History. In November he published *A View of the Lead Mines of Missouri*. The government owned the western lead mines, and while he was at Potosi, he developed his ideas about improving their management. He "determined to visit Washington and lay the subject before the President."[21]

Armed with the evidence of his scientific ability and the practical proposal he wished to make, he set out for the capital, where he "lost no time in calling on Mr. Monroe and the Secretaries of War & of the Treasury."[22] Henry was well received, and Monroe liked his proposal for enhancing the efficiency of the lead mines well enough to promote it in Congress. It called for outright sale or very long leases of the mines to private operation, but with a United States Superintendent over the entire operation. Henry hoped he would be *that* superintendent.[23]

Nor did he disguise his ambition so thickly that it might be overlooked. In the meanwhile, Secretary of War Calhoun was sufficiently impressed with the young scientist to recommend him for the Cass expedition then being organized. Henry's bold plan was working. The appointment "seemed to be the bottom step in a ladder which I ought to climb."[24]

When he returned once more from the West in the fall of 1820, his sights were still set on the mine superintendency, just beginning its weary trek through Congress. In the meantime his friend, Governor DeWitt Clinton of New York, offered Henry the use of his library for organizing the notes on the Cass Expedition. Since no immediately remunerative employment offered itself, Henry set to work on them, not only sending his separate report to Secretary Calhoun, much to the consternation of Douglass, but preparing the journal he had kept for publication in popular form. The book, entitled in the expansive style of the day, *Narrative Journal of Travels Through the Northwestern Regions of the United States Extending from Detroit Through the Great Chain of American Lakes to the Sources of the Mississippi River in 1820*, came out in May of 1821. The public, avidly curious about the frontier regions of the growing country which remained a mystery to the citizens of the eastern seaboard, acclaimed it.[25]

It also had its critics, and in August a series of six anonymous, barbed letters appeared in the Albany *Daily Advertiser*. Schoolcraft was hurt as well as angered by the criticism, which he attributed to Douglass. He had urged Douglass to get on with the business of a joint report and sent his own notes to him; further, he had in the book made a footnote reference to Douglass' forthcoming work. But Governor Cass assured him that Douglass was not the author of the letters, and the editor of the newspaper confirmed it. The truth was that Henry Schoolcraft never could accept criticism with grace; he invariably attributed it to petty vindictiveness.

But his career was progressing. Throughout the winter, he enlarged his correspondence with important men, especially in scientific circles. And the day after the book was published, he received an invitation from Cass to serve as secretary to a special commission for negotiating an Indian treaty at Chicago. Henry jumped at the chance to travel through areas of the country he had not yet seen—the valleys of the Miami, Wabash, and Illinois Rivers—and another opportunity to observe the Indians. He left New York in mid-June of 1821, but did not get back until October; an intestinal illness kept him flat on his back in Chicago long after the rest of the commission had departed.[26] Checking with his friends in Washington, Henry learned that War Secretary Calhoun had proposed the establishment of a military post and Indian agency at Sault Ste. Marie, and that he stood a good chance of getting the appointment as agent. It was not what he hoped for, but two irons in the fire were better than one.[27]

He spent the winter of 1821-22 as he had the previous one, preparing a memoir for the American Geological Society, to which he had just been elected, and attending to an already voluminous correspondence. "He who would rise, in science or knowledge, must toil incessantly."[28] Letters of encouragement for his work from three ex-Presidents—Adams, Jefferson, and Madison—gave that toil a sweet reward.[29] But correspondence, no matter how laudatory, did not supply him with food and clothing. In the spring he went to Washington to press his search for a job. At length Congress acted. President Monroe submitted his name, and on May 8, 1822 the Senate confirmed his appointment as United States Indian Agent for the Western Agency, to be moved from Vincennes to Sault Ste. Marie. It was not the job he really wanted, but it should be an interesting post where he would have a chance to pursue his nascent scientific interest in the American Indian. "At any rate, the trial of a residence on that remote frontier . . . was in fact made only as a temporary matter."[30] How often a "temporary" situation slips unobtrusively into the passage of years and decades; Henry would remain in the West for 30 years.

With his characteristic enthusiasm for travel and novel experiences Henry lost little time in removing himself and his possessions, after a brief visit home, to his future residence, via the new steamer *Superior*, which carried him all the way from Buffalo to his destination. His traveling companions through the voyage were Colonel Hugh Brady and his staff of 250 officers and men assigned to the task of establishing at Sault Ste. Marie the new military base Cass had negotiated for in 1820. They arrived at the tiny village in early July.[31]

This time John Johnston, squire become patriarch, was on hand to greet officialdom and offer his help and hospitality to the officers and their wives. Henry, who was a careful planner, had written ahead to Mr. Johnston requesting the privilege of boarding in his home,[32] as he knew from his visit of two years ago that the Johnstons were "then living in the only building in the place deserving the name of a comfortable residence."[33] Accommodation was an acute problem with the sudden influx of a large population. Some of the ladies found lodgings here or there, but many of them were obliged to share their husbands' tents.

Henry and Captain Brant, the quartermaster, rented a 12 by 14 log house from John Johnston. It had been the home of one of his men and now served the two newcomers for a shared office, in which they probably slept as well. But they, along with Dr. Wheaton and his wife, took their meals at the Johnston table.[34] To exacerbate the overcrowded situation, in addition to the military there arrived at the sleepy settlement suddenly come alive "followers and hucksters of various hues. . . . There was not a nook in the scraggy-looking little antique village but what was sought for with avidity and thronged with occupants."[35]

Within days of his arrival Colonel Brady called an assemblage of the Indians, at which he explained his purpose and function under the Treaty of 1820, and introduced Henry as the man who would look out for their welfare. Shingabawossin replied cordially, but Sassaba, resplendent in the gorgeous European attire he fancied, was as truculent as ever. His comments were not interpreted, but John Johnston rebuked him sharply when he had finished.[36] Within three months, however, Sassaba would make no more trouble. In drunken carelessness he stood up in his canoe as it came downriver toward the falls one day, and he, his wife, and child were lost in the swirling rapids.[37] Shingabawossin, along with Susan Johnston's brother, Waishkey, continued to provide a responsible liaison between the Indians of the Sault region and the agency for many years.

Construction of buildings for the new arrivals, and the refurbishing of ancient ones like Nolin's log house, was vigorously pushed all summer, and in August Henry moved into his new 36-foot-square, whitewashed, square timbered, three-room Agency. A large office, with a small anteroom and small bedroom, supplied him with entirely adequate space; a cast iron Montreal stove in the corner offered comfort, and the plastered walls represented luxury.[38] When the village finally acquired a saw mill, the men made up the first planks drawn from a maple log into a worktable for Henry.[39] By the time he moved into his house, he already had a good taste of what his duties involved—the supplications of pathetic Indians, like the forlorn fellow who had been ostracized by his band for conducting the Cass party to the sacred Ontonagan Rock in 1820; the relief of hardship and prevention of feuds generated by drunken murders (he asked Brady for an escort the first time he went to dispense aid on such an occasion); the frustrations of attempting to supervise the trade by searching the outfits for contraband liquor and granting licenses when "the whole old resident population of the frontiers, together with the new accessions to it . . . are determined to have the Indians' furs at any rate, whether these poor red men live or die."[40] Lawless traders would plague him throughout his tenure in the Northwest.

On September 6, he held his first dispensation of presents, a mode of payment for the land and propitiation against trouble. Among the recipients was Susan Johnston's brother, Way-ish-key (*Waishkey*, The First Born).[41] Henry was painfully aware from the beginning of his office that the single greatest difficulty in dealing with the Indians was ignorance of their language and the inability, even with interpreters, to communicate beyond the simplest routine ideas. This situation led to publication of a great deal of misinformation about the Indians, and Henry set himself the task of doing something about it. He determined not only to learn and publicize the customs and beliefs of the Native Americans, but to master the structure of their language.[42] This work occupied him all the rest of his life and earned his reputation as an ethnologist. He never did learn to speak an Indian language with any fluency, however.

On November 20 navigation closed. "We are now shut out from the world. . . . For some weeks past, everything with the power of motion or locomotion has been exerting itself to quit the place and the region, and hie to more kindly latitudes for the winter."[43] But Henry stayed on, devoting the winter to his studies. Although he spent considerable time reading the works of English explorers of the New World, English essayists and journals such as the *London Literary Gazette* and the *Edinburgh Review*, the arduous labor of his days and evenings focused on his determination to master, analyze and organize the Ojibway language. In this he was aided by his new friend, Mr. Johnston, often remaining at his house in animated discussion from 4:00 dinner until family evening prayers at bedtime.

The harsh winter served to draw the isolated little community very close, and now that the officers of the garrison had doubled the size of genteel society on both sides of the river a frequent round of dinners and parties occurred. Henry found many of these occasions interesting, as when the discussion at Mr. Sivereight's December 28 dinner on the Canadian side described the personalities of the great leaders of the North West Company, or when at Johnston's on the 30th the talk ranged from Greek politics through the Turkish Empire, the state of Ireland, and radicalism in England, to the unhappy relations between the philandering King George IV and his long-suffering Queen.[44] Nevertheless, he often grew impatient at the intrusion of social life, feeling that "the time devoted to these amusements, in which I never made much advance, would be better given up to reading, or some inquiry from which I might hope to derive advantage."[45] He resented even more the interminable visits from the Indians which duty required him to suffer. "No wonder that men in office must be guarded by the paraphernalia of ante-rooms and messengers."[46]

But for that part of the population less intellectual

and more social than Schoolcraft, presence of the garrison gave a luster to life at the Sault it had not previously enjoyed. One need no longer make a journey by canoe or dogsled to find congenial gaiety. Now officers from the British garrison at Fort Drummond and the Americans from Fort Mackinac visited here as well as each other, staying a week at a time during which the parties were continuous, including dancing at the Johnstons.[47] If that held little attraction for Henry, something more than language instruction did. Whether or not he had taken especial notice of Jane during his visit of 1820, within a few months of his arrival in 1822 he was conspicuously courting her.

Despite the remote location of her home, Jane Johnston had had opportunity over the years to meet eligible young men among the military officers and gentlemen traders of two nations, but no evidence exists of any particular romance in her life before Henry's arrival. He was in important respects quite different from the typical bourgeois of the northwest frontier—sober, punctilious, intellectual—and in just these respects the pair was well matched. Jane had been brought up to high standards of deportment and an absorbing intimacy with literary exercise of the mind. Henry was a man to be admired on both counts, and they spiced their courtship with playful little formal notes on both mundane and literary subjects:

> Miss Johnston presents her compliments to Mr. Schoolcraft, & begs he will have the goodness to send her the sixth volume of Goldsmith—Miss Johnston is sorry to interrupt Mr. Schoolcraft, but hopes he will pardon the intrusion.[48]

> As Mr. Schoolcraft seemed too much engaged to return (or even hear) Miss Johnston's salutation at Breakfast, she will not on that account, make known the cause of her present intrusion, until she has rendered the common politeness of wishing him, *a very good morning*. And now she feels herself at liberty to beg he would have the goodness to send her the Indian notes, if he has no occasion for them himself.[49]

> Miss Johnston presents her compliments to Mr. Schoolcraft & desires to tell him that her Mother begs his acceptance of the accompanying little moccuks of maple sugar. Miss Johnston begs leave to remind Mr. Schoolcraft of Shakespeare's Merchant of Venice, when Bessamio comments on the three caskets, one gold, one of silver & the last of Lead, in one of which, the picture of Portia, is contained, he repeats—'So may the outward shows be least themselves; the world is still deceived by ornament'. . . . Mr. Schoolcraft, may say the same of the unornamented moccuks, they are plain but the sweet they contain is not the less fine, & on that account he may be induced to accept them.[50]

Intellectual equality, though a necessity, was not a sufficient condition for Jane's ideal of marriage. Jane Johnston typified the genteel woman who has come to be described as "Victorian," even though Henry Schoolcraft entered her life some 15 years before that queen ascended her throne. A husband, like a father, was to be revered for the superiority of his knowledge, his moral judgment, and his strength of character. The female, brilliant and accomplished though she might be, represented the weaker sex in all things. A woman might marry beneath herself and, therefore, in fact be the superior, but in a proper marriage to an appropriate husband she would depend upon and defer to his leadership. In an anguished note of apology for an unintended offence to him she wrote:

> I cannot rest my dear friend, under the cruel and unjust imputation of a mean attempt at wit, especially as it is supposed to be uttered with the view of wounding the feelings of one to whose superior understanding I have always looked up with a kind of pleasing awe and admiration—I have always considered *witticisms* of any kind unbecoming to the delicacy of the female character, as

> they are generally thrown out with the hope of pleasing & attracting, or else with the fiend like intention of doing violence to the sensibility of the person to whom it is addressed. And to be suspected, let alone *charged*, and thought capable of such petty & despicable subterfuges pains me beyond enduring.... If you had listened, dearest Henry, to the explanation I was going to give you of the etiology of the word I put to you, you would have seen at once, that I could not have had the most distant idea of giving offence.[51]

She then went on to render Dr. Johnson's definition of the word "dunce" which, applied to her dearest Henry she intended only as a complimentary allusion to the scholarship of the medieval sage, Duns Scotus.

Henry, of course, forgave her readily, for, though humorless, he was not a vindictive man. But his beloved presented an unfortunate trait that he apparently glossed over at the time. For Jane Johnston the weakness of her sex was a literal fact, far more apparent in delicacy of health than in humility of opinion and discourse. To what extent Jane truly suffered and to what extent she indulged in hypochondria to manipulate family and friends is difficult to say. Although she complained a great deal she did so, at least in her youth, with a style that was considered feminine and even charming by the standards of her day. Everyone's health was a subject of greater concern and more exhaustive discussion than in the present time of advanced preventive medicine. Furthermore, despite frequent illness and pain (never precisely specified), she apparently performed her household duties with regularity and skill.

Little Indian servant girls did the meanest work and the fetching and carrying. But their capable mother Susan instructed each of the Johnston daughters in the domestic arts, both Indian and European; she obliged them to assist her in the management of that large household. Jane applied her fine needlework with equally artistic result to moccasins and leggings as well as dainty cambric underclothes. Her garden was her special pride and joy, vegetables for nourishment occupying an even higher rank than flowers for decoration. And neither she nor her sisters felt that their labor in the home conflicted with their status as ladies, despite Aunt Jane Moore's encouragement from Ireland to indulge hypochondria and eschew unsuitable domestic tasks:

> I was greatly grieved my Dearest Jane to hear that you had two nervous fevers. . . . I am grieved for all your sakes that female servants are so difficult to procure, for it is a sad . . . life for you young ones particularly. . . . I should think that in so large a place as Montreal you could not fail of meeting with some well behaved elderly decent woman that could dress your meat & wash for you. Your Papa should not mind the expense of bringing such a person & of giving her good wages, rather than let your sisters and you be complete slaves.[52]

Thus, despite her delicate health, Jane Johnston was well prepared for marriage, not only in the accomplishments domesticity required, but in knowledge and skills of particular value to Henry Schoolcraft. She was literate in the Ojibway language—indeed, she used it as well as English in her own poetics—and she was knowledgeable in the history and lore of the land of her maternal ancestors. She could be his helpmeet in many different ways, as he would be her protector and provider in all things. And for Henry, Jane provided more—her love. Evidence of the written word confirmed her love for Henry. But Henry did not commit his feelings to paper as often as she did (he did not even mention his marriage in his *Memoir*), although in later years their roles reversed, and she was less declarative of love than he. Nevertheless, Henry appears far more prosaic about the relationship than Jane. That may have merely reflected his colder personality, however; perhaps he loved her with all the passion of which he was capable.

> I read your kind note last night at a time and place, when I always think of you, if indeed you are ever absent from my mind. . . . how happy

> you make me by such tender and beautiful expressions respecting me. To merit them, is to merit what I most ardently desire. But how can you doubt that I reciprocate your thoughts, wishes, feelings . . . [53]

Certainly he was good to her; he loved her in his way, and she returned it in hers:

> I could not resign the first pen you have ever made for me, to its natural use, without first employing it to convey some of my sentiments . . . & of having the pleasure of signing the beloved name of Henry, and that of my own with it, before using it on any other object. Ever your affectionate Jane.[54]

> My dear friend, . . . I am happy you like the trifles I made you yesterday, & to convince you that I do not cease from thinking of you, even in sickness & pain, I have (with some exertion) made another today, which will, I hope, be of equal use to you, in your intended journey. . . . Yes, dearest Henry, . . . perhaps they will soon be the only memento's [sic] remaining of her, who is fast fleeting away, of her, who never knew how to hide her feelings & failings, . . . & whose sentiments for you will continue the same, notwithstanding—Farewell.[55]

> Will Mr. Schoolcraft, accept the accompanying little gift from *his Jane.* It is the first she has presented to him since their union. And may she flatter herself so far as to indulge the thought of its being prized by him, from its having been wrought by the hands of *her* whose *heart* is all his own.[56]

Despite Jane's morbid reflections on the transitory nature of life, especially her own, whose end she considered imminent for years, the courtship was both long and pleasant. Pleasant because of mutual feeling and the proximity which put them in each other's company at three meals a day, long probably because of Henry's policy of careful planning for his future. That undoubtedly included an appropriate marriage. If he were to stay in the Northwest there was no question that a Johnston connection was most advantageous. But he continued through the winter to cherish hopes of obtaining a post as superintendent of the government lead mines. In that case marriage to Jane might still be desirable, but in fairness to her, he could not commit himself until he had settled his future course. In the spring of 1823 he learned that congressional sentiment was moving to favor outright sale of the mines. Henry was deeply disappointed; he was convinced that if he had been on the scene to promote his proposal it might have succeeded.[57] He had never intended his present position to be more than temporary; now it looked as though temporary might last a long time. Nothing else appeared in the offing. He and Jane set their marriage date for the fall.

The wedding was a quiet family affair which took place October 12, 1823. Sault Ste. Marie did not yet have a clergyman in permanent residence. A subscription taken in October of 1822 raised an insufficient $107 for retention of a preacher, despite generous $20 contributions from Mr. Johnston and the Messrs. Ermatinger and $15 from Henry.[58] The wedding date was undoubtedly determined by the timing of Reverend R. M. Laird's visit.[59]

Two years previously an even quieter wedding had taken place in the Johnston household, on the occasion of a visit from James Wessimet, justice of the peace. Thirty years after he had pledged his word to her father John Johnston reaffirmed the love and devotion of a lifetime to his Susan, according to the rites and laws of man in the United States of America.[60]

While the formal marriage fulfilled a sacred promise, practical reasons existed for getting around to it. Legitimizing his wife and children was important to ensure their rights to inherit John's complicated property. Not only were there the claims for war losses, still hanging fire when the marriage ceremony took place in 1821, and the residue of the estate in Ireland which would fall to them after the death of his two sisters, but the real property at the Sault represented a considerable estate that was increasing in value as the outpost became a village. That property, too, was hedged about with difficulties.

As far back as 1785 Congress had passed a law which provided that all land not part of the original states would be purchased by the national government from the Indians, surveyed and laid out in townships and sections, and then sold to settlers. Subsequent legislation permitted persons whose claim to land in ceded territory derived from French or British grants to file statements of registration. A federal land office was established at Detroit in 1804 to administer these laws. Neither of them applied to Sault Ste. Marie, however, until Cass negotiated the Treaty of Cession there in 1820. The acreage ceded by the Indians comprised almost precisely the ancient French seigneury that had been granted by King Louis XV to Louis le Gardeur, Sieur de Repentigny, and Louis de Bonne, Sieur de Miselle, in 1750. But by 1822 the said tract was occupied by John Johnston, J.B. Nolin, the descendents of de Repentigny's "tenant," J.B. Cadotte, nine additional settlers, and the new Fort Brady. It was time for the claims of the numerous occupiers to be legally confirmed or denied, and a petition to that effect was filed in Congress.[61]

Lewis Cass and Duane Doty helped nurse the bill through the House and Senate during the winter of 1823, keeping Henry Schoolcraft and John Johnston apprised of its progress. In June the act was passed which provided that all persons who resided in the United States on July 1, 1812 and who had "continued to submit to the authority of the United States" should be confirmed in their possessions.[62] The government named three commissioners to examine the claims put forth and recommend confirmation or denial to the Commissioner of the General Land Office at Washington: William Woodbridge, Secretary of Michigan Territory; Jonathan Kearsley, Receiver of the U.S. Land Office at Detroit; and John Biddle, Register of the Land Office. At about the same time Congress established a district court at Detroit and appointed Doty as its presiding judge, while the territorial legislature appointed Henry Schoolcraft justice of the peace. Thus it was Doty and Schoolcraft who took depositions during the summer of 1823 at Mackinac and Sault Ste. Marie on behalf of the special commissioners.[63]

Doty had advised Schoolcraft as soon as the government passed the bill as to how claims and affidavits should be worded, and this information Henry surely passed on to John Johnston. The statements should describe the boundaries precisely, show when the settler first took possession, the specific dates of continuity, and "if he has been faithful to our government—state it; if he *has not—omit it.*"[64] In British law a formal deed of cession documented the Johnston claim of 300 feet of river frontage to a depth totalling 40 acres, bounded by unceded lands, "the old burying place of the Jesuits and . . . a lott [sic] of land belonging to Antoine Laundry,"[65] dated July 1, 1792 and witnessed by three white men, including Captain William Doyle, commanding officer at Fort Mackinac. And the potentially embarrassing question of his "continued submission to the authority of the United States" was quite easily resolved in the minds of two of the commissioners and their deposition-takers. Woodbridge and Biddle recommended confirmation of the Johnston claim along with eight others of the 12 filed. But Mr. Kearsley dissented on two important grounds.

Six of the nine claimants were speculators, who had recently purchased the land from settlers who had moved across the river into Canada. The three legitimate claimants with respect to long-term occupancy—Johnston, Ermatinger and Nolin—had all fought with the British in the War of 1812. Not only did they present no testimony to show their continued submission, but in light of general knowledge, such an inference could not be taken seriously. Woodbridge defended the majority opinion on the ground that no evidence existed to show that the claimants had *not* submitted, that guilt should not be presumed where it is not disclosed, and that their claims should not be disallowed on the grounds of hearsay and "general knowledge" that most of the inhabitants were British subjects in 1812-13 and therefore opposed the United States.

Kearsley's arguments were the more persuasive, however, and Land Commissioner Graham recommended in his 1825 report to Congress that the findings of the Michigan commissioners with regard to these claims be disallowed on the grounds that they had ignored the requirements of the law. Moreover, he did present affidavits declaring participation by Johnston, Nolin and Ermatinger on the British side in the war. Congress, accordingly, explicitly excluded Sault Ste. Marie from the act of land title confirmation it finally passed in 1828. Graham's report contained an additional small item of intelligence that placed those land claims in an even stranger limbo than congressional denial of their legitimacy. He had received a communication from one Mrs. Agnes Slacke of Dublin, Ireland asserting her claim to all of the ceded land at St. Mary's under the original seigneury grant of Louis XV![66]

Very few people at the Sault even knew that the seigneury had existed, and even they had virtually forgotten about it. But the law has a long grasp, and Mrs. Slacke set in motion one of the lengthiest, most unusual property suits ever to pass through the American court system. She had come into possession of the original deed by a circuitous route. The "silent" partner of the seigneury, Louis de Bonne, left a son when he fell in battle at Sillery in Quebec. In 1781 that son, Pierre Amable, took the oath of faith and homage at Quebec that was required for him to preserve his property interests under the 1763 Treaty of Paris.[67] Fifteen years later, in fact the day after American troops finally took over Detroit, he sold his part of the property to James Coldwell of New York. Coldwell, unable to tell which half of the original seigneury he had actually bought, searched for the de Repentigny heirs. He found de Repentigny's son, Louis-Gaspard, a French naval officer in Guadaloupe, where his father had served for a long time. Louis-Gaspard's rights were preserved, not by British law as were de Bonne's, but by a convention of 1800 between the United States and France, which provided that the citizens of either country should be permitted to inherit property without letters of naturalization. He refused Coldwell's offer to buy him out.[68] Two years later Coldwell sold his deed to Arthur Noble of New York,[69] and when Noble died the property went to his nephew, Mr. Slacke of Dublin. It was Slacke's widow, Agnes, who brought the whole thing to light again.[70]

Through a New York congressman she petitioned Congress four times between 1826 and 1836, but Congress rejected her claims for lack of proof of possession and the absence of any claim from the de Repentigny heirs. In 1841 two petitions came into Congress, hers and another signed by three daughters and a daughter-in-law of the now deceased Louis-Gaspard. Documentary proof of the inheritance was clear. It remained only to determine if the original grant was still valid. Another 20 years of petitions, hearings, and legal proceedings ensued, until a special act of Congress granted the claimants the right to sue in the U.S. District Court for Michigan. By this time the Sault Ste. Marie land titles had been confirmed, and most of the original litigants were dead, but their children carried on and were willing to accept compensatory land elsewhere.

For two years depositions were taken from Sault Ste. Marie to Guadaloupe, from Detroit to Paris, from Montreal to Washington. In 1864 Judge Ross Wilkins found for the plaintiffs that the grant had been made and ratified, that the title was still valid, and that the claimants were the rightful heirs. Appeal to the Supreme Court resulted in reversal in January 1867. The High Court, under Chief Justice Salmon P. Chase, whose brother so long ago had been a part of the military-commercial society of the Michigan frontier, concluded that the seigneury had, in fact, been abandoned, and that insufficient improvements had been made by the claimants to fulfill the conditions of the original grant.[71] A momentous decision for a handful of people—attorneys making and staking their reputations, and litigants losing such fortune as they had in the expensive pursuit of a distant cause.

As for the people actually living out their lives on the disputed soil, they were barely aware of the legal transactions. Nor did it matter much to the citizens of St. Mary's that until 1855 they held no valid paper entitling them to the land they inhabited and farmed. By then the original 12 claims had increased to 157, of which 121 the government confirmed.[72] As always they went about their business regardless of the machinations of national governments. John Johnston continued a modest Indian trade. He planted and harvested his crops. In 1823 he added a comfortable suite of rooms to his home for the private enjoyment of the newlyweds, Mr. and Mrs. Henry Rowe Schoolcraft.[73] His beloved Jane would not leave his roof after her marriage. She would await the joyous arrival of her first child in the same place as his dear Susan had done 30 years earlier.

Chapter Nine

Generations Arrive and Depart

One of the numerous sources of antagonism that erupted into the War of 1812 was the unsettled boundary between the United States and Canada. Under the Paris Treaty of 1783 the border was to strike the St. Lawrence River at the 45th parallel (the village of St. Regis, New York), then follow the middle of that river, and the Great Lakes and their connecting waterways to Lake of the Woods, where it would again meet the 45th parallel and continue westward along that line into the unknown. But no one actually surveyed the line, and the middle of the waterways remained undefined. Numerous islands in the St. Lawrence, St. Clair and St. Marys Rivers confused the issue further, not to speak of those non-existent islands in Lake Superior to which the treaty referred.

The 1814 Treaty of Ghent, therefore, provided for appointment of commissioners from the two nations to survey the boundary and fix its location. In the summer of 1817 the work began that would continue for 11 years (the survey could proceed only during the summer months in these northern waters), through several changes of commissioners and professional staff. Each nation supplied its own surveying vessel and crew to make independent measurements along each segment. The commissioners then compared their results and reconciled their differences before submitting the final recommendation. By and large the two parties were friendly, even sociable in the isolated circumstances of their work, but some serious technical disputes arose.

Although the survey began in 1817 the parties did not reach upper Lake Huron and St. Marys River until the summer of 1820. Major Joseph Delafield, an army officer also trained as a lawyer, was the American agent in charge of field operations, and Anthony Barclay represented the British Government. On August 2 the American schooner *Red Jacket*, chartered for the survey, and the British *Confidence* (originally Perry's *Tigress*, but captured by the British off St. Marys River in 1814),[1] met at St. Joseph Island to begin the survey that would allocate the three major islands in St. Marys River—Drummond, St. Joseph and Sugar—along with all the minor ones.

    A major question to be settled was whether the midline of the river should be determined with reference to the two mainland shores, or whether the middle should be defined with reference to the navigable channel only. For St. Marys River the latter seemed more logical, but then the question arose as to which was the best passage to Sault Ste. Marie and, therefore, represented the most logical boundary—Detour Passage between the Michigan mainland and Drummond Island, or False Detour Passage between Drummond and Manitoulin Island to the east. Since Manitoulin Island was indisputably Canadian, the American representative won the point in favor of False Detour Passage. Drummond Island, although occupied by the British garrison, was assigned to the United States; St. Joseph, which had always been British, remained so.[2] Thus the boundary commissioners precisely reversed the reasoning of the British military in 1815 when they evacuated Fort Mackinac to build a new post on the large uninhabited island they named in honor of Lieutenant-Governor Sir Gordon Drummond, instead of returning to the old Fort St. Joseph. A few weeks later the survey parties reported some disquieting news. Yet another island that no one had been aware of existed between Drummond and Manitoulin. What they had been calling the Grand Manitoulin was, in fact, a *petit* Manitoulin (later named Cockburn Island) and between these two, Mississagi Strait yielded yet another navigable passage. Actually this discovery served to reinforce the choice of False Detour Passage as the middle of the three courses.[3]

    Solving this problem left Sugar Island, just below

the settlement of St. Mary's, still in dispute. A fair distribution of land area would allocate it to the United States; furthermore, the best channel for ships lay east of the island through Lake George. But the British argued that the middle of the navigable part of the river, as well as the midpoint between the two mainland shores, carried west of the island. Despite Commissioner Barclay's compromise proposal that the main channel, wherever it was considered to lie, be declared free to the vessels of both nations—a safe condition under the Rush-Bagot Agreement of 1817 that disarmed the Great Lakes—the political destiny of Sugar Island was left hanging until enactment of the Webster-Ashburton Treaty of 1842.[4] Not that it made any difference to the Indian residents of St. Mary's, who continued to come from both sides of the river to harvest sugar from the magnificent stand of maples that covered the island.

Susan Johnston ran the biggest sugar camp of all, virtually living on the site during the early spring month of intense work. From time to time a lively party made up of her children, their friends, and officers and ladies from Fort Brady visited her. After the group inspected the oxhide buckets arranged to catch the dripping sap from the trees and the long temporary building containing some 20 huge kettles boiling over a log fire, they sat down to a potluck picnic, culminating in a candy pull and the sampling of the delectable sugar in its various forms.[5]

The 1821 survey season was fully occupied in Lake Erie and the Detroit River, but 1822 saw the commissioners ready to tackle Lake Superior. They actually reached Sault Ste. Marie for the first time and were, of course, hospitably received by Squire Johnston. Major Delafield's observations about the Johnston children, confided to his diary, coincided with the opinion most visitors formed about this "interesting" family: "his eldest daughter is most accomplished & certainly of interesting manners . . . Miss Charlotte is a fine-looking girl . . . Eliza much of the squaw in looks, & consequently kept in the dark, altho equally well behaved with her sisters . . . One son is in the Indian Dept, & a polite man; the other a trader, & I am told unpromising."[6]

The erroneous map by which the two parties had drawn up the Treaty of 1783 posed difficult problems at the western end of Lake Superior. The nonexistent Ile Philipeaux hardly mattered, but the treaty was unclear as to which river course leading westward to an unspecified "Long Lake" and thence to Lake of the Woods, was intended. Major Delafield declared for the Pigeon River, thereby reaffirming the interpretation made by the old North West Company almost 25 years before, and the British seemed to agree. But at the end of the 1823 season, after the work at Lake of the Woods had been completed, the British began to argue for St. Louis River much farther south, at present-day Duluth.

In retaliation, Delafield returned from Lake of the Woods via the Kaministiquia route to Fort William on the north shore and posed a new argument for that line. No compromise could be found, and this part of the boundary lay on the table in dispute, along with Sugar Island, when the commission adjourned *sine die* on October 27, 1827.[7] It, too, would await the Webster-Ashburton Treaty of 1842. The hosting of official visitors like the boundary commissioners, as they passed to and fro through the Sault, was now shared by John Johnston and his son-in-law. Henry Schoolcraft, as Indian Agent, was, after all, the chief civilian official in the region, and his 1827 appointment as justice of the peace added to his importance. As time passed, the two men came to share more and more of their personal, as well as their public, lives. Mutual esteem grew with the length of their acquaintance.

In his first meeting with his future father-in-law, Henry observed that he had "the manners and conversation of a perfect gentleman, the sentiments of a man of honor, and the liberality of a lord. He had a library of the best English works, . . . was a man of social qualities, a practical philanthropist, well-read historian, something of a poet . . . "[8] His wife Henry judged to be "a woman of excellent judgment and good sense."[9] The young man was enthusiastic about the arrangement to take his meals in "the hospitable domicil [sic] of Mr. Johnston, who has the warm-hearted frankness of the Irish character, and offers the civilities of life with the air and manner of a prince. I flatter myself with the opportunity of profiting greatly while under his roof, in the polished circle of his household, and in his ripe experience and knowledge of the Indian character, manners, . . . customs, and . . . language."[10]   Henry's early admiration was not disappointed; it grew into a strong affection.

John's opinion of his son-in-law was revealed not only in the intellectual discussions they enjoyed together, but also in consultation on family matters, confidences exchanged, and the entrusting to Henry of important business matters. If Henry had one failing it was his utter lack of humor. One might lightly observe to him on a day of torrential spring rains that even a duck needed rubbers, and Henry would respond with a patient explanation of the principle of webbed feet. If Henry's self-importance irritated John, he never let on. Perhaps he found it easy to forgive Henry's humorless pomposity in favor of his prudence, reliability, and sense of honor, a sorrowful contrast to the character of his own sons. Lewis's failings were, of course, an old story. While he was stationed at Drummond Island as a lieutenant in the British Indian Department, he was close enough to home both to remain part of the family circle and to keep his antics conspicuously before his exasperated father. But the transfer of Drummond Island to American sovereignty meant drastic change. Although the Boundary Commissioners made their decision in 1820, the island was not actually turned over to the Americans until 1828, after its official report was filed and accepted. The transfer removed the British military presence entirely from the area, and most of the resident traders followed the garrison to its new location at Penetanguishene, 200 miles away at the foot of Georgian Bay. The once busy village at Drummond became a ghost.[11]

As early as 1824, the government moved the officers of the Indian Department and their treaty distribution function to Amherstberg on the Detroit River. With them went Lewis Johnston. He did not perform any more capably in the Indian Department than he had in the military and continued to drink and gamble as excessively as ever. He found a new touch in his brother-in-law, on whom he presumed even before the marriage took place, writing on August 1, 1823 to request a loan of $160, "considering you a real friend," to be repaid with interest in two installments the following October and December. A week later he wrote again to acknowledge Henry's "truly friendly letter . . . and I accept with real thanks your kind offer of the draft on the Secretary of War, as it will then answer my purpose."[12] Almost a year later Lewis wrote to assure Henry that he had his money, but in view of the imminent move to Amherstberg he would need the funds for getting settled there. Would Henry mind waiting a bit longer? Perhaps Henry waited indefinitely, for the following year, 1825, poor Lewis was dead at the age of 32. Such was his power to charm that Henry, whose sober, industrious personality differed so sharply, penned a florid epitaph, compounded of truth and wish. It began:

> A manly form, a gen'rous heart,
> That ne'er unmoved, could meet or part;
> A sense of honor, high and clear,
> Above all guile—above all fear;
> Affection true, for kin or friend,
> Their hand to grasp—their fame defend—
> These all were his, who rests below,
> A parent's, brother's, sister's wo![13]

Lewis's last letter to Jane reveals his personality more poignantly than any other document. He wrote to her in February of 1825 from a friend's house near Sandwich, where he was spending a leave. He had been waiting to hear from her:

> but my hope and expectations have been greatly disappointed. I hope you are not getting in the way of the world, whose maxim is, no sooner out of sight, than out of mind . . . I received late last fall a long letter from our dear father, in which he complains bitterly of the unhappy state in which Major Cutler Keeps the Sault in, [sic] and expresses his anxious wish to leave it. Should I succeed in getting the Govr to sanction the grant of land which the Indians have given me on the river St. Clair, I shall try if possible to prevail on them to

> settle on it, the situation is beautiful and there is already 40 acres cleared on it, & I really think would please our Dear Mother. . . . You really will be surprised to see me . . . to see the change that has taken place in me, no more the same person. It is now 3 weeks that I have abstained from any thing like liquor, the consequence is that I am getting as strong as Sampson. . . . I should wish much that Mr. S. would purchase a book on farming for me.[14]

Always cheerful and hopeful, he was stricken suddenly while still at Sandwich, died and they buried him there, far from the family that loved him for all his faults.

By the 1820s disappointment in his second son was beginning to overlie John Johnston's despair for his first. In his early youth George had been a great help and comfort to his father. But as the family business contracted, George lived more independently, and his weaknesses became more apparent. In the fluid society of the frontier, half-breed or quarter-breed children could move either up or down in the social scale, depending upon personality and circumstance. George, like his older brother, aspired, indeed conformed, socially and intellectually to the white milieu of his father. He was well-educated, his manners were courtly, and he readily formed reciprocated friendships with the gentlemen of his acquaintance. He seemed not to identify with the Indian side of his heritage, alluding always to Indians in the third person with strong inferences of "otherness" than himself. Yet both brothers exhibited tendencies to irresponsibility and an unfortunate incapacity to tolerate liquor. George's alcoholism emerged later than Lewis's, and he was at all times a more capable and responsible person, but he suffered from an additional flaw of character. George was an incurable spendthrift.

Closeness to his father as he grew up imbued him with the principles and values of the parent he so fervently admired—devotion to God and family, a gracious generosity, courtesy, love of literature. But he also learned from his father a taste for elegance in dress and household that in George was untempered by John's prudence.

Whether he had the money to pay his bills or not, he ordered fine clothes, jewelry, and books whenever it suited his fancy or supposed "needs." One invoice of the American Fur Company at Mackinac in 1822 itemized:[15]

1 chased gold seal motto and device	40
1 superfine blue surtout	46
1 pair pantaloons & vest to match	25
1 tartan plain cloak	18
1 mixed pantaloons & vest	8
8 books	
"Young Man's Companion"	1
Caleb's "In Search of A Wife"	2.50
Milton's "Paradise Lost & Gained"	4
Johnson's "Pocket Dictionary"	1.50
"Whole Duty of Man"	2.25
Hoyle's "Games"	1.25
A Song book	1
Rose & Emilies	1.75
1 brass fishing reel	2
1 trunk	3
Packing of books, freight & interest	[28.75]
Total	$186

He was at that time a trader with the company. In October of 1822 he married Louisa Raymond,[16] of whom little is known. She was identified in subsequent letters and documents as an Indian, but may have been of mixed parentage, possibly the daughter of a canoe-man. She was certainly not of the same social status as the Johnstons.

John never commented in any remaining letters about George's marriage, but he probably disapproved of it. Louisa might be a nice girl, but John had reason to expect his son to marry someone more nearly approaching the conventional definition of a lady. Nor do any letters reveal his feelings about the arrival of his first grandchild, Louisa Maria, on September 2, 1823.[17] His expansive love undoubtedly included her, but he probably saw little of her, as George's family wintered with him at his various posts on Lake Superior.

Rather, it was the second baby, William Henry

Schoolcraft, born June 27, 1824,[18] who became the light of John's late years. With great reluctance he embarked on his journey to York for the hearing on his war losses soon after the birth. But Jane withstood childbirth better than her ailments, and he was reassured by Henry's letters reporting the healthy progress of mother and child. "I received your kind letter . . . yesterday evening, and am most grateful to the Almighty for you, my beloved Jane and my dear little grandson's good health as also for that of my dear Wife and all of my dear children, who I trust in God will in some respect recompence me for the sorrow, shame and disappointment the two eldest have given me."[19] Little Willy, along with the younger Johnston children, had an important responsibility.

But John was denied the joy of watching the child's development during his first year. Henry decided to spend the winter of 1824-25 in New York and Washington and appointed Captain N.S. Clarke from Fort Brady to handle the agency during the slow winter season.[20] His correspondence with important men and his collections and exchanges of natural specimens had grown continuously during his two-year residence at the Sault. Now it would benefit his reputation to spend some time in the East among his growing scientific acquaintance. Furthermore, he was preparing another manuscript for publication and wished to see it personally through the press. But his most important reason lay in the conflicts in authority that had arisen at St. Mary's.

Colonel Brady was succeeded at the fort that bore his name by Major Enos Cutler, and Henry had nothing but trouble with him. For example, Cutler wanted Henry, in his capacity as justice of the peace, to prosecute the operators of liquor shops in the village. Henry pointed out that his authority did not extend to the function of prosecuting attorney, but if Cutler wished to bring charges against named persons he would hear the case. The major demurred at this, and in apparent retaliation for Schoolcraft's refusal to do his bidding he refused to build the quarters for the Indian Agency that the War Department required him to provide. Henry recognized that conflicts between military and civilian authorities were almost inevitable on the frontier, "but there are, perhaps, few examples to be found where the former power has been more aggressively and offensively exercised than it has been under the martinet who is now in command at this post."[21] He determined that while he was in the East he would visit Secretary Calhoun in Washington and personally settle the issues of conflicting authority. Mending political fences in general, while reminding Washington of his presence in the world, was not a bad idea either.

In late September the entourage set out—Mr. and Mrs. Schoolcraft, their infant, his nurse, and ten-year-old Anna Maria Johnston.[22] The little girl would begin her formal schooling in New York.[23] It was Jane's first extended trip from home since her own childhood foray into "education abroad," and she was as glad to have her little sister for familiar company as the child was to enjoy the security of her adult sister's household. The family moved into rooms at 65 Barclay Street.[24] Henry relished the stimulation of city life, and he happily attended meetings of learned societies, conferred with fellow scientists, and worked over the final drafts of the new book, published in April, 1825 under the title *Travels in the Central Portions of the Mississippi Valley*.[25]

In January Henry left for Washington. It was the couple's first separation, and he wrote Jane frequent and detailed letters, describing the countryside and towns through which he traveled for three days by steamboat and coach, regretting that she could not see it too. "My thoughts lead me . . . perpetually . . . back to you, and to your little parlour in Barclay Street. What an interesting chain of thought is connected with the idea of a home, & a wife, & a child. What a new source of feelings, pleasures & anxieties does it open to me, of all of which, [sic] I formerly knew nothing."[26] He also reported favorably on his visits with John Calhoun. The Secretary assured Henry of his support, defined more precisely the Indian agent's authority, and "issued a peremptory order . . . to the commandant at the Sault, to put up my building during the present year."[27] He visited other dignitaries as well, including General Macomb, who extended warm remembrances to Jane's father and showed Henry a ring

Jane had presented him, fashioned from Lake Superior silver. Henry had never heard his wife speak of native silver and was surprised. Apparently, the Indians knew of it and used it long before the white man's discovery.

During the weeks Henry was away Jane missed him keenly. She suffered from a severe cough and had the doctor in so often for bleeding and consultation that his charges totalled almost $50.[28] Anxiety for her distant family measurably increased when her father wrote news like little eight-year-old John falling into a kettle of boiling lye. Fortunately, "Eliza was just coming in and caught him out in the instant, but the skin came off from the hip to the knee and from the elbow to the fingers. By a peculiar Providence of God his trunk . . . entirely escaped . . . he is [now] perfectly recovered and running about as usual without mark or maim."[29] But friends in New York were as attentive during Henry's absence as when he was there. Jane was, in fact, quite a social sensation. Her genealogy made her interesting in advance to a curious intelligentsia. To their agreeable surprise they were introduced to no rustic Indian princess, but a fashionable lady who "wrote a most exquisite hand, & composed with ability, & grammatical skill & taste. Her voice was soft, & her expression clear & pure, as her father . . . had been particularly attentive to her orthography & pronunciation & selection of words of the best usage abroad."[30]

Jane, for her part, did not consider herself an Indian. Dear Mama was not to be classed with "the poor, benighted children of the forest,"[31] who, having lost the self-reliance and dignity of their forebears, had become dependent upon the trader's alcohol and the Agent's handouts, too frequently shed one another's blood, and were becoming the most conspicuous members of the race. She shared the enlightened white man's patronizing pity for these demoralized people, but her own pride in her heritage reached back from the contemporary scene to her illustrious ancestors, of whom her mother and a handful of dignified older chieftains remained the few living examples.

On their way back to Sault Ste. Marie in late April of 1825 the Schoolcrafts stopped for a couple of weeks in Vernon, New York to visit Henry's family. When they left their group was enlarged by two—Henry's young sister, Maria Eliza, who would be enrolled at school in Detroit, and his youngest brother, James Lawrence.[32] The teenage boy had become a worry to his parents and to his older brother, as he appeared to be drifting into idleness and "evil pursuits with low companions." He was clearly a bright young man and had a most engaging personality; a new start on the frontier, with edifying employment as a clerk to his brother, might be the making of him.

On June 24, 1825, barely six weeks after their arrival home, Henry was off again, this time westward to Prairie du Chien for a convocation of all the northwestern Indian tribes.[33] Thus began a pattern of annual separation that, despite exchange of long and frequent letters, Jane would come to detest. But to Henry each one of his trips presented an opportunity to further his career. Admittedly, he had always relished new scenes in distant places and in the conflict between his love of travel and his love of home, ambition helped travel win out. Furthermore, he sincerely believed that the work he was called upon to do on these trips was of signal importance to the nation.

The formal relationship between the United States Government and the Indian tribes was anomalous from the start. The tribes considered themselves nations in the sense that they were entities independent from one another, and in this sense it was appropriate to deal with them as with foreign nations. But their political concept of nationhood was far different from the white man's definition. If individual American statesmen understood these differences, official policy rarely, if ever, reflected that understanding. To the extent that Indian relations were foreign relations, the United States (and Great Britain, for that matter) treated them in the same way they did European affairs—sending and receiving emissaries, negotiating treaties.

But some essential differences existed, even from the European point of view. First, the United States was in the process of conquering the Indian nations by infiltration. As that conquest progressed and the native populations became surrounded by Americans, their farms, and their villages, the fiction of Indian independent nationhood became harder to maintain. Yet no one at that time, neither the Indians nor the Americans, wished to consider them U.S. citizens. Their position within the society was, therefore, legally ambiguous and socially strained. Their growing economic dependence upon the white man, coupled with their ubiquitous health problem of alcoholism, added a third dimension to the relationship. From a humanistic perspective they became wards of the state. For 200 years American Indian policy has vacillated among these perceptions of the appropriate way to deal with Native Americans. Henry Schoolcraft experienced all of them.

Although Indian culture fascinated Henry, he never empathized with it. He looked upon it as a curiosity, to be studied and to be preserved in books and artifact collections, but not necessarily to be kept alive as a dynamic force. He was convinced, with all his kind, of the superiority of European Christian culture and sincerely believed that assimilation was the greatest benefit he and his government could confer on the native people. In the belief that this would eventually happen, he worked tirelessly to collect the oral traditions and language forms for scholarly preservation. To further these goals he traveled thousands of miles to exhort distant people as well as those who came to his agency door to reveal tribal customs.

While his wife and her family were the immediate instruments of his academic study of Indian culture, his father-in-law's views on the Indian problem and its solution undoubtedly influenced his own. Despite John Johnston's intimacy, love, and respect for the Indians, he believed, as demonstrated in his own family life, in the blessings of Europeanization.

> Within these thirty years there has been a great falling off in the industry integrity and hospitality of the Indians, which I impute chiefly to the facility with which they procure the means of intoxication. . . . Therefore I deem it impossible to reclaim them unless every species of spiritous liquor is completely shut out from them. . . . [The U.S.

> and Great Britain should] unite in establishing Missions and Schools. . . . the Indians when young, are gay, sprightly and acute, and are perfectly capable of being instructed and consequently improved, and their parents, whose natural affections are now sometimes drowned in the stupor of brutifying excess, would soon be taught to exult in the elevation of their offspring. . . . The more I reflect on the present state of the Indian population . . . I am the more convinced that as long as they remain in their present uncivilized and insubordinate condition it will be a work of great difficulty and labour to excite any number of them to listen to the truths of the Gospel or become so far stationary as to cultivate the soil to any substantial purpose or effect.[34]

Both the United States and Great Britain did have laws on the books prohibiting the sale of liquor to the Indians, the welfare aspect of relations, but that is where they remained. Two additional obstacles to constructive assimilation of Native Americans into European-American culture were inter-tribal warfare and nomadism. Perhaps these could be removed in the foreign relations mode—through treaties. Most of the treaties negotiated served the primary white purpose of land cession. By inference land not ceded belonged to the negotiating tribe(s), and the hope was that each would stay in his own territory. But they rarely did. Raids and territorial incursions, along with blood feuds and alcoholism, kept the pot boiling.

The treaty-making at Prairie du Chien in 1825 was an unusual event. For once the United States was demanding nothing from the 12 tribes assembled there. The War Department, represented by Lewis Cass and Henry Schoolcraft, called the convocation for the sole purpose of settling internal disputes and fixing their respective territorial boundaries. Perhaps peace among the Indian tribes would facilitate peace between them and the United States. But *amicus curiae* was a difficult role to play in these circumstances. Ancient rivalries resisted settlement, even when they used the Indians' own bark maps and drawings. The negotiations dragged on for weeks.[35]

Henry seethed with impatience. He missed his wife and baby dreadfully.

> My thoughts have often turned toward you, as I have proceeded westward, and with an intensity proportionate to the distance . . . . To be absent when our sweet boy is making his first attempts to speak & to walk, is indeed depriving me of a pleasure I had cherished in anticipation. My fears are that some accident may befall him in that *kitchen* where he so often goes, and where pots of boiling water are everlastingly over the fire. Do not laugh at my anxiety.[36]

His loneliness was most poignant in the late afternoons and evenings, when he endeavored to bring his wife closer by writing. "A weary wilderness lies between us. But although this inhospitable trace separates our persons, I trust it can never separate our hearts."[37]

> Oh my dearest Jane, believe me this long separation is painful to my heart. I could not know the strength of those ties that bind me to you, before this separation. I no longer feel myself capable of entering into the few amusements in which I once took pleasure. I feel as if it were doing injustice to you to act, or feel, or think, under any circumstances where you are not present to share the pleasure, or to appreciate the pain.[38]

Such passionate expression of emotion was uncharacteristic of Henry Schoolcraft, revealing, if momentarily, the depths of his love and longing.

Nor was he consoled by the pleasure of many letters from Jane in a land without postal service. She could only send letters when someone happened to be going Henry's way who could carry the messages of devotion, news about the baby's development, and her striving to live up to Henry's faith in her as a mother. The only thing that made his absence bearable for her was living in her father's house and enjoying the companionship and help of her mother and sisters.

A letter she addressed to "Henry R. Schoolcraft, Esq., U.S. Indian Agt. On his way to Lake Superior" never reached him at all. Nor did the last one she sent with her brother, George, on his way to winter at Lac du Flambeau, where he might intercept Henry on the way home. It was her most cheerful missive, full of dinner parties with friends from across the river—Lieutenant Bayfield, who was conducting the hydrographic survey of the lakes for the British government, and Hudson's Bay Company traders Mr. McBean and Mr. Mackintosh—as well as friends from Fort Brady, like Captain Dearborn and Dr. Pitcher. She also reassured Henry that "James' conduct has been perfectly blameless."[39] But Henry, coming home by a different route, was maddeningly delayed by weather on the lakes. By September 8 he was so impatient that, despite high winds, he ran the risk of sailing his canoe under reef to a depth of less than four feet. "I do not think myself ever to have run such hazards. I was tossed up and down the waves like Sancho Panza on the blanket."[40] Despite the pain of separation during the summer of 1825, the very next year Henry was off again. The Treaty Council of 1826 was actually called at the suggestion of Shingabawossin, now the acknowledged chief of the Sault Ste. Marie band.[41]

Although in a later time it became apparent that American officials and Indian leaders held divergent concepts of the role, meaning and inviolability of treaties, in this period many chiefs still had faith in the efficacy of the words and ceremonials imbedded in treaty-making. They were willing to trade alien, amorphous notions, such as intangible property rights in land and minerals, for concrete benefits in goods and services; Shingabawossin had his own agenda.

The government commissioned Henry to organize the convocation of the Lake Superior bands at Fond du Lac, which lay entirely within his jurisdiction, although Governor Cass and Thomas L. McKenney, United States Commissioner of Indian Affairs, joined him for the ceremonies. The impressive fleet setting out from Sault St. Marie, where Henry's new clerk, Francis Audrain, was left in charge of the agency, consisted of three large boats carrying a 62-man military detachment under Captain Boardman, four boatloads of provisions and presents for the Indians, and McKenney's canoe with the principal negotiators. Henry had organized carefully and with diplomatic liberality.

This time the negotiations proceeded smoothly. The Indians reaffirmed the 1825 Treaty of Prairie du Chien, settled some additional native boundaries, acknowledged U.S. sovereignty, and ceded to the United States the right to explore for and remove copper and other minerals. They received in return the usual guarantee of payments in cash and goods. And Shingabawossin won his request for establishment of a $1,000 annuity to finance an Indian school at St. Mary's. Although this traditional leader did not desire formal education for his own children, he wanted the option available for those of his people who did.[42] The United States Senate, in its wisdom, later struck out that clause when it ratified the treaty.[43] The other terms were immediately set in motion by efforts to remove the solid copper Ontonagon Rock for shipment east, but the natives' beliefs and inadequate tools frustrated accomplishment of that objective.[44]

Fortunately for Henry the 1826 trip lasted only a little over a month, for he sorely missed the "Dear partner of my soul"[45] whose health caused him no little anxiety that summer. The previous winter had been a miserable one, summed up in a letter John wrote to George, who was then trading at Lac du Flambeau.

> I have suffered more than ever by the rheumatism and have lost the use of my left leg up to the hip joint. My joints are so excruciating that I never know what a sound sleep is. . . . Your dear sister Jane narrowly escaped death last Novr. She had a little daughter stillborn, and between sickness and grief was brought to the verge of the grave, but thanks be to God she now enjoys her usual health, which however, was never good. . . . As to business it is very dull, and very poor returns are to be expected from the Indians who are too

drunken even to catch rabbits. Our fishing failed earlier than usual, which caused great distress amongst the debauched and impoverished Canadians.[46]

Nor was George any better off, "having . . . suffered shipwreck last September. Returns will fall short here, owing to the entire failure of bear, we are reduced very low in provisions, our fishing having failed us last fall."[47] But things were about to look up for George, whose second child, Henry William, born August 19, 1825,[48] added both joy and anxiety to the life of a father who had difficulty making ends meet.

Although Henry Schoolcraft had studied intensively the structure of the Ojibway language and would continue to do so for the rest of his life, he never learned to speak it with any fluency. Throughout his 20-year career among the natives of the frontier, he had to rely upon interpreters. And good ones were hard to find. For the Fond du Lac council of 1826 he wanted the most reliable transmissions he could get, and in May he wrote with elaborate courtesy to his impoverished brother-in-law that "I am desirous, if it is consistent with your engagements, to avail myself of your services at the treaty as confidential interpreter . . . for which you will be adequately compensated."[49]

For George this opportunity turned out to yield more than extra cash. In the course of his work he favorably impressed Commissioner of Indian Affairs McKenney, who concluded on this trip that the district was too large to be adequately supervised by one agent at Sault Ste. Marie. Schoolcraft was dependent upon traders of questionable reliability to report to him about conditions and deliver his messages to Indians hundreds of miles away. Furthermore, the only check he had on the traders he was supposed to be regulating was their spying on one another. On his return to Washington McKenney would arrange for official designation of a sub-agency at the western end of Lake Superior. In the meanwhile, he offered George a provisional appointment as sub-agent, to be stationed at La Pointe. From there he would deal with both the traders and the natives to see that U.S. laws were enforced, the Indians' allegiance secured, and the influence of foreign governments (i.e. Britain) minimized. Henry provided him with a small quantity of presents and provisions. Most importantly, the post, confirmed by the War Department a few months later, carried a salary of $500 per year.[50]

At last George had the opportunity to become the important man he always wanted to be, and he vowed to handle the assignment skillfully. Yet, in the end, it was his very desire for status that impeded his success. He tried to emulate his father in integrity and dignity, but somehow his strenuous efforts were never able to command the same respect from people that John inspired merely by being himself. George's moralistic demands and haughtiness antagonized his associates; he became enmeshed in petty quarrels, and, especially as his drinking problem worsened, his pretensions often appeared ridiculous.

Many on Lake Superior were dismayed by the appointment. Among these was Robert Stuart, American Fur Company agent at Mackinac since 1819, who had been dealing painfully with George for years. He masked his displeasure, but Henry knew that the appointment was "gall and wormwood to him"[51] when he wrote:

> I was much pleased to learn that Mr. George Johnston succeeded in obtaining an appointment which with prudence, may render him easy and comfortable, but . . . I understand that he has been already boasting, that he will show some of the Lake Superior folks *'who is their driver.'* Should he allow any foolish desire of revenge to get the better of his discretion, it will be sure to tend more to his own injury than those he may wish to punish. G. Johnston Indian Agent ought never to recollect the little petty quarrels of Geo. Johnston Indian Trader.[52]

Henry immediately warned George of the gossip and urged him to exercise self-control as he had not done heretofore.

You very well know that many eyes are upon you,

> *some* of which will rejoice to descry anything, however trivial in your conduct, that may be siezed [sic] upon to form an accusation. But I hope & trust, and with me, all your family hope & trust, that you will disappoint their malicious expectations. Abilities sufficient for the task I know you have, with zeal and industry adequate to their successful employment. But ability and zeal, & industry, are all unavailing without a cautious, economical and conciliating deportment. Exercise no act of authority without being sure that the authority is confided to you. . . . Magnaminity and a total oblivion to all the petty quarrels of the trade . . . however much against your inclinations, are in your *present* situation, virtues of the first order. . . . Act agreeably to those principles, in which one of the kindest of fathers has surceasingly instructed you, and you will always act well . . . [53]

Rather than take umbrage at Henry's admonishing tone, George was grateful for his interest and appreciated the wisdom of those words. His airs and graces had made him a rather lonely man in a rough society. "Long have I sought a friend in the country to direct me, and to whom I could unbosom myself without restraint." Feeling that he had found such a friend in Henry, he confessed his quarrels with his enemies made him "feel like Timon of Athens, a dislike to appear in the world. Now that I am here I begin to feel more independent and at ease . . . I again dread the moment I must appear in the civilized world. If it were not for the most endearing ties of parental & friendly affections and duty, I should never wish to make my appearance in it."[54]

George and Louisa spent three happy years in the comfortable little house he built at La Pointe, with bedrooms partitioned off, and the largest main room serving as combined kitchen and "Indian Hall."[55] The two *engages he* was allowed under a budget of $400 over his own salary had a separate smaller house of their own, and he had a small storehouse constructed as well. By the spring of 1827, they had cleared two acres of land;

the sub-agency would provide much of its own food.[56] And on December 17 of that year a third child, John George, was born.[57]

Henry was pleased with the way George took hold, reporting carefully all that was going on among the Indians and traders at the island, around Chequamegon Bay, and inland to Lac Court Oreille and Lac du Flambeau. George also sent him many interesting geological specimens and began to supply men like Lewis Cass and Thomas McKenney with Indian artifacts and curiosities. All of these men were proud of their cabinet collections, and George would supply each of them for years to come.

The journal he kept tells of his days spent chopping wood, fishing, building his house room by room, distributing supplies to Indians, and the comings and goings of the traders—Michel Cadotte, Jr. and Lyman Warren the principal men in residence at La Pointe, and Charles Oakes, Samuel Ashmun, Bela Chapman and John Aitken passing through. His work was much like that of a policeman, going out and seizing liquor from the Indians.[58]

Warren and Cadotte were imperious about their status at La Pointe, Cadotte by right of his wife, who considered herself the "princess" of the island (in fact, its name was later changed to her Christian name, Madeline). When George first arrived Warren welcomed him, expressing the "hope you will wink at some little alterations I have made in exchanging some of the men which you are sensible enough of that it is almost impossible to state at the Sault precisely as we want to place our men"[59]—in short ignoring the licensing regulations. But they never did get on; George despised Warren's "rouguery and rascality, meaness and lowness,"[60] and Warren never accepted his authority, nor anyone else's, George observed, from the President on down.

Pleasant times occurred too, as when he took his family sugaring in the spring and "hoisted sail in my new dog sleigh, and had a fine run . . . to the Mauvais River."[61] He spent many of the long winter hours reading and noting his thoughts about ancient history, the character of Socrates, Dionysius the Elder, Cleopatra, English history and the possibilities of preventing war by negotiation and conciliation, the work of Dryden and Addison.

> I have a spirit within me that soars above the common level of mankind, but alas; my misfortunes and those of my family have made a deep wound & impression in my susceptible heart. . . . But I trust I shall acquit myself to the satisfaction of my own feelings, and to the trust reposed in me, although culumnly [sic] malice, hatred and all uncharitableness, has been predominant in the civilized world, to the great scandal of enlightened minds, . . . —better it is to remain among the sons of nature, and in the deepest recesses of his wilderness and contemplate on the folly of the world and mankind— Lapoint [sic] March 15th, 1827, An Aborigine[62]

Although George controlled his drinking most of the time during these years, other habits were harder to shed. He tended as always, to exceed his authority, particularly when it came to spending money. He defended his overspending on presents for the Indians as humanitarian conduct necessary to their welfare and security of their allegiance. Despite the signature, "An Aborigine" in his notebook, George never identified himself as an Indian. He always spoke of them in the third person with paternalistic compassion. "The life the Indians lead is one of the most miserable. Half starving, smoaky [sic] lodges, buried in a filth of every description, and what is most surprising they seem to take everything regarding their state with such patience, that they actually seem happy under such circumstances."[63] Despite his concern for the Indians, according to at least one report, he did not incur their respect or loyalty. "The habits of the sub-agent at La Pointe . . . *are such*, that the Indians will not visit him. This branch of the agency . . . has actually cost the United States more than *five thousand dollars*, . . . & one, as it stands, of no utility."[64] In any case, Congress suspended appropriations for the sub-agency in 1829; George was instructed to close up shop and spend no more.

George's benefactor, Commissioner of Indian Affairs Thomas McKenney, was a worldly man, much taken by the entire Johnston family. He had a scholarly interest in the American Indian and between 1836 and 1844 would publish a multi-volume work on the subject that many considered definitive. In addition to being a scholar, however, he was also a politician and a gossip. Adroit handling of his political office had sent him on his western tour in 1826, and his penchant for gossip led him to write a book about it. In it he reported interesting tidbits (along with a good deal of description and history), like the fact that Governor Cass always traveled by canoe because sailing made him seasick.[65] He glowed in the warmth of the Johnston hospitality and penned vivid descriptions of the family in his book.

He described John as polished, intelligent and cheerful, Susan as tall and large, active and cheerful, capable, of strong character and vigorous intellect. Of Jane he wrote that she "would be an ornament to any society," and beautiful Charlotte, who dresses and sings well "would be a belle in Washington."[66] Ever after, in his official and investigative correspondence with Henry Schoolcraft, he referred back to the pleasure of his 1826 visit to Sault Ste. Marie and his esteem for the family.

But he carried his esteem in one direction just a bit too far. When he wrote Henry in April of 1827 telling of his plans for another western trip that summer, he sent a special message to Eliza and Charlotte that he would bring beaux for them and "expect to be lost in their superior charms." He would also bring copies of his book for them, as "It is rather a *ladies* book. I prefer the sex & their opinions."[67] Perhaps he preferred a little too much. Although he took care to include all the Johnston ladies in his gallantries, it became clear on the second visit that beautiful 21-year-old Charlotte was the primary object of his interest. He invited her to come to Washington as his protegé.

It seemed a splendid opportunity to enlarge her education and prospects from the home of an important person, who was middle-aged, married, and had a grown son of his own. But McKenney oversold himself and aroused the father's suspicions. His opinion of a " *certain person* has changed so much that he deems it necessary to retract his word & not permit sister Charlotte to go to Washington," where she would be so far from anyone to advise her and "check her too innocent and unsuspecting nature, devoid as she is of any knowledge of this world."[68] McKenney expressed "many, *many* regrets at the decision. . . As to expense, I had arranged it should cost her not a cent, & my home should have been hers. But it's over. The decision is made."[69] John Johnston, however, never had any regrets. In fact, the more he learned of McKenney the more thankful he was that second thoughts had prevailed over his initial impulse to folly.

By the winter of 1826-27 the hamlet of Sault Ste. Marie reached an estimated white civilian population of 150, including artisans such as a cooper, blacksmith, baker and tailor, as well as traders and merchants.[70] Adding the garrison at Fort Brady, they were now a large enough society to sustain a lively winter existence, even when ice shut them off from the world for six months. The military post conferred a special blessing on John Johnston. Its library enlarged the scope of his reading without the burdensome expense of importing all the books himself.[71] And the permanent presence there of a qualified physician enabled John to retire from medical practice. As for the population at large, "We pass the winter as usual, eating, sleeping, drinking and dancing &c &c."[72] Parties were a long tradition, but this year the intelligentsia of the community had something new to amuse them.

Henry Schoolcraft undertook to edit a small magazine entitled *Muzzeniegun*, the Ojibway word for book, or in English *The Literary Voyager*. Fifteen handwritten issues, averaging 24 pages, were circulated; the printing press had not yet arrived at the Sault. The little publication spawned a literary society, and each issue was read aloud at meetings before being circulated among interested readers. Members of the Johnston family and the editor himself contributed most of the articles, using pseudonyms in popular eastern fashion. Henry designated himself Alieca, while Jane alternated between Leelinau and Rosa.[73] John, calling himself Hibernius, entered into the spirit with several submissions. In January he wrote:

> To the Editor of the Literary Voyager
>
> Dear Sir, you have wish'd I should write for
> your paper,
> But of late I've become quite a pen and ink
> hater,
> Yet desirous sincerely my friends to amuse,
> I shall shake off my slumbers and draw on my
> muse.[74]

And in honor of St. Patrick's Day, March 17, 1827 he submitted a paean to his native Ireland.

Although the editor welcomed verse and fictional prose, the magazine focused on Indian tales and legends, including the oral history of the Ojibway tribe, as told by Susan Johnston in a series of articles. The bulk consisted of Henry's own writings, however—essays, poems, letters to his friends about his travels. Perhaps he had difficulty eliciting contributions from others. In the second issue he unbent enough to insert an apologetic letter from his little dog, Ponti, short for Pontiac, who in his "youth and indiscretion" had been unable to resist the temptation to chew up his master's valuable pages of Indian verb conjugations.[75] The long tribute to *The White Fish* reads as though it came from the irreverent pen of James Schoolcraft, beginning:

> Of ven'son let Goldsmith so wittingly sing,
> very fine haunch is a very fine thing
> And Burns in his tuneful and exquisite way
> The charms of a smoking Scots haggis display
> But 'tis often much harder to eat than discard
> And a poet may praise what a poet may want,
> Less doubt there shall be 'twixt my muse and
> my dish,
> Whilst her power I invoke, in the praise of
> white fish.[76]

Thus *The Literary Voyager* provided both fun and edification, filling the long weeks between infrequent mail deliveries from "below." As the village had grown, so had the frequency of its communication with the rest of the world. During the navigation season, mail and newspapers were delivered by every steamboat, but from November to April it must come overland from Detroit on the back of a sturdy fellow on snowshoes. In a good year this might occur monthly; normally only three or four such deliveries occurred a winter. Isolated communities like the Sault starved for news, and everyone circulated every newspaper or magazine that arrived until it was almost worn out. Then, when opportunity afforded, it was sent on to the even more isolated wintering traders like George Johnston.

All in all 1826-27 was a good winter at Sault Ste. Marie. The weather was mild (which did reduce maple sugar production); the family mostly enjoyed good health; John's rheumatism was much better; sixteen-year-old William was studying bookkeeping with John Hulbert, a merchant who had come to St. Mary's a couple of years previously as sutler to Fort Brady; Anna Maria, age twelve, and John McDouall, at ten, were away at school. Perhaps the most exciting event was "the scandalous conduct of Wm. Holiday (John Holiday's worthless son) who, not content to have spent his time in a constant round of gambling and debauchery with all the blackguards of the place, had the audacity to enter Mr. Schoolcraft's house in the night and attempt to debauch poor little Sophy [the maid] who was sleeping in the parlour. Luckily Mr. S. overheard him, got up, and the unprincipled monster fled."[77]

Then, suddenly in March, tragedy struck. God was "pleased to visit us all with his chastening rod by calling to himself our most beloved and promising little Willy."[78] The family was stunned. The swiftness with which an attack of croup carried off the little boy left all of them prostrate with grief. With blinded eyes Henry and Jane followed his little coffin to its place in the cemetery by the river, and John's voice broke with sorrow as he read the service over the remains of his adored grandson.[79] The bereft parents could not face returning to the house they had been renting since their return from New York two years before and sought refuge in the warmth of the Johnston home, in the rooms they had occupied before the child was born.[80] Here Jane could cry her lament on paper.[81]

> Who was it nestled on my breast,
> And on my cheek sweet kisses prest,
> And in whose smile I felt so blest?
> > Sweet Willy.
>
> Who hail'd my form as home I stept,
> And in my arms so eager leapt,
> And to my bosom joyous crept?
> > My Willy.
>
> Who was it wiped my tearful eye,
> And kiss'd away the coming sigh,
> And smiling, bid me say, 'good boy?'
> > Sweet Willy.
>
> Who was it, looked divinely fair
> Whilst lisping sweet the evening pray'r,
> Guileless and free from earthly care?
> > My Willy.
>
> ***************************
>
> My son! thy coral lips are pale -
> Can I believe the heart-sick tale,
> That I thy loss must ever wail?
> > My Willy.
>
> The clouds in darkness seemed to low'r,
> The storm has past with awful pow'r
> And nipt my tender, beauteous flow'r!
> > Sweet Willy.
>
> But soon my spirit will be free,
> And I my lovely son shall see,
> For God, I know did this decree!
> > My Willy.

They had no other way to cope than to believe in Divine Providence and Wisdom, and "the sweet consolation that he is now a pure and unspotted angel in the bosom of his ever adorable Saviour." But Henry mourned in the chilling thought that "Idolatry such as ours for a child, was fit to be rebuked."[82] Swift death of little children was a painfully common occurrence, yet in this instance even Doctor Zina Pitcher, who attended him, lamented his inability to save the child in a poem "To a Bereaved Mother."[83]

> I wail'd the impotence of art—
> Then wept to see the foeman's dart,
> Fix'd firmly in his bleeding heart,
> So fierce 'twas driven.

Inevitably new interests weave themselves over the scars, and for Jane and Henry Schoolcraft healing came through construction of the new agency building so long promised by the government. It was to be a very substantial two-story building, with 15 rooms and several chimneys, worthy of its position as home and office for the chief official of the county and the highest civilian officer of the United States government. Set on high ground in a grove of elms, maples and mountain ash, about half a mile east of the fort, it was sited a conveniently short distance from "Johnston Hall," as Henry liked to designate his father-in-law's home, with a splendid view of the rapids.[84]

The treaty conference of 1827 provided another distraction for the bereaved Schoolcrafts. In June Jane accompanied Henry on the first part of the voyage—by canoe to Mackinac, where they embarked on the steamboat *Henry Clay*, up from Detroit with Governor Cass, Commissioner McKenney, General Winfield Scott, and a large retinue of officials on board. The boat then continued on to Green Bay. Jane spent a few days there before returning with others to Mackinac, while the treaty-makers passed up the Fox River by canoe to the council at Butte des Morts. Another large convocation from many tribes gave Henry the opportunity to collect a lot of history and vocabulary during the weeks of negotiation, made lengthier by the Indian protocols of elaborate ceremony and oratory. Finally, on August 11 the treaty was signed which completed the system of Indian boundaries begun two years before at Prairie du Chien.[85]

Meanwhile, Jane had run into trouble at Mackinac. She realized soon after the agony of her little boy's death that even as she buried him, another child had begun to grow within her. Now, in her sixth month, signs of danger appeared. At Mackinac the Boyds invited her into their home, where she went immediately to bed to stay "as still & quiet as possible . . . without the least motion."[86] She would do everything in her power to see this precious pregnancy through safely. By late July it seemed safe to travel, and George, Charlotte and Eliza all came down to take her home. But the trip was a near disaster. They left Mackinac toward evening with a fair wind for sailing the canoe, intending to continue by moonlight to Drummond Island, as it was inadvisable for Jane to camp out in the open. Unfortunately, George fell asleep, the canoemen had access to the liquor, and they passed DeTour before anyone realized the error. By the time they retraced their course to Drummond it was sunrise and Jane was too exhausted to go on.

To avoid the expense of a waiting canoe, she told George to go on without her; she would hire another vessel when she felt strong enough. "I hope you will not blame me for acting so independently," she wrote apologetically to her husband. To add to her anxieties when she did reach home she found that her mother was ill. "What should I do if she should be unable to attend me placed as I now am in *daily fears*, without the support of your present & affectionate care."[87] But Susan, as always, recovered her buoyant health and remained as unstinting as ever in the tender care of her frail daughter.

The fall of 1827 was a busy time for the whole family. The Reverend Mr. Coe arrived at the Sault to teach the Indian children and preach to their parents. Working with him, Charlotte Johnston began to find her calling as a religious interpreter.[88]

John still carried on the fur business in a small way. But his transactions through Montreal were gradually reduced during the 1820s, after absorption of the

North West Company by the Hudson's Bay Company and the indisputable Americanization of the settlement on the south side of St. Marys River. He now dealt exclusively with New York suppliers. That fall he decided to pay them a visit. During a stopover in Detroit he was entertained by the city's civil and military leaders, and was hospitably received in New York by a number of Henry's prominent acquaintances.[89] The speed of travel by steamboat and stagecoach contrasted vividly with his earlier canoe voyages that required him to winter over in the cities of the East.

On his way down the lakes he enjoyed the cheerful company of young James Schoolcraft. James had begun a modest mercantile operation in the spring of 1826, perhaps with Henry as a silent partner. He combined a buying trip to New York with a visit to his parents at Vernon. After both men returned in November they celebrated another wedding. Henry's and James' sister, Maria, was married to John Hulbert, sutler and merchant, on his way to becoming a wealthy and prominent man.[90]

For Henry and Jane two subjects of unfailing delight happened that season: completion of their new home, which they named Elmwood, for the stately trees that adorned the property and their new daughter, Jane Susan Anne, who arrived at 3:30 p.m. on October 14, 1827, in perfect health.[91] Despite the sorrow that had so blighted their lives the previous spring, Henry was very happy and confided to his diary that he "had now attained that position of repose & quiet which were so congenial to my mind. The influence I exercised, the respect I enjoyed, both as an officer and as a scientific and literary man"[92] from the comfort of a book-lined, specimen-shelved home, with an accomplished wife and beautiful little daughter, made life quite complete for him. But more honor, yet, would take him away from his cherished family circle.

Although he did not seek the office, he was elected to the 13-man Legislative Council of Michigan Territory, which had been organized in 1823, and met at Detroit every spring. This kind of political activity was not to Henry's taste. In fact, he rather scorned party politics, believing that essentially only two kinds of parties were possible, a *promptly debt paying* & a *not promptly debt paying party*—a *non divorce* & a *divorce party.* I have been ever of the former class of thinkers . . . i.e. pay your debts & keep your wife."[93] Throughout his four years of service on the council he tended to find the duty irksome. He avoided the more controversial issues of the day, scorning demagoguery, and focused his attention on matters like incorporation of the Historical Society, the naming of counties and townships with "terse and taste," Indian names or his own creatively Latinized versions of same, and suppression of "the sale of ardent spirits to the Indian race, and to secure something like protection for that part of the population which [has] amalgamated with the European blood."[94] When the tediously awaited spring arrived in 1828 Jane and Henry began to embellish their already beloved Elmwood with plantings that were both useful and ornamental. Since girlhood Jane had been an enthusiastic gardener. Now Henry joined her in poring through the seed catalogues. On his way to the legislative council in May of 1828 he dispatched from the public gardens at Mackinac some young cherry trees to be planted around the house.[95] As in all things Henry took the lead, and though Jane labored hard and lovingly in the garden she sought only to defer to his wishes. She requested his permission to plant strawberry vines where he had planned a gravel walk and put the gravel walk below the terrace. She wanted all his plans carried out, so that she need only keep the gardening and farming going without worrying about making decisions to his liking.[96] When he was away she kept him minutely informed.

> My Father's men, his horse & ours, finished ploughing today & if it is *possible* to commence planting the potatoes tomorrow, it shall be done. There is no dependence to be placed in any Canadian, even the best of them will not fish or take an interest in their employer's business. . . . Descharme & Lalonde, were both absent all day & in consequence I did not sow, as I intended yesterday, the clover seed you sent—but shall do so

tomorrow, if I should, *myself* be under the necessity of preparing the ground; I have planted & sowed all the grain in the garden, except corn & the transplanting of the cabbage . . . I have Peas, an inch or two high, Carrots, Beets, Turnips, Radishes, Lettuce, Pepper Grass & some Pot Herbs coming on finely, the Cucumbers, M. Melons, Water Melons, Pumpkins & Squashes are all planted but not yet come out of the ground, neither is the parsnip or onion. I am still troubled by Men, Women Children & *Dogs* passing daily & hourly through the garden, the latter have trampled all over my young plants, not a single head of Asparagus has appeared.[97]

Henry worried about her overworking herself, but enjoyed the "Elmwood Diary" she sent him regularly that first summer.[98]

And it is not the less interesting to me, from knowing, that the hours you devote to it, are taken from the stillness of the night, when every mortal around you is wrapped in sleep, and there is no eye but that of Omniscience, to observe the traces of your pen. *Those* hours we have often enjoyed together, when the wild winds of winter have whistled around our dwelling; and I think, I may say, that whether passed in conversation or reading, they may be numbered amongst the happiest we have known. It is then, that we have been more truly than at any other time in the twenty four hours, *united in heart*, and have thought, & felt, & wished as one.[99]

He, in turn, told her all the Detroit gossip and sent her delicacies like lemons and vegetable soap.[100] He deliberately set aside a portion of his salary to buy for her the things she requested, like a bonnet in the present fashion as advised by Miss Trowbridge, "very large leghorn profusely trimmed. I will endeavor to hit your taste, which I know is not gorgeous."[101]

For once, however, Henry need not worry about

her. Jane enjoyed better health the summer of 1828 than at any other time of her life and took great delight in her home and her baby. Mrs. Coe, the missionary's wife lived with her for a while. ". . . an accession to my limitted [sic] family circle is very acceptable & desirable, it is so seldom I can conveniently leave home . . . to pay visits, & unless . . . we return calls of ceremony we are apt to be neglected, tho' I cannot complain of anything like neglect since your departure, yet to have one near you to interchange a sentiment, is very gratifying."[102]

Not only did she find time to keep the diary—"I suppose it has, more than once, given exercise to your risible faculties, as you have often laughed at my peculiarity of thinking, & the manner of embodying those thoughts in words"[103] —but to read, requesting that Henry get a number of books for her, including Baxter's *Saints Everlasting Rest*, Hanna Adams' *Letters on the Gospels*, Bunyan's *Pilgrim's Progress*, and similar uplifting works,[104] and to correspond with George at La Pointe. She sent him newspapers and some of her seeds for his garden,[105] and a message from their mother. Firstly, Susan requested some medicinal herbs, like slippery elm. Then "she begs to advise you to be very circumspect in your conduct, & tho' she wishes you to be so at all times, yet more *particularly* so *now*, for reasons best known to herself, & hope you will not repose *too much confidence* in persons whom you may suppose your friends, but are not so in reality."[106] Jane was worried about George. His grandiose ideas and susceptibility to flattery, especially from drinking companions, could only lead to trouble.

But she would soon have cause for other anxieties. In May, 1828 John decided to make another trip to New York to try and improve his business affairs, although "the tariff bill will cause me to curtail my little order almost one half; but if it fosters and promotes home manufacture I shall certainly acquiesce without regret."[107] He had not been well most of the winter, however, and postponed the start of his journey until August. Meanwhile, he helped Jane supervise the farm work at Elmwood and continued writing the reminiscences that Henry had begged him for years to put on paper, but which he got around to only that spring.

He was dealing again with John Jacob Astor and Ramsay Crooks, past differences having been resolved in the settlement out of court of a lawsuit John had initiated in 1824.[108] He planned only a brief stay in New York. When the furs arrived and he had sold them to Astor, he would return home

> as speedily as possible. . . . I shall retain the description of all I see for our little home circle; all that is rich, splendid and luxuriant is lost upon me. One smile of affection from those I love is worth all the rest of the world. Remember me with unabated affection to my dear wife, and Eliza, Charlotte, and Anna and to my dear William and John. May God in mercy bless you all and take you under his almighty protection is my daily prayer. Kiss and bless my dear Jane and her little Cherub for me.[109]

With this characteristic benediction he closed the last letter he would ever write.

A month later he arrived home on a small schooner, in a state of nearly total collapse. He had been attacked by typhus fever in Albany, but pushed himself to journey onward without help or medicine, so anxious was he to reach home and family.[110] By the time he got there he was dying, and a distraught midnight procession carried him semi-conscious on a stretcher from the ship. Susan's skilled ministrations revived him for a time next morning, to the extent that he sat up and cheerfully related the events of the trip to the family gathered around him and distributed presents to each of the children. By the next day he was worse again. Despite the most attentive efforts of his devoted friends, post surgeons Dr. Zina Pitcher and Dr. Edwin James, his condition continued to deteriorate, with shortening periods of remission, over the next four days. Finally, on September 22, 1828, surrounded by the family on whom he had lavished so much love and care, John Johnston quietly offered his last breath in prayer to the God who had ever been his guide and support.[111]

On the 24th he was laid to rest in the military

cemetery by the side of his little grandson. The officers of the garrison were his pall bearers, followed by the full garrison in dress uniform, to pay tribute to Sault Ste. Marie's first citizen.[112] A silver nameplate on the coffin, fashioned from two or three of the family spoons hammered together, was inscribed "John Johnston, Esq., Born Ireland, August 25th 1762, Died Sept. 22nd 1828, Aged 66 years 27 days.[113] His epitaph was penned by his admiring son-in-law.

> To mark the widow's grief, the daughter's tears
> The name a son bemoans, a friend reveres,
> Their own dear circle's honor'd joy and pride,
> Their earthly father, and their heavenly guide.
> For this, we raise thy lonely, simple tomb,
> Far from the world, and from thy native home.
> Warm was thy heart, and true to every fire,
> That love, hope, friendship, charity inspire.
> Yet not to laud thy worth, and polished mind,
> By fancy blest, and varied love rein'd.
> Oh flesh of our own flesh bone of our bone,
> Inscribe we here thy monumental stone.
> Ah Johnston no! the tablet mem'ry rears,
> Enbalms our love and sanctifies our tears.
> Accept oh sainted shade, the humble rite,
> And lead, oh lead us, to the realms of light.[114]

The sad news did not reach George until late October. When he had an opportunity to send a letter back he added his valedictory: ". . . he died as he had lived, in full reliance upon the merits of Jesus and I trust and firmly believed, that he is numbered with the blessed and just-made perfect."[115] Lewis Cass perhaps expressed it best. "He was no common man. To preserve the manners of a perfect gentleman, and the intelligence and information of a well educated man in the dreary wastes around him, and in his seclusion from all society but that of his own family required a vigour and elasticity of mind rarely to be found."[116]

John Johnston

Oshaw-guscody-way-quay (Susan) Johnston

George Johnston

John McDouall Johnston

Jane Johnston Schoolcraft

Anna Maria Johnston

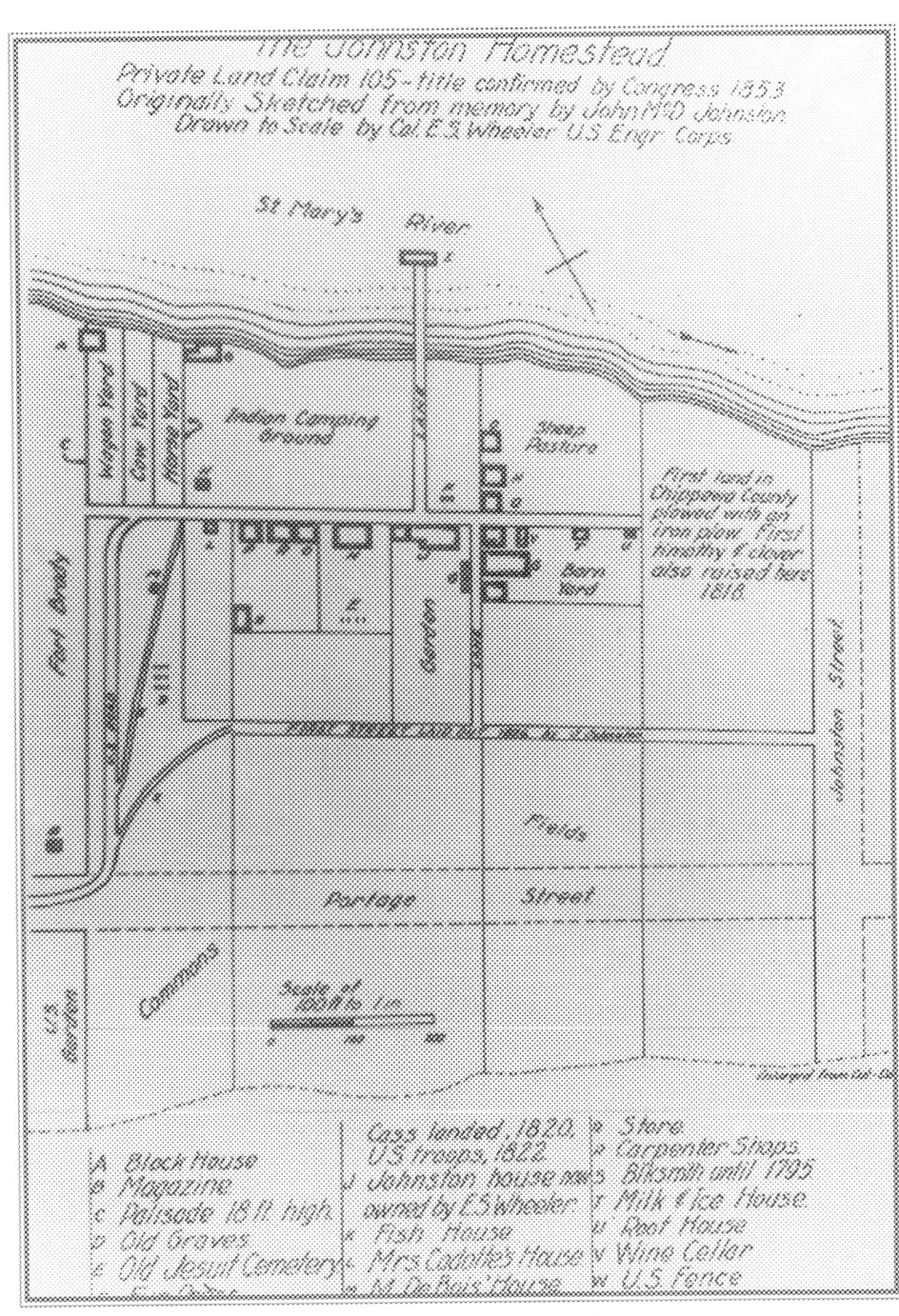

The Johnston Homestead

PART II

Chapter Ten

Of Morals, Rivalries and Village Tempests

In the 52nd year of its independence the United States of America spoke with a new voice. Andrew Jackson was elected President. The entrance of a frontier President into the White House was echoed 1500 miles away by the entrance of a frontier settlement into civic life. By the time Sault Ste. Marie lost its patriarch, its life support had largely shifted from fur to government, from private commerce to public service. The transformation actually began with the absorption of the North West Company into the Hudson's Bay Company in 1821. Abandonment of the Great Lakes route from Montreal to the northwest and the closure of Canadian posts on Lake Superior diminished the importance of the St. Marys portage, limiting its use to American traders. A year later, arrival of the United States Government, defined by the military establishment and the Indian Agency, signified the change in character of the little community.

In 1827 regular steamboat service opened the Sault to swift and easy communication with the outside world, at least in summer, and government appeared in yet another guise. The Territorial Legislature detached a new county from the enormity of Michilimackinac County, which extended from the Sault through virtually all of what is today the Upper Peninsula of Michigan, most of the Lower Peninsula, and all of Wisconsin and Minnesota east of the Mississippi River. The new entity included the northern half of the upper peninsula from Drummond Island to Wisconsin. They selected the name Chippewa County from among three that Henry Schoolcraft suggested, with Sault Ste. Marie as its seat. Governor Cass appointed Henry Chief Justice of the County Court, to serve for four years; a couple of months later he was elected supervisor for Ste. Marie Township as well.[1] John Hulbert was appointed Sheriff, Francis Audrain, Henry's assistant, was named Judge of Probate, and James Schoolcraft became Register of Deeds and Clerk of the Court.[2]

As the fortunes of the fur trade declined with scarcity of fur-bearers and demoralization of the Indian hunters, the government's role in the life of the village became more important. The number of licenses issued by the Mackinac Agency, of which the Sault was a branch, peaked in 1826 at 34.[3] But as the "fur" trade tapered off over the next decade it gradually became the "Indian" trade.[4] The village merchants might barter occasionally with the natives for fur; a beaver skin still bought a 3-point blanket or a bag of flour, and two beaver skins could be exchanged for a gun.[5] But increasingly the Indians paid for their goods with government-issued cash or credits. Between Fort Brady and the Indian Agency, Sault Ste. Marie became a dependency of the federal government—from the salaried officials and the merchants who supplied goods to them, to the Indians who received the goods and the Canadians who transported them. In the future, politics and the winning of government contracts would preoccupy its citizens. John Johnston's 36 years by the rapids of St. Mary's had spanned the transformation from wilderness to civilization. With his death the previous 200-year recorded history of the Sault was concluded; one way of life would be replaced by another.

For Susan Johnston the wrench of her loss was brutal and painful, though only her eyes might show it. She wrapped herself in the love of her children and grandchildren, as he would have done, and carried on the traditions she had shared for so long. The obligations of European hospitality shifted to her daughter and son-in-law, and the worldly Henry Schoolcraft played the role of counsellor. But Susan, who had never been a shrinking violet, a docile, dependent housewife, now, at 51, assumed the leadership of her family with characteristic firmness and dignity.

John had left her his good name, honorable reputation and high credit rating, but he left little of tangible assets. The contents of his home, as recorded in the typical under-valuation of the probate court inventory amounted to $1300. The most precious items were his gold watch at $100, his books at $100, 33 brass kettles worth $150, and 22 pounds of silver plate valued at $350.[6] The worth of the riverfront real estate was uncertain because land titles at the Sault were not yet cleared.

John had pursued his business to the very end, and Susan without hesitation, was determined to carry it on. She engaged young Henry Sibley, son of Judge Solomon Sibley of Detroit, as her chief clerk.[7] He wrote of her intentions to John's New York agents, who affirmed interest in serving Mrs. Johnston, whose "collection will be sure always to command the highest market values, as, except the Muskrats [whose price had recently declined], they are all of the best, and we should take particular pains under existing circumstances to sell them well."[8]

For the trapping end of the business Susan engaged her middle son, William, and when Sibley left her employ after only a few months, William took over the clerical work as well.[9] He was just 17 years old and had not been a particularly good student, but he had been apprenticed to the shrewd John Hulbert and was strongly motivated to conduct his mother's affairs successfully. That first winter was a hard one for him; he wrote George that trade was dull, the hunt poor, the Indians sick, and provisions low, but by spring Henry was reporting to George that William "gives promise of future efficiency & good management. He has been very active during the spring, and the returns are as good as usual."[10]

Susan had need of a steady and adequate income. In addition to herself, she had four children yet dependent on her. Eliza, her companion and help in the home, was a strange girl who did not fare well in society, whether white, Indian or mixed. Now 26, it was unlikely she would marry. The lovely Charlotte, on the other hand, was only 22 and did not lack admirers. Fourteen-year-old Anna Maria was still at school in the East, and John McDouall Johnston, at 12, was ready to begin his formal education at Mr. Taylor's school in Lowville, near Fredonia, New York.[11] Tuition payments imposed a heavy financial burden, but Susan would not consider curtailing the education John, and she, herself, for that matter, had deemed so important.

The quiet joy Susan took in her grandchildren lightened the burdens of responsibility. George occasionally sent little Louisa to stay with her for extended periods, and together they had great fun with Jane's new baby, whom everybody called Janee. Jane was both a source of womanly companionship and a responsibility added to the dependent ones at home, for during Jane's frequent spells of illness it was Susan who tended and comforted her. In the late summer of 1829, when Henry left for the second session of the Legislative Council at Detroit, she was far along in pregnancy. For Susan, in constant attendance, it would have been easier to have Jane at her own house. But Henry opposed such a move, so Charlotte stayed with her instead.[12] Either the baby was late or Jane miscalculated. She wrote to Henry on September 13, "You will probably be surprised to find that I have not yet come to the crisis that is to decide my life or death. . . . Pray for me my dearest—if it is the Lord's holy will to remove me hence, before you return, think kindly of me notwithstanding all my faults."[13] The child did not actually arrive until October 2—a boy weighing in at $8 1/2$ pounds.[14] He was named John Johnston.

Jane was under the care of a doctor, as two excellent physicians were stationed at Fort Brady, Zina Pitcher and Edwin James. Still Susan, wise in the ways of herbal medicine, continued to relieve much of the suffering in the community. She ministered to the townspeople and local Indians, as well as her own family, in the way she and John had done ever since they settled down by the river so long ago. Some of the best herbals came from the La Pointe area, and she frequently sent to George for her supplies. George for his part was carrying on his father's medical tradition there, although he obtained somewhat more modern supplies and advice from Dr. Pitcher:

> Presuming upon your experience in matters of this kind I have in a good measure dispensed with directions for use of the medicines sent herewith. The cough drops are for children of which you may give from 10 to 30 drops according to the age &c of the patient, in water. The adhesive plaster is to be spread warm upon strips of linen & used for cuts &c. The ointment of red . . . precipitate you will find of service in affections of the skin of which you doubtless have seen bad cases among indian [sic] children.[15]

When Congress deleted the appropriation for the sub-agency at La Pointe in May, 1829, George was directed to close it. He returned to the Sault, where his $500 salary as an assistant to Henry was continued for several years. He also continued to spend in a princely fashion. Perhaps the Indian in him could not adhere to the white man's "pay up or do without." One order from William Mitchell at Drummond Island included a blue coat for $25, and $4 for a black vest. His expenses from March 1 to August 31, 1829 totalled $1,011, of which he owed $264 to his brother, William.[16] In January of 1830 he ordered directly from William's supplier, C. Mills, $175 worth of merchandise, including such things as two dozen silver spoons for $42, one pair of sugar tongs for $4, four salt spoons for $2.50, one pair of candlesticks for $8, one coffee pot $4.50, one tea pot $3, $13.25 worth of books, 28 yards of carpeting at $25.[17] The bill was finally paid with three years' interest in 1833.[18] His account with James Schoolcraft for June 20, 1829 to May 27, 1831 included items like dishes, shoes, chessmen, water colors, books, silverware, brandy, fish hooks, violin strings, ribbon, whiskey, nails, nutmegs, ink stand, spices, blankets, silk, lard, gunpowder, handkerchiefs, candles, etc.[19] In short, he owed everybody money most of the time.

Nevertheless, merchants continued to extend him credit because that was what the frontier lived on. It was a pattern set long ago by the fur trade. William did not mind, as long as he and his clerk, John Hotley, continued to bring in good returns from the trade. 1830 was a lucrative year for them.[20] Yet Mills, his New York agent, decided not to supply the Sault with goods any longer. William had little choice now but to move into the orbit of the American Fur Company and take up an offer that Robert Stuart had proffered.[21] Independence was hard to maintain with the giant looming so close by.

Despite the dominance of the American Fur Company, business activity at the Sault was highly competitive, and the little village was subject to all the jealousies and rivalries that small towns are heir to—especially during the interminable, auto-digestive winters. Next to the American Fur Company, resentments focused on the Johnston-Schoolcraft family hegemony. Henry's position as senior civilian official, coupled with his humorless and sanctimonious personality, did little to assuage those antagonisms. Sometimes he sided with the majority in the community, and then they were happy to use him as their spokesman—as in the great Post Office fracas of 1825-26. The post office was then located in the fort, and Major Enos Cutler effectively denied civilian access by requiring people to pass through the guard house to get their mail. Henry carried the complaint to Postmaster General John McLean at Washington and forwarded to him the citizens' petition to place the post office elsewhere in the village.[22]

At other times, however, many people whispered, though they might not dare to shout, that the Schoolcraft-Johnston axis used Henry's power to their own advantage. One Isaac Butterfield informed Henry of gossip circulating in the winter of 1828 that Henry had intimidated the Indians into giving all their furs to John Johnston by threatening to withhold food, clothing and counsel from them. Both Henry and John were incensed. Henry assured his father-in-law that he never solicited advantages, and John replied that "In all the time you have filled the Agency here, such a base and unfounded calumny has never before been broached. It is equally dishonorable to you and to me and must have its origin in a heart fraught with the most degrading passions. . . . [my wife and son] deny having ever made use of your name to an Indian."[23] Henry lost no time in calling an Indian council at his office, at which he meticulously refuted the rumored charges, pointing out that he never even asked them, when they came to him for help, with whom they traded or for how much.[24]

In the fall of 1829 his compassion extended to old Jean Baptiste Perrault, "an aged Frenchman . . . whose reminiscences of life in the wilderness in the last century, had the charm of novelty."[25] Among those reminiscences was his first encounter with John Johnston at La Pointe in John's first year of trading. Now, however, he and his half-breed wife were living in poverty on the Canadian side. Henry invited them to spend the winter in warmer surroundings in a basement apartment at Elmwood. In return, Perrault, an educated and courtly man, gave Henry a daily lesson in French. In the spring the Perraults returned to their own home, where, at Henry's urging, Jean Baptiste began to write his memoirs.[26]

But resentments and accusations would simmer beneath the surface for many years to come. Nor was it surprising when the links were all put in place. Henry, at the top, disbursed government largesse in the form of goods and provisions to the Indians on the one hand, and in the form of purchases of those goods from his brother, James, and his brother-in-law, John Hulbert, on the other. The said brother and brother-in-law both held high county office. His brother-in-law, George Johnston, was on the government payroll as sub-agent and interpreter. His brother-in-law, William Johnston, traded with the very Indians to whom Henry made disbursements, and William also came onto the government payroll in later years. His brother, Abraham Schoolcraft, later set up as a merchant in Detroit who would also become a vendor to the government. No wonder the cry of nepotism raised its voice from time to time.

Henry never failed to attribute these accusations to "base calumny" and "petty jealousy," however, and never doubted the disinterested correctness of his own behavior. That the people he hired and purchased from happened to be members of his own family was only coincidental; he wasted not one penny of government funds on overpayments, and all was meticulously accounted for. As an unabashedly ambitious man, Henry Schoolcraft was exceedingly careful to remain precisely within the letter, if not the spirit, of laws and regulations. No matter what went on around him, he always managed to emerge with immaculate hands.

If Henry was unloved, though respected, at the Sault, his brother, James, enjoyed the opposite reputation. James' high good humor, friendly charm, and wild ebullience elicited smiles, not to say fondness, from all who knew him, although his respectability was at times marginal. It never sank lower than it did on the night of November 25, 1830.

A French ball, that scourge of respectable Northwest society, was held at the home of a Canadian known as Pêche. This festivity was invented long ago by fur-trading bourgeois as a way to entice French Canadian voyageurs into their employ and debt. The bourgeois would buy $20-$30 worth of liquor, rent a room, hire a fiddler, and invite all the men and their families to dance. In the course of the evening he presented a garland of colored ribbons to a girl, who became thereby Queen of the dance. She selected her King by attaching a ribbon to his coat while he was dancing, then confirmed the appointment with a kiss. The King so honored must give the next ball, even if he went into debt to the trader for it, which he usually did.[27] Now, in the 1820s and '30s, young men of a wild nature started a French ball cycle just for fun. By tradition they usually concluded in a drunken brawl. Indulged in only by the lowest classes, whose licentiousness was notorious, the respectable citizens of the community deplored these occasions of evil temptation to their impressionable young men.

Whether James Schoolcraft was still at the impressionable age was arguable, but when invited he attended these affairs with unfeigned enjoyment. No one was a direct witness to exactly what happened on the night of November 25. Everybody was thoroughly drunk. The usual kind of jostling and obscenity occurred, friendly or otherwise, and degenerated into impassioned belligerence. Suddenly silence clamped down on the sweaty crowd in the smoke-clouded room, as they pressed back in a circle around the prostrate form of a young soldier named Holmes, with James Schoolcraft standing over him, a dagger at his feet. None of them was more horror-stricken into sobriety than James, as he watched the trickle of blood spread over the man's shirt near the heart. A few people flashed into action and carried the wounded man to the post hospital, while others ran to fetch Dr. James from his quarters.[28]

In anguish, James waited for reports of the man's condition, but even after several days Dr. James could say only that the patient was hanging on to life. The ultimate outcome could not be predicted. At John Hulbert's urging, James made the sad journey to Mackinac Island to turn himself voluntarily in to the authorities on December 1; such a move would be to his credit later on.[29] He was immediately imprisoned, but at his arraignment next morning Judge Stuart refused to set bail on the grounds that the charge, and therefore the level of bail, could not be determined until it was known whether the victim would live or die. The charge could be murder.[30] James was despondent, and in a letter to John Hulbert talked of ending his own life.[31]

His friends at the Sault did their best to cheer him up and encourage him to hope for the best. Lieutenant Allen wrote him on December 5 that Holmes seemed to be improving, but even if he should die the men of the garrison felt certain that the charge would not be greater than manslaughter, and that James would not get more than a stiff fine and a relatively short prison sentence. After all, no direct witnesses came forward, and a good case could be made for self defense. A postscript added the next day, however, informed the prisoner that the patient was worse again.[32] Hulbert wrote him on January 11 that Holmes was having greater difficulty in breathing because of lung congestion from the wound, but everyone at the Sault, including the doctor, felt it was unjust to require the medical certificate before allowing bail. He went on to assure James that they were looking after his store.[33] And so it went on for weeks. Dr. James could not or would not predict whether the boy would live, and the magistrate would not set bail without a definite prognosis from the doctor.

Meanwhile, Henry, in Detroit for the winter session of the Legislative Council, had received the ugly news and was doing all he could for James from there. He immediately consulted Mr. Fletcher, John Johnston's attorney and now Attorney-General, and Judge Sibley. He was able to inform James that the trial would be held at the regular session of the Circuit Court at Mackinac on the third Monday of next July. Because it would be difficult to impanel an impartial jury there, however, the venue would likely be changed to Green Bay or even Iowa. He assured James of his loyalty and moral support, but went on to express his "deep regret & humiliation—not just [for] the notoriety of criminal atrocity," but the moral guilt and reckless passion. He regretted bringing James out from home to live at St. Mary's, where he did not seem able to withdraw from his "vile connections."[34]

To Jane, Henry communicated a somewhat kindlier attitude: "Poor, misguided boy! . . . . Whatever can be done for him I will do; but with a conscientous [sic] desire that whatever steps are taken may redound to his moral & spiritual good. . . . If this result can be obtained, if he can be made to see the error of his ways, & to forsake low company & evil deeds, imprisonment will be nothing, compared to the salvation of both body & soul."[35]

For active, high-spirited James, incarceration was an agony. His friends came to see him, tried to encourage him, brought him good things to eat. But he was also the captive auditor of preaching from the saintlier members of the community. Robert Stuart wrote Henry on January 25 that during the eight weeks of James' confinement "Both Mr. Ferry [the Presbyterian minister at Mackinac] & myself have labored with James, for his *spiritual* as well as his *moral* good, and *at times*, I felt much encouraged, he would melt into tears, like a child, went so far as to ask the prayers of the church &c. . . . but afterwards began to drink, people handing it in, as I understand thro' the Bars of the window. He has now given that up. . . . He receives all I say to him, with apparent kindness."[36]

Stuart was a little too self-satisfied. The very day he wrote that letter James broke out of jail. By the same token, James was one day too impatient. On that same January 25, Dr. James sent his certificate to Mackinac, declaring the patient would live,[37] and an Indian had been sent to bring James home. "How great was our astonishment," Jane wrote, "at the arrival of the Indian *alone*, on the 3d ultimo, and bringing news of James' escape from Mackinac . . . we were relieved of our fears by the arrival of James himself on the following day, very much exhausted . . . [but] his fatigue &c., had not in the least abated his natural vivacity and gayety."[38]

Henry knew his brother well enough to fear just such a move and wrote, too late, a warning "not to do any thing to give them who may wish to injure you a handle against you. If the door of the prison stands open do not walk out of it."[39] He went on to point out that any injustice James suffered would redound to his benefit at the trial. But Henry was not all preachy talk. He obtained from Judge Sibley and Attorney-General Fletcher written opinions that James' case was bailable at $500-$1,000, even if the man died, because the charge should properly be manslaughter. If these documents secured James' release, Henry advised him to go home, "dismiss from your sight your worthless friends, attend no French ball, and give up *drinking*. Pray, read the Bible, go to meeting, and you will earn everyone's respect, as even the *vile* respect the *virtuous*. You will acquire a character & standing you have never had."[40]

Now that the worst was over, Jane determined to help James to his new honorable life. A few days after his return she sent a note "inviting him to come & spend a quiet social evening with sister Anna M. & myself, & sent the sleigh to bring him down, so that he could have no excuse to decline coming." They spent the evening talking amiably, Jane gently pointing out the error of his ways and their damaging consequences. He promised to try and reform. "I have been enabled to pursue this course of conduct towards him ever since that evening & I am pleased to find that he comes oftener to Elmwood than I at first expected, but I perceive there is some other attraction besides my sage discourses that showed him so often to the now leafless shades of Elmwood. And he may fancy that either a *Rose* or a *Lilly* [sic] has taken shelter within its walls."[41]

But Jane's optimism was premature. By March she was writing Henry of her discouragement. When "a man came over from Mackinac, to take James, he was a good deal agitated, & said, if he had his pistols about him he would not care so much, as he would not suffer himself to be taken alive,"[42] though he always carried a dagger. In alarm, Jane tried to talk him out of such extravagance, and to get him out of the way until he could calm down she had Descharme and Baptiste take him by canoe across the river into Canada. Mr. Bethune, the Hudson's Bay factor,[43] received him there, but James soon realized that it was a mistake to run away, especially since the wounded man was quite recovered and "the affair settled with him."[44] He would go back and try to keep out of the way of the authorities. Or so he resolved. Apparently however, he did not stick to it, as a couple of weeks later Jane was still depressed about his moral state. He had "driven hope far, far away."[45] Legally the judge concluded the case by asking for payment of a fine and court costs. But psychologically the trauma of guilt and remorse haunted James for the rest of his life.

Of all Henry's problems as Indian Agent, control of the liquor traffic was the most stubborn of solution. Everyone recognized that Indians were peculiarly susceptible to chronic alcoholism. They did not seem able to enjoy an occasional drink, like the white man, and then go back to work. Rather, they drank constantly and to excess (for their capacity), becoming so stupefied and brutalized in the process that virtually every "frolic" resulted in injury, if not death, to some of their number—men, women, and children alike. Though everyone might agree that abstention was the solution, few were willing to give it a chance. Rather, the men who held the power to control, not to say eliminate, the liquor traffic shifted responsibility among themselves with the speed of a juggler's balls.

Henry issued the licenses to all traders out of Sault Ste. Marie or Mackinac (American citizens only and their bonded foreign, i.e., Canadian, boatmen) and each explicitly prohibited liquor for trading. It was not possible, however, to prevent the bourgeois and voyageurs from taking into the interior their allowances for personal use—one gill per day for each *engagé*; clerks allowed their wine.[46] In principle Henry and his sub-agents could stop any trader who violated the liquor ban, confiscate his contraband, and deny his license, but in practice enforcement was difficult. The Indian Agent was not a policeman. Although his staff, both full time and part time, numbered 14 people, most were laborers,[47] and he was in no position to inspect every canoe and effectively prosecute violators. He had to rely upon cooperation from the traders on the one hand, and the reports of jealous informants on the other. But, Henry complained to his diary, the citizens seemed to be in league against the law; if he appealed to the courts, nine-tenths of any jury would be offenders themselves.

The traders' favorite argument against suppression of the liquor traffic was a simple one: if A did not sell liquor to the Indians, B would, and thereby take A's business from him. The merit of this excuse varied with location of the trading post. Some traders could, in fact, avoid taking in any liquor (at least until another sharpie came in and broke the ban), others could get away with only small quantities, and still others insisted they could not survive in the trade without it. Robert Stuart, the American Fur Company agent at Mackinac, was a teetotaller himself, and cooperated with Henry as best he could. But he was also a realistic businessman and warned the agent that if he failed to control the Company's opposition, then Stuart, too, would have to trade liquor in self defense. Furthermore, whenever the opposition came from the Hudson's Bay Company, they had no choice but to sell liquor and would go over Schoolcraft's head to get special permits to do so. As a temperance leader Stuart continued to control sales by the glass in Mackinac taverns—while his employees sold it wholesale by the barrel.[48]

In any attempt to deal with the depravity of alcoholism, the stick of temperance needed also the carrot of religion. The fervor of faith was the best substitute for the fever of liquor. Although Reverend William Ferry had opened a mission on Mackinac Island in 1823, the church did not come to Sault Ste. Marie until the fall of 1828. (Curiously, Fort Brady employed two physicians, but no chaplain.) Just a few weeks after John Johnston died, Abel Bingham arrived as an emissary of the Baptist Board of Foreign Missions in Boston. He was a middle-aged man, who had been preaching among the Senecas of New York State, but never learned the Indian languages.[49] Nor was he a great success as a preacher. One irreverent listener described him as one who "thunders forth his orthodoxies, heterodoxies, and paradoxies, with as much energy and little success as usual."[50]

Bingham was fortunate in obtaining the volunteer services of Charlotte Johnston as interpreter when he first arrived. She was so enthusiastic about the message of faith that she would continue on with a story or sermon in her own words after completing the translation of his rather dull and prosaic message.[51] When the board appropriated $1,000 for the mission the following spring, they also budgeted $25 for Miss Johnston. In addition, they accepted Bingham's suggestion that a mission building be constructed and applied to the War Department for a grant of land. Most important, however, the board permitted Reverend and Mrs. Bingham to operate a boarding school for Indian boys and girls, if the expense could be covered within the $1,000 budget. If paying pupils were also taken, they should be able to accomplish it.[52] The school was probably more welcome at the Sault than the church. Among the earliest day students were George Johnston's two older children, for each of whom he paid tuition of $6 per year.

Although Henry welcomed the presence of a missionary to the Indians, he did not care much for Abel Bingham (or the Baptist sect, no doubt) and chose not to practice the faith with him. Rather, he made other plans for christening his children. When the fourth Legislative Council convened in May of 1830, Henry took Jane and the two babies with him to Detroit, along with their nurse and Aunt Charlotte. (George was left in charge at Elmwood, where he supervised some necessary repairs and painting of the Agency.)[53] There on July 4, Jane and Johnston Schoolcraft were baptised in the suitably dignified surroundings of St. Paul's Episcopal Church.[54] The family made a holiday of the whole summer, and during a recess of the council they journeyed to Niagara Falls, just for a look. Henry thought it was probably the first party ever to visit from the upper lakes purely for pleasure.[55]

Altogether, it was a happy interlude for Jane, after three difficult years in which she had mourned two tragic deaths, suffered childbirth twice, and endured three periods of separation from her husband. When Henry was gone from her she felt bereft, especially when she was ill and needed him to help her cope. Henry missed her too:

> However long I may be delayed, or where it may please Providence to carry me, or to put a final stop to my career, doubt not that you, & you only, are the exclusive object of my undivided love. It is the order of providence that man should be active, & woman quiescent. . . . But there has ever been but one primary object in my exertions—to provide a security . . . for you, and the dear little objects of our love. In the accomplishment of that object, it is necessary that I should keep myself from being forgotten & neglected, & to maintain that intercourse with my political friends, which is essential . . . to preserve my place.[56]

He may have been honest when he said it was necessity, not political ambition, that took him from her. But it was necessity of a kind that perhaps he did not admit to himself. Frequent absence was what made assignment to a forsaken place like Sault Ste. Marie tolerable. Interested as he might be in the ethnography of the American Indian, Henry Schoolcraft did not care much for their society and his day-to-day dealings with them. He vacillated between compassion for their plight and disgust at their behavior.

It was the latter that blew up another cause célèbre at the Sault during the summer of 1830. The episode had its origins about five years before, when Henry and Jane took into their employ a girl, who had been "born in iniquity" and at the request of her parents reluctantly raised by the Johnstons.[57] This was the same Sophy whom Henry had caught in bed with William Holiday in 1827. The Schoolcrafts kept her on, however, in the belief that Holiday was the villain and she the 14-

year-old victim. Then, during the winter of 1830, she ran away, presumably with a man. In the spring she turned up again—as a student at Bingham's missionary school.

Henry disapproved of the way Bingham ran his establishment in the first place, but this was intolerable—to allow a fallen woman to mix with the other pupils and be supported by charitable funds. Just before he left for Detroit, Henry wrote to Commissioner McKenney, complaining of Bingham's mismanagement in spending $1,000 to accommodate but 40 students; he illustrated his argument with the Sophy incident.[58] Furthermore, it was Henry's prerogative, indeed his obligation under regulations of 1819 and 1820, reconfirmed in 1828, to approve all admissions to the Indian School. Bingham was countermanding the agent's authority.[59]

McKenney promptly addressed a letter to the Mission Board in Boston, forwarding the complaints against Bingham. They, in turn, inquired sternly of their man in the field. Bingham was understandably apprehensive about the rebuke that Mr. Schoolcraft was capable of generating from such high authority and hastened to clear himself. Since Henry was out of town, Bingham could not confront him directly to clear up the misunderstanding. Therefore, he asked four prominent citizens of the village to send a supporting letter to the Mission Board, which would corroborate his own explanation—that he had not taken Sophy in as a "member of the mission family," that is as a boarder, but merely allowed her to attend classes.[60] John Hulbert, Dr. Edwin James, John Agnew, and Isaac Butterfield not only complied with the request, they even went a bit further. They justified their support of Bingham by pointing out to the Board that Mr. Schoolcraft tended to disfavor halfbreeds.

When Henry learned about the letter, he was furious at their insidious "attempt to show that all the halfbreed population of Ste. Marie's is on a par with respect to moral character." He found apalling their statement that this girl's reputation is "in every respect, as that of any other of the women of mixed blood in the settlement! The reputations of the women of mixed blood, in this settlement, embrace some of the most exalted and some of the vilest characters in it."[61] The three merchants and the doctor had trod dangerous ground in their letter, and Abel Bingham was reaping the righteous wrath of his antagonist. He wrote a conciliatory letter to Henry, explaining that he was neither condoning nor supporting Sophy, expressing regret that Henry had not come to him first and so avoided the unpleasant and embarrassing involvement of the board. He suggested that Henry might write both Mr. McKenney and the board to clear up the misunderstanding.[62]

But Henry would not be mollified. His reply to Bingham was full of hauteur and self-righteousness. Bingham was totally dismayed that Henry refused to recognize the damage he had done to the missionary's reputation, or acknowledge that he might have misunderstood what was actually done for the girl. "I would ask, is this the proper way to ease a burdened mind, & cultivate a good understanding between neighbors?"[63]

Henry was not particularly interested in cultivating a good understanding with the Reverend Bingham, however, and less than two years later they were at each other's throats again. This time Henry actually brought charges for 1) "interfering in the exercise of my official duties as Sub Agent for the U.S. government; and attempting to injure my standing with & influence with the Indians" by holding a secret meeting with certain chiefs and telling them "my standing at Washington [and St. Mary's] was low," that officers and citizens side with him, that the Indians "get most of their food at Fort Brady and only a little from me at Mr. Bingham's request, and that my wife and her family have used their influence with the Indians to prevent their baptism at Mr. Bingham's mission"; and 2) "taking advantage of the Indians' ignorance of letters to induce them to criminate [sic] themselves by getting their signatures to papers, of which they did not comprehend the true import."[64] Three prominent citizens acted as referees, and issued a finding that Reverend Bingham acknowledged his meeting with the Indians and his impression that Mr. Schoolcraft's relatives were sabotaging his baptismal efforts. But most of the rest of the charges came from a more insidious source, one that Henry was not in a position to prosecute.[65]

Its origins lay more than forty years back, on the south bank of the Ohio River, in a story that dramatically illustrates the interweaving of diverse lives in the Old Northwest. A family named Tanner had just taken up a Kentucky homestead. Little John, probably nine years old, disobediently wandered off from the house one day to pick walnuts by the river. He neither saw nor heard anyone approach. He only felt a hard arm encircle his chest, pinning down his arms as he was lifted aloft, while a dirty, rough hand clamped tightly over his mouth. Carried a long way through the forest, kicking ineffectually at the air, he was finally thrown down before a woman stirring a firepot in front of her teepee. A long time later he learned that he had been stolen by the Indians to replace the dead son of this woman. By this time the band had wandered so far from his home that he had abandoned all hope of being found. He had learned, too, to suffer in brave silence the indifference of the woman and the cruelty of his foster father and brother, which was worse when they were drunk. He had one small stroke of luck when, after two years of misery, the family sold him to Net-no-kwa, an Ottawa woman of renown and respect from L'Arbre Croche on Lake Michigan. With her he would continue to know the hunger that stalked all Indians, but he would also know kindness and loyalty—qualities he had almost forgotten in his short life.

As he grew older, John Tanner learned how to hunt and fish and provide for his adoptive family after Net-no-kwa's husband died. Most of the time he forgot he'd been born white, and very few English words remained in his head. He was an Indian in every respect except color, and even that darkened with years of exposure to sun, wind, smoke, and dirt. In the fashion of the forest Indian he roamed vast distances in search of game and fish to fend off the starvation that dogged their heels. As he grew more skilled he became the hunter to whom women and children and old people attached themselves. It was the way of the Indian, of whatever tribe. No thine and mine existed so far as food was concerned; either nobody starved, or everyone did.

Nor was life all suffering. He found friends, too,

as he wandered back and forth between Lake Superior, Lake Winnipeg, and the upper Red River. They hunted together; they gambled together; and they frolicked together on the *eau de vie* from the North West Company traders. And John found a wife in Mis-kwa-bun-o-kwa, Red Sky of the Morning. He had three children with her, but at some point her family turned against him. When he fell from a tree one day, severely injured, they did virtually nothing to care for him. Providentially, their camp was near the North West Rainy Lake post, in the charge of Dr. John McLoughlin. Under skilled medical care he recovered fully and moved west once more.

He and his family worked their way up the Red River to the North West Company's Fort Pembina. Nearby was the largest group of white people John had ever seen—the pathetic band of Hudson's Bay Company settlers from Fort Douglas, who hoped to sustain themselves for the winter on buffalo. But their hunting skills were minimal, and Tanner occasionally joined the Indians and Métis who hired themselves out as hunters for the settlers. He avoided direct contact, however. He had an uneasy feeling about white people, made up of fear, shyness and embarrassment. But in the early summer one of them could not be avoided. Thomas Douglas, Earl of Selkirk, was a thorough man, who looked into every aspect of his enterprises, and after his arrival he interviewed the hunters who had worked for his people. Fascinated by Tanner's appearance, he probed for his story. The year was 1817; John Tanner had been an Indian for over 25 years.

Lord Selkirk, not a man to be deterred from humanitarian enterprises, refused to believe, with Tanner, that his family was dead or lost beyond recovery. Selkirk promised to find them. The amazing fact is that he did. When he returned to civilization he simply placed an advertisement in the Louisville, Kentucky newspaper. Edward Tanner, brother to John, saw the notice and as soon as he could get away started out for Red River to find his long-lost brother.

By this time two years had passed since the encounter with Selkirk that aroused something like hope in John's mind for the first time since childhood. He decided to go south and see for himself if his family could be found. He started from the depot at Fort William, where his old benefactor, Dr. McLoughlin, was now in charge and arranged passage for John in a North West schooner to the Sault. A letter from McLoughlin to Charles Ermatinger got him an escort to Fort Mackinac, and from there passage was booked for him on a ship to Detroit, from which Lewis Cass took him almost all the rest of the way—to an Indian Council on the Miami River. There Cass turned him over to two men from Kentucky, who knew his sister and would take him the rest of the way "home." John was amazed at how much these white folks were doing to help him, for after 30 years with the Indians he had almost come to believe that all white men were mean and vicious.

His English was still very bad, but he gradually came to understand that his brother, Edward, had gone north to look for him at Red River. So John turned right around to go back and meet him. By some miracle, the two men caught up with each other in Detroit. By now everybody in Michigan Territory, it seemed, knew about John Tanner, the White Indian, and his problems. When they finally met, Edward took John to his home on the Mississippi.

He was barely settled into his new, strange way of life when he decided to return north for the three children of his second marriage, which had occurred at some time between the tree incident and the encounter with Selkirk.[66] After he found them his wife refused to go back with him, but the three children went willingly—to spend the next two years among people they never knew existed. One of them died in Kentucky, before John decided to return permanently to the north country, where he felt more comfortable.

In 1822 he placed the other two in school at Mackinac and took a job with the American Fur Company. It was not to his liking, however, and he set out to look for the family of his first marriage. When he found them the boy elected to stay with his mother's band, but his wife and daughters agreed to go with him. Shortly afterward John was shot from ambush. Apparently, it was pre-arranged by the faithless wife, who took her two daughters and left him to die. Tanner's almost incredible luck held, however, for he was picked up the next day by two men of the Hudson's Bay Company, now merged with the North West Company. He was taken to Rainy Lake, where his family had also gone, and left in the care of Simon McGillivray, half-breed son of William McGillivary. When the story was told, the wife was banished, but the two girls remained with their father. About a month later Major Joseph Delafield, the American boundary commissioner, visited at the post on his way back from Lake of the Woods. Tanner wanted to return to the States with him, but was still too weak to travel.

Once more, given enough time, he recovered his full strength. Later he returned to Mackinac with the children and for a few years worked from time to time as interpreter for the Indian Agent there, William Boyd. It was during this period that he told his story to Dr. Edwin James, then post surgeon, who arranged the dramatic tale for publication. Tanner even got a trip to New York in 1828 to help see the book through the press.[8]

Although he had now made his final choice to live out his life among white people, he never fully adjusted. Indeed, he was a man who belonged in neither society. Tall and lean, with long white hair, parted in the middle and pulled back behind his ears, [68] "Tanner was a singular being—out of humor with the world, speaking ill of everybody, suspicious of every human action, a very savage in his feelings, reasonings and philosophy of life, and yet exciting commiseration by the very isolation of his position. . . . [He was] morose, sour, suspicious, antisocial, revengeful and bad."[69] So judged Henry Schoolcraft.

Yet, when Tanner came to him with a letter of introduction from Lewis Cass, having been fired by the agent at Mackinac, Henry took pity on him. He did not really need another interpreter, but he hired him on a temporary basis, made regular when one of his other interpreters quit, for a dollar a day and $9 per month for housing.[70]

But Henry could not tolerate the man's tendency to insane rages any better than Boyd, and by the spring of 1830 had to fire him. Furthermore, Henry worried about the safety of Tanner's daughter, Martha, who was living with him at the time. During the Legislative Council of 1830 he secured passage of "An act authorizing the sheriff of Chippewa County to perform certain duties therein mentioned," namely to remove Martha Tanner to a missionary establishment or other safe place, with her consent, if need should arise. Any threats by her father to injure her "shall be deemed a misdemeanor, punishable by fine & imprisonment at the discretion of the court." This was "probably the only law ever passed in America attaching criminal consequences to injuries to a single private person,"[71] and it incurred for Henry Schoolcraft John Tanner's undying enmity. A few months later George Johnston reported that "Tanner has again made bold threats . . . in Doctor James presence, saying that had you still been here, he would have killed you."[72]

After leaving Schoolcraft's employ, Tanner went to work for Abel Bingham as interpreter, so it is entirely plausible that the referees of the Bingham-Schoolcraft controversy of 1832 were correct in finding Tanner responsible for the defamation of Henry Schoolcraft's character through insertion of his own words into the translations of Bingham's messages to the Indians. But the missionary apparently had a soothing effect on John Tanner, who served him ably, except for the occasional license he took to malign the Schoolcrafts. When not enraged, Tanner could be both pleasant and gentlemanly, and he got on well with the Bingham family.[73] In fact, through them he came to find the faith of his fathers, although prayer and Bible study never taught him to govern his savage passions, and he loomed over the Sault like a malignant shadow.

Chapter Eleven

Widening Circles

The assignment of Abel Bingham to Sault Ste. Marie in 1828 was not an isolated happenstance. Rather, it was part of an evangelical movement of religious fervor that was about to sweep the entire nation. John Johnston had been a devout man all his life and had ceaselessly, if gently, tried to transmit to his children the love of God and a strong faith in His wisdom and goodness. And all of them tried to live up to his precepts, although Jane and Charlotte were probably the most consistently observant. But John's piety was of a quiet, contemplative, philosophic nature, that took its teaching directly from the Bible, especially the Psalms of David that combined man's gift for expression with God's holy inspiration.

What entered his children's lives now was immersion in the admonitory teachings of the New Testament, a passionate longing for salvation through pure faith, the belief that prayer must be constant, self-criticism ruthless, morality stern, humility and profession of faith public. All the evils of this deeply troubled world could be laid at Christ's feet if people would truly believe in Him, with their hearts as well as their minds. As Jane and Henry and Charlotte eagerly read the tracts and sermons that came streaming off the printing presses, their conversations and their letters became first embellished and then absorbed in the teachings of the new revivalist faith.

For the Schoolcrafts the rather dull and unprepossessing Abel Bingham did not satisfy the need for inspiring preachments. Reverend William Ferry at Mackinac came closer to this ideal,[1] and when Henry went to Detroit for the council in November of 1830, he found a new strengthening of his faith in God, and himself. On February 7, 1831 he publicly joined the Church at Detroit.[2] He had written Jane significantly on Thanksgiving Day, urging her to look into her own heart "and see whether there is nothing there adverse to Christian principles. . . . it is the domestic conduct of a female that is most continually liable to error, both of judgment & feeling." He reminded her of the Biblical injunction to woman to forsake even her parents and cleave to her husband as her best guide and protector.

> Brought up in a remote place, without any thing which deserves the name of a regular education, without the salutary influence of society to form your mind, without a mother, in many things, to direct, & with an over kind father, who saw every thing in the fairest light, & made even your sisters & brothers & all about you to bow to you as their superior in every mental & worldly . . . thing, you must indeed have possessed a strength of intellect above the common one, not to have taken up some maxims & opinions & feelings, as false & foolish, as flattery & self deceit can be.[3]

Find out what they are, he admonished, and then pray to rid yourself of them. Do not expect much from other people, but trust only in God—and Henry Schoolcraft.

Henry's words carried pain, but Jane was grateful for his advice, as it helped her "to proceed in 'fighting the good fight of faith' for well I know, & have long mourned, without sincerely struggling, against the foes that assail me both *within* & *without*, but most particularly those of my own conjuring—and tho' you have *probed deeply* yet I thank you, because I know it was intended for my good. I have indeed imbibed 'false & foolish feelings as much as flattery & self deceit could make me' but alas who has not!"[4]

She read all the religious tracts she could get her hands on that long winter Henry was gone, including Thomas à Kempis' *Imitation of Christ*.[5] And she attended meeting as often as she could, especially since "Mr.

Bingham does a great deal better since he commenced writing his sermons."⁶ But Jane had more immediate and mundane troubles than theological arguments to remind her of the iniquity of the world. It seemed the Schoolcrafts were bound to be plagued by strange men in their servants' beds.

"A few hours after the departure of my dear Husband," she wrote Henry, "Mrs. Audrain came to see me & informed me that her *black man*, had slept *two nights* in this house (unknown to us) & that he had owned himself the father of Harriet's unborn child. Heaven preserve *me & my little ones* from the inmates of my own house!"⁷ Apparently a legal marriage raised no problem, as "Harriet has promised to marry her seducer & he is only waiting to get a coat made for the occasion, & in consequence I still *keep house*, but to tell the honest truth, I should far rather have taken shelter with my Mother [for] security, as well as to escape the disgrace attending Harriet, which will take place in a short time."⁸

But once the legal forms were satisfied Jane decided to swallow her pride, as Harriet was "an excellent servant & I believe her morals are not absolutely depraved. I keep giving her good books to read when she has leisure."⁹ The girl was finally married on December 7 and gave birth on the 25th. Susan, Mrs. Audrain, and Mme. Descharme all helped Jane with the delivery. And Susan loaned her daughter a servant until Harriet was well enough to come downstairs again.¹⁰

How much more painful, then, during this winter of soul-searching and church-joining, was the scandal and disgrace of James Schoolcraft. At least Jane's brothers were not as much of a worry at the moment. Henry did not want to leave too much to Providence, however, and decided to write Jane's 20-year-old brother, William, on the subject of French balls, meanwhile advising his wife that "if you could continue to revive the plan of an early *marriage* for him, with some suitable person from this quarter of the world, it would be his salvation."¹¹ The not so literary William appreciated Henry's interest.

> I heartily thank you for your Kindness, in pointing out to me that Evils and Dangers, which sur-

> round me, and those who degrade themselfs [sic] so far, as to go hand in hand with those who know no better in there [sic] vices. The scene that took place at one of their Balls has had no effect on them. They still have them night after night, and they think themselfs [sic] encouraged, by haveing [sic] the company of those who know the bad effect it has on society, But still attend them from mere wantonness. I am happy to say that those places have no pleasures, which would induce me to partake of them.[12]

While he was writing, he went on to inquire "wheater [sic] Mr. Hulbert is not obliged to pay taxes as well as we, For he has almost the Exclusive trade of all the Canadians. For it is tempting to them to purchase Liquor at 2/6 per gallon, when they have to pay 4/ in the Village. The Temperate Society is of no use when any of its Members [Hulbert was its leader] can dispose of Liquor at so low a rate."[13] Perhaps it was the hypocrisy of the John Hulberts and the Robert Stuarts of their world that induced men like the Johnston brothers, not to say James Schoolcraft, to fall off the wagon so readily.

If the young men of the family were having a struggle with their morals, the young women were busy improving their minds. Sixteen-year-old Anna Maria went to live with Jane the winter of 1830-31, while Henry was away. Jane worked with her to improve her writing skills; Anna Maria, in turn, started teaching three-year-old Janee to read and sew.[14] By March 7 she was writing that Janee "can now spell words of 4 letters, & for such a volatile little creature, I think she improves fast."[15] Little Johnston's achievement in life that winter was learning to walk.

The following winter, 1831-32, was a banner one for the saving of souls at Sault Ste. Marie. At last the Missionary Society sent out a pastor Henry considered suitable for himself and his family. Dr. Jeremiah Porter was a graduate of Andover and Princeton, and Henry was so well impressed he offered him "a furnished chamber, bed and plate, at Elmwood."[16] A third clergyman, in addition to Abel Bingham, was present in the village that winter, too. Reverend William Boutwell stayed over on his way to the Indians of the north shore of Lake Superior. With so many active preachers sending the warmth of their exhortations into the frozen air, the villagers flocked in unprecedented numbers to profess their faith and join the church. Included among them were Mrs. Johnston, her four daughters, and one son.[17] Susan, in fact, went beyond mere words to proclaim her faith. She subscribed the money to build a Presbyterian church.[18]

George Johnston had need of solace that winter. Two days before Christmas his wife, Louisa, died,[19] leaving him with three small children, ages four to eight. He continued living in the cottage he rented from his mother and hired Jeanette Picquette to cook, wash, mend, make clothes, clean, and look after the children for $3 per month.[20]

The smaller settlement on the other side of the river also received its representative of the organized church. The Canadian Sault had declined drastically from the flourishing days of the North West Company factory with its storehouses, residences, sawmill and boat yard. Consequently, far fewer whites lived on that side, but a substantial Indian village still thrived. In the summer of 1832 the Lieutenant Governor of Upper Canada, Sir John Colborne, appointed the first missionary to the Ojibways of Sault Ste. Marie. William McMurray, brought from Ireland to York by his parents as an infant, was just 21 years old, not yet ordained, but well trained by John Strachan, who later became the first Bishop of Toronto.

His new assignment got off to a very slow start, however, when he could find no one at York who knew how to get to the place; most of the people he knew had not even heard of it. Finally, at the Lieutenant Governor's suggestion, he went to Detroit to inquire from there, and eventually arrived at his destination in October. The Hudson's Bay factor lodged William in his house and provided space for the mission. But most important, someone recommended an interpreter to him—Charlotte Johnston. William felt his calling strongly, preached fervently to his flock, and opened a school for their edification,[21] but it was Charlotte's eloquent translations that made him as popular as he was. And it was Charlotte's family that gave him the warmth of a congenial social group.

One who might have benefitted from the pious atmosphere of the Sault during the winter of 1831-32 was not there. James Schoolcraft had gone down to New York State in the fall to look about for a new business opportunity, travelling with young John McDouall, who was returning to school. On the way they stopped to admire Niagara Falls.[22] James spent most of the winter at Albany, although he visited frequently at Vernon, a blessing to his mother who died in February.[23] His spirits alternated between exuberant fascination with the political stage on which Jackson, Van Buren, John Quincy Adams, Henry Clay, and the United States Bank were the principal actors,[24] and the despair and self-disappointment he associated with "many past follies, & more particularly the yet unsettled events of '25th Nov.'; I almost wish I were no mere mortal . . . it has been your *wish & desire* that I might rise under your guardianship to respectability . . . that this disposition has been *too* much slighted. But let this be as it may it can not be recalled. Therefore I will not dwell upon the subject."[25] Hovering in the background of his letters were the reports of cholera in New Orleans, brought in by a Spanish ship, and cholera in British cities. But nothing advantageous developed for him in the East, so he returned to the Sault in the spring with another stock of goods to sell. By the time he got there Henry was preparing for the road again. When he returned from Detroit in April of 1831 Henry had decided not to run again for the council.

Not only did it take him away from home too much, but President Jackson had expressed the view that federal officials should not be legislators, and he certainly did not want to offend the President in any way. Furthermore, he had instructions from Washington to make another expedition to the Indians of his large territory, as it was now four years since the last one. This time he had no treaty to negotiate, although he was charged to repress imminent hostilities among the tribes when he could. The major purpose was to inspect conditions of the trade and the conduct of the traders, with a view to recommending changes in the regulations, and to report all the statistical facts about the Indians that he could collect. In a new twist to Indian welfare policy he was instructed to take a surgeon with him to vaccinate the people against smallpox.[26]

In Detroit the previous winter Henry had met just the man for that job. Douglass Houghton, from Fredonia, New York, a graduate of Rensselaer Polytechnic Institute and assistant professor there of chemistry and natural history, was also a physician recently admitted to practice. He was all of 21 years old. Invited by the "leading men" of Detroit to give a series of lectures on scientific subjects, he arrived there in the fall of 1830. Not only the high quality of his lectures, but also the affability of his mischievous, fun-loving personality, won him instant popularity, both intellectual and social. So responsive were his Detroit friends, he later gave up his academic post for a medical practice in the western city. Schoolcraft's invitation to join the expedition as surgeon and botanist probably settled that decision, as the opportunity to travel the still little-known wilderness collecting scientific specimens was irresistible to a man of his voracious curiosity.[27]

The expedition set out from the head of the portage in late June, 1831—Schoolcraft, Houghton, Melancthon Woolsey, a young Detroit printer as statistical aide, Lieutenant Robert Clay commanding a small detachment of soldiers, and the usual crew of paddlers, guides, and interpreters. Jane, the two children, and the Misses Johnston, escorted by Lieutenant Allen, accompanied the party as far as Point Iroquois, where St. Marys River widens into Whitefish Bay.[28] Their day's outing concluded on the return with the Johnston girls and Lieutenant Allen shooting the rapids in the canoe, while Jane and the children got out to walk the portage road home.[29]

For the next two months the expedition pursued its course and objectives along the coast of Lake Superior, up the Chippewa River system to Prairie du Chien, and back via the Fox River to Green Bay—vaccinating, collecting demographic data, biological and geological specimens, and holding councils at strategic places. The canoes, supplies and Indian presents had been purchased from James Schoolcraft. In July he brought some supplements and mail to the party by light, fast canoe, and a package from Jane containing fresh butter, several pies, and a ginger cake. Henry and Douglass noted the presence of iron at many places on the south shore of the lake, and once again Henry exerted himself and his group to ascend the Ontonagan River to get additional samples of the fabulous copper rock, still in the place the gods had assigned to it. George Johnston joined the group at Ontonagan, and when they stopped at La Pointe for several days, they stayed in the house George had built there.[30]

Interesting as the 1831 voyage was, the expedition authorized for 1832 was the most exciting of all to Henry. At last he could take up again the unresolved quest of the Cass expedition of 1820—precise location of the source of the Mississippi River. Scientific research may have been the major purpose from Henry Schoolcraft's point of view, but the War Department had a more serious reason for financing an expensive and well-staffed expedition. Rumors of warfare on the prairies were reaching alarming proportions. If hostilities erupted (which later occurred, under the name of the Black Hawk War) the more northerly tribes above St. Anthony's Falls must be pacified and neutralized, to prevent their joining in. In addition, they would be inoculated with precious smallpox vaccine.

They organized the party of 30 similarly to the Cass expedition: Henry Schoolcraft, overall commander, in charge of researching history, archaeology, and language; Dr. Douglass Houghton, surgeon, botanist, and geologist, happily anticipating "the pleasure of a mental feast upon the hidden treasures of nature";[31] Reverend William T. Boutwell, chaplain; Lieutenant James Allen, commanding a small detachment of troops and in charge of topography; George Johnston, interpreter and baggage master. Their route carried them across Lake Superior, up the St. Louis River, across lakes, streams, and portages to the Mississippi, and finally to Cass Lake. There they established the base camp for further exploration in light canoes. Four days later, on July 13, 1832, after difficult passages and portages in blistering heat,

Henry attained the objective he had contemplated for 12 years—the source of the mighty Mississippi River. In his excitement he pushed ahead of the Indian guide, to be the first on its shores, and the first white man to travel the entire length of the river. He named the unimportant-looking, shallow little lake Itasca, from the Latin *Veritas Caput*, true head.

Allen's measurements proved it to lie two degrees south of the position assigned in the Paris Treaty of 1783. The group continued down the river to St. Peter's, finding, to their relief, that the tribes of the region were not involved with Black Hawk, and so proceeded back to Lake Superior via the St. Croix River.[32] They had counted 14,279 Chippewas (Ojibways) and Ottawas, 1,553 mixed bloods, and "259 persons of every description engaged in the trade."[33]

When they arrived home Henry was amused to find a missive from the dead letter office at Washington containing a diploma of membership in the Royal Geographical Society. It had been delivered first to St. Mary's, Georgia, since the envelope had simply been directed to "Henry R. Schoolcraft, Esq., U.S. AMERICA, a wide place to find a man in."[34]

Not that Henry was ever easy to find by mail in the summertime. The only way a letter could be delivered in the interior of the northwest wilderness was by casual Indian courier (often unreliable) or in the hands of a trader who happened to be going that way. Jane addressed two to him at La Pointe, to let him know that "we are still in the land of the living, but how soon we may be called to give up our spirits into the hands of Him who gave them, we know not."[35] The dread cholera had reached Mackinac, with five deaths in three days and was expected to arrive at the Sault any day. ". . . we have heard from Chicago the ravages of the cholera is ten fold worse than the scalping knife of the Black Hawk."[36] But she would resign herself to the will of God. The children were well, but "my own health has been much worse this summer than at any past time, my strength completely gone . . . if I am not numbered with the dead before that time," she would look forward to seeing her husband in August, "& should we never meet again in this vale of tears, think charitably to her, who would wish to have done better & forgive her failings."[37]

Jane's morbid outlook continued into the fall, when she wrote Henry during his brief visit to Detroit to confer with Secretary of War Lewis Cass, that she was under Dr. Houghton's constant care, and that he "says that unless a speedy check is put to my present disease, that it must unavoidably terminate in an affection of the lungs. My strength is gone, & I am gradually sinking into nonentity."[38] And the next day: "My health is so very [low] that I cannot attend to my domestic concerns, & at the *same time* pay attention to the minds & improvement of the children which are absolutely due to them & which I feel a heavy debt I owe them. . . . I never have discharged my duties as a Christian Mother as I ought—& if I would *now*, I *could not* . . . I am feeble beyond measure."[39]

But she did manage the strength to request him to bring back some preserved peaches, pears and quinces, as their stock of sweets was low, as well as the portrait of him that a Detroit artist had promised. She also reported the interesting gossip that Mr. Rice's sister had arrived and was reported to be a sensible woman, that Eliza was recovering from illness and might live until spring,[40] that she and the Binghams had united their little family prayer meetings twice, and that she hoped she and Henry could continue to manifest a spirit of charity.[41] Nevertheless, her health was clinically, as well as subjectively, very bad. James reported in a letter to George the following April that Jane "cascades blood very frequently."[42]

While making the trip that September Henry escorted Anna Maria as far as Detroit; she managed the voyage without getting seasick. Henry then placed her under the protection of a Mr. Browning for most of the rest of her way to Hadley, Massachusetts, where she would finish her education.[43] Anna Maria was a self-possessed young woman of 18, with a lot to report to Jane in her first letter. She was delayed five days at Albany with an ankle that she had sprained in getting out of the stage at Utica. Mr. Browning left her at a public house in Albany, but she found her way to the private boarding house of one of the Schoolcraft relatives, who was very kind and taped the ankle. Going on alone to Hadley, the stagecoach upset, with nine people in it.

> . . . my head struck against one of the posts and for a moment I saw sparks of fire and then all was over. When I recovered the first thing I knew was two gentlemen trying to pull me out of the Stage. . . . I find Hadley pleasant, the people are kind & agreeable, but they have some very singular *notions*. I see but little difference between Master & servant. They all eat at the same table and here no distinction is made. It was at first rather mortifying, but I hope through the grace of God I shall be enabled to conquer my foolish & wicked pride.[44]

The young innocent from the wilderness was apparently more delicately brought up than her more sophisticated eastern sisters. Mrs. Porter was kind, however, and sent a recipe for Mama's rheumatism: two ounces castille soap dissolved in warm water, 1/4 ounce turpentine, two [illegible] oil of rosemary, one pint alcohol, mixed together and coated on her arm every evening, after it had been rubbed vigorously with vinegar and red pepper.[45]

As Anna Maria went east to school, young John McDouall, now 16, was returning home for vacation from Mr. Taylor's school—a happy place enrolling ten students. Susan asked Henry to meet him at Detroit and give him money to get home, if he should need it.[46]

Even before Henry's fact-finding trip of 1832, the War Department had decided to consolidate the Indian agencies at Mackinac and Sault Ste. Marie, with Schoolcraft as director, at a $200 increase in salary. Mr. Boyd would be transferred to Green Bay. Henry was at liberty to reside at either place, with a sub-agent at the other.[47] For the first year he elected to remain at the Sault, where Francis Audrain continued to assist him, and dispatched George to Mackinac in the fall of 1832 under his old title of sub-agent.[48]

George was pleased about the move. Not only did he have status again, but he could enroll the children in

Mr. Ferry's school.[49] He was also able to perform little services for his sister, Jane, with whom he was very close and in frequent correspondence. "Many, many thanks for . . . having fulfilled so well the memorandum I troubled you with. I am very happy you did not take the articles out of the company's store on Mr. Schoolcraft's Act. as I had not his permission to get anything there on his credit, & I shall either send you the amount of the bill . . . by the winter express or give you the money myself in the spring."[50] George was like his father in his special love for the children of the family, and he doted on little Janee, whom he called his Wild Irish Girl, or his yellow-haired lassie.[51] He sent her a little workbasket that winter, and she returned the compliment with a pair of mittens for her cousin, John George, to wear to the Infant School.[52]

Although he had been earning a steady income for some five years, George continued to run up bills and debts with everyone. His promissory notes were circulated in a market of their own among the merchants, including his relations-in-law, John Hulbert and James Schoolcraft. They wrote to him frequently, pleading in the politest terms for him to pay up.[53] Although his boss, Henry Schoolcraft, disassociated himself scrupulously from the Indian trade, George, with his continually pressing need for money, sought silent partnership in commerce. William Mitchell, with whom he proposed equal investment in a store at Mackinac, was a little doubtful about the propriety, however, and wrote to Henry for his views before proceeding.[54] Consequently, they never concluded the agreement.

But George did go in with his brother when William, now 22, decided to strike out for himself in the summer of 1833, independent once more from the American Fur Company. They returned to their father's old New York agent, C. Mills, to purchase the outfit and arrange for selling the furs. But Mr. Mills had learned in earlier years that it was wise to deal with these men in cash. If he received a shipment of furs, then Mills would forward an extensive order of goods, as "it would be desirable to us on the onset to start without any old embarrassments in the way."[55] Somehow they got financed, however, and William proceeded to establish his wintering post at Leech Lake. He had 50 people there, in all, having allowed the women and children to come along with the men. Although this might be expensive in terms of provisions, the women did a lot of valuable work and took full responsibility for themselves, their baggage and their children at the portages, all on a much lower ration of food than the men.[56]

Ordinarily William hated writing, but that summer and fall his heritage emerged triumphant over his inclinations, and he wrote a series of 22 letters to Jane, describing in detail his journey inland and the operations of the fur trade.[57] They were remarkably unchanged from the heyday of the old North West Company, yet unknown to William, his letters were a swan song. He also bared his soul.

> You know how backward I have always been in communicating my feelings to any individual. . . . You know dear Sister how we was brot [sic] up by our dear departed Father, we were told to abhor all that was vile or base in our conduct one to another. . . . at that period of my life when I most needed his instructions was he called from us. . . . After that period I was left intirely [sic] to my own inclinations. . . . I commenced my career in aiding our Mother, for the first and second years my hopes were more than realized. But I dread to say that when we commenced business with the A.F. Comp, I met with bitter disappointment. . . .
>
> That disappointment made me thoughtfull, and then deep melancholy took it [sic] place; . . . I wanted to go to some solitary place, where I would be left alone . . . to meditate over my blasted hopes. Last spring these bitter thoughts returned with greater force, I entered into dissipation . . . with the idea that I might find a momentary relief; alas how disappointed the past appeared darker, and my stings of conscience more Keen; the deeper I went, the more wretched I felt. At last I saw my error, and formed my resolution to fly such desolating habits.[58]

It was January before he got around to writing George, with a troublesome crow quill, apologies, and another outpouring of his feelings.

> Although many think that I have no esteem or respect for my Friends or relations . . . they are deceived, if they only Knew my inward thoughts they would acquit me of that charge. I have . . . a few good Books and being almost alone for the greater part of the time, gives me time to read and meditate, and I hope that I shall return the penitent prodigal. . . . I have seen enough of the world, and the hypocrisy of those who pretend to be true and just in all their dealings one with another; I have also enjoyed what they call the pleasures of this world, But I now feel with double force my stings of consience [sic], and that I have drank [sic] the Venom of those pleasures, which are but for an hour, and I have felt and now feel the bitter anguish that accompanys those enjoyments.[59]

William's battle with liquor continued to see-saw, but his opposition to the American Fur Company could go only one way. Persuasive as he tried to be with the Indian hunters, they were too overawed and intimidated by the Company to switch their business. In one season William lost most of his and George's investment.

Although an infant school was opened at the Sault in January, 1833 by a Mr. and Mrs. Merrill, and attended by Janee and Johnston,[60] Henry decided to move his family and the agency headquarters to Mackinac for the following year. He went to Mackinac Island in May to arrange for necessary repairs to the agency house that would "unite elegance with comfort,"[61] buy some additional furniture from a man who was leaving, and plan his changes to the garden. A few weeks later the furniture, books, and Henry's large and still growing collection of geological, biological, and anthropological specimens were loaded onto a schooner at the Sault. Before departing he gave a look back to Elmwood "with fond regret at the trees I had planted, the house I had built, the walks I had constructed, the garden I had cultivated."[62] It had been a very happy 11 years of intellectual enjoyment and seclusion, and "it was not without deep regret that I . . . went back one step into the area of the noisy world . . ."[63,64]

If Henry found it painful to leave Sault Ste. Marie and its memories, how much more traumatic for his emotional wife, who had lived her entire life there and left behind a cherished family. Henry assured her that she would find many social advantages at Mackinac, that George would remain with them and that he relied upon Eliza to come and help her.[65] Then he went off to New York for seven weeks to arrange with Harper's to publish his book about the expedition to Lake Itasca.[66]

He traveled by steamboat, fast stage, and canal boat to Schenectady, where he took "the cars" for Albany, making 16 miles in an hour and ten minutes, then the steamboat the rest of the way.[67] Actually, he had hoped to go to Europe that summer, but his leave was denied by the War Department. His "friend high in influence . . . throws, with adroitness, cold water on the subject. He weights matters in scales which will only keep their equipoise at the place of the seat of govt; and . . . require their equipoise to be kept up by casting on the golden weights of political expediencey."[68] How difficult to be stationed so far from the seat of power and be denied opportunity to wheel and deal on one's own behalf.

Jane tried to make the best of things in his absence, although it got harder, not easier, with the years. Her strange, new surroundings depressed her. She was grateful when George brought her mother down to stay with her. The ladies of the village, led by Mrs. Robert Stuart, were attentive in their calls and invitations.[69] Nevertheless, she was lonely, as "all are seeking their own" and her health did not permit her to engage extensively in the visiting and parties that were the island's custom. She caught a heavy cold on the way home from a tea party in bad weather, and, confined to bed, she had only "my dear Mother to break the solitude of my sick chamber. I have felt indeed that I had got into a land of strangers."[70] Perhaps her mother's presence deterred even professing Christians from endeavoring to alleviate at least by their sympathy, the pain, not only of solitude but of body and mind—the one naturally the result of the other. "... I am hastening to the grave, [yet] I cling to life . . . I tremble in the long watches of the tedious night . . . with my guilty conscience . . . yes, guilty in a million of ways from my youth up even until now, of omission & commission."[71]

Her depression deepened as she wrote, and she begged Henry to pray for her, though she deserved nothing but wrath and indignation. She would put her anguish into the hands of her Redeemer. A few days later a ship arrived from below, "& to my great surprise & sorrow & mortification not a single line from you . . . I had tears—yes, tears, such as I never had before."[72]

A visit home to her beloved "St. Marie" in September revived her spirits with a lightness she must communicate. "I was pleased to learn that you manage to live so well, & contentedly in your *widowed* state, & since you have *so kindly* extended my furlough to the 1st of October, I have consented to stay a few days longer. . . . The children . . . are delighted to be with their Grandy & Aunty's." The ladies of the fort all called, and "express so much pleasure & cordiality . . . there is no formality or *stiff* ceremony among them." The previous day she took tea with two couples at the fort, then they went to meeting together at the old schoolhouse. "It is long since I passed so pleasant & profitable an evening," and at that day's Sabbath meeting the place was filled to overflowing. "O! What a different spirit seems to pervade the Religious exercise at this place to that of the cold, dullness of Mackinac."[73]

The joy of simply being home was enriched by a special celebration. A smooth working relationship between Charlotte Johnston and William McMurray had ripened into love, and they were married September 26, 1833.[74] Charlotte, at 27, was four years older than her Willy—an unusual circumstance in an age and place where men were customarily much older than their wives—but they were well suited to one another. Both of them balanced their sincere piety with a practical portion of worldly ambition and material good taste. William had not been in a position to consider marriage unless he was ordained; otherwise his future was highly uncertain. Therefore, during the summer of 1833 he went back to Canada (the north side of St. Marys River and Lakes Huron and Superior were all still Indian country) to seek formal ordination.

He had to track the Bishop all across Canada, from York to Kingston to Montreal. While in Montreal he negotiated with Charles Ermatinger for the handsome stone house the trader had built at the Sault in 1814, which still stands.[75] The feature event, however, was the ordination process, which he described in glowing detail with pardonable pride in a long letter to George, addressed as "My Valued Friend."

> I am happy to inform you that I was on the 11th Inst. [August] ordained a Minister of the Gospel. . . . The occasion was a most solemn one, and one that shall not be easily forgotten by me.

The grueling examination lasted three days and required him to compose a sermon from a given Biblical text within a specified period of time, to answer 19 long questions in writing, both without any references at hand except the Bible, to write the 25th Psalm in Latin, to pass a long *viva voce* examination, winding up with further examinations in Greek Testament and Cicero in Latin.

> The Bishop and his Examining Chaplain were very much pleased with my examination, and were exceedingly kind to me. The Chaplain made me a great many presents of valuable books, books which have been his companions since a boy, which was highly gratifying to me.[76]

Perhaps William did not yet understand the habits of his future brother-in-law, or perhaps he was anxious to show the love and good will he felt for his new family—"Home is dear to me, but the Sault still more so." In any event, he took pains to attend to all George's "little requests and purchases . . . with ease, and pleasure"[77]— collars, waist bands, a hat and case, and a shooting jacket, total $27. And while he was shopping in the East for his bride he bought household furniture and a "great many beautiful, useful things," according to Jane's judgment. "I see he is determined to live well and genteelly."[78] In October the newlyweds moved with their finery into the half of the Hudson's Bay Company house assigned to their use.[79] In the spring they would move into the Ermatinger stone house.

For Susan Johnston the winter of 1833-34 must have been especially lonely. Suddenly her children were almost all dispersed—George and Jane at Mackinac, William at Leech Lake, Charlotte across the river—and she always worried about them when they were far from her. In addition to Eliza, she had only the two youngest now close, both home from school at last. But young as she was, Anna Maria would not remain much longer in her mother's house; before she left it, heartache and scandal would occur.

At 19 Anna Maria was a striking girl, with sparkling black eyes and a proud, graceful carriage. She was beginning to acquire the habit of wearing mostly black, accentuated by red, which little Angie Bingham would so admire as "handsome and elegant" in the hope that when she grew up she would "sweep the train of my gown in the same grand fashion."[80] Three years earlier, at age 16, her vivacity and her sense of fun had attracted the lighthearted James Schoolcraft. While he languished in the jail at Mackinac that awful winter, one of his jocular friends wrote that he saw "Miss Maria this afternoon & asked if she had a 'sweet message,' [but she probably doesn't] trust this channel of communication, and said something about writing herself."[81] The fellow promised not to take advantage of Jim's absence, but served notice that later on he intended to contend for that "prize." On James' return to the Sault, Jane had ample opportunity to observe the attraction between the two while Anna Maria was living with her, and James was calling on her for counselling.

For the next two years they saw little of one another. James spent the winter of 1831-32 in New York, and the following year Anna was away at school. But they did exchange some letters, and during the fall of 1833 the romance began to blossom. Anna Maria confided to Jane that she had "told Mamma her feelings towards James, & that Ma referred her to Mr. S & myself whether she should receive James' visits or not. I told her in answer that Mr. S thought that both she & James might do better *otherwise*, & that he was sorry anything of the kind existed between them & I faithfully urged (warned) her not to see James *alone* any more & left her in the hands & care of a wise Providence."[82] A wise Providence apparently saw fit to allow the relationship to grow, though clearly nobody in the family trusted James to reform. Furthermore, it was Jane and Henry's judgment, and probably Susan's, that while he might be an irresponsible husband, Anna Maria was not the kind of person to steady him—she was too much like him.

But James was struggling determinedly to improve himself. He was working for his brother-in-law, John Hulbert, and living in the pious atmosphere of John and Maria's growing family. He had joined the church, took no wine "with the exception of . . . Mr. McMurray's dinner & with George, which I did out of courtesy" and took brandy only if necessary "to check a cholic."[83] Hulbert confirmed his good behavior.[84] If people had minded their own business a great deal of trouble and pain might have been avoided. But in a small wintertrapped town people do not; out of boredom, self-righteousness, and honest love, comes meddling.

The storm began one evening in early February, 1834, when the three Johnston women were sitting before the fire and talking. Susan had confided her anxiety about Anna Maria and James to Eliza, and Eliza took the opportunity to discredit James with her sister by a report she had heard that he had returned to his old ways and was drinking and whoring again. Anna Maria refused to believe this, but she was deeply troubled for James' sake, and told him about it as they walked home from meeting the next day.[85] He, of course, was hurt and angry, and after consultation with John Hulbert, who felt that was "a most *cruel, unjust,* uncharitable attack on his character, without the least foundation of truth,"[86] James wrote a note to Eliza. He demanded to know the source of the story and asked her to bring it before the church so that he might clear his name. "God knows I am bad enough . . . in my own eyes, and need not the slander of tongues. . . . I do not wish to create unhappy suspicions, . . . but I have seen enough to warrant the saying that if Eliza would bridle her tongue a little it would be to her benefit and to that of her mother."[87]

The note, couched in James' extravagant style, infuriated Eliza and her mother, who interpreted it as a threat from James to bring Eliza before the church. A confrontation with Anna Maria brought out her intention to marry James Schoolcraft, and her insistence that she had told her mother previously, and Mama had not disapproved. This Susan denied, asserting that she had no knowledge of Anna's intentions, and that if she insisted on going ahead with such a marriage her mother would "disown her . . . and entirely hide her face from her."[88] Anna Maria retorted that Mama better hold her tongue for " 'no person on earth should separate her from James.'"[89] At this point Susan sent for Charlotte to try and deal with the willful girl.

An even hotter argument ensued. Charlotte, according to Anna Maria's report to James, became so exasperated that she advised Mama to beat Anna Maria. "Seizing Maria by both arms, she calls on her mother to strike her, which waz [sic] accordingly done by inflicting blows over her shoulders with a pair of *fire tongs.*"[90] Perhaps even worse, out of the fury of the scene emerged the revelation that it was Charlotte who had told Eliza of the gossip about James, that allegedly emanated from "the ladies of the garrison," and that it was not generalized whoring of which he was accused. Rather, Anna Maria was reputed to be his "kept mistress."[91]

This news was more than James could tolerate. He launched a personal investigation to track down the source of the malice, questioning virtually all of the officers and their ladies, and the civilians as well, who constituted "all the *respectable* part of our community."[92] He then communicated the results of his survey to Charlotte. ". . . *all* without an *exception* deny to have in any manner so represented to you. . . . And the inference drawn from this, is: that a report so base, vindictive, and maliciouz [sic] calculated, so eminently calculated to blast and destroy the character of a female forever; and one too, designed to reflect dishonor, and to brand disgrace upon me, originated with yourself!"[93] James tried to phrase his two notes to Charlotte as politely as he could, but his audacity in even addressing her, and the threatening tone of one sentence—"I hope still that you may be able to clear up the matter. . . . If, finally you cannot do so farther proper steps will be adopted."[94] — brought William McMurray indignantly into the act. James "may think he can do as he pleases with the family on that side of the river," William wrote to Henry, "but not with Charlotte on this side of the river . . . my door is always open for him and we will give him audience, but to write notes as he did this morning is beyond bearing."[95]

Henry and Jane tried to avoid being sucked into the vortex of the controversy, but McMurray forced Henry into writing a letter of advice, which he tried to keep as cool as possible. And Jane felt she must write Charlotte of her distress over that sister's behavior

> . . . pleading ignorance of their attachment—*that* none of us can do for it has existed for years & you yourself have known more about it than I do . . . but Charlotte there is one thing I cannot approve . . . & that is your urging Mamma to [corporal punishment] towards Ann. Now that she is of age no one has a right to lay violent hands on her. . . . I do not [excuse] any of Ann's conduct for I have condemned it from beginning to end & I have told her so . . . forgive my frankness & candor, you know it is my nature never to gamble the truth. . . . [96]

James' judgment of the McMurray's behavior may have been harsh, but was probably accurate. "I think all that haz [sic] occurred so far haz been the effect of passion . . . rather than what in serious reflection, would have been deemed a duty. Mrs. Johnston . . . has had her feeling wrought upon, and carried to the pitch, by Charlotte & Eliza, with the assistance of the Rev.!"[97] McMurray's interference was particularly odious to James.

> ... condemning Maria & myself in *toto*, and a veto upon all intimacy between us. I don't know *why* Mr. McMurray should be deemed a standard by which *my* actions are to be judged ... What rank or pretention places Mr. McMurray above the ordinary, respectable inhabitant of this place ... instead of his appearing as the peacemaker, the reconciler of difficulties we find him coercive, ambitious and unrelenting. Instead of giving good pastoral advice to Anne, we find him attempting to force her into measures. Instead of attempting reconciliation, we find him threatening me with insults. In the place of forgiveness we observe resentment. Where love should reign, hatred predominates. Instead of the Ambassador of Christ, we see the secular man."[98]

Quite a condemnation of a man who had chosen the Church, and honestly strove to do his best—but not entirely undeserved.

In the end, of course, none of it mattered. James was denied the house for a while, but he and Anna Maria continued to meet outside and plan their future. In the spring Anna Maria moved in with Maria Hulbert, after John left for New York on his annual buying trip. ". . . the ill treatment of her sister Eliza, rendered her home any thing but a place of peace & contentment."[99]

James hoped to improve his material prospects and applied for appointment as sutler to Fort Brady, if Hulbert were to give it up as he hinted he might do. But Hulbert changed his mind, applied for reappointment himself, and James stayed on as an employee, at a $500 raise to $1,100 per year, plus a $500 bonus for giving up his application.[100] It was a good enough living, and on November 29, 1834 he and Anna Maria married. They forgot the bitterness of the previous winter and quietly moved in with Susan at the family homestead.[101]

Chapter Twelve
Chancery as a Way of Life

When the Johnston brothers succumbed to the power of the American Fur Company in 1834, they could not anticipate the drastic changes about to occur in the life of the Company and the Lake Superior fur trade. The old fox himself, John Jacob Astor, decided to retire that year and sold his fur business to Ramsey Crooks. Crooks, in turn, reorganized and decentralized. He designated La Pointe headquarters for the Northern Outfit,[1] and three years later the company buildings on Mackinac Island were sold and converted to a hotel.[2] Michilimackinac was falling from its century-old eminence as the great entrepot of the fur trade. On the other hand, Crooks added a new department to the company's Mackinac operations—fishing. To bring in the immense catch from several sub-stations on Lake Superior, the schooner *John Jacob Astor* was launched above the St. Mary's Falls in 1835, followed by additional company vessels in subsequent years.[3] The new fishing operation took up some of the economic slack at Sault Ste. Marie, where the Lake Superior catch was received, packed, and shipped to Detroit under the direction of former fur trader Gabriel Franchere.[4]

The transition from fur to fish in the Sault-Mackinac orbit reflected changes that were taking place in the Northwest as a whole. The advance in settlement of Michigan Territory, which accelerated in the 1830s, increased the demand for fish, but far more importantly, exerted enormous pressure on the demand for land. Negotiation for Indian cessions continued unabated, reducing the territory in which the natives trapped while replacing it with farms and villages that destroyed the habitat for many kinds of fur-bearing animals. As beaver virtually disappeared from the territory, muskrat and racoon assumed center stage. These animals could live with farmers, and the centers of high fur yield gradually shifted to the more populated lower Great Lakes.[5] Not that fur trapping or trading ceased on the upper lakes after the mid-1830s; it was simply less important.

In 1847 Crooks sold out the "tattered remnants";[6] the fur trade as the lakes had known it for 200 years was finished. By the 1850s "the voyageur had turned in his paddle for a hoe, and the Indian had retired in sadness and anger to a reservation."[7] From now on farmers would trap in the fall and winter for a forest version of egg money, trading their pelts at the village store.[8]

But by the mid-1830s, the sons of John Johnston had completed the shift from the independent life of their father to the federal government dependency of their village. George had worked for his brother-in-law and the United States government for eight years. Excessive pride, both born and bred, induced him to perform his duties with elaborate dignity and loftiness of manner. But the gravity he assumed when he was drunk made him appear ridiculous, when it did not actually antagonize people. Even Jane voiced her irritation at his going "on with a high hand in the name of 'Sub Agent and Interpreter for the United States',"[9] and Henry from time to time received anonymous complaints. Many believed that he owed his position only to his family connection with the agent. But Henry knew that George was a skilled interpreter, had a keen understanding of the psychology of both the Indian and the trader, and could be a conscientious official when he chose. Furthermore, he was genuinely fond of George, who despite his tendency to self-importance was an intelligent, loving and genial man. He also understood that it was hard for a man like George to tolerate inferiority with respect to his employment and income. After all, his father had been a true-born gentleman, and he had been raised as such.

Henry was admittedly vain about his large correspondence with important people. But George, too, corresponded regularly with men like Reverend William

Boutwell and Reverend Jeremiah Porter, now at Chicago, his English and Irish relations, and scientific men from the East who requested specimens directly from him rather than funneled through Henry. Perhaps Henry was not the only important man. Envy of their brother-in-law was never far beneath the surface in any of the Johnston brothers, although George kept it in check by a genuine friendship and a reciprocal tolerance for Henry's pomposity. The two men had much in common.

These conflicting emotions boiled to the surface one day in the fall of 1834, however, and pride won. The trivial incident occurred during the visit of an illustrious personage to Mackinac Island—Captain Tchehachoff of the Russian Imperial Guards. George, demoted once again from sub-agent to interpreter without loss in salary, was ready to leave his quarters for the office after breakfast when Captain Tchehachoff called. In courtesy, he stayed home with his visitor until nearly noon. When he arrived at the office

> I could distinctly perceive in Mr. Schoolcraft's manner, that a storm was brooding in his heart. Johnston soon came in and told his father that dinner was ready, and in the mean time told me that his sister wished me to make a doll bedstead. The gentlemen walked in to dinner, and I went to the blacksmith shop and commenced the bedstead, and so soon as I had finished it, I took it to the house, and presented it and returned to the hall, and commenced a conversation with the Capt. who [sic] I found smoking a cigar. Mr. Schoolcraft opened his room door and accosted me in pretty severe & angry language and said that he wished to see me in the office.[10]

Whereupon, to George's humiliation, although the door was closed, Henry proceeded to upbraid him for his absence during most of the day. Henry had been dealing with some Indians away from the office and sent for him twice, but he was not to be found at his desk. George apologized, explained where he had been both morning and afternoon.

> I remarked that I was always present and did not make it a practice to absent myself. He then observed that the office was never swept, and that I never went to the post office for his letters, a duty incumbant on an Interpreter, that I was deficient in the hour for opening the office. . . . I told him if he thought that I had not performed my duty, that he was at liberty to engage one who would.[11]

Then the fur began to fly, one word led to another, and George decided to "withdraw myself from the department. Mr. Schoolcraft's harsh course & tyranny [are] . . . not at all compatible for me to bear. His remarks this day were pointed, peevish and beyond endurance."[12] But departure from Jane and her children was hard for him, and he wrote to "My Beloved Sister. Permit me while my time is drawing nigh for my departure from this Island, in this way to pay a just tribute of grateful thanks for the love & tender kindness you have ever manifested towards myself and little orphan children, especially to Louisa."[13]

The question was where to go and what to do. As a first step he wrote to his old friend and benefactor, Lewis Cass, now Secretary of War (and, as such, Henry's boss). A recent letter from Cass contained a gratifying opinion of George's qualifications and "with this commendation, I once more launch myself to begin the world anew as I have been . . . compelled to this step by Mr. Schoolcraft's harsh disposition which . . . might be tolerated in Syracuse & in the time of Dionysius, but unfortunately we now live in a free form of Govt. and in too enlightened an age."[14] But there was little Cass could offer him, as Henry was the chief federal employer in the area. Furthermore, he wrote George, Henry had a very high regard for his brother-in-law and told Cass he deeply regretted the rift. The best advice the Secretary could offer was reconciliation.[15]

George tried, taking Cass's letter to the agency to show Henry, "who displayed such a haughty mein toward me, that I left him upon the same grounds I had before. . . . Should Mr. Schoolcraft feel there be any legal deficiency in the non performance of a duty I had most at heart, I trust that the department will grant me the priviledge [sic] of a hearing."¹⁶

Without a paying job in prospect, George turned his attention to other financial interests, a pursuit that gradually became a way of life for him even when he was gainfully employed. It reflected in part the federal gravy train psychology of Sault Ste. Marie—if he could not get a job with the federal government, he would press an assortment of financial claims against the U.S. Treasury—and in part what would become an almost obsessive Johnston family preoccupation with lost fortunes at home and abroad. Every few years one of them would revive old hopes of striking riches from their patrimony. George was not the only member of the family, or the community, to occupy himself in the prosecution of these kinds of financial claims. But he probably worked hardest at it.

As early as 1830 he had billed the Treasury for expenses incurred at La Pointe beyond the funds sent to him. Six years later the Treasury actually sent him a check for part of it, the $41.90 he had paid Joseph Default to help build his house.¹⁷ In the summer of 1834, before his break with Henry, he submitted an account to Elbert Herring, Thomas McKenney's replacement as Commissioner of Indian Affairs, for services as an interpreter from 1826 to 1830 and living expenses in the amount of $3,664.04. The Department had never provided for an interpreter at La Pointe, so George took it upon himself to act in that capacity between Indians and their traders. "Without an explanation and proof of these charges and services," came the reply, "or evidence that they have any sanction in precedents, it is impossible that this Department should act upon them. If the claim is admitted, it can only be admitted & paid under a special act and appropriation of Congress."¹⁸

After he lost his job, George engaged a Detroit lawyer, H.L. Cole, to collect the claim, offering a fee of $250 if he recovered the whole amount, $125 for half.¹⁹ Henry filed a statement that, indeed, George had not been paid for interpreter services or house rent during that time. But he had been paid as sub-agent, and he never convinced the Department that his interpreting constituted additional compensable services, although he tried again with another lawyer in 1843.

Recognizing that additional remuneration from the War Department was a long shot, which might take years to materialize, he turned to another prospect for funds that began to appear worthy of resurrection—an inheritance from Ireland. George had a cousin in London with the same name as he, a man who worked in the Inspector General's Office of the Customs House. John had corresponded with this relation, and the commonality of their names created a bond that induced George to continue. In the fall of 1833 he wrote a long letter containing all the family news, good and bad. In the latter connection he dwelt on his own disappointment at the reduction in his status and his dismal prospects. In his reply, addressed to George at "Sault Ste. Marie, Michigan Territory, Upper Canada," the London George commiserated sincerely. Things were pretty bad for him too—twenty years in the government service and still earning only £200 a year. He lamented with George the failure of the British Government to compensate his worthy father, and rekindled long-dormant hopes by promising to see what he could do. He also encouraged George in his claims against the family estate.[20] A few years later he would observe prophetically, "it is a singular fact that every man who married into our family prospered in life, while the old stock reduced both in quantity and quality."[21]

Wealth from Ireland became a more tangible possibility with a letter from Uncle Henry Kearney, with whom George also corresponded. Aunt Eliza passed away in May of 1834 and "By the demise of my late dear Wife your Father's family become entitled to a sum left in reversion to him by your Aunt Johnston" [John's Aunt Nancy Johnson].[22] There was, in addition, the £800 that John had left in the estate for the life interest of his sisters when he sold to McNeil, now due to his heirs. Payment of the latter claim necessitated that the original copy of the bond be presented to the authorities, even though it had been incorporated in the deed of sale. As near as Reverend Kearney could recall, John had the bond with him when he left Ireland at the end of his last visit.[23] Where was it now?

In December George answered his loving and preachy uncle in the same kind of pious, flowery tones, expressing condolences on his aunt's demise, and pleasure that she lived to enjoy her nephew's last letter. The bond had still not been found, although Susan thought it might be among some of John's papers now in Henry Schoolcraft's possession. George went on to inform his uncle that he considered the business of settling these legacies important enough for him to make a trip to Ireland for the purpose. "I think that I am called to this and I consider it a duty I owe to my family and to myself."[24]

At about the same time he wrote George, Reverend Kearney was also in touch with Henry Schoolcraft, whom he knew had assumed the mantle of family leadership after John Johnston's death. In fact, Kearney had informed Henry as early as 1829 that although Jane Moore's £50 legacy to her brother had already been settled, "there are other sums which Mrs. Johnston may calculate on after the demise of Mrs. Kearney . . . one is a sum of £500 (left by Miss Johnston, Mrs. Kearney's aunt), which after deducting a few small legacies would leave about £400. The other is a sum of £800 on Mr. Johnston's estate, now in the hands of Mr. McNeal [sic], which will revert to Mr. Johnston's children."[25] After his wife's death, Reverend Kearney informed Henry that the Bishop of Dromere was holding £461 of the original £500, in which John's sisters had held a life interest. After deducting specific bequests the residue was due the Johnston family in America. He asked Henry to obtain the necessary releases and powers of attorney to clear up the estate, and also to try and locate the lost bond.[26]

That missing document complicated settlement for years. Susan thought John left some of his papers with a Mr. Gale in Montreal about the time of his last visit to England, and that there might even be a will there as well as the bond in question.[27] But neither was ever turned up. Without a will, under English laws of primogeniture, George would inherit everything, provided the Johnston's marriage after the fact legitimized him in the eyes of the Crown. It was this knowledge (or hope) that inflated George's aspirations and induced him to contemplate an expensive trip abroad. Kearney sent John Hulbert, sherriff of Mackinac County, a power of attorney for George and Susan to sign that permitted him to settle his wife's reversion. Susan complied, but George refused until he could consult a lawyer, preferably in Ireland.[28]

It was James' observation that "George seemz [sic] to be of the opinion that *all* coming from Ireland comez [sic] for him, so doez [sic] not feel willing to sign any *papers.*"[29] Hulbert tried to convince him of the folly of making such a journey, "that his matters there could be settled through an agent, and with far less expense. But he has 'golden dreams' of 'Rich Relations,' who, beside paying the amount due him are to make him many valuable presents."[30] Nor was his principal relation in Ireland any more anxious for George to come than his family at the Sault was to see him go. In acknowledging receipt of the power of attorney, Kearney reported that George's letter intimating his intention to visit Ireland made a very bad impression, coming on top of his withdrawal from Henry's employment. It showed an instability and inappreciation for Mr. Schoolcraft's good offices that Reverend Kearney deplored.[31] He went on, in a subsequent letter, to say "I am aware of the grief and trouble produced by the immense expenditure of property by George in the absence of his Father, for I have it recorded in language of sorrow and disappointment from the dear departed friend himself."[32] While Mr. Schoolcraft understood business dealings, attorney's fees, and expenses which drained a legacy, Kearney made it subtly clear that he did not want a suspicious innocent like George interfering in his, Kearney's, conduct of affairs as the family agent.

In the end, George traveled no farther than Penetanguishene at the foot of Georgian Bay. On May 27 he was back at the Sault "in a high state of intoxication . . . He speakz [sic] very *large*—talks of recovering *his* war losses, and *his* this and *his* that . . . I think after a while he will find himself, 'himself again,' and all will go along quietly. I fancy the poor fellow haz [sic] spent the whole of his $250; and he has lost also his $4 a day for the whole time after his instructions reached this, which is about $120 more; so that his 'goose chase' haz

[sic] cost about $400."[33]

The instructions James referred to were transmitted in a letter from Henry to George, dated April 20, 1835, appointing him interpreter for a boundary survey to be run between the Chippewa and the Sioux. A similar letter was waiting for him from the commissioner at Washington.[34] The happy prospect of re-employment sobered George quickly, and he made immediate preparations to travel westward on his assignment, rather than eastward to frustration.[35] In the process, the estrangement from Henry was left behind.

Despite timely transmission of Susan's power of attorney, settlement of the Irish estate dragged on inconclusively. Meanwhile, other circumstances existed in the life of John Johnston that could be turned to profit by his heirs. William McMurray now entered the act. A new law had been passed in Canada regarding claims for war damage, and William offered to write a contact of his in York about filing a claim.[36] Thus, while Henry became the family's agent for obtaining the Irish inheritance, William McMurray, who never knew his father-in-law, became his representative to the government of Canada.

William had wholeheartedly joined the family circle as a full-fledged member right from the start. Within a few months of his marriage he had become personally involved in the troubled love affair between Anna Maria and James. And he spoke of "Mamma" and "Papa" in a sad letter to Henry in August, 1834.

> My Dearest Charlotte has suffered every thing, but death, but it has pleased God to spare her yet a little longer. . . on Thursday evening . . . a most beautiful Babe was given us, but not to gladden our hearts, for Alas! it was dead. Doctor Clark . . . was obliged to perforate the Brain of our Dear little son, to save poor Charlotte's life, but he assured us that it had been dead some hours. . . . He now lies buried on the left side of our Papa, and your own little Willy on the right. . . . Maria has been a little humbled by the loss of our dear Babe. She saw it when taken over to Mamma's . .

and then came over at my request to see Charlotte.[37]

But Anna Maria still suffered from the wound of Charlotte's cruel interference in her life; she did not visit again for a long time. A year later, on September 20, 1835, Charlotte was delivered safely of a healthy boy, whom they named William Strachan, in honor of William's illustrious mentor.[38]

It was William McMurray who kept George informed about the welfare of his children, who were living with their grandmother while he went off on the boundary survey in the summer of 1835 and on what James called his wild goose hunt in Canada the following winter. During that summer Louisa, now 12 years old, injured her knee. At first it appeared to be just one of those childhood accidents, although it was severe enough that the doctor feared she would be left with a residual stiffness. But it never did heal properly and continued to plague her into the winter. By January the doctor was "under the necessity of cupping it, and . . . is apprehensive that it will turn to a white swelling, in which case, it might cost her her life."[39] Susan was frightened. She dearly loved this eldest grandchild, whose sweet disposition endeared her to everyone. By spring William was happy to tell George that she was sufficiently better "to come to her meals and at times take care of [Charlotte's] little boy. It must be expected that her leg will always be stiff."[40] In fact, the leg troubled her all the rest of her life, and she became quite crippled, able to walk only with crutches.[41] The family pitied her greatly and always referred to her as "poor Louisa."

George was devoted to his children, but once the boundary survey was completed he was again unemployed. Shortly after his return he went off again to pursue nebulous schemes in Canada. He wrote James from Penetanguishene that he was going on to Toronto (as York was now known), but gave no address.[42] When his sisters or his children, whom he left in his mother's care, wanted to get in touch with him they could only send letters with an Indian from McMurray's band who was taking his dispatches express to Toronto, in the hope that

George could be found there. They needed to impart bad news about Louisa's leg and its worsening condition. And "your mother requests me to ask you to make some provision for the support and clothing of your two boys, George & William, by the very earliest opportunity. She says she is poor and finds it hard that you have left her this charge without a compensation."[43]

Louisa was staying with Charlotte and despite her illness could help with the baby. The other sad family news was Anna Maria's loss of her first child—stillborn on December 28. It was just as well, as the infant was malformed and could not have lived long, but Anna Maria's life hung in the balance for nine days.[44]

George spent the winter at Toronto, "doing, of course—nothing,"[45] in James' opinion. It was later rumored that he hired an attorney there to represent him in the matter of the Irish legacy that he, as eldest son, hoped to collect in its entirety.[46] But his refusal to sign the power of attorney with his mother that would enable Henry Kearney to collect on their behalf, may have jeopardized the whole settlement. Apparently, John McNeill now questioned whether he, in fact, owed the £800 that John Johnston had left in the property under the Deed of Trust, and the Bishop of Dromere, who held the legacy of Nancy Johnston, was requesting more time for its payment.[47]

Perhaps a Toronto attorney did have a sobering effect on George. When he returned to the Sault in the spring of 1836 with a stock of goods for opening a store,[48] he finally agreed to send his power of attorney to Ireland through Henry Schoolcraft, and leave the management of the business in his hands.[49] There it would lie dormant for yet another year.

When news of the October 1834 break between Henry and George reached Sault Ste. Marie, William lost no time in applying to Henry for the position his brother left vacant. His foray into independent trading the previous year had been financially disastrous, and with no obvious alternative near home, he had considered moving west of the Mississippi to try his luck in a distant place. Henry's acceptance of his application was a great relief. Unfortunately, he could not start promptly because his mother needed his assistance.[50]

Young John, who lived at home since his return from school and generally supervised the heavy work around the place, had fallen severely ill with what was described as inflammatory rheumatism. He was "very much reduced, and so weak that he has not been able to turn himself, nor indeed not been able to move in any way."[51] It would take him months to recover. Susan hired a man for six months, paying him $30 in advance, but then he, too, fell ill and she could not afford to hire another. William felt he had to stay, if only to see her wood chopped and hauled; by January John was well enough to do these chores.[52]

John had also been placed on the federal payroll after his return to the Sault, as interpreter at $360 per year.[53] But his conduct, like that of his brothers, was a constant worry to the more sober and responsible folk around him. Francis Audrain, Henry's sub-agent, reported shortly before John's illness that his behavior all year had been very bad, that he rarely showed up at the office before 11:00 or noon, and that he was abusive to his boss and to the Indians.[54] Unlike George and William, however, John would have little or nothing to do with religion, an attitude that caused great consternation in his loved ones.[55] After recovering from his illness his behavior was even worse. He played man of the house in making family decisions at the age of 19, but, having been replaced as interpreter, he did nothing to contribute to the support of his mother and sister.

"Mrs. Johnston requests," the reformed James wrote to Henry, "that you as the *Guardian* of her family will adopt some method by which John's conduct will be governed in and out of doors. Instead of being any kind of help now, he is a perfect drawback upon the resources of the family. He associates with the lowest blackguard company of the place, enters into all manner of excess, is bring [sic] disgrace upon himself, and discredit to his name. When his mother attempts to rebuke him, she receives a blast of French curses and abuse."[56]

Henry could do little about John's morals, but he could and did try to help the family financially in every way he could, not only through direct employment, but by using his contacts to pursue the more promising of the various claims they had inherited and to settle the deficient ones.

When John Johnston died he left a lawsuit pending against Colonel Cutler, who had been commander at Fort Brady. In late 1831 Congress found Cutler liable for the claim, and Susan's Detroit lawyer, Joseph Torrey, collected and deposited $1,000, less his fee, in the Bank of Michigan. It did not stay there long, however, as the executors of the late David David's estate had earlier presented their claim for $1,200. Apparently, John had agreed to pay this debt in four annual installments, but had made only one before he died. Henry handled the matter with Major Torrey, telling him that Susan "felt no disposition to take advantage of legal forms, but to fulfill the agreements of her husband, whatever they were, in good faith, agreeable to her means, & as soon as she had means."[57] David's Montreal executors agreed to renegotiate the remaining $750 on the loan, and arranged for a lawyer from Sandwich to call on Henry to collect it.[58]

Henry Schoolcraft was clearly the best off member of the family, although he felt obliged to keep struggling for larger income and greater security. In 1830 he had estimated his worth in cash, securities, and real property at $5,600.[59] In addition to his $1,400 annual salary, he received royalties on his books and had been able to make a few income-bearing investments—55 shares in the Bank of Michigan at $5 each, 10 shares of Michigan Steamboat Company, for which he paid $1,000. In addition, he bought land whenever he could spare the money and saw a remunerative potential, using surveyors going to distant places, like Wisconsin, as his knowledgeable agents. He felt it wise to draw his will at this time. He left everything to his wife and children, including such rights as he might have in Jane's £50 legacy from her aunt, Jane Moore, not yet recovered, and anything still collectible for the estate of John Johnston, including his losses from 1814. He left his personal property to Jane, his mineral and natural history collections and his library to his son, and his small gold watch, "a lady's watch in its pattern" to his daughter. "It is my wish that my son should receive a college education, & study divinity if he should be converted, and that my daughter should have the advantage of the education furnished by a female seminary."[60]

The children were pleasing to him as they grew up, and Henry enjoyed the life on Mackinac Island. More interesting people came through here than at the Sault, and he could choose from a wider range of friends among the larger resident population. The school was reasonably satisfactory for the children and the family could enjoy worthwhile outings to interesting geological formations on the island, like Arch Rock, Sugar Loaf, Henry's Cave, and so on.[61] A few fashionable people from Detroit were beginning to discover the unique combination of invigorating, healthful air and natural beauty that Mackinac offered, and were building summer cottages on the island. Henry predicted, in 1835, that in time it would become an important summer watering place for people from Chicago, St. Louis, Natchez, New Orleans, Cleveland, Cincinnati, and Buffalo, as well as Detroit.[62]

But Jane never cared for Mackinac as much as he did. During her summer at the Sault in 1835

> a thousand sad & pleasing recollections rush upon my mind; as I thus find myself once more, in reality under the roof of my beloved & ever-lamented Father's hospitable mansion—here where I first drew my breath—where I first claimed the names—the endearing, responsible names of Wife & Mother & where I found myself *childless* and *fatherless*.[63]

Janee spent most of her time across the river, where she became very much attached to her newest uncle, who quizzed her on her Bible and admired her intelligence. Johnston also liked to visit there, but he behaved better when his mother was around to control him. Jane's summer brought its moments of sadness too. "I have been to dear Pa's and Willy's grave. It is completely embowered by trees & looks so calm & peaceful."[64]

By the fall of 1835 the United States Government, pushed by land-hungry settlers, was again seeking land cessions from the Indians of Michigan Territory. In putting out feelers, Henry learned that the Ottawas of L'Arbre Croche and Drummond Island and the Chippewas of St. Marys River and Lake Superior were ready to sell their lands if the price were sufficient to pay their interminable debts.[65] Although the white man's accounting system remained largely a mystery to them, they hoped once and for all to get out from under its heavy burden and build a new, more promising life for themselves. To negotiate a treaty as close to their own terms as possible, they determined this time to send their delegates to Washington. Henry decided, almost at the last moment, that he should go with them to protect their interests;[66] in the end he played a leading role. His own interests also called for another visit to the seat of power to consolidate his political and scientific positions. In addition, he could perform important services for his mother-in-law.

For some time Susan had had virtually no regular income beyond what she earned herself from her fishing trips into Lake Superior and the 3,500 pounds of maple sugar she extracted each spring from her camp on Sugar Island[67] and shipped to Detroit for sale. She had a section of land for herself and one for each of her children under the 1826 Treaty of Fond du Lac.[68] Neither harsh weather nor illness ever kept her from the sugar bush once the sap began to rise in March.

Eliza suffered repeatedly from severe respiratory ailments, from which the family always doubted her recovery, although she would live longest of them all—to age 82. But she did exquisite needlework, some of which she could sell. She had, for example, supplied the bags for biological and geological specimens that Henry took on the expedition of 1831.[69] He took quite a few pairs of moccasins to Washington with him, of the kind she presented often as gifts to her family, paying her a good price in advance of his marketing them for her.[70] As the years went on she was able to sell her work to tourists and summer people, represented by her brothers or brothers-in-law who shielded her thus from the unladylike part of the business. But aside from these sources, the women were nearly destitute.

James informed Henry in October of 1835 that

they had no provisions for the winter, that he had already advanced them $400 and would probably be in for another $200. "I am about the poorest of the sons-in-law and can but ill afford this, and it seems somewhat hard. But an hundred yearz [sic] more it will matter little, at least with me."[71] Such was James' happy-go-lucky generosity. But he was worried about his own future as well.

He disliked working for John Hulbert, a dour, sanctimonious man, and hoped to go back into business for himself. Moving in and out of business on the frontier was a fluid process. Since the fall of 1834 he had held the contract for the winter mail, which was brought overland by snowshoe from Detroit and returned the same way approximately once a month. Once the road was built to replace the blazed trail it would be faster and cheaper, but James made a small profit anyway, much to everyone's surprise.[72] Nevertheless, he was dubious about how much room existed for him as a merchant at Sault Ste. Marie. He considered buying farm land in the Grand River Valley, but the $1,000 he expected to have saved by spring would not be enough. He therefore asked Henry to look out for something for him, too, while he was in Washington—for example, an order for a few thousand dollars in goods if Henry were to hold another treaty conference next spring.[73]

But Henry's most important mission was prosecution of two disparate claims on behalf of Susan Johnston. Firstly, as Oshaw-guscody-way-quay, she reminded Henry, she was of the same totem as the Drummond Island band, and if the island were to be sold by them to the federal government, she was entitled to a share of the proceeds.[74] Secondly, this last year of the Jackson administration was, perhaps, an auspicious time for a widow whose children were good Democrats to seek recompense once more for her husband's severe financial losses at the hands of American soldiery. Henry would lay the groundwork carefully for a new petition to be presented to Congress.

On his way down to Washington he stopped in New York to gather up letters from influential friends on her behalf, adding them to John Holiday's and George Johnston's eye witness testimony. Ramsey Crooks promised to testify on the validity of the claim and wrote to David David's executor, Mr. Lacroix, for copies of the invoices for 1814 and an affidavit that John Johnston was not connected in any way with the North West Company.[75] Crooks went even further and obtained an affidavit from Toissaint Pothier, now an "Honorable" in Montreal, who had been the recipient of Astor's original message to St. Joseph Island that the war was on.[76] Honorable Lewis Cass submitted testimony, detailing the invaluable services rendered to him by the Johnston family in 1820, describing Mr. Johnston as "a gentleman by education and habit" who, when war changed the status of the place where he was living, "behaved under these circumstances like a man of honor, and as his position prevented him from taking part in the war, his submission . . . could not be attributed to him as a fault. . . . He could not desert his family, and as he remained with them, he necessarily submitted to the authority which the British government established there."[77] A slight alteration of the truth, though Cass would have no direct knowledge of that. Finally, Henry obtained a copy of a letter Commodore Sinclair wrote two weeks after the seizure, acknowledging receipt of the goods on his ships, and pledging to submit the dispute to the proper court, plus affidavits from the appropriate court in Michigan that a search of the records showed that the case had never come up.

These documents and affidavits were submitted in support of the "Petition of the widow and administratrix of John Johnston, of the Falls of St. Mary's, in the Territory of Michigan, praying compensation for property seized and carried away by the American Army, during the late War with Great Britain," dated January 7, 1836, and referred to the Committee of Claims.[78] The petition established the petitioner's lifelong residence in the region, detailed the events of the war leading to the seizure, and certified Mr. Johnston's scrupulous avoidance of involvement with the North West Company, or any other, in peace or war. It also placed blame for the illegal acts of Major Holmes and his men on the head of Mr. Johnston's disaffected former employee who insinuated himself into the officer's confidence and deliberately misinformed him, thereby causing him to violate his express orders to respect private property, and attached an invoice for the lost and damaged property, showing an amount of £9,035 14 Halifax currency.

> Upwards of twenty-one years have now elapsed since these depredations were committed. . . . Time has shed its mellowing influence upon these transactions: death has put his seal upon many of the actors: but it has left the widow and her children as the victims of a loss, which is more and more felt, as years take from the ability of action, and add to the incapacity and uncertainty of age. . . . Having no longer a protector to look to, having exhausted her ingenuity of resource, and with the' infirmities of age fast pressing upon her, she now appeals to Congress for redress.[79]

The committee did not deliberate long. It did take the trouble to write Captain Sinclair about the matter, but he was unable to recall the incident. The committee then stated its conclusions succinctly. If the goods were private and "not the subject of capture, the party owing [sic] them had his remedy against the officer taking them for trespass. If they were public property they were liable to seizure. In no event would the United States be liable unless the seizure was unlawful and the treasury had been enriched thereby. . . . the petitioner is not entitled to relief."[80] So declared the Committee on Claims; so declared the 24th Congress.

Well, it was worth a try. The Indian claims were more promising, and they could be tracked on both sides of the street. Not only was there Oshaw-guscody-way-quay's claim to a share in the proceeds of Indian land "sales," but Congress was about to enact a clever scheme whereby traders could make good their bad debts from the Indian trade, retroactively, by collecting them from the annuities awarded by Congress in payment for those lands. Mrs. John Johnston and her children could also claim a trader's debts.

When the Lake Superior Chippewa chiefs started for Washington in February 1836, William pre-insured the family interests before they left the lakes. As Henry's deputy it was his job to talk to all the chiefs and verify that they were, indeed, willing to sell their land. While he was about it he also elicited from them recognition of his mother's claim to debts owing to his father and to him from 1814-1831. Furthermore, he sealed it in writing: "For value received by our young men, we the undersigned Chippewa Chiefs, do jointly promise to pay Susan Johnston the sum of Twenty Thousand Dollars . . . [as] consideration for claims which Susan Johnston has for provisions and clothing furnished our young men, and which we hold as justly due her, by them they were kept from freezing and from starvation, at a time when our country was unprovided with traders."[81] It was convenient, of course, that one of the six signatories was Susan's brother, Waishkey. Nor did this fact escape the notice of many local Indians, who resented Waishkey's status as a delegate, partly because he was not a Crane (the totem of the civil chiefs) and partly because of his cozy relationship to the Johnstons and the Schoolcrafts.[82]

Negotiations opened March 15, 1836 at the Masonic Hall in Washington between Henry Rowe Schoolcraft representing the United States and 24 chiefs of the Ottawa and Chippewa (Ojibway) nations. Thirteen days later a treaty was signed whereby over 16 million acres of land, comprising the lower peninsula of Michigan north of the Grand River and Thunder Bay and the upper peninsula from Drummond Island to Chocolate River, thence south to Green Bay, was ceded to the United States for $2 million, about $12 1/2$ cents per acre, including bogs and waste lands "which . . . in justice to the Indians was paid for at the same rate."[83] The government reserved Indian villages for them, and they had the right to use any portion of the land until whites required it for settlement.[84] The government set aside $300,000 from the purchase price to pay the Indians' debts and another $150,000 for the benefit of the halfbreeds of the area.[85] Of the remainder, $600,000 would be paid in specie, at the rate of $30,000 annually for 20 years, and $1 million pledged "to various useful or benevolent objects for their benefit."[86]

The treaty of 1836 was the crowning achievement of Henry's life so far, and he was jubilant.

> A treaty was signed today, by the Indians, which leaves to their unfortunate race, great advantages. . . . All that could be wished in the way of schools, missions, agriculture, mechanics &c &c, is granted. Much money will be annually distributed, their debts paid, their half breed relatives provided for, . . . & large presents given out. Rejoice with me. The day of their prosperity has been long delayed, but has finally reached them, in their lowest state of poverty, when their game is almost gone, and the country is shorn of all its advantages for the hunter state.[87]

It was Henry's dream to see red men turned into mechanically competent Christian farmers, and now, under the new treaty, they would be.

As for the traders' claims, a commission convened at Mackinac would adjudicate them, but no debts incurred before the War of 1812, nor debts of any citizen who did not leave the country during the British occupation, would be allowed.[88] Henry declined the office of commissioner for this purpose, "from the delicacy of deciding on the claims of my relatives."[89] But everybody got something—presents and some cash for Susan, money for each of the children under the halfbreed allowance (although Charlotte's claim was doubtful because she now lived on the British side of the river), and for the widow of John Johnston, acknowledgement by the Chippewa Nation

> For Medicine and medical attendance on men women & children of said bands for sustenance during their sickness, and the funeral expences of such as have died while at the Post between July 1794, and the establishment of the Indian Agency at this place in July 1822, inclusive at the rate of £50 Halifax Currency per Annum . . . [and] for fire wood furnished indigent families including corn potatoes and other articles of sustenance during

the period of their residence at Saut [sic] Ste. Marie at the rate of £25 per Annum.[90]

The total amounted to $7,820 and was paid over promptly.[91] John Johnston's compassion and generosity, for which he neither sought nor expected recompense, came home to benefit his beloved wife when she was most in need.

But the family was dissatisfied with the allowance for bad debts of 1813-1816, when John Johnston's trade was larger than it was from 1816 to 1828. "Yet the 12 latter years, during which he dealt on a capital diminished to about 1/3 is taken as the data [sic] in making the allowance for outstanding Indian debts on the former period of 4 years. The estate claimed $14,440 for actual outstanding debts on this period, & was allowed $4,800 based on an estimated average loss on the *succeeding 12.* "[92]

No books or records existed for 1813 to 1816, which caused difficulty, while records for the subsequent period did exist. All that could be produced was the original invoice for the goods John bought in Montreal in 1814—$5,985 worth—verified by a copy from the invoice book of the late David David. For 1816-1820, the period of the Johnston co-partnership with Astor, one half the losses shown for the Lake Superior region on the books of the American Fur Company was acceptable. But the family claimed, in addition to the settlement for the 1813-1828 period, that, because it was an Indian debt, they should be recompensed on moral grounds for losses incurred by John Johnston from 1794 to 1813. These were actually estimated for the 1794-1816 period at $18,750,[93] or one fourth (the customary proportion derived from general experience) of the estimated total capital of $75,000 employed in the ceded region. Which specific claims the government allowed and what adjustments they made, is not known, but eventually they paid a total of over $32,000 to the Johnston family.[94] Presumably, the Johnston brothers got enough to tide them over frequent periods of unemployment. For all the family the payments were timely in seeing them through the hard times caused by the Panic of 1837.

Although Henry might celebrate the Treaty of 1836 in his sincere belief that he had obtained justice and golden opportunity for the Indians, a long run view would conclude that "the elaborate charade of Indian treaties and land purchase was only the political and diplomatic window dressing necessary to disguise a subsidy to the fur companies for persuading or coercing their customer-employees to come docilely to the treaty table. Not only did the traders collect direct payments from the government; they also reaped a substantial percentage of the money nominally given to the Indians."[95] These payments carried most of the traders through the recession of 1837. It has been estimated that between 1835 and 1838 the American Fur Company, in all its branches, received more then two thirds the value of its stock from this source.[96]

On a personal level, the terms of the treaty opened a Pandora's Box of controversy over the estate of John Johnston and precipitated a nasty quarrel between the Schoolcraft brothers. Johnston had died intestate, with few tangible possessions to be distributed among his widow and the four adult children. What little existed went to Susan, who was still supporting three minors. But now, eight years later, all the children had attained majority, and suddenly a substantial estate existed, after all—close to $50,000, in fact. Henry stage-managed the distribution on his return to Mackinac, and in the fall of 1836 forwarded three checks to the Sault: about $2,200 each for Charlotte and Anna Maria, and $1,800 for Eliza and John together, with an accompanying memo of explanation that he had reserved $25,000 for Susan and over $9,500 each for Jane and William, Jane's portion being inclusive of her inheritance from Ireland.[97] When the letter arrived, James exploded.

> As you requested I have *endeavored* to explain it 'to the girls'. I presume I speak correctly when I say that *girls & boys* are all very much dissatisfied. . . . By what authority do you invest $25,000 of the Estate's money in Mrs. Johnston's favor? By what authority do you appropriate about $9,500 to the use of William, and about $9,223 to

> Jane in ready cash, without applying the same sums to the use of the other children?. . . . I should never have opened my mouth upon this subject, had Anne been treated with any thing like proportionate justice.[98]

Henry's reply indicated that the estate of John Johnston and the separate trader's claims of William and his mother were getting mixed up. The large amount paid to William included Indian debts owed to him as a trader in his own right, and the $25,000 paid to Susan included the $7,800 award she had received from the Indians for her personal charities to them. Moreover, she had authorized Henry to invest it for her. As for the large amount paid to Jane, most of it constituted her dowry, promised many years ago by her father, but never actually paid.

> The repayment of the claim would never have been presented by me, had not the estate by which it was owed been able to pay it. Jane's marriage portion was presented, and urged by Mr. Johnston himself, . . . in conformity with his English notions . . . He took pride in it, regretted his low circumstances, which prevented his doing more, and confirmed the gift the week before our marriage . . . He never, however, found himself in a situation to pay a dollar, & I never asked him. [99]

John had originally expected to dower his daughters from the two Irish legacies from his sister and his aunt, but he had needed to invest that cash in his business when it arrived in 1821 and had never been in a position to extract it again. Susan confirmed her recollection of his intentions in a message transmitted to Henry through William McMurray.[100]

But James was still not satisfied.

> Your love of money must have prevailed over your sense of justice, and Christian correctness of principle when you appropriate $6,976.92 from the Estate of Mr. Johnston within your own purse . . . you have no right to take the money belonging to

> the estate, and appropriate it to the provisions of Mrs. Moore's legacies, or any other person's legacies, or will. In my last conversation with you upon the subject of the Irish affairs you express[ed] a half way opinion that George might recover the whole. *You appear now to have secured yourself,* even should George succeed. This I suppose is upon the 'bird in bush' principle. If anything is due to Jane . . . from Ireland she should by all means have it; but she should wait the results of the provisions of such legacy or will.[101]

At the time Henry was too busy to respond to his brother's indignant tone and severe accusations. A month later he told James just what he thought of him.

> When I received your violent & abusive letter. . . I determined, whatever my feelings were, that I would not descend to answer it, according to its virulent temper. Though you had forgotten the respect due to me, I did not forget that which I owed myself. . . . I had taken a deep interest in time past, in leading your mind from the mists & errors, in which youth, hot blood & Satan had bound you, and I was not disposed to turn on my heel, & merely exclaim ingratitude! If *you* had in your zeal after 'dollars and cents' as you say, forgotten that you were my brother, *I* could not forget that I was yours.[102]

He had hoped that explanation would induce James to apologize for drawing hasty and emotional conclusions, but

> Not a feeling of compunction—not a word of apology! On the contrary you say . . . 'that you do not know that your views are materially changed.' . . . that I have acted an *unjust, illegal, grasping* part, without a *sense of right,* or a particle of *propriety,* or *Christian principle.* [103]

If that was the way James really felt, perhaps they should not correspond at all. Of course it was not. James found it galling to be placed so often in a position of moral inferiority to his unfailingly correct brother. He knew intuitively that Henry had feet of clay, but he could never succeed in exposing them. Nevertheless, he did not want estrangement, and his natural good will soon emerged in apology and an attempt at self-explanation for his apparent frivolity and impulsiveness.

> I assure you I have moments of serious reflection, & perhaps too, when others least think, it is but in the moments of gaiety or excitement that I seem to be a thoughtless man, but *scenes impressed so strongly upon my mind, and always before me cannot be erased.* The reflection, too, that my life cannot be long (the complaint of the head is becoming more & more frequent) leads me naturally to serious reflection. But enough of this; man cannot be his own judge—neither does it become me to write my panegyric . . . [104]

James had not involved himself in the issue of the Irish estate before this, but now he, too, felt that he must do so to protect his wife's interests, and, incidentally, his own. Settlement was becoming more and more urgent, both financially and psychologically, as the brothers and sisters became more acrimonious about it. Their venal attitudes would have caused great sorrow to the father whose financial legacy outranked the moral legacy he had hoped would survive him.

Chapter Thirteen

Restlessness

After a slow start the Territory had grown at an accelerating pace over the decade between 1825 and 1835. As early as 1834 Michigan applied for statehood, but Congress refused to act until Michigan and Ohio settled their border controversy. It arose from the provision of the Northwest Ordinance of 1787 by which the boundary ran eastward from the southern tip of Lake Michigan to Lake Erie, not then accurately mapped. By the time surveys placed this line accurately, Ohio was an important state and the growing town of Toledo was encroaching on land technically defined as Michigan. Skirmishes, both legal and physical, heated up the dispute during the summer of 1835; they became known as the Toledo War.

In December 1835, President Jackson directed Congress to settle the matter, and during the next session the compromise was hatched that offered Michigan the western Upper Peninsula in exchange for conceding the Toledo Strip to Ohio. On those conditions Congress then enacted admission. Controversy raged within the Territory during the summer of 1836 between the assenters and the dissenters, who also divided between Democrats and Whigs. Henry Schoolcraft, who appreciated more than most the natural resources of the Upper Peninsula, supported acceptance of the compromise, and wrote some letters to Democratic newspapers to that effect. But he was otherwise too busy with his own affairs to participate actively in the debate. Nor was Chippewa County represented in the conventions (at Ann Arbor in September and December of 1836) that first refused, then accepted, the compromise. Without much help from its oldest settlement Michigan became a state in January 1837.[1] Before Henry went to Washington in the fall of 1835 he had seriously considered changing his situation, as the possibilities of future attainment in his present circumstances were uncertain. "I was not married when I accepted my present office . . . now I have a wife & children, whose happiness, constitutes my happiness. It is the great object of my life & exertions to provide for you, and to leave you, the means of living, when I am gone."[2]

But his political winter away from his family paid off. Congress reorganized the conduct of Indian affairs in the West and passed a bill "to invest the Agent at Michilimackinac with the authority and duties of Superintendent of Indian Affairs in the Lakes."[3] The enlarged jurisdiction not only enhanced Henry's status, but happily required him to move back into civilization at Detroit, while permitting him and his family to spend their summers at Mackinac and Sault Ste. Marie.[4] It was an ideal arrangement that afforded him the congenial intellectual environment he craved, while allowing his wife to spend a good deal of time with the family that was so important to her well-being.

During the six months Henry was away, Susan wanted Jane to live with her, so that she could "attend to her closely in case of sickness."[5] But Jane knew that Henry preferred her to remain in their own home and for the children to attend the school at Mackinac. Her brother, William, was with her, and conscientiously took upon himself the responsibilities of man about the house in addition to his duties as Henry's agent. He had become active in the church and entirely sober. Nevertheless, Jane had a difficult winter. She was short on servants, and the children were sick a great deal, including a serious bout with whooping cough. She was up half the night with them and had to attend to the cooking herself during the day.[6] In addition, a 15-year-old Indian girl her parents had adopted in infancy, and she took into her home a few years later, was dying of consumption, and Jane nursed her tirelessly to the end in April.[7] During the periods of crisis she managed, out of necessity, but the toll was heavy.

By spring she was a nervous wreck. But when

the March express was ready to leave she made certain to get a letter off to her husband, though her arm was bound up from her having been bled that morning. She had great need to pour her heart out, as well as

> tell you *myself* that I am in the land of the living . . . my domestic duties (at least some of them) [are] a sore trial to my faith & patience & to mind & body. [I want] all the little *nameless* kind attentions, so necessary to the comfort of a weak, nervous invalid . . .[8]

She went on to give him the news, including the fact that the children were back in school and that with the help of a servant she made 17 dozen candles from the tallow of a cow they killed. Finally, "I am, like my paper, *exhausted*, but not so, my love and affection for my ever dear Husband, on whom the Lord preserve from *all* evil prays your ever affectionate Jane Johnston Schoolcraft."[9]

To his frustration, Henry was delayed in Washington for another two months after the conclusion of the great treaty, until Senate ratification.[10] He was eager to get back and arrange for his new life in Detroit. They would need new servants, and he "endeavor[ed] to get a black, married or single, or a foreigner, as we shall probably have company during the summer, and cannot possibly get along without them."[11] He also brought home, as always, the long list of things Jane and the children needed, like hose and boots. Jane relied upon Henry to observe the styles for her and to shop accordingly. "Fur capes are still in vogue," he wrote from Detroit. "I have therefore purchased one. I observed yesterday, in the church going throng, that most ladies still wear straw, some velvet bonnets. I have ordered one of the latter."[12] And from New York he reported that ladies were wearing silk cloaks with large sleeves and black velvet or silk bonnets, with fur capes. In addition to finery Jane needed him to bring something else—"a good quantity of Laudanum."[13] This opium derivative was the common nostrum for aches and pains, and Jane came to rely upon it more and more to get her through her dreadful headaches. After her death people whispered that she was addicted, but no documentary evidence exists either to confirm or deny the suggestion.

On August 28, 1836 the first fruits of Henry's great treaty were harvested. Over 4,000 Indians camped on the beaches at Mackinac Island to receive their treaty payments—$150,000 worth of merchandise and food distributed directly to individuals, $150,000 similarly distributed to their half-breed relatives on the basis of carefully prepared lists, and $220,000 paid to the Indians' creditors. "The Indians went away with their canoes literally loaded with all an Indian wants . . . and a practical demonstration was given which will shut their mouths forever with regard to the oft-repeated scandal of the stinginess and injustice of the American government."[14]

After Jane and Henry moved to Detroit in October of 1836, William McMurray took on the responsibility of corresponding with them on Susan's behalf and keeping them informed about family affairs. He had succeeded in getting about $500 for Susan from the Canadian government under the new war claims bill. Susan's news of the family included improvement in John's behavior, Eliza's illnesses, William's broken leg, the mild winter weather, and her final visit (so she promised) to the sugar bush. She forwarded a request that Henry procure for her a good yoke of cattle and an oxcart, 20 bushels of oats for planting, and a light plow to replace the one she wore out, and asked that portraits be made of Janee and Johnston.[15] She assured her son-in-law that she approved of the investment he made for her and sent him "my thanks for his protection and assistance to the fatherless & widowed; may God reward him for it. He has done *much much* more than even my own sons, for me, and I can never repay him."[16]

Her son, George, was a particular trial to Susan at this time. Apparently, he was well enough off financially because Henry was investing in land for him—$581 worth in Oakland County, at $1.25 an acre in the fall of1836; [17] $1,000 in Saginaw Valley, recently ceded; and $2,000 in the Cass Farm, which that gentleman was selling off at Detroit in the spring of 1837.[18] The money undoubtedly came from the payments he had received under the 1836 treaty—as a halfbreed on the one hand,

and as a mercantile creditor on the other. But by midwinter he was drinking heavily again, so heavily that the doctor feared he might kill himself before spring and sent a discharged soldier over to take care of him.[19] George attributed his illness to other causes, "the rheumatism I have experienced this winter has been severe, sometimes preventing me to cross the room, but through the influences of divine providence and the indefatigable [sic] exertions of Doctor Porter, I think I now feel much better."[20] Henry William and John George were both attending the garrison school,[21] but the following year he sent them to Washington A. Bacon's school on Jefferson Avenue in Detroit, where Henry had enrolled Johnston. Mr. Bacon charged $3 per week for their board, because they ate as much as men,[22] but he was good to them, and they were happy there. Twelve-year-old Henry William wrote,

> I like my school very well. We study arithmetic, Geography, read write, spell and write compositions. . . . John George knows the multiplication table and the subtraction table and addition table all by heart . . . We have got a new suit of broadcloth clothes. . . . When we go to church we sit with Uncle Henry as Mr. Bacon has no pew. . . . James gave us half a dollar and we bought a pair of skates and as soon as it was frozen we went and skated on the commons . . . but we never skated on the river because you told us not to.[23]

John George, age ten, added a note full of "tells" and "sends":

> Tell Antoine to take good care [of] Bull and Hector and not entirely forget Brandy [dogs?] . . . tell grandmother to send Mrs. Bacon some cake sugar because she is very good to us and mends our stockings. I hope you will not forget to send our bows and arrows.[24]

Louisa was at Mr. Garvey's school at Mackinac and was quite happy living there, although she fell a good deal with her crutches.[25] Her Uncle William, sub-agent at Mackinac while Henry wintered in Detroit, kept his eye on her.[26] He, too, used his treaty payments to invest $3,000 in the Cass Farm. He was lonely by himself in the big Agency house, although plenty of starving Indians were coming in for help.

> Dear Jane how I long to see you all; and above all I want you to see how I get along in keeping house. I have a discharged soldier for cook, waiter, and in fact a Jack of all trades; he is an Irishman of steady habits and very faithful. I wish frequently as I sit down to my solitary meal that you were all here to partake of my . . . white fish; what is all the eastern luxury, which only gratifies nice and fastidious appetites, to be compared to this our Northwestern staff of life. . . . All my Indian visitors always ask about you, for they find no one in the kitchen, with a soothing hand to feed them.[27]

Mackinac Island was changing rapidly, becoming less Indian and more white. So assured was peace that the government evacuated the garrison in 1837 and no longer used the fort.[28] Over Henry's objections, the government closed the mission, too, that year, dispersed its boarding students, and sold its property for summer homes among other things.[29] To accommodate more summer visitors they converted the American Fur Company buildings into a hotel.[30] Finally the government had closed an era—the fur trade at Mackinac. Nevertheless, the government expected the Indians to visit every summer to receive their presents and annuities under the Treaty of 1836. Henry obtained authorization to build a dormitory for housing them, both during the annual distribution and at such other times as they came to the agency for aid and service.[31] Ironically, only two more years of treaty payments would occur at Mackinac. After 1838 the government moved the site to Grand Rapids and the conduct of Indian affairs on the upper lakes diminished substantially in importance.

The handsome dormitory that opened in 1838 served its original purpose only once. The government was going to appoint William its first Keeper.[32] But, at 26, he had had enough of celibacy. "As regards my future course in life" he wrote to Henry "for advice as my relation and friend. . . . Whether it would be proper for me to marry Susan Davenport . . . I think she has an amiable disposition, [he had written earlier to Jane that she "is good looking, very lively {with} considerable natural good sense; disposition below par"[33]] and though she has not had the advantages which others have, still she is little inferior to them in other qualities. . . . I have not carelessly thought of it, I have prayed to God to bless me, if consistent with his holy will, & who has so far extended his mercy & bounty to me in all things."[34] And He continued to do so. William and Susan were married that year[35] and were ultimately blessed with five sons and three daughters.[36]

While William seemed to be finding himself at last, James Schoolcraft began to drift again. He had straightened up after his very happy marriage to Anna Maria. Her gaiety matched his own. "Maria gives a party tonight, and az [sic] I am to make up the mail before *I make up to the females* this evening, it iz [sic] all important that I hurry," he closed a letter to Henry.[37] They were as much in love as ever. On another occasion, when Anna Maria was planning a visit to Mackinac he admonished Henry to "treat her well, *for she is a first rate woman!!*"[38] But after they lost the baby in December of 1836 things did not go so well for them. James suffered a debilitating illness that Dr. Porter was unable to diagnose conclusively. He bled James profusely and suggested to Anna Maria that if it were dropsy he would not live long. "What will become of me, if the Lord should see fit to take him from me, I know not. He is & always has been the kindest & best of husbands to me."[39]

James survived to spring. Although somewhat better, he was very weak, suffered from severe headaches, and his hand shook when he tried to write. He concluded that a better climate and another doctor might improve his health and dissolved his partnership with John Hulbert.[40] Withdrawing $3,400 profit and his initial capital of $2,000, he and Anna Maria left for Detroit to seek medical aid and new prospects.[41] Despite the terrible heat of the summer of 1837, the new medical treatment prescribed by Dr. Zina Pitcher was working; James was able to walk a bit about the city and attend church.[42] But by August Anna Maria was ill and went home to recuperate. "I fancy however her main Project is to see her mother & friends; if the truth were known; I suspect she is home sick."[43] James now decided that he wanted to spend the rest of his life as a gentleman farmer in the Detroit area.[44] He felt sufficiently better to go at the project with his usual gusto. At first he thought he would buy a place three miles out on the Grand River Road, cleared and fenced, with a good house and buildings for $5,000. Then he saw one he liked on Orchard Lake, six miles from Pontiac, which after they had completed the new railroad would be only a three-hour ride from Detroit. With a good house and fences it could be bought "for $1500 in *Bank bills* or $1200 in specie."[45] Ultimately he bought neither because by September of 1837 he was letting contracts for the construction of a house, in Detroit, to be finished in December.[46]

Meanwhile, he and Anna Maria stayed on at the American Hotel, despite the expense, and enjoyed the society of the city. "Gov Mason haz [sic] gone east, and tis said for the purpose of being married. Maria attended a [party] at his house on Saturday evening (my health not permitting me to go) which waz [sic] her debut among the town. According to her, much formality exists among a certain class of first class society."[47]

The McMurrays, too, shared the general feeling of restlessness and the desire to improve their situation that was, in fact, a national phenomenon. They had done well at the Sault, Archdeacon Strachan writing that "I feel a great pleasure in congratulating you on your general success in your Mission—a great deal must and ought to be attributed to your amiable spouse the daughter of *my old friend Mr. Johnston* a Gentleman of excellent family & great acquirements and one whom I highly esteemed."[48] But national policy was changing, and the government was withdrawing support from the Sault mission. Not only was William's future there uncertain, but with a family to support he wanted to improve his status.

He and Charlotte and the baby went to Toronto during the summer of 1837 to see his bishop and discuss their future with him. To their dismay they made the long journey in vain. Once again the bishop had traveled eastward, this time to Gaspé at the farthest extremity of Quebec; he would not return until August. They could neither afford to wait at an expensive hotel nor chase him down, so they returned home in disappointment. Nevertheless, their short time in the city included a pleasing social round of calls and invitations, including one to attend the opening of Parliament, and another to dine with Lieutenant Governor Sir Francis Head.[49]

In addition, William took the opportunity to engage a prominent lawyer of his acquaintance, Clarke Gamble, to pursue once more (on the British side) the matter of John Johnston's war damages. The possibility of cashing in on John's misfortune was still too alluring for the son-in-law, as well as the sons, to give up. Sir Francis promised to help by laying the matter personally before the Executive Council and to take whatever other steps he thought useful. Moreover, in addition to damage claims, John Johnston, having served in His Majesty's forces was, or should be, entitled to a grant of land in Upper Canada. William was happy to report that "I have secured it beyond a doubt, having obtained the certificate from the Adjutant Generals' Office for 800 acres, with directions that I should take it to the Surveyor General's Office and locate it wherever vacant lots were to be found."[50] He left this matter in Gamble's care as well.

Twenty minutes before the McMurrays' steamboat was due to depart at the conclusion of their visit, two women rushed up to them breathlessly. The one who was an acquaintance introduced the other as Anna Brownell Jameson. The well-known authoress and unhappily-married wife of the Attorney General of Canada was planning a trip to the West to gather material for a "work upon the female character of the inhabitants,"[51] and grasped the opportunity to meet a native of that distant place beforehand. "I must confess that the specimens of Indian squaws and half-caste women I had met with, had in no wise prepared me for what I found in

Mrs. MacMurray [sic]. [Her] figure is tall . . . with that indescribable grace and undulation of movement which speaks the perfection of form."[52] They took to each other immediately and Mrs. Jameson was delighted to find that "there is some chance of my reaching the Island of Michilimackinac, but of the Sault Ste. Marie, I dare hardly think as yet—it looms in my imagination dimly described in far space, a kind of Ultima Thule."[53]

Only a few weeks later she arrived at Mackinac to find that Charlotte had arranged her reception. The Schoolcrafts were expecting her as a guest in their home, although at the moment Jane was confined to her room with illness. When they did meet, Mrs. Jameson was "charmed with Mrs. Schoolcraft. When able to appear, she received me with true lady-like simplicity. The damp, tremulous hand, the soft, plaintive voice, the touching expression of her countenance, told too painfully of resigned and habitual suffering."[54] As with Charlotte, they had immediate rapport. Jane told her a great deal about the Indian way of life, the language she spoke with her bilingual children and her servants, and of the famous storytellers. "Her own mother is also celebrated for her stock of traditional lore, and her poetical and inventive faculties, which she inherited from her father."[55] She found Jane to be "proud of her Indian origin; she takes an enthusiastic and enlightened interest in the welfare of her people, and in their conversion to Christianity, being herself most unaffectedly pious. But there is a melancholy and pity in her voice, when speaking of them, as if she did indeed consider them a doomed race."[56]

Late in July, Jane took the children for a visit to the Sault and invited her sophisticated guest to travel with her by canoe. Long after steamboat service arrived at the Sault, the family continued to travel by the old conveyance, perhaps to avoid schedules with their attendant delays and to attain privacy. The journey through uninhabited wilderness, camping out around a fire among islands of primeval forest, and even the swarming and voracious appetite of northern mosquitoes, captivated the visitor by their novelty. But what interested her most was the prospect of meeting the remarkable mother of her two new friends.

> Large in person . . . a countenance, open, benevolent, and intelligent, and a manner perfectly easy—simple, yet with something of motherly dignity, becoming the head of her large family . . . she is eloquent, and her voice, like that of her people low and musical. . . . I observed that not only her own children, but her two sons-in-law . . . both educated in good society, the one a clergyman and the other a man of science and literature, looked up to this remarkable woman with sentiments of affection and veneration. . . . She received me most affectionately . . . and when I said anything that pleased her, she laughed softly like a child. . . . She set before us the best dressed and best served dinner I had seen since I left Toronto, and presided at her table, and did the honors of her house with unembarrassed, unaffected propriety.[57]

Mrs. Jameson tried to learn a few words of Ojibway, to everyone's amusement, and mastered most easily the lovely name of Neengay (mother) with which she addressed Mrs. Johnston.[58] A visit to Waishkey's lodge and a stroll along the river front on George's arm ("and I had much ado to *reach* it"[59] taught her more of the dignified Indian way of life. Then, to climax her visit, she embarked with George in an Indian canoe for the breathtaking seven-minute ride down the rapids. She was the first European woman ever to do it, and "had not even a momentary sensation of fear, but rather of giddy, breathless, delicious excitement."[60] For her bravery she was awarded the Ojibway name of Wasa-ge-won-qua, Woman of the Bright Foam.

Her departure from the McMurray's home came too soon, but she was eager to go to Manitoulin Island with them to observe the distribution of presents there. Susan paddled across the river to give a few last minute things to Charlotte and embrace her new "daughter" in a last farewell. Then she "got into her little canoe, which could scarcely contain two persons, and handling her paddle with singular grace and dexterity, shot over the blue water, without venturing once to look back!"[61]

Other visitors to the wild Northwest authored books about their experiences and brought the Johnston family to public notice, most notably William McKenney. But the book that emerged from Anna Jameson's pen two years later, *Winter Studies and Summer Rambles in Canada*, presented the most vivid description recorded, before or since, of this family, its surroundings, and its history and customs on the aboriginal side. But she presented her valedictory privately to Jane. "I must be thankful for what I have gained, what I have seen & done! . . . . I remark generally that the propinquity of the White Man is destructive to the Red Man . . . they are a noble race brought near to us, a degraded & stupid race, we are destroying them off the face of the earth. May God forgive us our tyranny, our avarice, our ignorance."[62]

Anna Jameson was not the only glamorous person to appear at Sault Ste. Marie in the summer of 1837. Henry's new sub-agent, James Ord, was a mystery man, who aroused much speculative gossip in the little village. He and his beautiful wife remained quite aloof from the community, and they were rumored to receive unknown visitors of "quality" during the night. Letters arrived in the post office from abroad with impressive seals on them. Some said he was a natural son of the king of England or the king of France, but no one really knew.[63] Unlike all the other employees of the agency, no birthplace appeared on the personnel list opposite the name of James Ord.[64]

Despite his failure to find and consult the bishop, by November 1837, William McMurray had made up his mind to leave the Sault and missionary work, though he hoped to remain in the ministry. "I have had perhaps as many trials since my residence with [the Indians], in trying to bolster their deplorable condition, as almost any other person . . . yet I feel myself more called upon to relinquish them and to endeavor to find some more tranquil place, where my services can be appreciated and where I feel I can be more useful."[65] That winter he and his family moved in with Susan so that Charlotte would be closer to medical care in her advanced state of pregnancy. Too often the river was impassable from ice floes and the post doctor could not get through to the

Canadian side.[66] John Henry was born January 5, 1838.[67]

By now the McMurrays began to feel they could not get away from the Sault fast enough, so fed up were they with its atmosphere. "The Sault seems to be getting worse every day. Nothing is heard of but balls and drinking, in the former of which I am sorry to say John participates freely."[68] William hoped that Bishop Samuel A. McCoskey of Michigan would find a pulpit for him in the Pontiac area, but he would take up farming there if he had to.[69] Henry had bought some Oakland County lots for him.[70] John was thinking about leaving the Sault, too, with all its iniquities, and William urged Jane to encourage him in this. "Your mother says that if we all go and settle near Pontiac, she will also go, and endeavor to persuade Waishkey also."[71]

But the mass migration never occurred. Susan left home March 3 to select a new sugar bush; her old one had been destroyed by a storm last summer. Her announced "final" sugaring the previous year of course was not. She still fished every fall as well, having made 23 barrels of whitefish and herring in 1837. The third week in April the family was horrified to see her stumble up to the house from the canoe landing with one side of her face drawn, greeting them with slurred speech. Fortunately, the stroke had been a mild one,[72] and by the end of May she was sufficiently recovered that Charlotte was willing to leave her.

Once more the McMurrays traveled in search of a bishop—and once more he eluded them. This time it was the Bishop of Michigan, who had gone off to Chicago. They hung around Detroit waiting, and visited the church in Pontiac where William hoped to be assigned.[73] But the prospect was so uncertain that after a few weeks they went on to Toronto to see what might be available there. The only firm offer William turned up was a post as assistant curate of two small combined parishes, Ancaster and Dundas. He was inclined to turn it down, however, as he much preferred a post in Michigan. Bishop McCloskey, when finally contacted, had several other possibilities besides Pontiac, including Ypsilanti and Dexter.[74]

While he was in Toronto he went to see Clarke

Gamble, the lawyer he had hired the previous year. He recommended that the family execute a deed in McMurray's favor so that the patent for the Canadian land due John Johnston's heirs could be issued to him and he (McMurray), in turn, could issue separate deeds to each of the other heirs. William sent it on to Henry for action, urging him to hurry so that the land could be selected before the choicest parcels were gone. Meanwhile he talked to Gamble about filing for additional acreage in the name of Lewis Johnston who had died before he ever had a chance to take up the award that was due him.[75] William also had some new ideas about the two sets of family claims on the other side of the Atlantic—the old war losses and the Irish legacy. He was becoming as enthusiastic about resurrecting the family fortune as George had been a few years before. And William was only slightly more realistic.

In fact, it was contemplation of the patrimony issuing from the father-in-law he never knew that induced William to stay in Canada after all. If he left now to take up American residence it might jeopardize the various claims. He would make the sacrifice for the sake of the family and accept the Ancaster-Dundas job. In connection with the war losses he had a different suggestion. ". . . if the family could unite and subscribe $125 each, making in all $1000 it would be sufficient to bear our expences [sic] to England, . . . where Charlotte might lay it in person before Her Majesty . . . and I am sure the decision would be favorable . . . . I have no particular desire to go to England, unless for the benefit of the family,"[76] but friends in Toronto could arrange the audience, and he could attend to the Irish business at the same time.

But now that Henry was living in Detroit, he was less inclined to be enmeshed in family affairs. The intellectual life of the city pleased him—in informal exchange of ideas with like-minded men, and in formal associations like the Historical Society, the Algic Society, and the Lyceum, all of which he was instrumental in founding. He continued to be elected to membership in academic societies all over the country and abroad. In March of 1837, Governor Mason appointed him a regent of the University of Michigan, now building a new campus at Ann Arbor. He completed the first volume of his *Algic Researches* that year, a diffuse work that reproduced a great many of the legends and stories he had heard, as well as his own observations about Indian life and language. He took up the study of Hebrew grammar, teaching it to his children as well, to compare it with the Indian. He was prone to accept the hypothesis that the Indians represented some or all of the ten lost tribes of Israel.[77]

Although Jane enjoyed the easier domesticity and social life of the new state's capital city, she missed her family and was always happy to return to Mackinac for the summer. In 1837 she decided to stay on for the winter. Henry's nephew, Francis Shearman, also wintered there in the dual capacity of sub-agent and tutor to the Schoolcraft children, as the only school on the island did not open this year. Shearman and Ord at Sault Ste. Marie were the last two appointments to the office of sub-agent that the government would make. Shortly thereafter the Commissioner of Indian Affairs adopted Henry's recommendation for abolishing sub-agencies and raising the pay of interpreters. Henry also proposed establishment of a normal school to train interpreters in Indian grammar, but the government rejected that idea.[78] William was now interpreter for his father-in-law, Ambrose Davenport, who also worked for the War Department at this time.[79] While Jane lived at Mackinac, Henry stayed at the American Hotel, where James and Anna Maria were living until they finished building their house. He shared some of James' enthusiasm for politics and current events, especially his support for the Canadian rebellion.

> The [sympathies] of every friend of constitutional liberty are with the Canadians. They demand only what is right—a popular & free representation—the power to elect counsellors &c. [80]

But Jane's life was filled with more immediate concerns.

> I cannot enter into the subject of Politicks. [sic] I am content to . . . leave *this* subject to *Men*, altogether, as I think Women have a more appropriate sphere in domestic duties. Both Mrs. Stuart's letter & my sister Anna's were filled with politicks, [sic] & I care not to be called *unpatriotic*, so long as I obey the laws of the land I live in, without *intermeddling* in the *obvious* duties of the *other* sex. Yet I feel interested in the Canadians, I hope they wil [sic] succeed in their efforts for freedom, perhaps the U.S. will aid them.[81]

One wonders why she chose to winter at Mackinac. Management of the household with an impudent serving girl, location of the agency office in her home with the traffic it involved, as well as her distress when she observed its mismanagement (the government would move the office to the Indian Dormitory when it was completed in 1838), the raising and education of children aged eight and ten, loneliness, and her own ill health, all combined to make life very hard for her.

> The dear children are doing well under Francis' teaching, tho' Johnston requires stricter care & watchfulness than I can give him, he is so independent & boisterous I cannot at all times manage him. I have given the whip to Francis . . . but he is loathe to use it. . . . Janee. . . obeys implicitly, & cheerfuly all that is commanded her, & is learning household duties speedily. . . . *I cannot attend to all the family concerns* in my *present weakness*. . . . I have had a great deal to *oppress me, public & private*, & how often have I wished you here! William is too much engrossed in his own happiness to think of *me* or *mine*, & I seldom see him or his Wife, but she is *excusable*, she is preparing for a stranger, but I am alone all the time & I think it is not right, as I am so weak & faint. Excuse my telling you all I *feel* & *fear*, I have no one else to go to but you, on this side of the grave, & perhaps I shall not long trouble you,

& no doubt it will be a blessed day, when you are released from such a mortal coil.[82]

Her handwriting shook, which may have been attributable to the fact that "the palpitations of my heart is so great at times, that I know not what to do."[83] She depended more and more on medication to relieve her pains and anxieties, but when she ran out she could not so readily replace it.

In response to a request William McMurray wrote to say "I am sorry to say that I have no Laudanum . . . but I have Opium and will in the morning ask the Doctor here how it is to be made and send you his receipt. I hear it is very simple, but am ignorant of the quantity to a quart of Brandy or High Wines."[84] Meanwhile, Henry sent her some digitalis from Detroit. He had been unable to reach Dr. Pitcher to ask about its efficacy, but he had heard it was good for nervous complaints. In the same letter he responded to her views on politics and women: "Ladies may be intelligent on the subject without being stigmatized as politicians. Every mother should know her rights, & be able to tell her children theirs."[85]

But Jane continued to be preoccupied with her personal troubles.

> I have had *trials* and *sorrows*, such as I did not at all anticipate when you left me . . . I have often thought that *public* duties bring their own fame and reward, but the unobtrusive duties of domestic life are not *even* thought upon; with all its cares & troubles & *incessant* appeals to forbearance and patience; nor is a word spoken, in praise or encouragement to the devoted person who sacrafices [sic] health & *ease* in the fulfillment of these oft neglected duties, & yet human nature is the same in *Man* or *Woman.* Perhaps the latter requires more encouragement.[86]

Despite her illness and anxieties she retained her absorption in her husband. "I beseech you to tell me all you *do, feel, fear, hope* & *expect* temporally & spiritually, & how,

& where you are lodged, whom you visit &c as you used to do, on similar separations, for none on earth can feel more interested than your own Jane."[87]

One interesting distraction for the family during the early summer of 1838 was a visit from their English cousin, George Johnston. The poor man was robbed of his portmanteau soon after his arrival in New York in March, losing most of his money, his gold watch, new clothes, and gifts he had brought for the family, about £150 worth in all. As his pension from the Customs House, from which he had just retired, was only £75 a year, it was a heavy loss.[88] But he made his way to Mackinac in June, nevertheless, where he met the American George, Jane, Henry, William, James, and Anna Maria. Then he went on to the Sault for a longer stay, where he boarded at Mrs. Cadotte's and enjoyed visits with Susan, Eliza, and poor Louisa.[89]

In the early summer of 1838 Henry made a quick trip to Washington (2,000 miles round trip in 25 days),[90] where he settled accounts at the Treasury, had three treaties ratified that he had drawn, and tended his political fences. His planning for the following year signalled important changes in his family's life. After only two years in Detroit he obtained permission to live wherever he chose. After the 1838 payments were made to almost 5,000 Indians, the Schoolcrafts moved east—the children to start boarding school and their parents to spend the winter of 1838-39 in New York City. They made a holiday of the trip. Leaving New York "in the cars" on December 12, they stopped first at Princeton to enroll Johnston at Round Hall School, and then at Philadelphia to enroll Janee at the Misses Guild's School, arriving in Washington for the holiday season, where they took lodgings "at my excellent friends, the Miss Polks."[91] After two weeks of parties and political calls by Henry, they returned to New York the way they had come, this time leaving the children at their respective schools, while Jane and Henry took up residence at 62 Greenwich Street.[92]

Jane missed her children dreadfully and felt quite cut off and alone in the large and growing city. The children had never been "absent from me more than a few days since their birth & not having any others near me to lavish the overflowing of a Mother's foolish, fond, heart, I have indeed been at times a sad picture of forlornness, but I know it is for their good & I strive to feel reconciled."[93]

Henry missed the children, too, but took the view that "without education, children grow up, like the beasts to perish." His hopes for them "are especially based, on that mixture of the Anglo Saxon blood, which they derive from their father, and the *eastern mind* so strongly exemplified in the *Algic* race. Without the *former*, the result is, a want of *forsight*, [sic] and *firmness* —two traits, that man *cannot* spare, and *excell* in the sterner duties of human life."[94]

To add to Jane's anxieties, George wrote that Mama had suffered another mild stroke, and Johnston, whom she felt was too young at age ten to be separated from his mother, was not happy at his school. Fortunately, Janee was contented, and Jane was overjoyed to hear from her.

> I felt very anxious to hear from you as *poor, dear, little* Johnston had written twice to me since I left him . . . he begs very hard to come to us & seems to be quite unhappy. . . . I am much pleased to learn that you have resumed your Music. You do not say anything about drawing, I hope you will not give it up, unless it interferes with more important studies, as we wish you rather to possess the *substancials*, [sic] more than the *ornamentals* of education. . . . I send you a list of misspelt words as you wished I should, remember to have your diction-ary beside you when you read or write.[95]

Jane Schoolcraft was not the only one to be lonely and home sick that winter. Her sister, Charlotte, living at Dundas in Upper Canada since September did not "know how I can even live so far from my friends; for this part of the country seems quite out of the world to me; but I hope at no distant day we shall go back to Michigan where we hope to find a permanent home. Dear Jane it would not be much out of your way if you could . . . pay us a visit on your way up to Mackinac. I need not say how happy we should be to see you both . . ."[96] Although lonely, the McMurrays were living very comfortably in a new brick house, with nine rooms and three acres of ground.[97] And the children gave them great joy. "Willy . . . is becoming very intelligent indeed and is constantly full of strange questions. John Henry has grown quite large and handsome, he is just beginning to stand alone, and can say a few words; I am sure his name sake would be proud of him if he could see him."[98]

William could not say he was unhappy with his situation. Both Dundas and Ancaster were pretty places, among fertile hills, with about 1400 people living in the former and 1000 at the latter.[99] His duties were very different from missionary work, with much sermon preparation, but his parishioners were kind to him and appreciative. Like Charlotte, however, he did not feel at home there. Although the cost of living was lower than in Michigan, his $700 per year salary was barely enough to live on after paying $120 rent. And living so long on the frontier "has made me too much of a *Republican* to live much longer in Canada,"[100] although when civil war seemed imminent during the 1837 rebellion he could not "think otherwise than that the Canadians are in fault, and that they will be speedily brought to their senses."[101] His continuance there was justified, in his own mind, only by its benefit to the family claims.

His attorney advised him to bring the war losses to Parliament when it convened at Toronto in February of 1839. He wrote Henry to send affidavits of the same kind that he had used before Congress three years earlier, only this time Mr. Ramsey Crooks should "add in his affidavit that Mr. Johnston was absent from home, and assisting Colonel McDouall at . . . Mackinac, as I suppose he can, for he was there I believe at the time, it would still add something to the strength of the claim."[102] The arguments used before one government would not do for the other. But William was certain the time was propitious, "as we may expect that the family will be brought into notice at House, [sic] by the appearance of Mrs. Jameson's work; in which I have every reason to believe they will be favorably mentioned. This seems Providential, and I think will do something for us."[103]

Parliament could and would do nothing, however, and a year later the McMurrays petitioned the Governor General of Canada. "Yours is not a case," came the answer, "in which any relief can be afforded in this Province, and that relief, if obtained at all, must come from the Home Government . . . "[104] If Reverend McMurray would draw up a statement addressed to the Secretary for the Colonies, His Excellency the Lieutenant Governor would send it along in his dispatches. William had gone precisely the same round that his unknown father-in-law had chased 20 years before. But the well-wishers among his Toronto friends convinced him that he was now in the home stretch, and he reiterated his old suggestion that each member of the family chip in $200 for him and Charlotte to "undertake the fatigue" of going to England (and Ireland). "Charlotte's appearance at Home would excite a good deal of interest, and by letters that we can obtain here, to persons of influence at court, there is not the *least doubt of our success.*"[105]

But the family was not about to finance a trip abroad for the McMurrays. Certainly not for the 1814 losses, which the rest of them had finally written off. After two and a half more years of trying through petitions to England that were turned down, William finally did too. As for the Irish estate, in September 1837, Henry Kearney wrote that McNeil finally acknowledged that the £800 John left in the estate by Deed of Trust for his sisters did not become his, McNeil's, property after they died. "This is now entirely given up, and Mr. McNeale [sic] agrees to the decision of our lawyers, that, at the death of Mrs. Kearney, one moiety (400 pounds Irish) became payable to the representatives of Mr. Johnston and at my decease, the other half." He had just been paid £54 interest on that money, but was keeping it to defray expenses, "altho'. . . much less than I feared . . . yet still I have been obliged to incur some expence and must incur much more" before everything is settled.[106]

Between April 1837 and April 1838 a sum of about £597 was transmitted to Henry as family agent in three drafts. This probably represented the £50 due from

Jane Moore's estate and what remained of the £500 legacy from Aunt Nancy Johnston. But additional sums are unaccounted for, perhaps emanating from an additional legacy of Jane Moore to John. The total amounted to some $2,900 to be divided eight ways.[107] The rest of the inheritance re-mained in limbo.

McMurray had fared best in obtaining the Canadian land grant. "I have at length after great difficulty, succeeded in securing the land for your deceased Father's services during the late War," he wrote George. "But before the Deed will be given by the Government it is necessary that you should make an assignment of it to me . . . because you are residing without . . . this Province, secondly to save expense and expedite our getting it, which we would not have done had I not as one of the family been residing here, and thirdly to enable me to give transfer Deeds to each member of the family."[108] Notwithstanding his elaborate and detailed explanations of the hows, whys, and wherefores, of the legal requirements, William McMurray found his Johnston brothers-in-law overly cautious, not to say suspicious. Getting affidavits or powers of attorney out of them necessitated a long campaign.

Chapter Fourteen

The Wheel Turns

As the decade of the 1830s drew to a close the Lake Superior stepchild of the new state of Michigan and its "capital," Sault Ste. Marie, were about to leap in a new direction. The Schoolcrafts' good friend, Douglass Houghton, had given up his successful Detroit medical practice in 1836 to concentrate on making a fortune in real estate on the one hand and promoting the advancement of science on the other. He persuaded Governor Mason and the State Legislature to establish a state geological survey in 1837, the first so sponsored in the nation. Houghton was, of course, appointed director.[1]

He and his tiny field staff got to the Lake Superior part of the survey in the summer of 1840. Five months of crawling around the steep, forested crags that lay in a swath, striated with swamps, along the length of the desolate Keweenaw Peninsula revealed the presence of rich veins of copper ore beneath the surface. Another summer of work in 1841 confirmed the findings including maps, and the first miners arrived in 1842.[2] By 1843 the nation's first mineral boom was on. The hoard of prospectors must come through Sault Ste. Marie upbound, where enterprising merchants supplied them with gear and transportaton, and the ore that returned downbound had to be portaged around the rapids. Consequently, the village boomed too, to the consternation of respectable folks. "The most striking feature of the place is the number of dram shops . . . the roar of bowling alleys and the click of billiard balls."[3]

These developments still lay in the future when Indian affairs were reorganized again in the summer of

1839 after the Ottawas decided to move in large numbers back to their ancestral home on Manitoulin Island.[4] In the general shifting around the department decided to make the native village on Grand Traverse Bay, where there had been a mission for several years, a focal point for the education and training of Indians in agriculture and mechanical arts. Henry offered George Johnston the post of mechanic there, at a salary of $600.[5]

George had not had steady employment since he resigned from the Indian Agency in 1834. He had worked only on temporary assignments as an interpreter on special missions for the Indian Department; he had done some translating for Reverend O'Meara, McMurray's replacement at the Sault,[6] and he had taken a flier at a commercial venture or two. He had even volunteered to raise a force of half-breed Chippewas to "aid in the subjugation of the 'Southern Indians',"[7] during the tragic Second Seminole War, but was turned down because the department had sufficient manpower at its disposal.

Despite these disappointments, George had lived handsomely on the proceeds of Indian debt payments to trader Johnston and treaty payments to Kah-men-tay-ha, son of Oshaw-guscody-way-quay. Under the Treaty of 1836 he had filed, in addition to his own claims, for a share of the proceeds from the cession of his late wife's ancestral lands. This vast tract fronted for 13 leagues on the Lake Superior shore near the Black River and extended inland to its headwaters. Louisa, or Way-se-ge-mon-aqua, as the eldest, had inherited through her grandfather, Gitchy Gansinay, and George claimed inheritance from her.[8]

When ready cash gave out (he had invested quite a bit in Detroit and Oakland County real estate) he ran up bills—such as one that totaled $176 for silver cutlery, candlesticks, coffee and tea pots, rings, books, and 38 yards of carpeting.[9] He requested people like his brothers-in-law McMurray[10] and James Schoolcraft (Henry was more skittish) to buy things for him when they traveled below, then took forever to pay them back. He was negligent in meeting the bills for his sons' education, especially after Bacon closed his school to work for the University of Michigan.[11] The boys had been happy there, were nicely behaved, and had done well scholastically; Bacon was a good teacher and a warm human being. In June of 1838 he asked in the politest of terms for George to pay 32 weeks of board for the two children at $3 per week, tuition at $12.50 per quarter, books, new shoes, laundry, etc., a total of $268.[12] In August he appealed to Henry Schoolcraft, who acted as the boys' guardian in Detroit, for assistance in the collection.[13] In December he was still pleading with George.[14]

With the prospect of a new job in hand, the 43-year-old George, after eight years of widowhood, decided to remarry. The lady of his choice was Mary Rice, a 36-year-old woman from Boston, who had come to live with her brother at the Sault several years before and was assisting the Binghams in the instruction of Indian girls. He had been seeing her off and on for years, and they were married July 16, 1839 at Mackinac.[15] Mary was a "bright, capable, energetic woman,"[16] warm and extremely well liked. She was appointed interpreter at Grand Traverse at a salary of $300. Together, the newlyweds did not do badly.[17]

Louisa remained with her grandmother, but they took John George, age 12, with them, and Henry William, now 14, was apprenticed to John Hulbert for three years. Hulbert, in turn, "obligates himself to board and clothe said H.W. Johnston in a proper and respectable manner (endeavoring at all times to facilitate his improvement as clerk in the merchantile [sic] business) and in the event of the faithful performance of the duties required of him to pay him the sum of One Hundred Dollars at the expiration of said three years."[18] Hulbert's first report of him was a good one.

> I sincerely hope that before spring opens he may be a scholar in Grammar. He has commenced that study and will soon begin to parse. I am endeavoring to teach him music too and think that these two studies will afford him more pleasure & great benefit this winter than reading & history. He is no great singer but I think will blow the flute well by little practice. He is sometimes lonesome and I often pity him when I see him

inclined to play with such boys as I cannot place on a par with him.[19]

James Schoolcraft was back in the area too. His sojourn as a gentleman farmer in southern Michigan was short-lived, and in the summer of 1838 Henry appointed him keeper of the Indian Dormitory at Mackinac at an annual salary of $600,[20] later raised to $1,000.[21] He presided over the building that was constructed that summer (and still stands) for "receiving their visits, and transacting their business, both during the payment of the annuities and at other seasons, together with rooms for storing and issuing provisions . . . and apartments for temporary visitors."[22]

William Johnston was shocked when he learned of the appointment. He had fully expected the job to be his; Henry had virtually promised it.[23] Henry's excuse for substituting James was that William was again active in the Indian trade, and therefore disqualified for the job. Nor could he be allowed to work as an interpreter. In his distress William wrote a letter of protest to the commissioner of Indian affairs, who, in turn, inquired of Henry. Henry justified his action by submitting a statement, signed by several merchants of the village, that William had gone into trade.[24] When William learned of this he became very angry, an anger that seethed within him for over a year before he took his revenge.

Meanwhile James and Anna Maria were happy living at Mackinac, and their happiness brimmed over on March 4, 1839, when "our Maria 'bro't forth' a *nice little* (about a 5 pounder) daughter which with the mother is *doing well*. We call the little Miss, Helen Maria Evalyn. The Helen after [our] sister Helen, the Evalyn for romance, and the Maria to render the whole a little musical."[25]

Jane was the first to arrive back at Mackinac after the family's winter in the East, Henry having stopped off at Detroit. The time until the children arrived home from school seemed interminable to her.

I have got the house all arranged & fit for your & the children's occupation, it looks *so* comfortable,

> & every thing is *so* clean that I wish you here to enjoy your own home. . . . I keep employing myself in patching & mending the furniture & sundries little things that are necessary. I have been so much on my feet since I moved into the house that my limbs and feet are swelled every evening as big as my head, but I get Eliza to rub me with the camphor & flesh brush before going to bed & I get up in the morning *fresh* for the days work.[26]

Much debate occurred in the family about the wisdom of Jane housekeeping, rather than living with James and Anna, but her joy at being home again helped her to overcome her infirmities. She might not be able to cope when her household was full and busy, but in anticipation of its completion she was fired with ambition.

She had only about a month to enjoy her children, and part of that time they were sick, before they were off to school again, outfitted with new clothes and linen. Henry transferred Johnston to Wolcott Marsh's school in Brooklyn, where he was happier than last year, although Mr. Marsh reported a problem in the boy's occasional lying and his tendency to go places that were off limits.[27] Janee had done well at the Misses Guild's School, getting all Ps (for perfect), except one G (for good), as she was a very conscientious girl. Hard for her, then, was the minor tragedy she suffered on her return.

> The five dollars that you gave into my charge, I did not take out of the box that Mother had put them in; for fear of losing it; but it was either taken or got out in some way I know not how . . . . I hope you will not feel unpleasantly about it, as I think it was not through carelessness, [but] I have not money to buy anything on Christmas. I have not heard from Johnny lately; I hope he will come here on Christmas, for I am very homesick.[28]

To maintain the two children at school cost Henry $670 for all expenses, including 75 cents to extract four of Johnston's (presumably first) teeth.[29]

Henry and Jane spent the winter of 1839-40 at

Mackinac, so perhaps he was aware of the storm building up around him, with William at its eye. Henry Schoolcraft antagonized many people, not the least those he helped, by his sanctimonious manner and insufferable propriety. *He* never seemed to make an error of business judgment, or slip even momentarily in his morals. Moreover, he wore his authority heavily and behaved like a tin god in his domain. Yet he lived quite handsomely on a salary of $1,500 a year.[30]

The suspicion that he managed a good deal of private consumption on his public expense account had long smoldered at the Sault, along with resentment at his flagrant nepotism. Now a beneficiary of that nepotism, scorned, made up his mind to expose the superintendent (Henry's new title) as a political hack feeding at the public trough. In March of 1840 William went personally to Washington to lay his charges before the commissioner of the Indian Bureau, T. Hartley Crawford.[31] His reception there led him to believe that "the Department was predisposed against [Henry] and wanted only a cause to proceed against him and his removal is talked off [sic] as if it had been decided on."[32] Thus he wrote James, for whom he felt neither enmity nor jealousy. "I can assure you that my feelings toward you are those of a brother."[33]

But William misjudged the simplicity of the matter. The commissioner appointed an investigator and arranged a hearing for Henry, in which he was given the opportunity to answer each itemized charge with supporting evidence.[34] Henry could, and did, marshall an array of records, invoices, and character references from important persons to refute a primarily verbal and poorly documented case against him—brought, after all, by an unreliable and unsophisticated halfbreed. He had not been cultivating friends in high places all these years for nothing. William's grandstand play was doomed to failure.

William's chief support came from John Biddle, longtime merchant at Mackinac and political foe of Henry Schoolcraft, and Samuel Abbott, another leading Whig trader. They and others wrote letters to the Michigan delegation to Congress, and even to Congressman Duane Doty of Wisconsin, containing charges against Henry.[35] In addition, they submitted a petition for his removal from office. Given the instigator of the whole business, charges of nepotism were not exactly in order. But misuse of public funds for private benefit and withholding goods and services the government gave to the Indians were serious enough offenses in themselves. To top it off William threw in assertions of mismanagement that maligned his own brothers—"that George Johnston is employed as Carpenter at Grand Traverse, without knowing any thing about the business; & that John Johnston is employed as farmer at the same place without any knowledge of such a vocation . . . that the Interpreter at Grand Traverse [Mary Johnston] cannot speak Indian . . . He has gotten up a long list of charges, which will be found as destitute of trust, and as frivolous, as those I give as specimens affecting you."[36] So wrote James, who was not deceived about William's vindictiveness, despite the friendly letter.

The Court took depositions at Detroit and Sault Ste. Marie in May, in which "William swore the whole hog [but] crossed his own oath upon examination by Henry. . . . If William ever stood *low* he now stands *lower*. He attempted to prove that his *mother* had conveyed moccasins from this place that belonged to the Indian Department!"[37] Henry went down to Washington in June of 1840 to defend himself. He was equipped with his carefully preserved records and a deposition from his wife that answered 20 questions derived from the formal list of charges. Her testimony affirmed that needy Indians called frequently at their home (which until 1838 had been the same building as the office), that she often acted as interpreter for them, that they were never turned away without food, medical aid, or clothing according to their need, however inconvenient their calls, and were often supplied from the Schoolcrafts' private stock by her own hands.[38]

In addition, glowing letters of character reference were sent by important people to President Martin Van Buren, as well as Commissioner Crawford.[39] The letter to the President from R.D. Turner, member of the Michigan legislature, summed up their view of the case as a political ploy: "A faction covered by the pretence of seeking to expose fraud and corruption, have been aiming a secret blow at an administration and a party, which is the object of its bitterest hatred and ceaseless hostility." The prejudice and hostility against Mr. Schoolcraft can be "traced . . . to what I believe to be its true and *only* cause, namely, the faithfulness with which Mr. Schoolcraft discharged his duties." In trying to counteract the cupidity of the traders and protect the Indians, the letter went on to say, he arouses enmity and jealousy. Last fall's Democratic election victory, in which the Schoolcraft brothers were very active in a bitter contest, made matters worse, and his enemies combined to use "William Johnston [as] a very fit and ready tool. . . . Desperate in his fortunes, and known by all here, from his own avowal, to be personally hostile toward the Agent. Such is the man who has been a principal actor in this business."[40]

With William's character discredited and the traders' motives exposed as political, Henry was not unduly worried. "I have been most kindly, & even cordially received by the President . . . and Mr. Crawford, also by Mr. Calhoun," he wrote Jane. "I would do injustice to my feelings & opinions not to assure you, that I have no fears for the result. The whole matter will end, as it began, in smoke."[41] He was right, of course. On receiving the investigators' report, Commissioner Crawford came to the conclusion "that the management of the superintendent has been marked with ability, and that there is nothing to impeach his honor or integrity."[42] Henry was exonerated and turned the whole affair into a rather pleasant visit at the capital.

He stopped off to see Johnston in Brooklyn on the way down, and when he got to Philadelphia to visit Janee she asked to go along with him to Washington. She had been impatient since April for her August vacation.[43] She was doing well in her studies, and as he was not averse to showing off his 13-year-old young lady, he agreed. He took her to parties, dressed in demure white, where she met many famous and important people, including the President.[44] She made a favorable impression, and Henry was proud of her. But as the visit dragged into several weeks Janee became "tired of the city, and most anxious to return. She says she is wasting her vacation & will have but little time at Mackinac. She is admired here, and has recd [sic] both attentions & compliments, beyond those due to her age, but not beyond her modest worth, good sense, good looks, and uniformly amiable deportment."[45]

Jane was regretful that Johnston did not also get a visit to Washington.

> It would be worth many months of study, I think, to him *now*, he is so much older, & would be more observing I have been thinking, if you could get a worthy, intelligent man . . . to become his Preceptor *at home* it might be less expensive to fit him for College & Janee might finish her Education under such a Teacher, . . . & a great comfort to us both it would be to have them with us. For my own part, I do not expect to enjoy their blessed, cheerful company long, anyway, with one step in the grave, I may say, and they—ready to bound off into the stirring scene & conflicts of active life, will soon make a separation *inevitable.*[46]

She knew, of course, that it was futile to suggest taking the children out of school, that Henry would never hear of it. But they had been taken away from her so young, and she was so desperately lonely for them. Henry was kind to her—he was buying her dresses in Washington and was sending up a piano so that Janee could practice when she was at home[47]—but what she wanted most was her children.

More and more her letters seemed only to recite a litany of complaint. Trouble with surly servants plagued her as usual. And "*sometimes* we have turns of *fear* at night, surrounded by the yells of inebriate french [sic] & Indians, & often by the riots of *sailors* on shore. I have often wished for a good Brace of Pistols beside my little bed, & by the way, it would not be amiss to add a pair to your list of purchases for private use, set jesting aside."[48]

Mixed in with the troubles, major and minor—"the barrel of apples spoiled, but John put them in a barrel of rain water to get vinegar; all the corned beef is gone, no chickens killed lately, and the fish money I have used up, so come home before I am starved to death"[49]—some tidbits of pleasant news came through. William's Susan had a large boy (Jane was not speaking to them, of course; Anna Maria had gone to see them); John visited from Grand Traverse, where he is very satisfied with his job and is helping in the garden; "Sister Ann, has just been in to see me, & brought me as a present, from my poor, dear Mother, a beautiful little shawl of pale, orange colour"[50] However, the case filed against Henry placed her in a difficult position. "I have been the first to feel the effects of the *depositions* taken here last Month, as nothing now can be done without first ascertaining whether it is *public* or *private* service that is demanded, & *not a little* pride, is manifested when any thing is to be done for the house. It is hard to bear refusal, with the addition of *jaw* & impudence from that cause, I would rather do every thing myself, if I could."[51]

In addition to poor health she complained of loneliness—only the letters from him and the children enabled her to "bear, with sufficient patience & fortitude the many lonely hours I spend, without a soul to exchange a rational idea with for days on days together—& if *you* complain of having nothing to say, how am *I* to fill up a letter to you."[52] Yet when

> James & Ann . . . had been preparing to give a large party . . . I declined going . . . only by your side, would I like to appear in public, especially as *some* of the company are not altogether exempt from abetting those who . . . injure you—& today, I feel more & more pleased that I did not go, as they so far fought the rules of that very World they have hitherto dreaded to offend . . . by *dancing* ! & Mr. Hulbert acted as musician!—Monstrous—the very savages would point at them, & upbraid them.[53]

Dancing was bad enough, but Henry's and James' father had died that summer, and Jane took her mourning seriously, though to her disgust James and Anna Maria did not put on mourning clothes.[54]

After all the dust settled the one who suffered

most from the attempt to unseat Henry Schoolcraft was George Johnston. Despite the aspersions to George in the content of the charges, William assured him that "All the stories Mr. Schoolcraft told about my trying to injure you all is false. The government looks to him only, he is responsible. All the others obey his orders & the Ind Dept do not look to you for errors which he may have committed."[55] It was not George's alleged incompetence that lost him and his wife their jobs, however, but the evidence of nepotism which made the Commissioner of Indian Affairs most uncomfortable in exonerating Henry. George was the sacrificial lamb. At least Henry had the grace to express regret and to tell George that he had shown the investigator a letter from Cass commending George's important services to the country, as well as his offer to enlist a company of halfbreeds for the Florida war, but this evidence was probably not passed on to Crawford.[56]

But excuses brought no income to the family, which was about to grow by one more mouth. Benjamin Saurin was born September 25, 1840.[57] And the following spring another chicken came home to roost, when John Hulbert wrote George to say he was sending Henry William over in the mail boat.

> I am very sorry to say that he has disobeyed me in various things some of which may appear trifling in themselves but lead to unhappy results . . . he has neglected to keep the sabbath properly & grossly violated it, has associated with *low* company &c &c. He has been quite inactive & inattentive in business . . . tho I have taken much pains to make him respectable . . . I shall give him $5 to take with him and send him well clothed . . . shoud [sic] any pay be justly due I will settle with you another time.[58]

So much for the future of a bright and promising boy.

George fell back on his old stand-by—filing "claims" for a living. The one he had put in several years ago for his first wife's ancestral lands had availed nothing, but he would try it again now that a new opportunity arose. He sent a message through missionary Sherman

Hall at La Pointe, to "My Grand Father," Chief Buffalo. Having just learned that the chief was about to sell his land east of the Montreal River, George hoped he would remember his grandchildren, Louisa, Henry William, and John George, who were neglected when Chief White Crow sold his lands.[59]

But the British side of the family more successfully asserted land claims. George and the others had finally acquiesced in a power of attorney for William McMurray and in September of 1841 he succeeded in acquiring one more bit of property on the good name of John Johnston. "The quantity of land for a Captain's allowance is 800 acres, which must be located in certain districts, but as this was so much culled over, I was advised to make application to be allowed to take up Crown lands in lieu of Militia lands."[60] Since Crown lands were worth twice as much, he obtained 400 acres in Maidstone Township near Windsor. To save the expense of a survey for division he planned to send each member of the family a deed for his or her share, and strongly recommended that they keep it in one parcel until prices rose for a profitable sale. At the moment the government upset price was £8 Halifax currency, or $1.60 per acre, but William doubted it could be sold yet for that much. Taxes were $3.33 per year, and legal expenses came to $10 for each member of the family.[61]

It was clear by now that the McMurrays were going to stay in Canada, despite their often expressed wish to return to Michigan and their protest that they could not live properly on the salary paid by the two congregations. Henry showed little sympathy. "I had a letter from McMurray yesterday," he wrote Jane. "He is tired of Canada & will come back, at all events, and when he has been in Michigan a few months, will be tired here & wish to go somewhere else. He is living beyond his means, has squandered away money in travel abroad and is blown about by unsteady purposes."[62] Charlotte received a more sympathetic hearing from her sister when she apologized for the delay in answering letters.

> But my dearest sister my pen would not have been inactive so long had I only consulted my

> wishes; for there is not a day, no not an hour passes that I am not with you all: distance, time or absence, can never remove from my heart the sincere attachment I have for you all. My only apology is, constant employment on account of bad servants, which is my greatest complaint.

She hoped to visit home in the spring if some windfall occurs, because

> I shall wait long enough if I should depend on Mr. McM's small income to do so. [But William's] labours are wonderfully blessed in this place as well as in Ancaster, his Churches are well filled every Sunday, and he has two flourishing Sabbath schools. He seems to be very much beloved by his congregations, he is blessed far beyond his expectations.[63]

Perhaps these rewards of satisfaction, despite hard work for little pay, convinced William that he should make do with what the Lord allotted him and not chase ephemeral fortune. After corresponding with Henry throughout the winter of 1840 about a chaplaincy at Mackinac, two events occurred in the spring that convinced him to stay where he was. After a miscarriage the previous year, Charlotte was "safely confined [May 28, 1840] . . . and has presented me with another *immense* Boy. . . . She never had so favourable a time, for which we have great reason to be thankful."[64] They called him James Saurin. Even more significant for their future, William "was admitted to the *higher order* of the Ministry (a Priest in the Church of God) by the Bishop of Toronto, on the 12th of April. It is a *fearful responsibility* which I have taken."[65] He was now eligible to be appointed Rector to his two parishes and filled the vacancy recently opened; the future looked much brighter. The parishes were about to build a splendid new church, expected to be the handsomest in Canada and seat 600 people. William was responsible for raising the $6,000 in subscriptions.[66] He had found his calling.

It was now Henry Schoolcraft's turn to face a

change in the winds of fortune. In the election of 1840 the Whig Party attained power, and the days of Henry's long political appointment were numbered. After the inaugural of President William Henry Harrison, he went to Washington to see what maneuvering room was left to him. Jane wrote him from Detroit of talk against him and his associates, now that they had lost favor and power. Then

> last Friday evening . . . Johnston . . . stopped at the P.O. knowing how anxious I was to hear from you, & exulting handed me a letter having the Washington P. Mark & the handwriting being very much like yours, I tore it open (though it was addressed to you) not the least doubting it was for me—and sure enough! its contents providence designed I should be the first to know in this place, as a fact. It was a letter from Mr. Cochrane, announcing the appointment of Mr. R. Stuart to your Office . . . I could not restrain my tears.[67]

Henry, though disappointed, even affronted in light of what he considered his scrupulous impartiality in the conduct of his office, nevertheless received the setback with mixed emotions. He worried about money. Now it was his turn to cast about for a new source of income. On the other hand, he had lived on the frontier for 21 years, craving more of the personal interaction with men of importance and learning than he had been able to achieve through voluminous correspondence and brief, infrequent visits to metropolitan centers. Nor was residence in the hinterland favorable to promoting his books or the education of his children. A change might even improve his wife's health. He decided to move permanently to New York, where opportunities abounded for a man of his talents.[68]

For a start he planned a magazine, to be published simultaneously there and in London. It would focus on his favorite topics—Indian language, legends and characteristics. When William McMurray wrote to applaud the idea he reiterated his hope that the

Schoolcrafts would visit at Dundas on the way to New York, as they needed to discuss so much family business.[69] Moreover, the McMurrays were much easier to reach now that regular steamer service was available between New York state and Hamilton, Ontario, and they lived only five miles from Hamilton on macadamized roads.[70]

But the visit was not in the offing for this year either. Robert Stuart, who had retired from the American Fur Company and moved to Detroit in 1833, was anxious to move into the agency as promptly as possible for the conduct of the summer business with the Indians. Henry went to New York in June to find housing, leaving Jane to pack up for the move, with James' assistance in selling off their furniture and effects.[71] James had his hands full with his own affairs, however, as Anna Maria gave birth to a son at the beginning of the month and was very ill. "We are all up side down here, both at the Dormitory and at Jane's," he wrote George a month later.[72]

It was a hard time for Jane, although she was too busy to indulge the emotional response to the transplantation of her life. She worked slowly, so as not to exhaust herself, and as always, in crisis her mother moved in to help her. Despite her strokes, Susan's health was good, but her eyes were giving her trouble. John George escorted Louisa on a four-day trip from Grand Traverse to Mackinac, so that she and Janee could visit. The two girls were close cousins, and Janee was happy to give Louisa the assistance she needed. But Jane found it much harder to manage Johnston when John George was there. The two of them went racing around the place against Henry's orders, and she feared for the kind of trouble they might get into together that Johnston might avoid if left to himself.[73]

Yet Jane's spirits remained remarkably high, for a while at least.

> I found the touching lines you wrote on your departure . . . I know not why! but hope & trust, in brighter days, predominate with me, & anticipation of peace & comfort glance before me, like

the beautiful, softened beaming of the sun, awhile, before it leaves the World to rest, after a furious storm that bent (not broke) the plants & shrubs, leaving them refreshed by the rain, ready to bloom afresh with renewed vigor on the morrow. & my trust is—that the Lord will prepare the way before you & that all will work together for good to us in the end.[74]

But she also endured some righteous anger.

The selling off, of the furniture & the necessary consequences attendant on similar proceedings make our stay here any longer very unpleasant, & absolutely uncomfortable. We have been exposed to the prying curiosity of persons who felt privileged to come & ransack the whole house in pretence of seeing what was to be purchased . . . the purchasers are so unaccommodating as to take all they buy immediately away. . . . In addition to this harrassing state from without, we have had continued trouble from that unsconscionable [sic] perverse creature in the Kitchen—all the other trials are as a drop in the bucket compared to what I have endured from that foul-mouthed old hag.[75]

Perhaps the distress associated with the speedy stripping of the house and the prying of curiosity seekers to see how the mighty had fallen was just as well for taking the edge off the wrench of departure from a beloved homeland. Finally, by mid-August all was in readiness—the furnishings sold, the treasures of a lifetime packed up, the last farewells repeated—and the family embarked on the steamer, followed by the railroad, to their new home at 224 West 19th Street, New York City.

The winter of 1841-42 passed pleasantly enough for Jane, with the distractions of visits to and from old friends. If she missed her parental family, the feeling was returned in kind. Anna Maria wrote in November that they anxiously awaited a first letter, that "poor Mama despairs altogether of ever seeing you again, and the only comfort she expects is to hear from you often."[76]

Charlotte had written her almost immediately upon her arrival in New York.

> My dearest sister . . . altho' averse as I am to letter writing . . . I some times feel very homesick and fancy that I am forgotten by my dear relations . . . I have never received an answer to a letter I wrote you . . . I think it is about two years now, I do not know whether you ever received it or not. But my dear Jane if I had written to you as often as I intended, since I last wrote, you would have been tired of my correspondence . . . I think you would be pleased with this place, and if ever you should find N.Y. not healthy, you should come and spend a few months with us, it is very healthy here.[77]

To Charlotte's joy a letter came in the spring telling of Jane's intention to visit at last. Henry's publishing venture enabled him finally to make the trip to Europe that he had yearned for the past ten years. But Jane did not feel up to the long ocean passage.[78] With the children together at Mr. and Mrs. Parsons' school at Albany,[79] she would spend the time of his absence with the sister to whom she had always been closest. Jane offered to make herself useful while visiting the McMurrays by instructing their children. Charlotte could only

> pray earnestly to him who ordereth all our goings and doings . . . that we may not meet with disappointment in this our long wished for meeting, that it may prove for the comfort and good of us all, for the benefit of our never dying souls. . . . I have been in Canada for four years and I have not seen a single old friend that I could converse with about old times, let alone open my mind to, excepting the time Brother William passed through on his way to Washington, and he stayed only a few hours with us, and his visit I must say was of such a nature that I did not enjoy it much.[80]

On April 30, 1842, Henry took Jane up to Dundas. They arrived at tea-time, Jane reclining on the sofa to take hers, as she was exhausted from the trip and had a slight cold. She went to bed early, leaving Henry to sit up talking with William until midnight. At four o'clock the next morning Henry was on his way again.[81] By May 4 he was back in New York, at the Astor House. "I have just sent my baggage aboard the Roscoe and am ordered to be on board myself tomorrow morning at an early hour. So I sat down to bid you adieu." He had paid all his debts and arranged his affairs, should he go down in the Atlantic Ocean. He had told the children to be economical because he had no fixed income, "and I give you the same advice . . . you must aid me—*you must hold up my hands*, by letting me see that you are at the age of 42 adequate to the [letter blotted] which is set before you. . . . Remember me affectionately to all. Once more, & finally, adieu!"[82]

The sisters enjoyed three weeks of comradeship and talk of old friends and home. Jane was as frail and feeble as ever but happy. On the evening of May 22 Charlotte helped her undress and get into bed, then went downstairs for a few minutes. On returning to the room to say goodnight Charlotte's own blood seemed to stop in her veins as her sister failed to answer the cheerful words. While she stood rigid in fear Jane stopped breathing before her eyes.[83] It was unbelievable. Jane had ailed and predicted her own demise for so long that they had all become accustomed to it. No one, not even Jane herself, truly expected her to die so suddenly.

By the time the news reached Henry in London, she was long buried in St. John's churchyard at Ancaster. He wrote to his forlorn 15-year-old daughter on June 16.

> Yesterday's mail from America, brought me the heart rending news from Dundas. Little did I anticipate such a result, when I left your poor mother. . . . I was impressed with the feeble & wasted state of her frame, on the trip, although it was nothing different, perhaps, from what it had been long previous. . . . . But how little we know

of our destiny, and how blind we are to all that is in the path before us!

> The bitterest reflection arises from her having, apparently, *died alone in her chamber.* . . . But we have the assurance from her habitual faith & constant reliance on her bible & supplication, that her end was peace, . . . that she is gone to join . . . the redeemer in heaven. . . . There, she will recognize her father, our dear Willy, and his little sister, and her brother Lewis to whom she was tenderly attached.[84]

His eulogy was of private remembrance.

> When I first saw her in 1820, her refinement, taste, propriety of manners, purity & delicacy of language, correctness of sentiment, were such as few females, in any rank or station possess . . . she was, so long as her health permitted, a most devoted mother . . . and her attention & care, in the superintendence & management of the house during my frequent & long absences as a public agent . . . were such as few, are able successfully to encounter. Her taste in literature, was chaste. She wrote many pretty pieces, which I have carefully [preserved]. Let us cherish her memory, and let us take occasion from her loss, to love each other, more & more, and strive to make ourselves examples of excellence in all that is worthy and noble.[85]

The tragic news from Dundas was not a shock to Susan—she had somehow known she would never see her beloved daughter again. But she was nonetheless grief-stricken and wished only that she could have nursed the child herself, as always. She wanted Jane's remains to rest at the Sault beside the father who adored her and her first two children.[86] But, for reasons known only to himself, Henry overruled her fond wish and insisted upon leaving the grave where it was. To honor Jane he ordered a handsome marble monument, inscribed[87]

JANE

Wife of Henry Rowe Schoolcraft, Esq.

Born at St. Mary's Falls
January 31st 1800

She died May 22nd 1842, in the arms of her sister, during a visit to Dundas, at the house of the rector of this church, while her husband was absent in England, and her children at a distant school. She was the eldest daughter of Jno. Johnston Esq. and SUSAN, daughter of

WAUBOJEEG

A celebrated War Chief and Ruler of the Ojibway Tribe. Carefully educated, of polished manners & conversation, she was early fitted to adorn society, yet of retiring & modest manners. Early imbued with the principles of true piety, she patiently submitted to the illness which for several years marked her decline, and was inspired through seasons of bodily and mental depression with the lively hope of a blessed immortality.

> Here rests, by kindred hands enshrined,
> All of the Loved One, earth could bind,
> The brow, the eye, the heart, the hand,
> So gentle once, so kind and bland.
> Death came unlooked for, yet his tread,
> She met so calm, so free from dread;
> Like angels, winged to happier spheres,
> She smiled to quit a world of tears:
> We mourn not then, as those who see,
> No glorious, bright eternity;
> But while this stone fond hands upraised,
> Grief best bespeaks our love and praise.

Chapter Fifteen

Accounts Closed

The political turnover of 1840 altered not only the fortunes of John Johnston's descendents and their spouses, but the personal relations among them. When Henry Schoolcraft moved to New York, he began the withdrawal from the family's complicated affairs that his wife's death completed. He continued to correspond from time to time with his brother and brothers-in-law, but he shed the burden of leadership he had carried for some 15 years. Each of the others was now on his own, to deal with the suspicion and mistrust, the shifting alliances and antagonisms that arose periodically among them as best he could, without Henry to take command.

After George lost his appointment as mechanic at Grand Traverse in 1840, he and his family stayed on in the house he had built there. They had nowhere else to go. But by September 1841, Robert Stuart, acting superintendent of Indian Affairs in the Whig administration, ordered him to vacate. George refused to do so until he was reimbursed the $222.50 of his own money invested in the house.[1] Stuart advised him to submit the bill, but vacate in the meanwhile or "rigorous measures" would be taken that "exclusive of the odium that would attach to your character . . . would cost you ten times more than the property is worth."[2] But the War Department refused to allow his unauthorized additional expenditure on a house that had been financed by the government—an old story with George.[3]

Yet he wanted nothing more than to farm at Grand Traverse. To that end he hoped to sell the Detroit property Henry had bought for him with the claim settlements emanating from the Treaty of 1836, pay off his debts, and buy a "good lot of land, and carry on a small safe business."[4] Accordingly, in August of 1841, he invited John Hulbert to buy out his $2,000 interest in the Cass Farm,[5] paying George $1,000 in goods and crediting the remainder against George's outstanding debt with him. But the depression resulting from the Panic of 1837 had not yet worked itself through. Hulbert would offer no more than $300 for George's interest in a property on which Henry had failed to maintain the payments, so the whole was about to revert to Cass anyway.[6]

George wasn't the only one who wanted to convert to cash his shares of the family-owned real estate bought with the proceeds of the treaty settlements. During the summer of 1839, while Susan was visiting with William and Anna Maria at Mackinac Island, she "consented to have the property divided . . . H.R. wants Ma to keep the place at the Sault & have no part in the property at Detroit—Mama does not wish it, & says an equal division must be made."[7] In August of 1841 George and James agreed to a division such that three of the ribbon lots were divided among the six children (excluding William, who was not, apparently, an original participant) with a separate deed for each, two lots reserved for Susan, and two lots retained by Henry in trust for the heirs.[8]

John Hulbert tried to convince both James and William McMurray that all of the heirs should put up more money to save the Cass property during the hard times in order to reap the future benefit of which he was certain. But either they could not or would not; several of them wanted out of the whole arrangement. Two years later Hulbert informed George that the property had, indeed, reverted to Cass and was therefore a total loss to both Henry and George, as was George's interest in another Detroit property he had bought with Schoolcraft and Hulbert. Furthermore, George's interest in a third parcel wasn't worth the amount of his debt to Hulbert, but Hulbert would settle for the real estate and $800 cash.[9]

Dissatisfaction with Henry Schoolcraft's accounting for the awards arising from the Treaty of 1836 surfaced again in September of 1843. Susan and William testified before the District Attorney at Sault Ste. Marie that Susan had never received $8,200 due her, as Henry alleged.[10] James supported them in a letter to Henry.

> If obliged to give evidence in court . . . all the heirs, will be obliged to state that they knew nothing of the transfer of the claim to you, or of your deposits in trust, as you term it, with Abraham [Schoolcraft]. . . . to show a *bona fide* transaction [you should] make an *actual* deposite [sic] of the funds, with me, now the only and legal agent of the Estate, as appointed by Mrs. Johnston. . . . My Powers from Mrs. Johnston are dated 6th of February last, up to which time you, as the agent of Mrs. J. had a legal right to retain the money.[11]

Henry's records are incomplete in this matter, but apparently he did ultimately distribute the proceeds in July of 1844.[12]

Although George was unable to raise cash to buy land, he built another house at Grand Traverse anyway, just in time for Mary to present him with a second son, James Kearney, October 2, 1842.[13] He was farming and traveling to the Indian camps in winter to do a little trading for furs, with his older boys along to help. The land there had not yet been surveyed, but custom allowed that "so long as the country does not come into the market, so long can we enjoy the priviledge [sic] of preemption without taxes to pay."[14] James Schoolcraft had encouraged him with his opinion that "Any person may *squat* on any of the public lands, before or after survey, and obtain his 160 acres after the lands are brought into market. . . . make my best bow to Madame, and remember me to all your children, not forgetting the young *Yankee*. When do you expect another; I am told the Yankee girls are terrible in that way, so I expect to hear from you again *soon*, or rather from your *better half*."[15]

After the inauguration of Harrison in March of 1841, James Schoolcraft expected his dismissal as keeper of the Indian dormitory to arrive at any moment. Meanwhile he continued to enjoy life on Mackinac Island. He was "engaged on my own work, at a weekly called the 'Bee'. It is perfectly a 'private concern', written wholly by myself, & composed principally of *fun* & *satire*, and is only seen by a few 'chosen spirits', among them Lt. Phelps, who is much pleased with what he calls my 'Pindar' style. I have given two parties this winter, besides *small affairs*, which has had a tendency to keep up the life of the place."[16] In November he was still in the job, and in fact remained in office until April, 1842. In anticipation of a necessary move, however, Anna Maria and the children spent the winter of 1841-42 with her mother at the Sault. But the taste she had had of big city life in 1838 spoiled her for the frontier village, and

> in the spring I shall try and prevail on him to go into business with Hulbert at Detroit . . . my cough increases, and I find this climate far too severe for me and then the prospects of a winter here is perfectly horrid . . . there is no society. . . . Oh! I wish it had been my lot to live in a city, the constant change and bustle would just suit me; but tis of no use to wish what I cannot get, and I must learn to be contented, though the lesson is hard. . . . I think I shall have to go to work and study something, to make the time fly . . . [17]

It was a harsh winter for them all. John was unable to find a job after he lost his $500 a year government appointment as farmer at Grand Traverse, and his mother was "in a bad way for eatables [and] cash."[18] James was virtually supporting them. And many deaths occurred from whooping cough that winter among the children of the Sault. Fortunately, the Schoolcraft babies escaped. The little boy, for whom they could not decide on a name, was dubbed Niagara Falls by his father. He grew fast, walked early, and danced when his Uncle John played the flute.[19] It was another year before the little fellow was finally christened Howard.[20]

When James finally lost his job in April of 1842 he had a hard time deciding where to settle. Susan was "anxious for me to remain at the Saut [sic], and says positively, if we go away also, she will seek her relatives at La Pointe and end her days with them. I would have no objection to remain here provided I could make the *ends meet.*"[21] He ultimately decided that he could, by opening a store that he hoped would prosper by selling at lower prices than his competitors.[22]

He also decided to activate his long standing interest in politics in a bid for elective office. He ran for the State Legislature in the fall of 1842, won handily, and was re-elected in 1843.[23] Chippewa County remained Democratic. In his usual wry way James took neither himself nor his colleagues too seriously. "Very little has been done by us *Honourable* men this winter. I always held that it was rather a disgrace than otherwise to be a member of the Michigan Legislature, and this winter's experience has not had the tendency to alter this opinion."[24] But his seat in the house enabled him to promote a project of signal importance to his constituency—construction of a lock and canal to bypass the rapids of St. Marys River.

In the first year of statehood, 1837, the legislature appropriated $25,000 for the project and asked Congress to donate land to finance the full estimated cost of $112,500. In September, 1838 a contract was let with a Buffalo firm, Smith and Driggs, to begin construction. When the advance party arrived at the Sault, Lieutenant Root, in command at Fort Brady, cautioned them that the canal must not interfere with the millrace, but Aaron Weeks, construction boss, insisted on excavating exactly there. Root called out the troops, and the workers dropped their shovels. So concluded the first attempt to build the St. Marys Canal.[25]

The state of Michigan continued its appeals to Congress for funding, and in 1840 a bill for donation of 100,000 acres for the project went as far as a third reading. Then Henry Clay rose to ridicule expenditure on such a large project "beyond the utmost verge of civilization, if not in the moon."[26] In 1844 James Schoolcraft was "almost certain" that the canal bill would pass, and the project, combined with "copper fever," should bring prosperity to the Sault.[27]

Sailing ships had been built from time to time on Lake Superior ever since Louis Denis, Sieur de la Ronde, commandant at La Pointe, built the first one in 1734 for his prospective venture into copper mining. Now, 110 years later, copper was again demanding ships. Instead of setting up a building yard, as the North West Company and American Fur Company had done, a new method was devised for bringing in ships that were constructed more economically in big shipyards below—hauling them across the portage on rollers, propelled by horse and capstan. The 55-foot schooner, *Algonquin*, built at Cleveland in 1838, was the first vessel hauled over in 1840. Intended for the fish and waning fur trade at first, she went into the copper trade after 1842. By 1845, when the boom moved into high gear, more shipping was desperately needed.[28]

In response the first steamboat, the 118-foot propeller *Independence*, was hauled over the portage. Several vessels followed in the next few years. But the launching of ships into Lake Superior did not solve the entire problem of the bottleneck. Equipment and merchandise still had to be hauled over the portage to be ferried by the ships upbound, and the returning copper had to be hauled across to vessels waiting below the falls. One Sheldon McNight and his gray horse held a commanding lead in the freight portage business, and in 1850 he and J.T. Whiting built a mile-long strap railway to carry a larger volume in carts pulled by horses. These two entrepreneurs understandably opposed the canal.[29] For ten years the threat to their near-monopoly was only a minor one.

While James was pursuing his political career, more sadness was in store for Susan after Jane's death. Her brother, Waishkey, died of consumption on November 27, 1842.[30] She, herself, continued her accustomed round of activities, the fall fishing and spring sugaring, and looking after her youngest daughter, who was almost as plagued with ill health as her oldest had been.

Shortly before the dawn of November 27, 1843, Susan awoke in distress, barely able to breathe. She sent for Anna Maria and the doctor, who bled her and applied the cupping glass. After a while she felt well enough to recite her morning prayers and get up for breakfast with the family. But by ten o'clock she was back in bed, with the doctor and Anna Maria at her side. Aware of what was happening to her, she would like to have seen and talked with George once more, but her greatest regret was for Evalyn and Howard. The little ones came to see her every morning and she felt badly that next time "when they come to see Grandma, she would be gone."[31] Within moments she was gasping for breath again, and as Anna Maria raised her up she died in her daughter's arms. The probable cause of her death at age 66 was coronary occlusion.[32] She was laid to rest in Riverside Cemetery next to her husband and the little lost grandchildren.

Although James' optimistic 1844 prediction about the Sault Canal was a decade premature, his own fortunes were rising at the time. He returned after the legislative session with an appointment as sutler to Fort Brady, a post he had sought for ten years.[33] And he was about to get in on the copper bonanza himself. Meanwhile, concerned about Anna Maria's health problems during the difficult Sault Ste. Marie winters, he sent her and the children south to spend the season with Charlotte at Dundas. James remained for a while in the old homestead, but was not happy with his housemates.[34]

Two years earlier, on September 10, 1842, John had married Justine Piquette.[36] Apparently the family didn't care much for her. William McMurray concluded that "This seals his fate. He will be nothing in future, but a companion for the Frenchmen of the place."[36] Their first child, Spencer Norval, was born March 27, 1843, and Anna Maria (known as Miss Molly) came along October 25, 1844.[37] James, after a couple of weeks of living with them, "found things too much *a la pickette*," and moved to rooms at Fort Brady. "For our amusement in the garrison we have a Theatre, a nine-pin alley & Billiard table—and this, with now and then a *Ball* will make up the sum total of our amusements." He added as an afterthought in his letter to George, "Old Mr. Perrault is dead."[38] Did he know of the connection to John Johnston that dated back 52 years?

James also had the family's endless business affairs to keep him occupied that winter. None of the Johnston sons was sophisticated or steady enough to assume management of their mother's affairs, and two of her sons-in-law lived far away during the last few years of her life. On February 6, 1843, she gave the son-in-law closest to her the power of attorney to act in her behalf.[39] James had now "officially" replaced Henry as her agent.

Not infrequently he was irritated by both Henry and William McMurray's handling of the tangled affairs John Johnston left behind him. James' antipathy to his brother waxed and waned. When Henry was planning his trip to Europe in the spring of 1842 it seemed eminently sensible for him to make a detour to Ireland and settle the estate there once and for all. Working through Kearney was an excruciating procedure. Nor was it difficult to detect in the man's convoluted letters a cunning to his perpetual stalling that probably enabled him to cream off a goodly part of the legacy for "expenses." In Henry's opinion, "The taking out of letters of administration by Mr. Kearney when there were Heirs living, *legal heirs*, & without their sanction or knowledge, was a sufficiently singular proceeding, to cause the heirs in America, to pause and doubt."[40]

To settle matters in Ireland it was necessary that one representative of the heirs be designated agent for them, and that required that they all sign a release to that effect. McMurray told Henry that James refused to sign because Henry was to be the agent, and suggested that he, William McMurray, be named instead.[41] In James' opinion McMurray "is a very queer *minister*, too fond of money, and possessed of rather too high notions of his own importance."[42] But he finally agreed to sign, persuade George and William to do likewise, and forward the document to McMurray, who would get it to Henry before he sailed on May 9, 1842.[43]

One year later Henry Kearney wrote that "The transaction with Mr. McNeale [sic] is nearly come to a conclusion—I expect the money to be paid in to my acct in a few days . . . Counsel advises that the money is to be paid in one sum to the administratrix . . . and she is to distribute it to the heirs."[44] When McMurray heard this he was angry. It was directly contrary to his expectation that the money was to be turned over to him for distribution. Because of James' interference and Kearney's overcautiousness, more paper would have to travel back and forth across the Atlantic, entailing further delay in obtaining the money they were all so anxious to get.[45]

McMurray's discomfiture did not bother James, however. "McMurray writes to Mrs. Johnston about the Irish affairs, about once a month. Mrs. J has placed the matter in my hands and of course I do all that is necesary to call for the money speedily, and communicate with Mr. Kearney, of which Mack is not aware, or I presume he would save his ink & paper."[46] But he was not so amused when he learned in November that Kearney was retaining £600, leaving only £200, or $100 a piece, for the heirs. Now he regretted having sent the release.[47]

It appeared that the high-born relatives in Ireland had found a way to use the vaunted British legal system to deprive the country bumpkins in North America of their patrimony. After questioning in 1836 whether he owed the £800 to John Johnston's heirs that had been left in the estate for a life interest to John's now deceased sisters, John McNeil had conceded in 1837 that he did. Henry Kearney then asserted that he retained a life interest in his dead wife's £400 half, and that only the widowed Jane Moore's £400 half was due John Johnston's heirs; McNeil concurred. The Judge of the Prerogative Court required that an administrator be appointed to manage the £800. William Saurin, Bishop of Dromere, who was next of kin and had been holding the funds and disbursing the interest heretofore, kindly declined in favor of Henry Kearney. The Bishop, himself, died in the spring of 1842. The £200 conceded in 1843 was, therefore, the remainder from Jane Moore's half of the original £800, less legal and administrative expenses incurred since her death nine years earlier. The rest would be forthcoming after he, Kearney, died.

All of this Kearney explained in letters to America, but Mr. McMurray received the information "unbecomingly . . . [To] write in contemptuous language of the Solicitor and Lawyers, who happen to be truly Evangelical and exemplary Christians, is not the way to remedy any supposed evil connected with the case . . . my business correspondence has not been made more agreeable by being transferred from you [Henry Schoolcraft] to others . . . you understood those matters much better."[48] Therefore,

Kearney had asked his solicitor, Mr. Maddock, to write James and McMurray directly. This he did, and quoted the original 1789 deed of trust, which stated that after the deaths of the sisters and their husbands the £800 would revert to the estate.[49] McMurray obtained another expert opinion, however, from Robert Jameson, Anna Jameson's husband, now vice chancellor of the Court of Chancery in Toronto. He judged from the contents of Maddock's letter that Kearney's interest in his wife's £400 terminated at her death. Once more William suggested that the family put up the money for him to go to Ireland to obtain settlement.[50] Rejected again.

Henry participated one more time in the controversy when he answered Kearney's letter, explaining that when he left

> the Lake region . . . I turned over to my brother James the subject of the Irish claims . . . and I feel no disposition . . . to resume them, or take any active agency. . . . I only knew the subject, as one, in which the family had been left very much in the dark by the late worthy John Johnston, who however, was noted for mismanaging all his business affairs—a man indeed, whose *heart* . . . appeared to be umpire in all questions of this kind.

But Henry was not deluded by legal machinations. John Johnston had told him that certain sums would revert to him after the death of his sister, Eliza Kearney, and Henry didn't recall that

> you made any claim, at this time [1834] to a part, or any part, of the claim, said to be due, from Mr. McNiel [sic]. . . . It now appears, from what I hear from Canada, and from St. Mary's, that your claim has increased by time & correspondence, that it has absorbed the better part of the sum, & that it is, a matter referred to solicitors. . . . If you have a just claim . . . so be it. And if you . . . have no just claim, surely the moral onus must rest, not with us, but with you.[51]

Although William McMurray was now stage manager of the Irish inheritance, Susan's death in November of 1843 opened a new theater for wrangling over the family heritage—the riverfront property at Sault Ste. Marie. Congress had not yet confirmed the land claims at the Sault, but lack of a valid deed did not trouble her heirs.

James' first task, as her designated administrator, was to take a complete inventory of her personal effects. Their value totaled $413, and when he put them up for auction they realized $34.[52] As this was all that was available to pay her debts, James took it in partial satisfaction of the $600 she owed him when she died. John Hulbert also put in a claim for $650, which James thought could be satisfied by turning over to him her interest in the Detroit real estate. As for the balance of her debt to James, the only asset remaining was the real estate at the Sault—over 750 feet of river frontage that would some day, James was sure, be highly valuable. One third belonged to Susan and could be sold to satisfy her debts. The remainder, divided six ways, left 106 feet for each of the John Johnston's remaining heirs.[53] At first James thought he would build on the site if he could assemble more than Anna Maria's share. He bought out William's interest, and inquired of George if he was willing to sell.[54] Apparently George was not.

Eliza was not too pleased with James' management. She "seems to consider herself the *Commander in Chief*," James complained, "and I shall be *obliged* to set her right before long as she is getting beyond endurance."[55] The McMurrays and George each invited Eliza to come and live with them so that she would not be alone. But she was determined to spend the remainder of her days in the house in which she was born and where she had lived for 42 years.[56] She was a withdrawn, taciturn woman, settling comfortably into eccentric middle age. "From what I have read of Nuns," the English George Johnston had written five years earlier to his American cousin, "I think your sister Eliza would have made a very strict one. She is very silent."[57]

Angie Bingham was impressed quite differently by the "most picturesque of this famous family," who was very kind and told wonderful stories to the children "with her own peculiar language, intonation and pride," and served "the sponge cake no one else could make so deliciously delicate as she. She kept a young Indian maid, Equa-zham-shis, who followed her everywhere. In winter Miss Eliza wore

> a long blue pellise, or cloak with wing-like capes . . . trimmed with black velvet; a copper-colored satin bonnet with round, high crown and broad front; a long green . . . veil tied over the front with a ribbon, always drawn to one side, and held back by her right arm. In summer she wore a blue-black silk gown, a bonnet with a heavily embroidered black lace veil, drawn over the face and reaching nearly to the feet, or a large green calash made like the top of a covered buggy, with rattan cords shirred into folds up or let down, managed by a ribbon attached to one side.[58]

It was never easy for Eliza to make ends meet, however, and she was obliged to accept family charity from time to time, over and above what her needlework earned her. By the summer of 1844 she was already asking Henry to dispose of the New York real estate[59] he had bought with part of her treaty money—a 25-foot lot on 91st Street between Sixth and Seventh Avenues (Central Park had not yet obliterated that block), for which he realized $268.[60]

William Johnston, too, was in severe financial straits. The treaty money was spent, and every so often another mouth appeared to be fed. Without sound prospects, he swallowed such pride as remained and turned once more to the old family mentor. "For two years," he wrote Henry, "I have done but very little of any thing, and our misunderstanding with all connectd with it, being like a cloud over me . . . I came to a determination to commence anew in business & foresake dissipation for my spirits now feel light."[61] Even after turning over to James his share of the Sault Ste. Marie property he couldn't command $200 to get started with, as James, without the other shares, could not sell the lots. He asked a loan from Henry, with his word and his share of the Irish estate whenever it came in as security, at 10 percent interest. Henry understandably declined.[62]

As an alternative, William opened a school at Mackinac Island the winter of 1844-45 and enrolled about 25 pupils. Apparently education was too uncertain a field of employment because the following spring he was writing again, expressing the hope that Henry would be reinstated as Superintendent of Indian Affairs. Pending such a happy turn of events, he would greatly appreciate a strong recommendation to support his application for keeper of the Indian dormitory at Mackinac Island. Although the government would discontinue the dormitory in another year, according to a provision in the Treaty of 1836, so many people were applying that William needed a boost. As for drink, "I hope I have thrown it aside for this life."[63]

If the Johnston brothers were suffering hard times during the mid-1840s, James Schoolcraft was more self-assured than he had ever been. With the sutlership as his economic base, he was eager to join the lucrative speculation in copper mining leases. He associated himself with a group of investors, led by Andrew Talcott, that included James B.Campbell, A.B. Gray, and James Paul. What these men needed most was guidance in the rough terrain of the copper range and an influential presence in dealing with the Indians. James could not himself bring those talents to the group, but his brother-in-law, George Johnston, could. And George was always on the lookout for a promising business venture (a third son, Samuel Abbot, was born to Mary December 2, 1844),[64] and James was the catalyst to bring it all together.[65] He arranged a prospecting trip for the summer of 1845, but warned George to "Keep dark—it is known that we are going, and every one is anxious to know where, and they wish to get interested with us. Keep dark and mysterious."[66] He also offered his brother Henry a piece of the action.

But the trip for which he held such high hopes turned into a fiasco. The Indian guide he and George obtained led them to the right area, but then lost his way. "He made all sorts of stories, and finally he came to the sage conclusion that the rock had *sunk.*"[67] Yet James was confident that "The best region of Country is as yet untouched . . . & which thus far still remains a secret. *It is on this side of the Anse bay.*"[68] They would make another trip next spring to locate it precisely, and then they would be in a position to auction their knowledge to the highest bidder.[69]

James did not make the trip to the copper range in 1846. He did go to New York that winter to make further arrangements with Talcott. In Detroit, on the way down, he met Richard R. Lansing and talked about working together; others as well sought him out, as copper fever continued to rise. George was an important element in his deals, however, and his unreliability both exasperated and penalized James. When he and Lansing arrived at Sault Ste. Marie in early May, George was not there as James had asked him to be. A little later in the month a Mr. Whiting offered an equal interest for each of them in his Copper Rock Company, but James, after hanging on as long as he could, had to turn it down when George didn't appear. Then a Mr. Holland came up with another proposition when James assured him George would be there soon. "I have again misled these gentlemen; so that another good chance has escaped. All this had caused me a deal of mortification . . . Do you intend to come this way this year at all?"[70]

George turned up eventually, and by late June he was at Agate Harbor, exploring for Talcott at a salary of $50 per month.[71] He was on the lookout for other jobs as well, offering his services to Samuel Hastings' Eagle Harbour Company at the same time he was working for Talcott.[72] He was still living at Grand Traverse, deeply discouraged by the condition of the Indians there. "They certainly were a more innocent people in their natural state, and then possessed a certain pride of integrity and honesty, but at present this is all vanished away . . . leaving them . . . relics of depravity . . . [who] cannot exist among white men. . . . The present missionaries, farmers and mechanics are of little service to the Indians. It is a public expense benefitting the former only." The solution he favored was "their removal to a territory they can claim as their own . . ."[73] James stayed on at the Sault with his family, but he worried about Anna Maria. She was pregnant again and not at all well. He insisted she go to Detroit to consult with Dr. Zina Pitcher, in whom the family retained its confidence of many years' standing. She left on July Fourth.[74] An odd thing occurred that night after the boat's departure. John Tanner's little white house on the river, just below the agency, suddenly burst into flames. No one could get near it to extinguish the fire because powder had been placed around the building which exploded every so often. The house was totally destroyed, but no evidence of a trapped occupant appeared in the ashes. Nevertheless, John Tanner was never seen again.[75]

With Anna Maria away, James spent the lonesome holiday with some of his drinking buddies across the river. He returned home on the fifth to recuperate. On the sixth he went about his usual activities, and after dinner started out for the woods beyond his house, to supervise some boys he had hired to clear the land. One youngster passed him on his way down the road to get a drink of water. Two others remained at work among the thick trees that James was just entering. All three were startled by the sudden crack of gunfire. They converged together on the fallen body—hit at such close range that he was literally knocked out of the soft shoes he was wearing. James died instantly from a musket ball and buckshot directly to the heart. No one was in sight. But "the wretch must have stood within four feet of him; the woods on the right of the road are very thick—on the left they are partially cleared—but you can see where he had broken the boughs so as to have a clear view of the road."[76]

But who? And why? The villagers all knew. The murderer was John Tanner, the White Indian, whose insane, uncontrollable rages had grown worse as he aged. Within weeks the reward money subscribed for his capture was up to $600, but after a posse came back empty-handed on the first day no one was brave enough to go back out after him.[77] Two weeks earlier Tanner had gone to his former mentor, Reverend Bingham, and asked if he could live in his old room at the mission and eat at the table with the family; he could not stand the loneliness of his existence any longer. Bingham refused, out of fear of Tanner's violent temper. Clearly the old man was on the thin edge, and Bingham suggested to Major Kingsbury, the commanding officer at Fort Brady, that Tanner should be incarcerated. But he had done nothing to warrant this, beyond the threats he had uttered for years against Henry Schoolcraft.[78]

He held Henry responsible for depriving him of his daughter in 1830. And several years after that he had brought home a new wife from Detroit, a chambermaid at Woodworth's Steamboat Hotel, whom he treated so badly that some of the neighbors helped her escape on a boat for Detroit, where she sued for divorce. He held the Schoolcraft brothers, their brother-in-law John Hulbert, and Abel Bingham responsible; no doubt they all helped the unfortunate woman. Tanner threatened at one time or another to kill them all.[79] Obviously, James was the first and easiest target. Tanner had set fire to his house and disappeared. Wasn't that sufficient evidence of his guilt?

Or was it? The soldiers at Fort Brady and some of the townspeople knew of another enemy James had, Lieutenant Bryant P. Tilden with whom he had allegedly quarreled over a girl. Shortly after the murder, Lieutenant Tilden was transferred to Texas, along with most of the garrison, to fight the Mexican War. There Tilden was court-martialed with others for burglary and murder, and sentenced to hang. General Butler remitted his sentence, however, and he returned to the U.S., resigned his commission in 1848, and became a surveyor and geologist in the east.[80] At the time of his court martial he wrote Reverend Bingham that he was also being charged with James Schoolcraft's murder, and asked for an affidavit of innocence from the townspeople.

Bingham circulated a statement to that effect, which many people signed. Among others, one important man held out, the respected Judge Samuel Ashmun. Evidence implicating Tilden consisted of the military-type buckshot cartridge found at the scene. Evidence linking Tanner was the burnt page of a mission hymnal that was used for wadding the musket ball, also found at the scene.[81] Forty years later Angie Bingham ran into Tanner's daughter, Martha, at Mackinac Island. Martha said she had received a letter in 1858 from the recently widowed Mrs. Tilden in which she told of her husband's death-bed confession of James' murder. But still no conclusive evidence emerged; Martha had burnt the letter.[82] Tanner or Tilden? No one would ever know for sure.

For Anna Maria Schoolcraft it hardly made much difference who had widowed her at the age of 30 and orphaned her babies. Her beloved James was gone, and she had to face the world alone. At the time of James' death all the men in the family—George, William, John and John Hulbert—were away on Lake Superior. Eliza was left to cope with the funeral arrangements and all the sad business attendant upon a death.[83] She dispatched the Schoolcrafts' man, Edward, to Detroit to bring Anna Maria home; Maria Hulbert came with her.

But she had little time then to indulge her grief. Provision must be made for hers and her children's future. "I have taken letters of Administration, but cannot have a bond signed till I can find some responsible person to do so. . . . I applied to Captain Kingsbury to give me the Sutlery but he had refused on the excuse that he is going away . . . Lieut. Westcott who relieves Kingsbury has promised it to me, but whether his single recommendation will be sufficient I don't know."[84]

A woman sutler? Not likely. She did not get the appointment, of course, and John Hulbert became the administrator of James' estate. He left $14,000 in debts, which Hulbert hoped to satisfy through the sale of his assets, including the Sault Ste. Marie real estate, with enough left over to keep Anna Maria and the children.[85] A bigger problem was where she could live. It was impossible to share "the homestead with Eliza, of whose treatment she complains bitterly. Her trials are sufficiently severe without being increased by the unkindness of friends."[86] Then, on October 3, 1846, little Minnie was born, three months almost to the day after her father's death.[87] When Anna Maria recovered she decided to remain where she was.

Another strange element in the bizarre events surrounding James Schoolcraft's death was the way in which his brother, Henry, received the news in Washington. Senator Dickenson handed him a copy of the *New York*

Express that reported a July 10th telegraphic dispatch from Buffalo reporting "the death of Mr. Henry R. Schoolcraft, late Indian agent, at Sault St. [sic] Marie. He was murdered by a halfbreed, named Tanner, last week. The murderer is at large, pursued by the entire population."[88] Henry wrote immediately to the editor of the paper. "I fear this news forbodes evil at the time & place mentioned to some person of my name in Michigan. I have a brother, & several nephews, residing in that state. The person called Tanner, is a kind of outlaw . . . capable of the most foul deed. . . . I shall be happy, indeed, if the active rumour . . . proves a mistake or a hoax."[89] A letter of condolence to Henry from Ramsey Crooks the next day confirmed that the report was neither a mistake nor a hoax; James was dead.

With Henry's abdication and James' death, family leadership now rested in the hands of William McMurray, where he had always wanted it. He was beginning to feel more comfortable in his situation at Dundas, especially after "my beautiful new church was dedicated last month." To celebrate he baptized the new baby, Charlotte Elizabeth Jane, born July 12, 1843, the day the church opened.[90]

At the time of James' death the Irish inheritance was still in legal limbo. It had been stalled since the spring of 1844 when Kearney's lawyer explained to McMurray why the heirs would get only £200 from the original £800. Not only did he protest this settlement, but William McMurray added a few sharp words to the correspondence flowing to Ireland. In August of 1846 McMurray received a final offer from Kearney and Maddock to "compromise the difficulties . . . which I think we had better accept."[91]—£50 for each heir. As they now numbered six, that offer raised the total from £200 to £300. The only alternative remaining was a suit in chancery that would certainly eat up whatever legacy remained. If the rest of the family couldn't agree to trust McMurray and authorize him to sign off for them all, then he would settle independently for Charlotte's share and they might lose out entirely.[92] In November George forwarded his certificate and power of attorney to Dundas, as did William, John, Eliza and Anna Maria.[93] The widower Henry Schoolcraft was no longer a participant. At any rate, he had been in possession of Jane's share of the Irish estate ever since he took it out of the Indian treaty settlement in 1837.

Despite the transmission of papers in November of 1846, it took another year and a half before the money actually arrived on the American side of the Atlantic in March of 1848. After McMurray deducted £13 8 shillings 11 pence in expenses from each share,[94] the six heirs received less than $200 each from their Irish fortune. Whether any part of Eliza Kearney's £400 share was distributed to them after Henry Kearney's death is not known. Perhaps by that time none of the family was willing to invest another 14 years to claim it.

Distribution of the Irish inheritance did not quite discharge William McMurray's self-imposed obligations. He was still holding onto the land grant he had acquired in John Johnston's name in 1841 at Maidstone Township near Windsor, Ontario. Despite impatient requests from time to time from the always impecunious George, he did not find a buyer until October of 1849. The price negotiated was $1 per acre, 60 cents less than the government's upset price had been eight years earlier. Dividing $400 seven ways—Jane's children participated this time—yielded $57.14 each. But, of course, there were expenses to deduct for taxes and transaction costs and even some expenses left over from the Irish affair, leaving a balance of $25.80.[95]

At last, 21 years after John Johnston died, McMurray wrapped up the tag ends of the man's tangled accounts—with one exception. The willow-draped land on the bank of St. Marys River, where he had settled.

Chapter Sixteen

Expectations Lost and Attained

Three deaths in four years and dispersal of the family during the early 1840s invoked a sense of loneliness and made the Johnstons' customarily prolific correspondence even more important to them. George reached out immediately to his poor, orphaned niece and nephew, still at school in Albany when their mother died in 1842. Young Johnston Schoolcraft replied with gratitude and longing "to see you or any others from home. When I saw Uncle James [who visited the school on his way to New York] it made me very homesick. . . . I hope you will write soon, and tell me all the news of the Sault St. Mary's, and every thing you can think. If you see Grand Ma will you please to tell her that I thank her a thousand times for those mocuks of Sugar."[1] While they remained at school the children spent much of their vacation time with the McMurrays at Dundas or the Schoolcraft relatives at Vernon. Only rarely did they get back to the Sault Ste. Marie-Mackinac homeland they loved.[2]

The correspondence between Johnston and his Uncle George, initiated in the summer of 1842 continued over the years, as the young man confided his hopes and disappointments to his loving uncle. By the fall of 1846 he was 17 and entered the world of business as a clerk in a New York shipping firm.[3] Janee was living with her father in Washington. During a visit to South Carolina, possibly as a guest of John Calhoun, Henry met Miss Mary Howard of Grahmville. They were married in Beaufort on January 13, 1847.[4] The marriage "surprised everyone and none more so than Jane and myself. She is a Southern lady. I cannot say I like her, and altogether do not think father did right, but I must respect & obey her I suppose."[5] Johnston's first job lasted a year and was followed by a series of positions—in a New York lawyer's office, at a newspaper in Utica, New York—culminating in a clerkship to his father at the War Department.[6]

The federal government re-hired Henry to write his multi-volume definitive work on American Indian ethno-graphy.[7] Johnston was living at home as well, but after two years was ready to move out as "I find it utterly impossible to get along with my southern stepmother, so strange and selfish is she in all her movements, & father being blinded to all her faults."[8] He not only left home, but also left his job, and would, in fact, be a rolling stone looking for a place for the rest of his life, blaming misfortune and his stepmother for the frustration of his hopes. He continued to long for the warmth of extended family, inquired of each one by name in his letters, sent magazines to Louisa in almost every letter to George, and occasionally asked for a sweet remembrance, a small mocuk of maple sugar.[9]

Janee was less homesick after the first few years of bereavement, as she was caught up in the Washington social whirl. In 1849 she was betrothed to the well-known novelist and poet, Charles Fenno Hoffman, who had been a friend of Henry's for about ten years.[10] A week before the wedding he was stricken by mental illness and confined to an asylum near Baltimore. William McMurray, who had come to Washington to perform the ceremony, took the stricken Janee home with him for a winter of recovery in Dundas.[11]

Dundas was also the place of refuge for Anna Maria after her terrible loss. The McMurrays had invited her to come to them the first year after James' death. But she stuck it out at the Sault until the fall of 1847 when she and her children went to live with Charlotte and her family.[12] Although she enjoyed the warmth of family life, Anna Maria found Dundas an even duller place to live than Sault Ste. Marie, and she was "pretty hard up . . . [despite having] rented my store at the Saut [sic] to Mr. [Edwin] Hulbert again for one year."[13] Nevertheless, she began to keep company with Oliver Taylor, a young clergyman. While her relationship with him could in no way match the love affair with James Schoolcraft, he was a good man and no other alternative existed but remarriage for a widow with three young children. "I never knew what it was to be pinched for money before and there is no one I can look up to for assistance."[14]

Taylor was searching for a congenial pulpit as William McMurray had done over a decade earlier, hoping to secure one in the United States.[15] The possibilities included Maumee City, Ohio, Ypsilanti and Ann Arbor, Michigan. The final arrangements had not yet been made when he and Anna Maria were married in William McMurray's church on October 24, 1850. "It was quite a gay affair. . . and the only drawback to it was that all her relatives could not be present. Charlotte exerted herself to have it pass off well, and invited some 60 or 70 persons to be present; for whom she prepared a very nice supper. . . . The Bridal party left early the next morning for Detroit—Maria took all her children with her with bag and baggage."[16]

In the end Reverend Taylor took a parish in Pontiac, Michigan, where his ready-made family settled in comfortably. But their happiness was destined to last only 16 short months. On February 19, 1852, Anna Maria died at the age of 38, probably of tuberculosis.[17] Oliver Taylor took up the burden of his wife's children with kindly devotion. He sent the girls to Detroit for their housing and schooling and placed Howard at a school in Lodi, but they returned to him for their vacations.[18] Two years later the girls were back in Pontiac living with him. Taylor must have been a lonely man, perhaps without any family of his own, as he kept in close touch with his brothers-in-law, attended to their errands and business affairs in the Detroit area, and sent things to Eliza as well as doing chores for her, like having her glasses repaired. But Taylor was paid very little for his clerical services and was sinking deeper into debt during these years, even though he was farming as well as preaching. As they grew older Evalyn and Minnie tried to help him as much as they could. By August of 1854 he had remarried, but continued as a father to the three Schoolcraft children, the girls living with him, and Howard apprenticed to a Detroit merchant.[19]

Sault Ste. Marie was something of a boom town during the 1840s, the jumping off place for prospectors, miners, speculators, and suppliers, bound for the copper range. All goods as well as people, including the military sent to establish Fort Wilkins at the tip of the Keweenaw Peninsula to keep the peace (that was never broken) between Indians and miners, had to be transshipped across the portage. Modest fortunes were made in storekeeping and transport.

Although he would always struggle just to make ends meet, let alone accumulate even a modest fortune, George Johnston moved back to Sault Ste. Marie in October of 1846.[20] Eliza Ann Jane was born there on December 20.[21] Soon after his dismissal from government service, while still living at Grand Traverse, he had turned again to the fur trade. He was loosely associated with one L.Y. Birchard between 1841 and 1844.[22] Birchard was optimistic about the profits still to be made and painted rosy pictures of what he and George would accomplish together.[23] But those were the twilight years of the fur trade on the upper Great Lakes, and George was shrewd enough to shift his focus to the rising star of copper mining. He formed associations with several different men and syndicates during the latter half of the 1840s, but little of the talk and correspondence seemed to extend beyond a season or two of planning for George's generous cost estimates and occasional trips into the field.

He was essentially unemployed most of the time after his return to the Sault and continued to use his time writing letters to potential backers in either the mineral or Indian trades. He described himself in these letters as "a plain son of the forest,"[24] "a son of nature, untutored in the schools [whose] intercourse has chiefly been with the wild Indians."[25] Yet he shrewdly assessed the future of the Lake Superior region in mineral wealth, the currently flourishing fish trade, and lumbering, as "the timber for spars, masts and lumber is endless and Lake Superior is destined to supply the eastern world."[26] George's pitch to many of the capitalists he addressed was that the Indians knew where to find copper, but "they are averse to disclose [the information] to white men, through a religious or superstitious fear, and such information they would not hesitate to divulge to me from ties of consanguinity."[27] To insure the Indians' confidence and their "producing good specimens, and pointing out good veins and . . . localities . . . liberal action & not stintedness is the essential trait needed" when offering to buy.[28]

One man actually sought out George. Having met him during a brief visit to Grand Traverse in 1842, Edward Clarke of Worcester, Massachusetts, wrote in December 1847 that he was ready to buy claims and operate one or more copper mines.[29] But after a visit to Sault Ste. Marie the following July he apparently began to cool. Yet George had placed a good deal of faith and hope in this proposition, declining other employment opportunities during the summer while he waited for Clarke, and even boarding two men he had hired.[30] It was the usual story of his misunderstanding another's intentions and overreaching authority. Clarke had expected to pay expenses in traveling to mineral localities that George knew about, but "you never have been employed or retained as an explorer by me or any one else through me . . . [I believed] you to be honest although the evidence of every man was against you in this place with one solitary exception."[31]

George offered his services in locating mineral lands on both sides of the international border. During the summers of 1848 and 1850 he explored the area around Bruce Mines and up the Thessalon River on the north shore of Lake Huron in Canada West, on behalf of the Montreal Mining Company.[32] His longest and most promising association beginning from about 1850 to 1854 was with Truman Smith, a Connecticut senator, interested at first in Michigan's copper range; later George steered him to the Bruce Mines area. Smith paid George's expenses and fees from time to time, which was more than many of his other contacts did,[33] but by May of 1854 Smith was reporting that his partners seemed to be pulling out. "I think it best to state to you fully & frankly my apprehensions . . . . If you can make any other disposition of your knowledge for the benefit of yourself & family you are at liberty to do so."[34]

Clearly George could not rely on copper mining to support his family. In 1856 and 1857 he tilted at iron mining in collaboration with Algernon Merryweather. He made an exploratory trip to the Gogebic district in 1857, but these efforts, too, resulted in frustration and disappointment. Meanwhile, he continued during these years to seek other means. In June of 1847, he made a rather outlandish proposal to Cass that he be appointed to accompany a group of chiefs from the La Pointe area who would like to visit the United States and Europe and earn their way by performing difficult dances.[35] Apparently George's career as an impressario never progressed beyond that letter. Two years later he was writing to Ramsay Crooks to look out for an explorer's job for him,[36] and to a Colonel S.S. Bliss in Washington, reminding him that they had met 14 years earlier and asking his assistance in obtaining appointment as sub-agent at Sault Ste. Marie.[37]

In the fall of 1853 Henry Gilbert, Indian agent at Detroit, hired him to take $1,468 worth of presents to the Indians at L'Anse, from which he could deduct his expenses. These came to $96.75, including George's salary of $2 per day; he tried to add another $50 to his compensation for additional funds he had laid out, but that did not work.[38] In the spring of 1854 he finally got a job as interpreter at the Sault.[39] His first assignment was to attend the treaty payments at Fond du Lac, followed by negotiations for a new treaty "ceding the north shore of Lake Superior [now Minnesota], the richest mineral country on Lake Superior."[40] As usual, he claimed entitlement to more than the stipulated salary on the ground that he had performed extra services as commissary, messenger, and door keeper.

It is unlikely that George's additional claim was ever seriously considered, but he held onto the job until September 1855. Then Gilbert fired him because his "treatment of myself individually in making unfounded charges & complaints without first suggesting his grievance to me, has been so gross as to destroy all those intimate and confidential relations that should always subsist between the Agent and his employees."[41] George heard that Gilbert complained that he "fussed with the department," doubtless in reference to George's penchant for writing letters to Washington.[42] How he felt about his replacement he didn't say. His youngest brother, John, got the last job George ever held.[43]

Nor did he fare much better in collecting for his free-lance work. In 1837 Reverend O'Meara replaced William McMurray as Anglican missionary to the Indians of Sault Ste. Marie. Shortly thereafter George translated many of the prayers for him into the Ojibway language. As O'Meara learned the language he undertook to translate the entire New Testament, and engaged George from time to time to edit his work. Although O'Meara claimed sole authorship, George "begrudge[d] him not the worldly honor he claims. . . . There is a god of truth who knows, and who has seen and witnessed my labors."[44] But being paid for his work was another matter. "I have relied wholly upon your word, when you stated to me, that you was [sic] authorized by the Bishop to employ me for revising your transaction, *and that you would pay me well.*"[45]

When business deals, attempts to sell off real estate, jobs, and free-lance assignments all failed he could always follow the well worn path of government claims. Although George referred to his government service "in the midst of lawless savages, in perils seen and unseen" when he sent bills for reimbursement,[46] he nevertheless strenuously claimed his rights to participate in government payments to Indians and halfbreeds, basing his claims on the recognition afforded him by the chiefs of those lawless savages. "In 1844 & 45 at a public council held by the chiefs, the halfbreeds of that region [La Pointe] were admitted participants at the annuity payments in common with their Indian relatives."[47] George and one other were specifically cited and received their shares at the annual payments of 1853 and 1854. In the treaty of 1854, for which George acted as interpreter, the government would award to halfbreeds and heads of families 80 acres of land, but somehow Gilbert struck his name and his three older children, born at La Pointe of an Indian mother, from the list.[48]

In short, George billed Washington for his services, while at the same time claiming pension payments as a halfbreed. In many of these letters he reiterated his history, dating from his old appointment as sub-agent in 1826 and even recapitulated the history of his grandfather, Waub-o-jeeg, from whom his entitlement derived. To supplement his requests to congressmen and senators he wrote to Lewis Cass for support, as he always did. "The lands owned by my ancestors, have passed away into the hands of the government, and I am left as it were without space for burial."[49] In addition, some old trader claims still existed against the Indians. In 1856 Congress appropriated another $60,000 to satisfy these, and George put in his bid for $1600 allowed him by chiefs in council in 1837 and supported by affidavit from present chiefs.[50] Once more "notwithstanding the miserable state of health I was in, I have lost no time making out a perfect statement of my claims, and copying my letters of correspondence since 1837—to the present time, this occupied me over a week writing, sometimes not quitting till one or two o'clock in the morning."[51] In August of 1857 he actually received a check for $239.64. He had promised Mary a trip to visit her relatives in New Hampshire if the payment came through. But after all the voluminous correspondence and laborious copying of documents his halfbreed claims were never satisfied.

While the claims and the get-rich-quick mineral schemes were pending, George found a way to provide for his family on a more regular basis. In 1853 he and Mary began to take in boarders. The time was propitious as Sault Ste. Marie was beginning to attract summer vacationists. The village was described in 1854 by one visitor as an "irregular scattering of houses," mostly frame, a few log, and a few stores selling mainly birch-bark boxes with porcupine quill trim. "There are plenty of drinking shops, and a liberal suply [sic] of bowling alleys and billiard tables; there are two good hotels, a good many others of doubtful complexion."[52] Nevertheless, over the years the Johnstons attracted a select, if small clientele.[53] Samuel Whitney of Detroit, visited quite regularly with his young family, and they even discussed some prospects of George going into a store with him. Whitney also kept a yacht at the Sault, the "Northern Light," looked after by George, and in the summer of 1856, he hired young Benjamin to crew for him. George's longtime friend, Charles

Trowbridge, and his family were additional regulars.[54]

In 1855 the family moved to the Baptist mission building after Abel Bingham left the Sault. George and the boys renovated it "for the accomodation of transient or season boarders; and for families who desire to spend a few weeks in the summer season, at this delightful and healthy spot. The table always supplied with the best the market affords. Sail and Row-Boats, kept for the accommodation of visitors. Guides to the Trout streams, and other fishing grounds."[55] This was probably George's most successful commercial venture, perhaps due largely to Mary's role in its operation.

Despite his troubles George was no worse off than the other members of the family. His brothers William and John were also vulnerable to intermittent employment, mainly as interpreters at Mackinac and Sault Ste. Marie, respectively, and had large families to support. In addition, William was for several years clerk of Mackinac County.[56] John carried goods across the portage with his ox team.[57] Eliza continued to live in the family homestead, making one foray to a distant place when she visited Charlotte in Dundas in the summer of 1849.[58] She subsisted on a pittance, although in 1850 William McMurray sold her Detroit real estate, and after deducting fees and expenses took charge of the proceeds so that interest of about $30 would be paid to her semi-annually. He also sent her provisions from time to time.[59] Eliza tried to reciprocate by playing hostess to distant family members when they visited Sault Ste. Marie, especially her Schoolcraft and McMurray nieces and nephews.

The McMurrays were now the most well-off members of the family, although they had struggled for a long time; only in 1851 did they give up boarding students to ease the burden on Charlotte.[60] In addition to his thriving church, William had found his calling as a fund-raiser. The price he paid was extensive traveling "over thousands of miles and . . . preach[ing] to tens of thousands of people in all the principal churches of the chief cities of the Union"[61] on behalf of Trinity College, but he was very happy in the work and attained honors as well as a steady income. Columbia College, "the oldest and best in the United states, [sic] conferred upon me the Degree of

Doctor of Divinity. This was no doubt in compliment to our Church, but the honour fell upon me . . . So now you see your humble servant, is entitled to The Revd Dr. McMurray!!!—So much for being a public man, or rather acting in a public capacity."[62]

Despite his success William McMurray grasped every opportunity to secure the future of his children. In September of 1850 he and Charlotte took their oldest son, William, now aged 15, to Toronto to register him as a chief of the Ojibway nation, taking the name of his great-grandfather, Waub-o-jeeg. One would have expected this right to descend through George to his eldest, John George, but as they were Americans and this was a British ceremonial, young Willy was the next in line. His father hoped to reinforce the claim by buying from Anna Maria a medal that "Mama . . . repeatedly offered . . . to James but of course it would have been of no use to him—she left it to Howard as a *memento* of what his grandmother had been. In her last conversation to me, she said that she would have given it to you [George] but you could demand your right from the government as well without it."[63] The origin of the medal is unclear, but the value of an established Indian lineage was far more than ceremonial. Important claims to land and treaty payment shares existed and his Indian lineage established thereby, and a chieftanship was worth a good deal more than an ordinary tribal membership.

Actual payment of these claims usually required affirmation of their validity by the Indians, a frequently frustrating procedure. For example, according to family understanding Susan Johnston's kinsmen had allowed her an $8,000 claim against one of the treaty investment funds (which one is not clear). In 1851 the Secretary of the Interior, to whom responsibility for Indian affairs had now been transferred from the War Department, decided to sell the trust fund investments and distribute the proceeds. Somehow Susan Johnston's name was omitted from the list and application by the family to the secretary was initially rejected. William McMurray was "determined to leave no stone unturned"[64] in pressing for a re-opening of the beneficiary list, as it was his understanding that the chiefs had sworn an oath on the legitimacy of her claim in the U.S. District Court at Detroit. He worked through his Washington connections other than Henry Schoolcraft, because his former brother-in-law feared losing his job, now at the Interior Department, and "I do not wish to take any step that would be in the least prejudicial to Henry, but, why should I remain quiet, and see the whole debt fund paid out, which it will be, without endeavoring to get our own!"[65]

But McMurray was too late. The Acting Commissioner of Indian Affairs informed him that the funds had already been disbursed, but suggested that the family could apply to them for Susan's share. George, as eldest son, was the appropriate candidate for that assignment. McMurray was thoroughly disgusted with Henry Schoolcraft, who was on the scene, "in the very office" where all this was taking place; even though his position was delicate, he could have let McMurray know about it in time to take action.[66] It is doubtful that any of the $8,000 was obtained. When, on a trip to Detroit, McMurray searched the court records, he could not find the Indians' allowance that he had been so certain was there.[67] So ended the last attempt at Indian claims.

The indisputable legacy of Susan Johnston to her children, however, was the landed estate on the riverfront at Sault Ste. Marie. At the time of James' death in 1846 her estate had still not been settled. As he had contributed more to her support than the others, Anna Maria hoped to be repaid before the remainder of the estate was divided. This suggestion did not go down well with the other members of the family, especially Henry Schoolcraft looking out for his children's interests. "There is no law to give a preference in the matter of indebtedness to the estate of James. Each of the heirs is equally entitled to a share of the personal property, houses & other appurtenances . . . I have always found Anne reasonable & I think she would be readily made to see than any arrangement, of the kind . . . mention[ed], would, by giving an undue preference to herself, be injurious to the other heirs & consequently liable to revision."[68] William McMurray, on the other hand, who deplored the suspicion and bickering, and did not want to make matters any more painful to Anna Maria than they already were, suggested dividing the debts equally, as well as the assets.[69]

Susan's will was finally probated in 1848 and the property was divided into seven equal parts, one for each of her surviving children and one for Jane's children, with the house deeded to Eliza.[70] Platting gave each of them two lots, one on the river side of the road, now Water Street, and one on the landward side. By the early 1850s, when the long-sought canal began to look like a real possibility, McMurray was anxious to sell Charlotte's share,[71] and Oliver Taylor hoped to realize enough from Anna Maria's shares to buy a good farm near Pontiac in Oakland County.[72] As James had bought William's interest before he died, Anna Maria actually had two shares, now four lots. George and John were also hopeful of making profitable sales. But the strength of their opportunity depended upon Congressional confirmation of the ancient land grant.

Congress finally acted in 1855, to legalize land claims that had been in dispute for over 30 years, although final settlement of the suit brought by the heirs of de Bonne and de Repentigny would not occur for another dozen years after that. Nevertheless, canal fever was high enough by 1853 that Oliver Taylor was offered $1100 for Anna Maria's lots. Anxious though he was for funds, he declined in the expectation that land prices would rise even higher once the canal was a certainty. A year later he sold for $1200.[73]

Eliza, always hard up, sold her back lot in the summer of 1851 to Edwin Hulbert for $250; he then divided it in two and sold them immediately to people who put up frame cottages. Both George Johnston and Henry Schoolcraft were distressed by the low price for which she was willing to settle.[74] Henry was the only member of the family who did not wish to sell, but if he had, he valued the riverfront lot at $3,000 and the back lot at $1,500 in 1851.[75] Then in the spring of 1852 he was incensed at George for

> caus[ing] the entry for my lands to be made in the name of my children. By what authority have you done this thing? Neither by my *request* nor by an

colour of law. . . . There is no will in this case [from Jane] & I am the *legal representative* & the title cannot pass to them without *me.* I have ever designed the property for them & still do so but I feel this act is a piece of high-handed injustice & indignity. . . . I requested you to take care of the property by fencing it in, but nothing besides. I filed my claim here in the General Land Office, & will take care of it. . . . John has been wandering about, and not only has no money to make such entries, if I approved them, but is wholly incompetent to manage or keep any property.[76]

Poor George had meant to be helpful. When a land officer appeared at the Sault in the fall of 1851 to file claims under an 1850 "act to provide for the examination and settlement of all claims for land at the Sault Ste. Marie in Michigan,"[77] he told George that unless the claim was filed immediately it would miss the deadline and be lost. George was aware that he did not have authority over the property, but when he examined the partition deed under Susan's will he saw "'that the parcel of land is awarded and set apart and made the sole property of the heirs of the late Jane Schoolcraft,'"[78] and reported this wording to the officer.

In 1855 Samuel Whitney offered to buy the "lot on the River in front of your house [for] $200, the lot Between Portage St. and the River lot $350, the lot from Portage St. South $300,"[79] to be paid in three installments. It is likely that George accepted the offer because three years later land prices were again depressed at the Sault. George observed that houses that formerly rented for $150 per year were being let for $24. He attributed this state of affairs to the new city that was being planned at Mackinac "which will be the center of attraction for capatallists [sic]."[80]

This was just one more downswing on the canal roller coaster Sault Ste. Marie had been riding since statehood in 1837. In 1852 Congress at last donated 750,000 acres of land and granted right of way through Fort Brady for construction of a canal at least 100 feet wide, 12 feet deep and with a lock measuring 60 by 250 feet, provided that construction was begun within three years and the project completed within ten. But Congress did not count on Charles T. Harvey, a 23-year-old employee of the Fairbanks Company of St. Johnsbury, Vermont, who came to the Sault that summer to investigate mineral resources. He returned to the head office full of enthusiasm for the canal project. The Fairbanks brothers contacted venture capitalists of their acquaintance, including Erastus Corning of Albany, John W. Brooks and James Joy of Detroit, and August Belmont of New York. They, along with some others, won the contract Joy guided through the Michigan legislature during the winter of 1853, and incorporated the St. Marys Falls Ship Canal Company, capitalized at one million dollars.

The Michigan bill was even more demanding than the Congressional act, requiring that the work be completed within two years from the letting of the contract, and at Harvey's urging the lock dimensions were increased to 70 by 350 feet. The irrepressible Charles Harvey was appointed general agent.[81] He moved into the Schoolcrafts' old Agency House, from which he immediately began ordering supplies and recruiting workers from Detroit, where his agents met immigrant ships. George Johnston and his son, John George, were involved in locating and submitting specimens of limestone for construction, which they sent in from Echo Lake, the Neebish Rapids area, St. Joseph Island, Drummond Island, and Campment d'Ours Island in the St. Joseph Channel.[82]

Working through the winter of 1853-54 as many as 2,000 men labored to dig and buttress the mile-long canal. But Harvey was no engineer, and by the spring of 1854 progress was disappointing and the construction of inadequate quality. John W. Brooks, vice president of the canal company and general manager of the Michigan Central Railroad, an accomplished civil engineer, was placed in charge of construction. Harvey, relieved of technical responsibilities, continued to manage the ancillary functions of purchasing, accounting, labor recruitment, housing, and so on.[83] With this appropriate division of managerial labor the project was completed in 22 months, coming in at just under the million dollar estimate.[84] On April 19, 1855, Charles Harvey opened the coffer dam sluice gates to fill the canal, which was officially received by the state of Michigan on May 21. The water was let out again, perhaps for some last-minute repairs, and the canal refilled between 1:00 and 11:00 a.m. on June 18, in time for the steamer *Illinois* to inaugurate the system. After so many years of anticipation the first locking was not destined to proceed smoothly. A block of wood fouled one of the gates on the lower of the two locks, and the upper gates were blocked at the miter sill by two feet of earth that had washed down from the embankment. It took the *Illinois* eleven hours to lock through, with help of the steamer *Baltimore* and a winch to pry the upper gates open.[85]

Nevertheless, it was a gala occasion for the citizens of St. Marys River and Lake Superior. They lined the shore to watch the spectacle, the three Johnstons still living at the Sault doubtless among them. It may be supposed that 59-year-old George would reflect on how different was the scene of his childhood when his parents were just beginning their adventurous life together, when only a few log houses stood on the untamed riverbank, when the only activity was the fur trade, when birch-bark canoe was the only form of transport, when neither minister to sustain faith nor doctor to sustain health nor government agent to sustain law were available, when civilization with its comforts and its iniquity lay almost 1,000 miles and six weeks of arduous travel away. Now a town of almost 2,000 people[86] in all occupations of business, government and the professions bustled among the frame houses, shops, offices and mills that lined the platted streets, and the arrival of modern engineering brought swift contact with the entire world. Sault Ste. Marie had come in from the frontier.

Epilogue

Today no known descendents of John Johnston and Oshaw-guscody-way-quay (Susan) are living at Sault Ste. Marie. But hundreds of them are scattered throughout the United States and Canada, in all walks of life, uniformly proud of the bi-racial heritage that gave them life.

George

George later viewed the opening of the St. Marys Lock and Canal as a misfortune for Sault Ste. Marie. "The condition of this place is truly deplorable, the opening of the Ste. Maries Canal has literally killed the place, and the inhabitants are leaving the country, and nothing but empty houses are seen in the village."[1] Certainly the St. Marys Lock and Canal destroyed the carrying trade across the portage, and the commercial boom that construction had brought was over. George lived another six years, sad ones in which his meager fortunes declined even further.

Mary died of cancer on September 25, 1858.[2] Her four children ranged from 12 to 18. After that, George apparently gave up the boarding house, and his life seemed to fall apart. He spent hours writing letters to dignitaries of his acquaintance in business and government, still seeking restitution for old grievances and losses. In 1859 he wrote to the Secretary of War asking permission to occupy one of the vacant officers' quarters at Fort Brady, as he had no money to pay rent and for once a merciful government responded.[3] He even went so far as to try and revive the old 1814 war loss with the

Canadian government. His letters became longer and more rambling and his handwriting shakier.[4] He described his condition as analagous to an Indian he had known at La Pointe in 1827, who when fishing through the ice one day suddenly found himself adrift on a floe in Lake Superior. "On perceiving his condition, he ran to and fro upon the Ice, but finding no prospect of escape, and in agony he writhed down and covered himself up with his blanket, resigning himself to his fate . . . . I know not what to say or do, my only alternative is . . . to lay down and cover myself up with my blanket, and resign myself to the will of providence."[5] Two years later he did just that. On a cold day in March of 1861 his neighbors noticed his absence from the village. A search party went out on snowshoes to look for him and found him slumped in the snow across the canal near the rapids, frozen to death.[6] He was one month short of 65 years old.

Louisa never married and, never in good health, continued to live with her father, receiving occasional gifts from her more fortunate relatives to brighten her life.[7] She outlived him by only a few years.

Henry William lived much like his uncles did, in a variety of storekeeping and government jobs. At one time George tried to get an army commission for him, perhaps for the Mexican War, but without success.[8]

Henry married and was survived by two daughters, Mary Louisa, who became a Mrs. Scott, and Margaret Angelic, later Mrs. Fuller. A son died in infancy.[9]

John George, the more promising of the two sons of Louisa Raymond Johnston, also sought employment in the Indian service, but how he earned his living we do not know. He married and fathered two sons and a daughter. He lived mostly at Bay Mills near Sault Ste. Marie and was buried there.[10]

Benjamin Saurin, George's eldest son with Mary Rice, was the most promising of all the children. He did well in school, and lived for a time with the Trowbridges in Detroit, where he "endeared himself to us very much indeed . . . he has developed a kindness of heart very seldom met with in boys of his age . . . he has gained the esteem of his fellow scholars & the hearty approbation of his teachers.[11] He came home to a clerkship in Mr. Hatch's store.[12] But Benjamin's promise was not to be fulfilled. He was killed in the Civil War. So were his two brothers, James Laurence Kearney and Samuel Abbott, all barely into their twenties.[13]

Eliza Ann Jane, only 12 when her mother died, was sent east to live with her mother's sister, Hannah. Her future beyond 1858 is not known.[14]

Jane

Henry Schoolcraft's great six-volume historical and statistical work on the American Indian was published between 1850 and 1857 by the Bureau of Indian Affairs, after ten years of labor. By this time he was badly crippled with arthritis, and could walk only on crutches. The last few years of his life he was bedridden.[15] Mary cared for him faithfully. An assertive woman, with many connections, she also vigorously pursued his literary and economic interests.[16] Henry died December 10, 1864, leaving everything to her except for personal mementos from his first wife, which went to Jane, the real estate at Sault Ste. Marie, any Indian claims yet to be paid, and any sums that might yet be forthcoming from the United States Government or the United Kingdom with respect to John Johnston's war losses of 1814.[17]

After Jane's tragic disappointment in her engagement to Charles Fenno Hoffman in 1849, she met her stepmother's half brother, Benjamin Howard, on a visit to South Carolina. They were married in 1855 and settled in Richmond, Virginia. No children were born of this marriage, but many esteemed Jane throughout her life as a benefactress to charitable causes.[18] She died November 25, 1892, aged 54.[19]

John Johnston Schoolcraft, on the other hand, never found himself. Letters written to his Uncle George display a cheerful personality and lively interest in public affairs similar to his unfortunate Uncle James, but he never lasted long in a job and drifted around the country seeking fulfillment.[20] Finally, he enlisted during the Civil

War, served from 1861 to 1864, and was wounded at Gettysburg. He never recovered his health and died in April 1865 at the age of 36.[21]

Eliza

Eliza lived on in the family homestead until she sold it to L.A. Harris in 1870 for $400.[22] Where she lived after that is not known; it is unlikely that a difficult personality like hers could have gotten along well in the home of a relative. She lived another 14 years, however, until June 28, 1884.[23] Dying at age 82, she lived the longest life of any member of her family and was buried near her parents.

Charlotte

Charlotte, although never a very healthy woman, continued as her husband's helpmeet in his successful career. Not only was William McMurray effective and tireless in raising money for Trinity College, but he was active in church governance beyond his own parish. In 1857 the family moved to Niagara, where he became rector of that parish and later its first archdeacon.[24] In 1864 he went to Great Britain on a fund-raising trip for Trinity College. Wined and dined as an honored guest at many important functions, he attained the zenith of his clerical career when he was invited to preach at St. Paul's Cathedral on April 24.[25]

Charlotte died January 17, 1878, at the age of 71. In November of 1879, William, then 69, married 43-year-old Amelia Baxter. He enjoyed 15 years of his second marriage until his death May 19, 1894 a few months before his 84th birthday.[26]

The McMurray children were all promising in their youth, and their parents carefully nurtured their education. William Strachan studied four years for the law; the bar admitted him in 1859.[27] He practiced in Welland, Ontario until his untimely death from tuberculosis in November 1864 at the age of 29. He had married

Elizabeth Hamilton, but their only child, three-year old Juanita, had died ten months before he did. [28]

John Henry, a young giant of 6'2", went into business, first near home, and then in a mercantile house in New York, where in 1856 he was earning $1,000 per year.[29] In 1867 he married Elizabeth Wittaker, and they had five children. Four grew to adulthood, of whom three married and left numerous progeny. John Henry was not destined to live long either, however, and died in Chicago, where he was president of the Chicago Cab Company, September 22, 1885 at the age of 47.[30]

James Saurin looked toward the church,[31] then switched to law, which he practiced in Toronto. He was married to Elizabeth Fuller October 5, 1864. They had six children, not all of whom lived to adulthood or married. James' date of death is not known.[32]

The youngest McMurray child, Charlotte Elizabeth Jane, was sent to school in Toronto and later married Hamilton Hartley Killaly. They had four sons and one daughter. Charlotte died in 1928.[33]

William

William continued to live at Mackinac Island with his family until his death November 15, 1863 at the age of 52.[34] At the time he was serving as clerk of Mackinac County.[35] His widow, Susan, survived until 1899.[36]

Of their eight children, William, Jr. died in the Civil War, holding the rank of second lieutenant.[37] Most of the others—Louis Saurin, Charles, James Rice, George Edgerton, Maria, Marian Louisa, and Jane—married and had children.[38]

Anna Maria

At least part of the time that Anna Maria was living in Dundas after James died, Evalyn was in school at Detroit. Grieving for her father, she also missed her mother dreadfully and her baby sister. "How is little Minny I wish I could see her I hope she will not forget me again I felt very badly when you went away and very lonesome I would like to be with you very much when you keep house will you have me live with you" she poured out in an unpunctuated letter to her mother at the age of nine.[39] She was a naturally cheerful girl, however, and even after losing her mother at the age of 13 she continued her schooling and was devoted to her kindly stepfather. She spent a good deal of time with her Aunt Charlotte as well.[40]

After the McMurrays moved to Niagara, they developed social and church connections in Buffalo, New York, and probably through them Evalyn met William Ketcham Allen of that city. Oliver Taylor apparently provided for her wedding, however, which took place in Pontiac October 13, 1858. They settled in Buffalo, where Evalyn was prominent in church and charitable circles until she died of Bright's Disease at the early age of 50, in 1889.[41] Her two sons married two sisters, and from them a continuous line descends.[42]

Howard Schoolcraft resembled his cousin Benjamin in appearance and mannerisms, "like two peas," as George described them.[43] He also seems to have inherited his father's happy-go-lucky personality. After he finished school at Lodi, Oliver Taylor arranged an apprenticeship for him with a Detroit merchant. But he did not stay there very long. In 1856 he went to Albany, perhaps to see what his Schoolcraft relatives could do for him. When he stopped at Dundas to visit the McMurrays, William observed that he "seems indolent, and not disposed to exert himself . . . I fear he will not do much."[44]

By 1859 Howard had gone to California to seek his fortune. After a short stint in the army (he was not subject to the Civil War draft) and a few years in other jobs, he was sent by a mining company to La Dura, Mexico to help set up a mining and milling operation. There he became engaged to a Mexican girl of good family. His work on occasion took him to Guaymas, and more than once marauding Indians attacked him and his party on the road. The first time, they drove off their attackers.[45] The second time he and his companions met the same fate as his father. The Indians ambushed and killed them in early 1867.[46] Howard was then 26 years old.

Some time after Evalyn was married, her little sister, Minnie, went to live with her in Buffalo. There she married George H. Dorr.[47] They had at least one son, Eben Pearson.[48]

John McDouall

John McDouall lived on at the Sault, working as the last interpreter and also working at the locks. He died of a stroke in 1895 at the age of 78.[49] He and Justine, who died at 90 in 1913,[50] had ten children: Spencer Norval, 1843-?, Anna Maria, 1844-1928, Charlotte Jane, 1847-1912, Eliza Susan, 1849-1913, James Lawrence, 1851-?, John McDouall, Jr, 1851-1893, Howard Lewis, 1854-1933, Henry Gilbert, 1856-1897, William Meddaugh, 1858-?, Archibald Winfield, 1862[51] Some of them added an "e" to the end of the family name and were known as Johnstone. Many of them married and had children and continued to live in the Sault Ste. Marie area, but no descendents dwell there at present.

The Johnston Family Historical Society was formed in 1985 and held a reunion at Sault Ste. Marie in 1992 celebrating the bi-centennial of the Johnston settlement there.

ENDNOTES

Chapter One

[1] John Johnston to Henry Schoolcraft, February 26, 1828, Library of Congress, Papers of Henry R. Schoolcraft, microfilm, Reel 4, Container 8. Hereafter referred to as Schoolcraft Papers. All of the family history and early biographical material that follows is found in the series of five letters John Johnston wrote to Henry Schoolcraft between January 14 and April 28, 1828.
[2] Ibid. By present-day reckoning he was actually beginning his 29th year.
[3] Henry Rowe Schoolcraft, "Memoir of John Johnston," *Michigan Pioneer and Historical Collections,* Volume XXXVI, 1908, p. 81. Hereafter referred to as "Schoolcraft, 'Memoir of John Johnston.'"
[4] Jack Loudan, *In Search of Water,* Belfast, William Mullan and Son, 1940, p.11.
[5] R.W.M. Strain, *Belfast and Its Charitable Society,* 1961, p. 183. Hereafter Strain, *Belfast.*
[6] Loudan, *In Search of Water,* pp. 11-12.
[7] John Johnston to Henry Schoolcraft, January 19, 1828, Schoolcraft Papers, Reel 4.
[8] Ibid.
[9] John Johnston to Henry Schoolcraft January 14, 1828, Schoolcraft Papers, Reel 4.
[10] Strain, *Belfast,* pp. 185-186.
[11] Loudan, *In Search of Water,* p. 15.
[12] John Johnston to Henry Schoolcraft, January 19, 1828, Schoolcraft Papers, Reel 4.
[13] Ibid.
[14] Ibid.
[15] John Johnston to Henry Schoolcraft, February 26, 1828, Schoolcraft Papers, Reel 4.
[16] Ibid.
[17] Schoolcraft, "Memoir of John Johnston," p. 82.
[18] John Johnston to Henry Schoolcraft, March 1, 1828, Schoolcraft Papers, Reel 4.
[19] Ibid.
[20] Ibid.

21 Ibid.
22 John Johnston to Henry Schoolcraft, April 28, 1828, Schoolcraft Papers, Reel 4.
23 Charles W. Chapman, "The Historic Johnston Family of the Soo," *Michigan Pioneer and Historical Collections,* Vol. XXXII, p. 328. Hereafter Chapman, *The Johnstons.*

Chapter Two

1 Grace Lee Nute, *The Voyageur,* New York, D. Appleton and Company, 1931, pp. 25-26.
2 Harold A. Innis, *The Fur Trade in Canada,* Toronto, University of Toronto Press, 1956, p. 14. Hereafter Innis, *The Fur Trade.*
3 Ibid., p. 64.
4 Ibid., pp. 52-54.
5 Alexander Mackenzie, *Voyages from Montreal,* Toronto, The Radisson Society of Canada, 1927, p. 96.
6 Innis, *Fur Trade,* pp. 96-112.
7 Ibid., pp. 168-169.
8 W. Stewart Wallace, ed., *Documents Relating to the North West Company,* Toronto, The Champlain Society, 1934, p. 3. Hereafter Wallace, *Documents of the North West.*
9 Innis, *Fur Trade.* p. 210.
10 Wallace, *Documents of the North West,* pp. 6-9; Marjorie Wilkins Campbell, *The North West Company,* New York, St. Martin's Press, 1957, pp. 31-34. Hereafter Campbell, *The North West Company.*
11 Gordon T. Davidson, *The North West Company,* New York, Russell and Russell, 1918, pp. 226-230. Hereafter Davidson, *The North West Company.*
12 Nute, *Voyageur,* pp. 26-27.
13 Ibid., pp. 27-31.
14 Ibid., pp. 13-19.
15 Eric W. Morse, *Canoe Routes of the Voyageurs,* St. Paul, Minnesota Historical Society and Toronto, The Quetico Foundation, 1962, pp. 16-18. Hereafter Morse, *Canoe Routes.*
16 Ibid., p. 29; Nute, *Voyageurs,* pp. 38-40.
17 Nute, *Voyageurs,* pp. 51-52, 56-59.
18 Morse, *Canoe Routes,* p. 21.
19 Nute, *Voyageurs,* p. 62.

[20] John Johnston to Henry Schoolcraft, April 28, 1828, Schoolcraft Papers, Reel 4.
[21] John Johnston to Henry Schoolcraft, June 10, 1828, Schoolcraft Papers, Reel 4.

Chapter Three

[1] L. R. Masson, *Le Bourgeois de la Compagnie du Nord-Oest,* New York, Antiquarian Press, 1960, p. 160. The journal was not preserved.
[2] Description of a typical trader's house is found in William Johnston, "Letters of 1833," *Michigan Pioneer and Historical Collections,* Volume 37, 1909-10, p. 196.
[3] Nute, *Voyageurs.* p.79.
[4] John Johnston to Henry Schoolcraft, June 10, 1828, Schoolcraft Papers, Reel 4. All of the biographical material in this chapter is contained in this letter.
[5] William W. Warren, *History of the Ojibway Nation,* Minneapolis, Ross and Haines, 1957. The Ojibway stories in this chapter are found in this book. Hereafter Warren, *Ojibway Nation.*
[6] Ibid., pp. 76-90.
[7] Ibid., pp. 104-105.
[8] Ibid., pp. 109-111.
[9] Grace Lee Nute, *Caesars of the Wilderness,* New York, D. Appleton Century, 1943, pp. 58-66, Hereafter Nute, *Caesars;* Louise P. Kellogg, *The French Regime in Wisconsin and the Northwest,* Madison, State Historical Society of Wisconsin, 1925, pp. 109-111. Hereafter Kellogg, *The French.*
[10] Kellogg, *The French,* pp. 146-151.
[11] Nicolas Perrot, "Memoir," in Emma Helen Blair, *The Indian Tribes of the Upper Mississippi Valley and Region of the Great Lakes,* Cleveland, Arthur H. Clarke Co., 1911, p. 173. Hereafter Perrot, "Memoir," in Blair, *Indian Tribes.*
[12] Warren, *Ojibway Nation,* pp. 141-145.
[13] Philip P. Mason, ed., *The Literary Voyager or Muzzeniegun,* East Lansing, Michigan State University Press, 1962, pp. 39-42. Hereafter Mason, *Muzzeniegun.*
[14] Warren, *Ojibway Nation.,* pp. 219-220.

15 Ibid., pp. 194-195.
16 Anna Brownell Murphy Jameson, *Winter Studies and Summer Rambles in Canada*, New York, Wiley and Putnam, 1839, Volume 2, p. 239, Hereafter Jameson, *Winter Studies*; Mason, *Muzzeniegun*, p. 42.
17 Jean Baptiste Perrault, "Narrative of the Travels and Adventures of a Merchant Voyageur in the Savage Territories of Northern America," *Michigan Pioneer and Historical Collections*, Volume XXXVII, pp. 564-565. Hereafter Perrault, *Merchant Voyageur*.
18 Ibid., p. 565.
19 Chapman, *The Johnstons*, p. 311. Translation by John Johnston.
20 Warren, *Ojibway Nation*, pp. 242-246.
21 Chapman, *The Johnstons*, p. 350. Translation by John Johnston.
22 Mason, *Muzzeniegun*, pp. 55-56.
23 Warren, *Ojibway Nation*, pp. 253-255.
24 Jameson, *Winter Studies*, Volume 2, p. 225.
25 Ibid., p. 242.
26 Ibid. Chapman, *The Johnstons*, p. 312.
27 Thomas L. McKenney, *Sketches of a Tour to the Lakes*, Minneapolis, Ross and Haines, 1959, p. 183. Hereafter McKenney, *Sketches*.

Chapter Four

1 Jameson, *Winter Studies*, V. 2, p. 242.
2 Ibid., p. 244.
3 There is some doubt about where the couple wintered 1792-93. The land grant to John Johnston for acreage on St. Marys River is dated July 1792, and Anna Jameson reported his settlement there in 1792, as did George Johnston in his letterbook in1844. But in the Territorial Papers there is a deposition of John Johnston to Henry Schoolcraft, then justice of the peace, dated October 31, 1825, that states he settled at the Sault in 1793.
4 Reuben Gold Thwaites, ed., *The Jesuit Relations and Allied Documents*, Cleveland, The Burrows Brothers, 1899, Vol. LV, pp. 107-115. The year 1668 seems to be

widely accepted as the founding date, but *The Jesuit Relations* for 1667-69 make it clear that Father Nicolas opened the mission in 1667, with Father Jacques Marquette succeeding him there in 1668.
[5] Perrot, "Memoir," in Blair, *Indian Tribes*, p. 221-224.
[6] Thwaites, ed., *The Jesuit Relations*, pp. 107-115.
[7] Innis, *Fur Trade*, pp. 51-53.
[8] La Jonquiere to Minister, October 5, 1751 in Edward D. Neill, *History of the Ojibways*, Minneapolis, Ross and Haines, 1957, p. 434.
[9] F. Clever Bald, *The French Seigneury at Sault Ste. Marie*, Sault Ste Marie, 1937, pp. 5-8. Hereafter Bald, *French Seigneury*.
[10] Ibid., p. 12.
[11] Alexander Henry, *Travels and Adventures in Canada and the Indian Territories Between the Years 1760 and 1776*, Chicago, The Lakeside Press, 1921, pp. 180-184. Hereafter Henry, *Travels*.
[12] John Johnston, "An Account of Lake Superior," in L.R. Masson, *Le Bourgeois*, Vol. II, pp. 146-147.
[13] The sobriquet derived from the way in which General Anthony Wayne's cavalry cut down the Indians with their long sabers in Ohio in 1794 and 1795.
[14] 1845 copy of Original Grant of Land, dated July 1, 1792, in Johnston Collection, Bayliss Public Library, Sault Ste. Marie. Hereafter Johnston Collection.

Chapter Five

[1] Samuel Flagg Bemis, *Jay's Treaty*, New Haven, Yale University Press, 1962, pp. 454-455.
[2] F. Clever Bald, *Michigan in Four Centuries*, New York, Harper & Row, 1961, p. 92. Hereafter Bald, *Michigan*.
[3] Joseph and Estelle Bayliss, *Historic St. Joseph Island*, Cedar Rapids, The Torch Press, 1938, pp. 23-28. Hereafter Bayliss, *St. Joseph Island*.
[4] Bemis, *Jay's Treaty*, p. 455.
[5] Quoted in Henry R. Schoolcraft, "Memoir of John Johnston," p. 75.
[6] Mackenzie, *Voyages*, pp. 50-52; John MacDonnell Diary in Charles M. Gates, ed., *Five Fur Traders of the North*

West, St. Paul, University of Minnesota Press, 1933, pp. 93-94. Hereafter Gates, *Fur Traders*.

[7] McKenney, *Sketches*, pp. 181-182.

[8] Harold A. Innis, *Peter Pond*, Toronto, Irwin and Gordon, 1930, pp. 79, 85-87, Hereafter Innis, *Peter Pond*; Innis, *Fur Trade*, pp. 231-232; Campbell, *The Northwest Company*, p. 9; Morse, *Canoe Routes*, p. 36.

[9] Campbell, *The North West Company*, pp. 50-51, 99-100, 134-135; Davidson, *The North West Company*, pp. 47, 49; Perrault, *Merchant Voyageur*, pp. 587-589; Masson, *The North West Company*, Vol. 1, p. 17.

[10] Masson Collection, M. G. 19 C1, Public Archives of Canada, pp. 27-31. Hereafter Masson Collection; Davidson, *The North West Company*, p. 225; Wallace, *Documents of North West Co.*, passim.

[11] Wallace, *Documents of North West Co.*, pp. 85-88.

[12] A Statement of the Amount of Capital Employed by John Johnston and Jno. Johnston and Company, 1813-1823, Schoolcraft Papers, Reel 18.

[13] Ross Cox, *The Columbia River*, Norman, University of Oklahoma Press, 1957, p. 339.

[14] Henry R. Schoolcraft, *Personal Memoir of a Residence of Thirty Years with the Indian Tribes on the American Frontier*, Philadelphia, Lippincott, Grambo and Company, 1851, p. 107. Hereafter referred to as Schoolcraft, *Memoirs*.

[15] Chapman, *The Johnstons*, p. 344.

[16] Undated brochure in Emerson Smith Papers, Box 2, Michigan Historical Collections, Bentley Historical Library, The University of Michigan.

[17] Cox, *The Columbia River*, pp. 338-339.

[18] John J. Bigsby, *The Shoe and Canoe*, London, Chapman and Hall, 1850, p. 127. Hereafter Bigsby, *The Shoe*.

[19] Cox, *The Columbia River*, pp. 338-339.

[20] Schoolcraft, *Memoirs*, p. 135.

[21] McKenney, *Sketches*, pp. 181-182.

[22] Campbell, *The North West Co.*, pp. 117-118.

[23] Masson, *Le Bourgeois*, Vol. 1, pp. 22-29.

[24] Campbell, *The North West Co.*, p. 72; Douglas McKay, *The Honourable Company*, Toronto, McClelland and Stuart, 1949, p. 43. Hereafter McKay, *The Honorable Company*.

[25] Marjorie Wilkins Campbell, *McGillivray, Lord of the North West*, Toronto, Clarke Irwin and Company, 1962, p. 49. Hereafter, Campbell, *McGillivray*.
[26] John Johnston to George Johnston, September 8, 1813, George Johnston Papers, Box 8, Burton Historical Collections, Detroit Public Library. Hereafter Johnston Papers.
[27] Handwritten Johnston Family Record, Johnston Family Papers, 1822-1936, in Michigan Historical Collections, Bentley Historical Library, The University of Michigan. Hereafter Johnston Family Record.
[28] *Dictionary of National Biography*, Oxford University Press, Vol. XVII, p. 822.
[29] Donna J. Seltzer, *Flint Genealogical Quarterly*, April 1959, Vol. 1, No. 2, typescript in Emerson Smith Papers, Box 2. Hereafter Seltzer, *Flint*.
[30] Johnston Family Record.
[31] Ibid.
[32] Mason, *Muzzeniegun*, p. 71 footnote.
[33] Jameson, *Winter Studies*, Vol. 2, p. 240.
[34] Johnston Family Record.
[35] Jameson, *Winter Studies*, Vol 1, p. 240.
[36] Johnston Family Record.
[37] Masson, *Le Bourgeois*, Vol. II, pp. 138-139.
[38] Campbell, *The North West Company*, pp. 113-114; Morse, *Canoe Routes*, p. 127.
[39] On 1820 receipt for barrel George Johnston shipped from St. Marys to Amherstburg, Johnston Papers, Box 1.
[40] John Askin Papers, Burton Historical Collection, Detroit Public Library, Vol. 19, p. 294 footnote. Hereafter Askin Papers.
[41] Minutes of the Proceedings of the Beaver Club, 1807-1827, Public Archives of Canada, MG 19 B3.
[42] Lawrence J. Burpee, "The Beaver Club," Canadian Historical Association, *Annual Report*, Ottawa, 1924, pp. 73, 79-82, hereafter Burpee, *The Beaver Club*; Campbell, *North West Company*, p. 164.
[43] Masson, *Le Bourgeois*, Vol. 1, p. 52 footnote.
[44] John Johnston to Roderick McKenzie, July 15, 1807, Public Archives of Canada, Masson Collection, MG 19 C1.
[45] Schoolcraft, "Memoir of John Johnston," p. 77.
[46] John Johnston to George Hoffman, August 21, 1808,

in Solomon Sibley Papers, Burton Historical Collection, Detroit Public Library. Hereafter Sibley Papers.
47 John Askin, Jr. to John Askin, Sr., August 17, 1808, Askin Papers.
48 John Johnston to George Hoffman, August 21, 1808, Sibley Papers.
49 Ibid.
50 Schoolcraft, "Memoir of John Johnston," p. 61; Cox, *The Columbia River*, p. 338.
51 Schoolcraft, "Memoir of John Johnston," pp. 61-64.
52 John Johnston to George Johnston, December 7, 1813, Johnston Papers, Box 8.
53 Letter from Montreal, 1813, quoted in Henry R. Schoolcraft, "Memoir of John Johnston," p. 76.
54 Ibid., pp. 58-59.
55 Henry Kearney to John Johnston, January 29, 1819, Schoolcraft Papers, Reel 18.
56 Dictionary of National Biography.
57 Schoolcraft, "Memoir of John Johnston," p. 61.
58 Ibid., p. 60.
59 Ibid.
60 Campbell, *McGillivray*, p. 174.
61 Mackenzie, *Voyages*, p. 81.
62 Campbell, *North West Company*, p. 165.
63 McKay, *The Honorable Company*, pp. 133-134.
64 Campbell, *McGillivray*, p. 212.
65 Campbell, *North West Company*, pp. 198-199.
66 Davidson, *The North West Co.*, pp. 144-146; McKay, *The Honorable Co.*, p. 134.
67 Campbell, *North West Company*, pp. 200-202.
68 Schoolcraft, "Memoir of John Johnston," pp.59-61.

Chapter Six

1 Campbell, *North West Company*, pp. 186-187.
2 Ibid., p. 111.
3 Wallace, *Documents of North West Co.*, pp. 224-229.
4 Ibid., pp. 239-245; Campbell, *North West Company*, pp. 167-168; Campbell, *McGillivray*, pp. 161-162.
5 Campbell, *North West Company*, p. 113-114.
6 Edward H. Capp, *The Story of Baw-a-ting*, Sault Ste.

Marie, Canada, 1904, pp. 117-119. Hereafter Capp, *Baw-a-ting*. (This description of the canal is taken from the Canadian Archives of 1886 and 1889.)

[7] To Proprietors from Alexander Mackenzie, June 4, 1799, June 16, 1799, to Bennett from William McGillivray, January 7, 1800, Letterbook of the North West Company, 1798-1802, typewritten copy, Masson Collection, MG19 B1 V1-3, Public Archives of Canada. Hereafter Letterbook of the North West Company.

[8] David Lavender, *The Fist in the Wilderness*, Garden City, Doubleday and Company, 1964, p. 42. Hereafter Lavender, *The Fist*.

[9] Treaty of Peace Between the United States of America and His Britannic Majesty, Article II.

[10] Campbell, *North West Company*, pp. 112-113; Davidson, *The North West Company*, pp. 104-106.

[11] Bayliss, *St. Joseph Island*, pp. 26-28. The first payment, which took place in 1798, was one of the earliest instances of a policy and practice that assumed major importance, on both sides of the border, as settlement of the West accelerated land "purchase" from the Indians. The British called these annual gatherings of large numbers of Indians "the giving of presents," the Americans called them "treaty payments."

[12] Campbell, *North West Company*, pp. 186-187; unaddressed letter of Charles Roberts (probably to Isaac Brock) July 12, 1812, "Copies of Papers on File in the Dominion Archives Relating to the War of 1812," *Michigan Pioneer and Historical Collections*, Vol. 15, p. 101. Hereafter War of 1812 Papers.

[13] Another version of the story places these events at Mackinac Island the following year. It is more likely that the coats made on St. Joseph proved so warm and serviceable that the practice was continued and the garment received its name later on. Walter Havighurst, *Three Flags at the Straits*, Englewood Cliffs, Prentice-Hall, 1966, pp. 111-113. Hereafter Havighurst, *Three Flags*.

[14] Unaddressed letter from Charles Roberts, July 12, 1812, War of 1812 Papers; Observations of Toussaint Pothier, War of 1812 Papers, p. 142; Neill, *History of the Ojibways*, p. 460.

[15] Unaddressed letter from Charles Roberts, July 12,

1812, War of 1812 Papers, p. 101.

[16] Statement of George Johnston "To the Public of the State of Michigan," Detroit, 16th July 1844, George Johnston Letterbook, Michigan Historical Collections, Bentley Historical Library, The University of Michigan. Hereafter Letterbook.

[17] Havighurst, *Three Flags*, pp. 117-119; Bayliss, *St. Joseph Island*, pp. 56-63.

[18] Statement of George Johnston, July 16, 1844, Letterbook; Schoolcraft, "Memoir of John Johnston," p. 66.

[19] Charles Roberts to Isaac Brock, July 17, 1812, War of 1812 Papers, p. 108.

[20] Havighurst, *Three Flags*, pp. 122-123.

[21] Bayliss, *St. Joseph Island*, p. 63.

[22] "A Statement of the Amount of Capital Employed by John Johnston and Jno. Johnston and Company," Schoolcraft Papers, Reel 18.

[23] John Johnston to George Johnston, September 8, 1813, Johnston Papers, Box 8.

[24] John Johnston to George Johnston, September 17, 1813, Johnston Papers, Box 8.

[25] Copy in Bayliss Public Library, Sault Ste. Marie, Michigan. Original document in private collection of Charles Wheeler.

[26] John Johnston to George Johnston, September 8, 1813, Johnston Papers, Box 8.

[27] John Johnston to George Johnston, September 17, 1813, Johnston Papers, Box 8.

[28] Seltzer, *Flint*.

[29] Johnston Family Record.

[30] John Johnston to George Johnston, September 8, 1813, Johnston Papers, Box 8.

[31] Memorial of Lewis S. Johnston, January 20, 1820, *Michigan Historical and Pioneer Collections*, Vol. 23, pp. 366-367.

[32] John Johnston to George Johnston, September 17, 1813, Johnston Papers, Box 8.

[33] Unaddressed letter of Isaac Brock, July 29, 1812, War of 1812 Papers, p. 124.

[34] John Johnston to George Johnston, September 8, 1813, Johnston Papers, Box 8.

[35] Elsie McLeod Jury, "U.S.S. Tigress-H.M.S. Confiance,

1831-1831," *Inland Seas*, Spring 1972, pp. 3-4. Hereafter Jury, "U. S. S. Tigress."

36 Letters of Brigadier-General Henry Proctor, mostly to Sir George Prevost, dated July 4, July 6, July 13, August 18, August 26, August 29, 1813, War of 1812 Papers, pp. 330-365.

37 John Johnston to George Johnston, September 17, 1813, Johnston Papers, Box 8.

38 Usher Parsons, "Account of the Battle of Lake Erie," Walter Havighurst, ed., *The Great Lakes Reader*, New York, The Macmillan Company, 1966, pp. 138-145, Hereafter Havighurst, *Great Lakes Reader*; Proctor to de Rottenberg, September 13, 1813, War of 1812 Papers, pp. 377-378.

39 Usher Parsons to George Johnston, April 15, 1857, Johnston Papers, Box 7.

40 Jury, "U. S. S. Tigress," p. 6.

41 Schoolcraft, "Memoir of John Johnston," p. 66.

42 Campbell, *North West Company*, p. 189.

43 A. H. Holmes to Mr. Johnston, July 23, 1813, copy, George Johnston Letterbook.

44 Jameson, *Winter Studies*, Vol. 1, p. 240.

45 Johnston Family Record.

46 Schoolcraft, "Memoir of John Johnston," pp. 66-68.

47 Ibid., p. 67.

48 Memorial of John Johnston to Rt. Hon. the Lords Commissioners of His Majesty's Treasury, December 27, 1819, *Michigan Pioneer and Historical Collections*, Vol. 25, p. 668; 1824 affidavits by John Holiday and George Johnston, Public Archives of Canada, Department of Finance, War of 1812 Losses, RG 19 E5A Vol. 3757.

49 Havighurst, *Three Flags*, pp. 125-126; Schoolcraft, "Memoir of John Johnston," pp. 68-70.

50 John Johnston to George Johnston, August 8, 1814, Johnston Papers, Box 8.

Chapter Seven

1 John Johnston to Jane Johnston, quoted in Schoolcraft, "Memoir of John Johnston," p. 72.

2 Ibid., p. 71.

3 Ibid., p. 64.
4 John Johnston to George Johnston, September 17, 1813, Johnston Papers, Box 8.
5 John Johnston to "My Dear Boys," November 12, 1814, Johnston Papers, Box 8.
6 Copy of David David's Account, Public Archives of Canada, Department of Finance, War of 1812 Losses, RG19 E 5(a). Vol. 3757, Claim Number 1823.
7 Ibid.
8 John Johnston to "My Dear Boys," November 12, 1814, Johnston Papers, Box 8.
9 Schoolcraft, "Memoir of John Johnston," p. 73.
10 Minutes of the Beaver Club, 1807-1827, MG 19 B3, Public Archives of Canada. Hereafter called Minutes of the Beaver Club.
11 Burpee, *The Beaver Club*, p. 91.
12 Schoolcraft, "Memoir of John Johnston," p. 74, footnote.
13 Ida Amanda Johnson, *The Michigan Fur Trade*, Lansing, Michigan Historical Commission, 1919, pp. 124-128. Hereafter Ida Johnson, *Fur Trade*.
14 George Johnston to Robert Stuart, September 22, 1842, Johnston Papers, Box 4.
15 Samuel F. Cook, *Drummond Island*, Lansing, R. Smith Printing Company, 1896, pp. 29-36.
16 Fred Landon, *Lake Huron*, Indianapolis, Bobbs Merrill, 1944, p. 221.
17 John Johnston to George Johnston, July 24, 1816, Johnston Papers, Box 8.
18 John Johnston to George Johnston, November 20, 1815, Johnston Papers, Box 8.
19 Davidson, *The North West Company*, pp. 144-146.
20 McKay, *The Honorable Company*, 135-138; Campbell, *North West Company*, pp. 202-208.
21 Campbell, *North West Company*, p. 211.
22 Certificate in Johnston Collection, Bayliss Public Library, Sault Ste. Marie, Michigan.
23 Campbell, *North West Company*, pp. 212-213.
24 Campbell, *McGillivray*, p. 218.
25 Campbell, *North West Company*, p. 222.
26 McKay, *The Honorable Company*, pp. 143-144.
27 Campbell, *North West Company*, pp. 214-218;

Davidson, *The North West Company*, pp. 147-150.
28 Campbell, *McGillivray*, pp. 228-229.
29 *The Sault Daily Star*, June 18, 1970, special section.
30 Campbell, *North West Company*, p. 226.
31 Ibid., pp. 226-230.
32 McKay, *The Honorable Company*, p. 148; Campbell, *North West Company*, pp. 238-239.
33 Wallace, *Documents of North West Co.*, p. 2.
34 This son's middle name is sometimes spelled McDougall in the literature, but all of the genealogical records and "official" family documents use the spelling given here.
35 Johnston Family Record.
36 John Johnston to George Johnston, October 16, 1816, Johnston Papers, Box 8.
37 John Johnston to George Johnston, November 9, 1816, Johnston Papers, Box 8.
38 William McGillivray to John Johnston, June 22, 1817, Schoolcraft Papers, Reel 18.
39 Minutes of the Beaver Club.
40 Nute, *The Voyageur*, p. 203; Lavender, *The Fist*, p. 233.
41 John Johnston to George Johnston, January 15, 1817, Johnston Papers, Box 8.
42 Statement of the Amount of Capital Employed by John Johnston and Jno. Johnston and Company, 1813-1823, Schoolcraft Papers, Reel 18.
43 Ramsey Crooks to George Johnston, December 15, 1818, Johnston Papers, Box 1.
44 John Johnston to George Johnston, January 12, 1819, Johnston Papers, Box 1.
45 Ibid.
46 John Johnston to George Johnston, n. d., Johnston Papers, Box 1.
47 Copy of letter dated August 20, 1821, Lewis Cass Papers, Box 3, Bayliss Public Library. Hereafter Cass Papers.
48 David David to John Johnston, September 14, 1817, Schoolcraft Papers, Reel 18.
49 John Johnston to George Johnston, October 30, 1818, Johnston Papers, Box 1.
50 Ibid.
51 Schoolcraft, "Memoir of John Johnston," p. 79.

52 Henry Kearney to John Johnston, January 29, 1819, Schoolcraft Papers, Reel 18.
53 Memorial of John Johnston, December 27, 1819, *Michigan Pioneer and Historical Collections*, Vol. 25, p. 668; Certificate of Lt.-Col. Robert McDouall, December 17, 1819, ibid., p. 664.
54 Copy of letter dated 13 February 1820, signed Bathurst, in Public Archives of Canada, War of 1812 Papers.
55 J. McNeale [sic] to John Johnston, March 29, 1819, Schoolcraft Papers, Reel 18.
56 Eliza Kearney to John Johnston, March 20, 1819, Schoolcraft Papers, Reel 18.
57 Schoolcraft, "Memoir of John Johnston," p. 79.
58 William McMurray to Henry Schoolcraft, May 31, 1844, Schoolcraft Papers, Reel 34. Letter quotes the original deed as quoted in letter from Irish solicitor.
59 Schoolcraft, "Memoir of John Johnston," p. 82.
60 Henry Kearney to John Johnston, February 26, 1818, Schoolcraft Papers, Reel 18.
61 John Johnston to George Johnston, January 15, 1817, Johnston Papers, Box 8. It has been suggested by one researcher that Lewis fathered two daughters by the wife of Jean Baptiste Cadotte, Jr. The evidence is slim and inconclusive, however. Partly it is based on the word in this letter that I read clearly as "falsehood," which has been read as "fatherhood." One of the girls, Sophia, was raised in the Johnston household as a servant, but she remained illiterate. It is very unlikely that John Johnston would have allowed a granddaughter, even an illegitimate one, to grow up in his home unable even to sign her name. While it is true that both girls are mentioned in various documents as Johnston, they are identified equally often as Cadotte. So far the question remains unresolved.
62 Ibid.
63 Schoolcraft, "Memoir of John Johnston," p. 79.
64 David David to John Johnston, May 17, 1821, Schoolcraft Papers, Reel 18.
65 Copy of Letter from B. Wilmot to Hon. Robert Peel, October 20, 1822, Department of Finance, War of 1812 Losses, Public Archives of Canada, RG19 E 5(a),

Vol. 3757, Claim Number 1823. Hereafter Department of Finance.
66 John Johnston to Peregrine Maitland, October 1823, ibid.
67 Affidavit sworn at Drummond Island, July 1, 1824, ibid.
68 Statement of Board of Claims, 6th August 1824, ibid.

Chapter Eight

1 "Reminiscences by George Johnston of Sault Ste. Marys, 1815," *Michigan Pioneer and Historical Collections*, Vol. 12, pp. 605-607.
2 Ibid., pp. 607-608.
3 Lavender, *The Fist*, pp. 42-43.
4 Johnson, *Fur Trade*, pp. 103-104, 147; Wilcomb E. Washburn, "Symbol, Utility and Aesthetics in the Indian Fur Trade," *Minnesota History*, Vol. 40, Winter 1966, p. 202. Hereafter Washburn, *Symbol in Indian Trade*.
5 Henry Schoolcraft to Major E. Cutler, July 31, 1824, Schoolcraft Papers, Reel 18.
6 Clarissa Headline and Milton N. Gallup, eds., "The Diary of an Early Fur Trader," *Inland Seas*, Winter 1962, pp. 299-305, Fall 1963, p. 32, Winter 1963, pp. 280-281. Hereafter Headline, *Diary of Fur Trader*.
7 McKenny, *Sketches*, pp. 184-186.
8 Henry Rowe Schoolcraft, *Narrative Journal of Travels Through the Northwest Regions of the United States*, Albany, E. and E. Hosford, 1821, pp. 71-78; hereafter Schoolcraft, *Travels;* Schoolcraft, *Memoirs*, pp. 49-50; Joseph and Estelle Bayliss, *River of Destiny*, Detroit, Wayne University Press, 1955, pp. 74-75.
9 Journal of James Duane Doty, *Wisconsin Historical Collections*, Vol. 13, p. 180.
10 Ralph H. Brown, ed., "With Cass in the Northwest in 1820," Journal of Charles C. Trowbridge, *Minnesota History*, Vol. XXIII, p. 144.
11 "Johnston Reminiscences," p. 609.
12 Ibid., p. 610.
13 "Johnston Reminiscences," pp. 609-611; Trowbridge Journal, pp. 145-147; Schoolcraft, *Travels*, pp. 135-139.

[14] Lewis Cass to Colonel Boyd, August 20, 1821, Cass Papers, Bayliss Public Library.
[15] Schoolcraft, *Travels*, pp. 174-176.
[16] Schoolcraft, *Memoirs*, pp. 49-50; Chase S. and Stellanova Osborn, *Schoolcraft, Longfellow, Hiawatha*, Lancaster, Pa., Jacques Cattell Press, 1942, pp. 349-350. Hereafter Osborn, *Schoolcraft*.
[17] Schoolcraft, *Memoirs*, p. 53.
[18] Osborn, *Schoolcraft*, pp. 302-318.
[19] Ibid., pp. 319-320.
[20] Schoolcraft, *Memoirs*, pp. 18-42.
[21] Ibid., p. 40.
[22] Ibid., p.43.
[23] Osborn, *Schoolcraft*, pp. 329-330.
[24] Schoolcraft, *Memoirs*, p. 44.
[25] Ibid., pp. 55-63.
[26] Ibid., pp. 64-69.
[27] Ibid., p. 73.
[28] Ibid., p. 75.
[29] Ibid., p. 77.
[30] Ibid., p. 88.
[31] Ibid., pp. 88-89.
[32] Henry Schoolcraft to John Johnston, July 6, 1822, Schoolcraft Papers, Reel 2.
[33] Schoolcraft, *Memoirs*, p. 93.
[34] Ibid., p. 94.
[35] Ibid., p. 95.
[36] Ibid., pp. 96-97.
[37] Ibid., p. 119.
[38] Ibid., p. 109.
[39] It was used by the interpreters for counting out the payments. When John McDouall Johnston became the last of the interpreters at the Sault, he acquired the table. At his death it went to Judge Joseph Steere, who donated it to the Carnegie Library, now the Bayliss Public Library, at Sault Ste. Marie. Stanley Newton, *The Story of Sault Ste. Marie and Chippewa County*, Sault Ste. Marie, The Sault News Printing Company, 1923, pp. 155-156. Hereafter Newton, *The Story*.
[40] Schoolcraft, *Memoirs*, p. 117.
[41] Ibid., p. 117.
[42] Ibid., pp. 106-107.

43 Ibid., p. 127.
44 Ibid., pp. 127-136.
45 Ibid., p. 141.
46 Ibid., p. 143.
47 Ibid., pp. 153-154.
48 Note dated December 26, 1822, Schoolcraft Papers, Reel 18.
49 Note dated September 2, 1823, Schoolcraft Papers, Reel 18.
50 Note dated May 19, 1823, Schoolcraft Papers, Reel 18.
51 Note dated January 27, 1823, Schoolcraft Papers, Reel 18.
52 Jane Moore to Jane Johnston, January 15, 1818, Schoolcraft Papers, Reel 18.
53 Henry Schoolcraft to Jane Johnston, October 24, 1822, Schoolcraft Papers, Reel 2.
54 Jane Johnston to Henry Schoolcraft, March 6, 1823, Schoolcraft Papers, Reel 18.
55 Jane Johnston to Henry Schoolcraft, May 2, 1823, Schoolcraft Papers, Reel 18.
56 Jane Schoolcraft to Henry Schoolcraft, Christmas Day, 1823, Schoolcraft Papers, Reel 18.
57 Schoolcraft, *Memoirs*, p. 167.
58 Subscription, dated October 1822, Schoolcraft Papers, Reel 2.
59 Family Record, Schoolcraft Papers, Reel 66; Copy of entries in Schoolcraft Bible in Osborn Papers, Lake Superior State University Library, Sault Ste. Marie.
60 Certificate signed by James Wessimet, April 29, 1835, in Johnston Collection, Bayliss Public Library.
61 Bald, *The French Seigneury*, pp. 16-19; *Territorial Papers of the United States*, Vol. XI, Michigan, 1820-29, p. 256.
62 J. D. Doty to Henry Schoolcraft, June 16, 1823, *Schoolcraft Papers*, Reel 2.
63 Bald, *The French Seigneury*, p. 20.
64 J. D. Doty to Henry Schoolcraft, June 16, 1823, *Schoolcraft Papers*, Reel 2.
65 Document in Johnston Collection, Bayliss Public Library.
66 Bald, *French Seigneury*, pp. 20-22.
67 Ibid., p. 15.

68 Ibid., p. 16.
69 Indenture of July 18, 1798 in Michigan Historical Collections, Bentley Historical Library, The University of Michigan.
70 Bald, *French Seigneury*, p. 22.
71 Ibid., pp. 23-32; Brief of Alfred Russell, U. S. District Attorney, *Louise Pauline de Repentigny and Others vs. The United States of America*, Detroit, 1864; "The United States v. Louise Pauline de Repentigny et. al.," *United States Supreme Court Reports*, 18 Law ed., Book 18, The Lawyers Cooperative Publishing Company, 1901, pp. 643-646. Hereafter The U. S. Supreme Court.
72 Chapman, *The Johnstons*, p. 306.
73 Osborn, *Schoolcraft*, p. 520.

Chapter Nine

1 Jury, "U. S. S. Tigress," p. 14.
2 Robert McElroy and Thomas Riggs, eds., *The Unfortified Boundary*, the Diary of Joseph Delafield, New York, privately printed, 1943, pp. 66, 281-292. Hereafter Delafield Diary in McElroy and Riggs, eds., *The Unfortified Boundary*.
3 Ibid., p. 298.
4 Bayliss, *River of Destiny*, pp. 69-72.
5 Schoolcraft, *Memoirs*, pp.162-163.
6 Delafield Diary in McElroy and Riggs, eds., *The Unfortified Boundary*, p. 370.
7 Ibid., pp. 69-73.
8 Schoolcraft, *Memoirs*, p. 93.
9 Ibid., p. 107.
10 Ibid., p. 100.
11 Cook, *Drummond*, pp. 79-82; Bayliss, *River of Destiny*, p. 135.
12 Lewis Johnston to Henry Schoolcraft, August 9, 1823, Schoolcraft Papers, Reel 2.
13 Undated scrapbook, Johnston Papers, Box 9.
14 Lewis Johnston to Jane Schoolcraft, February 13, 1825, Schoolcraft Papers, Box 18.
15 Invoice dated July 26, 1822, Johnston Papers, Box 1.
16 The Johnston Family, typescript list of names and

dates, Johnston Collection, Bayliss Public Library. Hereafter cited as The Johnston Family.
[17] The Johnston Family.
[18] Family Record, Schoolcraft Papers, Reel 66.
[19] John Johnston to Henry Schoolcraft, July 16, 1824, Schoolcraft Papers, Reel 2.
[20] Schoolcraft, *Memoirs*, p. 200.
[21] Ibid., pp. 187-188.
[22] Ibid., p. 201.
[23] Receipt "For Education of Miss Anna Maria Johnston," April 1825, Schoolcraft Papers, Reel 3.
[24] John Johnston to Jane Schoolcraft, January 15, 1825, Schoolcraft Papers, Reel 2.
[25] Schoolcraft, *Memoirs*, p. 207.
[26] Henry Schoolcraft to Jane Schoolcraft, January 13, 1825, Schoolcraft Papers, Reel 3.
[27] Henry Schoolcraft to Jane Schoolcraft, January 17, 1825, Schoolcraft Papers, Reel 3.
[28] Jane Schoolcraft to Henry Schoolcraft, January 12, 1825 and receipt from Dr. Washington Murray, Schoolcraft Papers, Reel 3.
[29] John Johnston to Jane Schoolcraft, January 15, 1825, Schoolcraft Papers, Reel 3.
[30] Schoolcraft, *Memoirs*, pp. 207-208.
[31] Jane Schoolcraft to Henry Schoolcraft, July 5, 1825, Schoolcraft Papers, Reel 23.
[32] Schoolcraft, *Memoirs*, p. 208.
[33] Ibid., p. 213.
[34] John Johnston to Colonel Trimble, January 24, 1822, Schoolcraft Papers, Reel 18.
[35] Schoolcraft, *Memoirs*, pp. 214-217.
[36] Henry Schoolcraft to Jane Schoolcraft, July 13, 1825, Schoolcraft Papers, Reel 18.
[37] Henry Schoolcraft to Jane Schoolcraft, July 20, 1825, Schoolcraft Papers, Reel 18.
[38] Henry Schoolcraft to Jane Schoolcraft, August 17, 1825, Schoolcraft Papers, Reel 18.
[39] Jane Schoolcraft to Henry Schoolcraft, August 1, 1825, Schoolcraft Papers, Reel 3.
[40] Schoolcraft, *Memoirs*, p. 235.
[41] Mason, *Muzzeniegun*, p. 31.
[42] Ibid.

43 Schoolcraft, *Memoirs*, p. 300.
44 <u>Ibid</u>., pp. 242-245.
45 Henry Schoolcraft to Jane Schoolcraft, August 4, 1826, Schoolcraft Papers, Reel 19.
46 John Johnston to George Johnston, January 14, 1826, Johnston Papers, Box 1.
47 George Johnston to John Holiday, February 27, 1826, Johnston Papers, Box 1.
48 The Johnston Family.
49 Henry Schoolcraft to George Johnston, May 30, 1826, Johnston Papers, Box 1.
50 Lewis Cass to George Johnston, August 20, 1826 and Lewis Cass to Henry Schoolcraft, August 20, 1826, Johnston Papers, Box 1.
51 Schoolcraft, *Memoirs*, p. 246.
52 Robert Stuart to Henry Schoolcraft, August 29, 1826, Schoolcraft Papers, Reel 3.
53 Henry Schoolcraft to George Johnston, September 30, 1826, Johnston Papers, Box 1.
54 George Johnston to Henry Schoolcraft, September 26, 1826, Schoolcraft Papers, Reel 3.
55 To Henry Schoolcraft, February 12, 1827, Letterbook, Johnston Papers, Box 9.
56 George Johnston to Henry Schoolcraft, February 12, 1827, Schoolcraft Papers, Reel 4.
57 The Johnston Family.
58 Journal, Johnston Papers, Box 8.
59 Copy of Lyman Warren Letter to George Johnston, September 17, 1826, Letterbook, Johnston Papers, Box 9.
60 1828 Journal, entry of November 10, Johnston Papers, Box 8.
61 <u>Ibid</u>.
62 Notebook, Johnston Papers, Box 9.
63 1828 Journal, Johnston Papers, Box 8.
64 Henry Schoolcraft to George Johnston, November 3, 1829, quoting a letter Indian Agent Taliaferro at St. Peters had forwarded to him from the War Department, Johnston Papers, Box 1.
65 McKenney, *Sketches*, p. 146.
66 <u>Ibid</u>., pp. 185-186.
67 Thomas McKenney to Henry Schoolcraft, April 17,

1827, Schoolcraft Papers, Reel 4.
[68] Jane Schoolcraft to Henry Schoolcraft, August 17, 1824, Schoolcraft Papers, Reel 4.
[69] Thomas McKenney to Henry Schoolcraft, August 17, 1824, Schoolcraft Papers, Reel 4.
[70] Bayliss, *River of Destiny*, pp. 81-82.
[71] Schoolcraft, *Memoirs*, pp. 81-82.
[72] C. F. Morton to George Johnston, February 20, 1827, Johnston Papers, Box 1.
[73] Mason, *Muzzeniegun*, p. 2.
[74] John Johnston to Henry Schoolcraft, January 27, 1827, Schoolcraft Papers, Reel 19.
[75] Mason, *Muzzeniegun*, pp. 23-26.
[76] Ibid., p. 43.
[77] John Johnston to George Johnston, March 26, 1827, Johnston Papers, Box 1.
[78] Ibid.
[79] Mason, *Muzzeniegun*, pp. 148-150.
[80] Schoolcraft, *Memoirs*, pp. 260-263.
[81] Ibid., pp. 261-262.
[82] Ibid., p. 263.
[83] Mason, *Muzzeniegun*, p. 159.
[84] Schoolcraft, *Memoirs*, pp. 274-275,
[85] Ibid., pp. 265-268.
[86] Jane Schoolcraft to Henry Schoolcraft, July 11, 1827, Schoolcraft Papers, Reel 4.
[87] Jane Schoolcraft to Henry Schoolcraft, August 7, 1827, Schoolcraft Papers, Reel 4.
[88] Charles F. Morton to George Johnston, October 22, 1827, Johnston Papers, Box 1.
[89] Schoolcraft, "Memoir of John Johnston," p. 84.
[90] Charles Trowbridge to Henry Schoolcraft, November 6, 1827, Schoolcraft Papers, Reel 4; Charles Morton to George Johnston, October 27, 1827, Johnston Papers, Box 1.
[91] Family Record, Schoolcraft Papers, Reel 66.
[92] Schoolcraft, *Memoirs*, p. 275.
[93] Ibid., p. 276.
[94] Ibid., p. 328.
[95] Henry Schoolcraft to Jane Schoolcraft, May 8, 1828, Schoolcraft Papers, Reel 19.
[96] Jane Schoolcraft to Henry Schoolcraft, May 19, 1828,

Schoolcraft Papers, Reel 19.
[97] Jane Schoolcraft to Henry Schoolcraft, June 5, 1828, Schoolcraft Papers, Reel 19.
[98] Henry Schoolcraft to Jane Schoolcraft, May 18, 1828, Schoolcraft Papers, Reel 19.
[99] Henry Schoolcraft to Jane Schoolcraft, June 15, 1828, Schoolcraft Papers, Reel 4.
[100] Henry Schoolcraft to Jane Schoolcraft, May 17, 1828, Schoolcraft Papers, Reel 19.
[101] Henry Schoolcraft to Jane Schoolcraft, June 7, 1828, Schoolcraft Papers, Reel 19.
[102] Jane Schoolcraft to Henry Schoolcraft, June 4, 1828, Schoolcraft Papers, Reel 19.
[103] Ibid.
[104] Jane Schoolcraft to Henry Schoolcraft, June 14, 1828, Schoolcraft Papers, Reel 19.
[105] Jane Schoolcraft to George Johnston, July 9, 1828, Johnston Papers, Box 1.
[106] Jane Schoolcraft to George Johnston, August 6, 1828, Johnston Papers, Box 1.
[107] John Johnston to Henry Schoolcraft, May 30, 1828, Schoolcraft Papers, Reel 19.
[108] Robert Stuart to William Woodbridge, June 8, 1824, and John Johnston to William Woodbridge, August 13, 1825, William Woodbridge Papers, Burton Historical Collection, Detroit Public Library.
[109] John Johnston to Henry Schoolcraft, August 14, 1828, Schoolcraft Papers, Reel 19.
[110] Charlotte E. J. Killaly, *History of John Johnston of Sault Ste. Marie, Michigan*, Typescript in Johnston Collection, Bayliss Public Library, p. 17. Hereafter Killaly, *John Johnston.*
[111] Schoolcraft, "Memoir of John Johnston," pp. 84-86; Henry Schoolcraft to Henry Kearney, September 30, 1828, Schoolcraft Papers, Reel 4.
[112] Schoolcraft, "Memoir of John Johnston," p. 82.
[113] Howard L. Johnston to Leslie Warren, February 15, 1931, private correspondence. The letter contains a tracing of the nameplate, then in his possession.
[114] Schoolcraft, "Memoir of John Johnston," pp. 86-87.
[115] George Johnston to Henry Schoolcraft, February 22, 1829, Schoolcraft Papers, Reel 19.

[116] Lewis Cass to Henry Schoolcraft, November 18, 1828, Schoolcraft Papers, Reel 19.

Chapter Ten

[1] Schoolcraft, *Memoirs*, pp. 259-263; Lewis Cass to Henry Schoolcraft, April 9, 1827, Schoolcraft Papers, Reel 4; Notice of Election, June 4, 1827, Schoolcraft Papers, Reel 4.
[2] Bayliss, *River of Destiny*, p. 216; Francis Audrain to George Johnston, March 27, 1827, Johnston Papers, Box 1.
[3] Twenty-second Congress, First Session, Senate Document 90, p. 79.
[4] Rhoda R. Gilman, "Last Days of the Upper Mississippi Fur Trade," in Malvina Bolus, ed., *People and Pelts*, Winnipeg, Pegus Publishers, 1972, p. 104. Hereafter Gilman, "Last Days," in Bolus, ed., *People and Pelts*.
[5] Ibid., pp. 43-44.
[6] Order of Judge of Probate, July 20, 1829, Schoolcraft Papers, Reel 19.
[7] Jane Schoolcraft to George Johnston, January 14, 1829, Johnston Papers, Box 1.
[8] Clapp and Ehringer to Henry Schoolcraft, April 26, 1829, Schoolcraft Papers, Reel 19.
[9] Henry Schoolcraft to George Johnston, May 23, 1829, Johnston Papers, Box 1.
[10] Ibid.
[11] George Johnston to Rev. Uncle, March 20, 1831, Letterbook.
[12] Jane Schoolcraft to Henry Schoolcraft, September 13, 1829, Schoolcraft Papers, Reel 19.
[13] Ibid.
[14] Jane Schoolcraft to Henry Schoolcraft, October 5, 1829, Schoolcraft Papers, Reel 19 and Family Record, Schoolcraft Papers, Reel 66.
[15] Zina Pitcher to George Johnston, August 5, 1828, Johnston Papers, Box 1.
[16] Receipt, Johnston Papers, Box 1.
[17] George Johnston to Chephas Mills, January 24, 1830, Letterbook.

[18] George Johnston to Mills and Company, April 9, 1833, Letterbook
[19] Account statement, June 10, 1829-May 27, 1831, Johnston Papers, Box 1.
[20] George Johnston to Henry Schoolcraft, June 12, 1830, Johnston Papers, Box 1.
[21] William Johnston to Henry Schoolcraft, June 12, 1830, Schoolcraft Papers, Reel 20.
[22] Schoolcraft, *Memoirs*, pp. 238-239; Henry Schoolcraft to John MacLean, January 20, 1826, Schoolcraft Papers, Reel 19.
[23] John Johnston to Henry Schoolcraft, February 12, 1828, Schoolcraft Papers, Reel 4.
[24] Speech to the Indians, February 13, 1828, Schoolcraft Papers, Reel 4.
[25] Schoolcraft, *Memoirs*, p. 333.
[26] Ibid., 333-334.
[27] William Johnston, "Letters of 1833," *loc. cit.*, pp. 138-139.
[28] Samuel Lasley to Henry Schoolcraft, December 7, 1830, Schoolcraft Papers, Reel 5.
[29] Jane Schoolcraft to Henry Schoolcraft, December 6, 1830, Schoolcraft Papers, Reel 20.
[30] Samuel Lasley to Henry Schoolcraft, December 7, 1830, Schoolcraft Papers, Reel 5.
[31] Jane Schoolcraft to Henry Schoolcraft, December 6, 1830, Schoolcraft Papers, Reel 20.
[32] L. Allen to James Schoolcraft, December 5, 1830, Schoolcraft Papers, Reel 5.
[33] John Hulbert to James Schoolcraft, January 11, 1831, Schoolcraft Papers, Reel 5.
[34] Henry Schoolcraft to James Schoolcraft, December 25, 1830, Schoolcraft Papers, Reel 5.
[35] Henry Schoolcraft to Jane Schoolcraft, December 8, 1830, Schoolcraft Papers, Reel 20.
[36] Robert Stuart to Henry Schoolcraft, January 25, 1831, Schoolcraft Papers, Reel 20.
[37] Robert Stuart to Henry Schoolcraft, January 31, 1831, Schoolcraft Papers, Reel 5.
[38] Jane Schoolcraft to Henry Schoolcraft, January 31, 1831, Schoolcraft Papers, Reel 20.
[39] Henry Schoolcraft to James Schoolcraft, February 11,

1831, Schoolcraft Papers, Reel 5.
[40] Ibid.
[41] Jane Schoolcraft to Henry Schoolcraft, January 31, 1831, Schoolcraft Papers, Reel 20.
[42] Jane Schoolcraft to Henry Schoolcraft, March 7, 1831, Schoolcraft Papers, Reel 20.
[43] Ibid.
[44] James Schoolcraft to Henry Schoolcraft, March 7, 1831, Schoolcraft Papers, Reel 20.
[45] Jane Schoolcraft to Henry Schoolcraft, March 20, 1831, Schoolcraft Papers, Reel 20.
[46] Francis Audrain to George Johnston, August 4, 1827, Johnston Papers, Box 1.
[47] A list of names of all persons employed in the Agency between the first September 1829 and the first September 1830, Schoolcraft Papers, Reel 20.
[48] Schoolcraft, *Memoirs,* pp. 326-327.
[49] John Cumming, "A Puritan Among the Chippewas," *Michigan History,* Vol. 51, Fall 1967, pp. 213-216. Hereafter Cumming, "A Puritan."
[50] Unsigned letter to James Schoolcraft, January 5, 1832, Schoolcraft Papers, Reel 5.
[51] Cumming, "A Puritan," p. 216.
[52] L. Bolles to Abel Bingham, June 4, 1829, Bingham Family Papers, Michigan Historical Collections, Bentley Historical Library, The University of Michigan.
[53] George Johnston to Henry Schoolcraft, May 22, 1830, Schoolcraft Papers, Reel 5.
[54] Family Record, Schoolcraft Papers, Reel 66.
[55] Schoolcraft, *Memoirs,* p. 334.
[56] Henry Schoolcraft to Jane Schoolcraft, September 12, 1829, Schoolcraft Papers, Reel 19.
[57] Henry Schoolcraft to Abel Bingham, August 30, 1830, Schoolcraft Papers, Reel 5. This is one of the girls who, it has been suggested, might have been an illegitimate daughter of Lewis Johnston.
[58] Henry Schoolcraft to Thomas McKenney, August 25, 1830, Schoolcraft Papers, Reel 20.
[59] Henry Schoolcraft to Abel Bingham, August 30, 1830, Schoolcraft Papers, Reel 5.
[60] Abel Bingham to Henry Schoolcraft, August 25, 1830, Schoolcraft Papers, Reel 5.

[61] Henry Schoolcraft to Abel Bingham, August 30, 1830, Schoolcraft Papers, Reel 5.
[62] Abel Bingham to Henry Schoolcraft, August 25, 1830, Schoolcraft Papers, Reel 5.
[63] Abel Bingham to Henry Schoolcraft, August 31, 1830, Schoolcraft Papers, Reel 5.
[64] Statement of January 11, 1832, Schoolcraft Papers, Reel 21.
[65] Statement of Bela Chapman, Samuel Ashmun, and [illegible], January 14, 1832, Schoolcraft Papers, Reel 21.
[66] Edwin James, ed., *A Narrative of the Captivity and Adventures of John Tanner*, Minneapolis, Ross and Haines, 1956, *passim*. The only source for the events of his life is Tanner's own narrative, in which dates and intervals of time are vague. Hereafter James, ed., *John Tanner*.
[67] Ibid., *passim*.
[68] Mrs. Angie Bingham Gilbert, "The Story of John Tanner," *Michigan Pioneer and Historical Collections*, Vol. 38, p. 199. Hereafter Mrs. A. B. Gilbert, "John Tanner."
[69] Schoolcraft, *Memoirs*, p. 315.
[70] Statement by Henry Schoolcraft, February 18, 1832, Schoolcraft Papers, Reel 21.
[71] Joseph H. Steere, "Sketch of John Tanner, Known as the 'White Indian', " *Michigan Pioneer and Historical Collections*, Vol. 22, pp. 246-247. Hereafter, Steere, "John Tanner."
[72] George Johnston to Henry Schoolcraft, January 26, 1831, Schoolcraft Papers, Reel 20.
[73] Mrs. A. B. Gilbert, "John Tanner," p. 99.

Chapter Eleven

[1] Henry Schoolcraft to Jane Schoolcraft, November 24, 1830, Schoolcraft Papers, Reel 20.
[2] Schoolcraft, *Memoirs*, p. 343.
[3] Henry Schoolcraft to Jane Schoolcraft, November 24, 1830, Schoolcraft Papers, Reel 20.
[4] Jane Schoolcraft to Henry Schoolcraft, December 6, 1830, Schoolcraft Papers, Reel 20.
[5] Jane Schoolcraft to Henry Schoolcraft, March 8, 1831, Schoolcraft Papers, Reel 20.

[6] Jane Schoolcraft to Henry Schoolcraft, January 4, 1831, Schoolcraft Papers, Reel 20.
[7] Jane Schoolcraft to Henry Schoolcraft, November 19, 1830, Schoolcraft Papers, Reel 20.
[8] Jane Schoolcraft to Henry Schoolcraft, November 27, 1830, Schoolcraft Papers, Reel 20.
[9] Jane Schoolcraft to Henry Schoolcraft, December 6, 1830, Schoolcraft Papers, Reel 20.
[10] Jane Schoolcraft to Henry Schoolcraft, January 4, 1831, Schoolcraft Papers, Reel 20.
[11] Henry Schoolcraft to Jane Schoolcraft, December 8, 1830, Schoolcraft Papers, Reel 20.
[12] William Johnston to Henry Schoolcraft, January 26, 1831, Schoolcraft Papers, Reel 20.
[13] Ibid.
[14] Jane Schoolcraft to Henry Schoolcraft, January 26, 1831, Schoolcraft Papers, Reel 20.
[15] Jane Schoolcraft to Henry Schoolcraft, March 7, 1831, Schoolcraft Papers, Reel 20.
[16] Schoolcraft, *Memoirs*, p. 398.
[17] Ibid., pp. 400-401.
[18] Ibid., p. 431.
[19] The Johnston Family.
[20] Agreement of January 1, 1832, Johnston Papers, Box 2.
[21] Hugh D. Maclean, "An Irish Apostle and Archdeacon of Canada," *Journal of the Canadian Church Historical Society*, Vol. XV, September 1973, pp. 50-52. Hereafter Maclean, "An Irish Apostle."
[22] John McDouall Johnston to George Johnston, January 6, 1832, Johnston Papers, Box 2.
[23] James Schoolcraft to Henry Schoolcraft, February 20, 1831, Schoolcraft Papers, Reel 5.
[24] James Schoolcraft to Henry Schoolcraft, February 1, 1832, Schoolcraft Papers, Reel 5.
[25] James Schoolcraft to Henry Schoolcraft, February 15, 1832, Schoolcraft Papers, Reel 5.
[26] Schoolcraft, *Memoirs*, pp. 347-348.
[27] Edsel K. Rintala, *Douglass Houghton*, Detroit, Wayne University Press, 1954, pp. 1-12; Alvah Bradish, *Memoir of Douglass Houghton*, Detroit, Raynor and Taylor, 1889, pp. 9-17.

28 Schoolcraft, *Memoirs,* p. 350.
29 Jane Schoolcraft to Henry Schoolcraft, June 27, 1831, Schoolcraft Papers, Reel 20.
30 Schoolcraft, *Memoirs,* pp. 353-396.
31 Douglass Houghton to Henry Schoolcraft, April 3, 1832, Schoolcraft Papers, Reel 5.
32 Schoolcraft, *Memoirs,* pp. 405-421.
33 Francis Audrain to George Johnston, November 24, 1832, Johnston Papers, Box 2.
34 Schoolcraft, *Memoirs,* p. 423.
35 Jane Schoolcraft to Henry Schoolcraft, July 16, 1832, Schoolcraft Papers, Reel 5.
36 Jane Schoolcraft to Henry Schoolcraft, July 25, 1832, Schoolcraft Papers, Reel 5.
37 Ibid.
38 Jane Schoolcraft to Henry Schoolcraft, October 9, 1832, Schoolcraft Papers, Reel 5.
39 Jane Schoolcraft to Henry Schoolcraft, October 10, 1832, Schoolcraft Papers, Reel 5.
40 Jane Schoolcraft to Henry Schoolcraft, September 18, 1832, Schoolcraft Papers, Reel 5.
41 Jane Schoolcraft to Henry Schoolcraft, October 9, 1832, Schoolcraft Papers, Reel 5.
42 James Schoolcraft to George Johnston, April 15, 1833, Johnston Papers, Box 2.
43 Henry Schoolcraft to Jane Schoolcraft, September 26, 1832, Schoolcraft Papers, Reel 21.
44 Anna Maria Johnston to Jane Schoolcraft, October 10, 1832, Schoolcraft Papers, Reel 21.
45 Ibid.
46 Jane Schoolcraft to Henry Schoolcraft, September 18, 1832, Schoolcraft Papers, Reel 5.
47 Schoolcraft, *Memoirs,* p. 404.
48 Henry Schoolcraft to George Johnston, August 20, 1832, Johnston Papers, Box 2.
49 Bill for Board and Tuition, Johnston Papers, Box 2.
50 Jane Schoolcraft to George Johnston, November 12, 1832, Johnston Papers, Box 2.
51 George Johnston to Henry Schoolcraft, May 22, 1830, Schoolcraft Papers, Reel 5.
52 Jane Schoolcraft to George Johnston, November 12, 1832, Johnston Papers, Box 2.

[53] Various bills and letters from James Schoolcraft and John Hulbert, Johnston Papers, Box 2.
[54] William Mitchell to Henry Schoolcraft, February 19, 1833, Schoolcraft Papers, Reel 6.
[55] C. Mills to George Johnston, June 26, 1833, Johnston Papers, Box 2.
[56] William Johnston, "Letters of 1833."
[57] Originals in Schoolcraft Papers, Reel 21.
[58] William Johnston to Jane Schoolcraft, January 13, 1834, Schoolcraft Papers, Reel 22.
[59] William Johnston to George Johnston, January 14, 1834, Johnston Papers, Box 2.
[60] Schoolcraft, *Memoirs*, p. 432.
[61] Henry Schoolcraft to Jane Schoolcraft, May 11, 1833, Schoolcraft Papers, Reel 6.
[62] Schoolcraft, *Memoirs*, p. 440.
[63] Ibid., p. 441.
[64] Elmwood was occupied by sub-agents for the next seven years; during the 1850s it was the home of Charles Harvey, the man who supervised construction of the first lock and canal; during the Civil War it was used for government offices; later it reverted to private residence under several owners; in 1898 it was sold to the Lake Superior Power Company for office use until 1922, when the building was closed. Restoration began several years ago under the auspices of the Chippewa County Historical Society. Undated brochure in Emerson Smith Papers, Box 2.
[65] Henry Schoolcraft to Jane Schoolcraft, May 11, 1833, Schoolcraft Papers, Reel 6.
[66] Schoolcraft, *Memoirs*, pp. 442-443.
[67] Henry Schoolcraft to Jane Schoolcraft, June 23, 1833, Schoolcraft Papers, Reel 21.
[68] Schoolcraft, *Memoirs*, p. 438.
[69] Jane Schoolcraft to Henry Schoolcraft, May 13, 1833, Schoolcraft Papers, Reel 6.
[70] Jane Schoolcraft to Henry Schoolcraft, June 24, 1833, Schoolcraft Papers, Reel 6.
[71] Ibid.
[72] Jane Schoolcraft to Henry Schoolcraft, June 29, 1833, Schoolcraft Papers, Reel 6.
[73] Jane Schoolcraft to Henry Schoolcraft, September 22,

1833, Schoolcraft Papers, Reel 6.
[74] Jane Schoolcraft to Henry Schoolcraft, June 24, 1833, Schoolcraft Papers, Reel 6; Maclean, "An Irish Apostle," p. 52.
[75] Maclean, "An Irish Apostle," p. 52.
[76] William McMurray to George Johnston, August 19, 1833, Johnston Papers, Box 2.
[77] Ibid.
[78] Jane Schoolcraft to Henry Schoolcraft, September 22, 1833, Schoolcraft Papers, Reel 6.
[79] William McMurray to Henry Schoolcraft, October 5, 1833, Schoolcraft Papers, Reel 6.
[80] Mrs. Thomas D. Gilbert, "Memories of the 'Soo'," *Michigan Pioneer and Historical Collections,* Vol. 30, p. 629.
[81] Unsigned letter to James Schoolcraft, January 5, 1832, [misdated], Schoolcraft Papers, Reel 5.
[82] Jane Schoolcraft to Charlotte McMurray, March 4, 1834, Schoolcraft Papers, Reel 6.
[83] James Schoolcraft to Henry Schoolcraft, March 1, 1834, Schoolcraft Papers, Reel 6.
[84] John Hulbert to Henry Schoolcraft, February 9, 1834, Schoolcraft Papers, Reel 6.
[85] James Schoolcraft to Henry Schoolcraft, February 9, 1834, Schoolcraft Papers, Reel 6.
[86] John Hulbert to Henry Schoolcraft, February 9, 1834, Schoolcraft Papers, Reel 6.
[87] James Schoolcraft to Henry Schoolcraft, February 9, 1834, Schoolcraft Papers, Reel 6.
[88] William McMurray to Jane and Henry Schoolcraft, February 11, 1834, Schoolcraft Papers, Reel 6.
[89] Ibid.
[90] James Schoolcraft to Henry Schoolcraft, February 14, 1834, Schoolcraft Papers, Reel 22.
[91] Undated letter from James Schoolcraft, entitled "Copy of my first note to Mrs. McMurray," Schoolcraft Papers, Reel 21.
[92] Ibid.
[93] Undated "Copy of my second note to Mrs. McMurray," Schoolcraft Papers, Reel 21.
[94] "Copy of my first note to Mrs. McMurray," Schoolcraft Papers, Reel 21.

⁹⁵ William McMurray to Henry Schoolcraft, February 11, 1834, Schoolcraft Papers, Reel 6.
⁹⁶ Jane Schoolcraft to Charlotte McMurray, March 4, 1834, Schoolcraft Papers, Reel 6.
⁹⁷ James Schoolcraft to Henry Schoolcraft, February 27, 1834, Schoolcraft Papers, Reel 6.
⁹⁸ James Schoolcraft to Henry Schoolcraft, March 1, 1834, Schoolcraft Papers, Reel 6.
⁹⁹ James Schoolcraft to Henry Schoolcraft, April 19, 1834, Schoolcraft Papers, Reel 6.
¹⁰⁰ James Schoolcraft to Henry Schoolcraft, August 23, 1834, Schoolcraft Papers, Reel 6; John Hulbert to Henry Schoolcraft, December 29, 1834, Schoolcraft Papers, Reel 22.
¹⁰¹ James Schoolcraft to Henry Schoolcraft, December 30, 1834, Schoolcraft Papers, Reel 22.

Chapter Twelve

¹ Gilman, "Last Days," in Bolus, ed., *People and Pelts*, pp. 105-108.
² William Johnston to Jane Schoolcraft, March 15, 1837, Schoolcraft Papers, Reel 26.
³ Otto Fowle, *Sault Ste. Marie and Its Great Waterway*, New York, G.P. Putnam's and Sons, 1925, p.406. Hereafter Fowle, *Sault Ste. Marie.*
⁴ Grace Lee Nute, *Lake Superior,* Indianapolis, Bobbs Merrill, 1944, pp. 174-178.
⁵ James L. Clayton, "The Growth and Economic Significance of the American Fur Trade, 1790-1890," *Minnesota History*, Vol. 40, Winter 1966, pp. 212-214.
⁶ Gilman, "Last Days," in Bolus, ed., *People and Pelts*, p. 120.
⁷ Ibid., p. 129.
⁸ Ibid., p. 130.
⁹ Jane Schoolcraft to Henry Schoolcraft, November 27, 1830, Schoolcraft Papers, Reel 20.
¹⁰ Statement of October 4, 1834, Johnston Papers, Box 2.
¹¹ Ibid.
¹² Ibid.

[13] George Johnston to Jane Schoolcraft, October, 1834, Letterbook.
[14] George Johnston to Lewis Cass, October 6, 1834, Letterbook.
[15] Lewis Cass to George Johnston, October 22, 1834, Johnston Papers, Box 2.
[16] George Johnston to Lewis Cass, December 12, 1834, Letterbook.
[17] Treasury Department to George Johnston, December 20, 1836, Johnston Papers, Box 3.
[18] William Ward to George Johnston, August 13, 1834, Johnston Papers, Box 2.
[19] George Johnston to H.L. Cole, October 18, 1834, Johnston Papers, Box 2.
[20] George Johnston to George Johnston, April 24, 1834, Johnston Papers, Box 2.
[21] George Johnston to George Johnston, April 7, 1837, Johnston Papers, Box 3.
[22] Henry Kearney to George Johnston, August 12, 1834, Johnston Papers, Box 2.
[23] Ibid.
[24] George Johnston to Henry Kearney, December 17, 1834, Johnston Papers, Box 2.
[25] Henry Kearney to Henry Schoolcraft, October 5, 1829, Schoolcraft Papers, Reel 19.
[26] Henry Kearney to Henry Schoolcraft, August 31, 1830 [misdated in another hand], Schoolcraft Papers, Reel 20.
[27] James Schoolcraft to Henry Schoolcraft, December 30, 1834, Schoolcraft Papers, Reel 7.
[28] John Hulbert to Henry Schoolcraft, February 7, 1835, Schoolcraft Papers, Reel 23.
[29] James Schoolcraft to Henry Schoolcraft, February 7, 1835, Schoolcraft Papers, Reel 23.
[30] James Schoolcraft to Henry Schoolcraft, February 27, 1835, Schoolcraft Papers, Reel 23.
[31] Henry Kearney to Henry Schoolcraft, March 6, 1835, Schoolcraft Papers, Reel 23.
[32] Henry Kearney to Henry Schoolcraft, May 25, 1835, Schoolcraft Papers, Reel 23.
[33] James Schoolcraft to Henry Schoolcraft, May 27, 1835, Schoolcraft Papers, Reel 23.
[34] Ebert Herring to George Johnston, March 27, 1835,

Johnston Papers, Box 8.

[35] George Johnston to E. Herring, May 27, 1835, Letterbook.

[36] William McMurray to Henry Schoolcraft, May 21, 1835, and James Schoolcraft to Henry Schoolcraft, May 21, 1825, Schoolcraft Papers, Reel 23.

[37] William McMurray to Henry Schoolcraft, August 23, 1834, Schoolcraft Papers, Reel 22.

[38] James Schoolcraft to Henry Schoolcraft, October 1, 1835, Schoolcraft Papers, Reel 23.

[39] William McMurray to George Johnston, January 20, 1836, Johnston Papers, Box 3.

[40] William McMurray to George Johnston, undated, Johnston Papers, Box 3.

[41] William Johnston to George Johnston, March 27, 1837, Johnston Papers, Box 3; William McMurray to George Johnston, February 16, 1859, Johnston Papers, Box 8.

[42] James Schoolcraft to Henry Schoolcraft, January 11, 1836, Schoolcraft Papers, Reel 24.

[43] James Schoolcraft to George Johnston, misdated January 19, 1830, Johnston Papers, Box 1.

[44] James Schoolcraft to Henry Schoolcraft, January 11, 1836, Schoolcraft Papers, Reel 24.

[45] James Schoolcraft to Henry Schoolcraft, February 16, 1836, Schoolcraft Papers, Reel 24.

[46] Henry Schoolcraft to James Schoolcraft, October 9, 1836, Schoolcraft Papers, Reel 26.

[47] Henry Kearney to Henry Schoolcraft, August 7, 1835, Schoolcraft Papers, Reel 23.

[48] William McMurray to Henry Schoolcraft, March 9, 1836, Schoolcraft Papers, Reel 24.

[49] William McMurray to Henry Schoolcraft, November 11, 1836, Schoolcraft Papers, Reel 26.

[50] William Johnston to Henry Schoolcraft, November 17, 1834, and William Johnston to Henry Schoolcraft, December 30, 1834, Schoolcraft Papers, Reel 7.

[51] William McMurray to George Johnston, July 19, 1834, Johnston Papers, Box 2.

[52] William Johnston to Henry Schoolcraft, December 30, 1834, Schoolcraft Papers, Reel 7.

[53] Statement of First Quarter 1834, Schoolcraft Papers, Reel 22.

[54] Francis Audrain to Henry Schoolcraft, May 28, 1834, Schoolcraft Papers, Reel 22.
[55] James Schoolcraft to Henry Schoolcraft, February 27, 1835, Schoolcraft Papers, Reel 23.
[56] James Schoolcraft to Henry Schoolcraft, October 18, 1835, Schoolcraft Papers, Reel 23.
[57] Henry Schoolcraft to Jane Schoolcraft, December 22, 1830, Schoolcraft Papers, Reel 20.
[58] Executor of David David's Estate to Joseph. W. Torrey, February 17, 1831, Schoolcraft Papers, Reel 20.
[59] Henry Schoolcraft to Jane Schoolcraft, December 22, 1830, Schoolcraft Papers, Reel 20.
[60] Will dated October 2, 1835, Schoolcraft Papers, Reel 7.
[61] Schoolcraft, *Memoirs*, p. 480.
[62] Ibid., pp. 512-513.
[63] Jane Schoolcraft to Henry Schoolcraft, July 5, 1835, Schoolcraft Papers, Reel 23.
[64] Jane Schoolcraft to Henry Schoolcraft, July 16, 1835, Schoolcraft Papers, Reel 23.
[65] Schoolcraft, *Memoirs*, p. 465.
[66] Ibid., pp. 524-526.
[67] Jameson, *Winter Studies*, Vol.2, p. 246.
[68] Chapman, *The Johnstons*, p. 313; Mason, *Muzzeniegun*, p. 31.
[69] Receipt dated June 14, 1831, *Schoolcraft Papers*, Reel 20.
[70] Anna Maria Schoolcraft to Jane Schoolcraft, September 30, 1835 and William McMurray to Henry Schoolcraft, October 10, 1835, Schoolcraft Papers, Reel 23.
[71] James Schoolcraft to Henry Schoolcraft, October 18, 1835, Schoolcraft Papers, Reel 23.
[72] James Schoolcraft to Henry Schoolcraft, February 27, 1835, Schoolcraft Papers, Reel 23.
[73] James Schoolcraft to Henry Schoolcraft, September 1, 1835 and James Schoolcraft to Henry Schoolcraft, October 23, 1835, Schoolcraft Papers, Reel 23.
[74] James Schoolcraft to Henry Schoolcraft, September 17, 1835, Schoolcraft Papers, Reel 23.
[75] Henry Schoolcraft to Jane Schoolcraft, December 12, 1835, Schoolcraft Papers, Reel 23.
[76] Ramsey Crooks to Henry Schoolcraft, January 19, 1836, Schoolcraft Papers, Reel 24.

[77] Lewis Cass to Henry Schoolcraft, January 30, 1836, Schoolcraft Papers, Reel 24.
[78] 24th Congress, 1st Session, House of Representatives, Document No. 47.
[79] Ibid., p. 2.
[80] Report of the Committee of Claims, misdated in another hand March 2, 1830, Schoolcraft Papers, Reel 5.
[81] William Johnston to Henry Schoolcraft, February 20, 1836, Schoolcraft Papers, Reel 7.
[82] James Schoolcraft to Henry Schoolcraft, March 9, 1836, Schoolcraft Papers, Reel 24.
[83] Schoolcraft, *Memoirs*, pp. 534-535. One hundred and thirty-six years later the United States Government decided that justice had not been done. In 1972 an additional $10.3 million was awarded to the descendents of the treaty-makers, culminating a re-evaluation of the land that the Indians had requested in 1948.
[84] Schoolcraft, *Memoirs*, p. 534.
[85] List of names of chiefs who attended treaty and text of treaty, Schoolcraft Papers, Reel 24.
[86] Henry Schoolcraft to Jane Schoolcraft, April 10, 1836, Schoolcraft Papers, Reel 24.
[87] Henry Schoolcraft to Jane Schoolcraft, March 28, 1836, Schoolcraft Papers, Reel 24.
[88] List of names of chiefs who attended treaty and text of treaty, Schoolcraft Papers, Reel 24.
[89] Henry Schoolcraft to Jane Schoolcraft, April 10, 1836, Schoolcraft Papers, Reel 24.
[90] Undated statement headed "The Chippewa Nation to Mrs. Susan Johnston," Schoolcraft Papers, Reel 25.
[91] Account of Estate of the late John Johnston, n.d., Schoolcraft Papers, Reel 67.
[92] "Claim No. 23 Estate of Jno. Johnston," Schoolcraft Papers, Reel 25.
[93] Undated memorandum beginning, "Mr. Johnston commenced trade at Lapointe . . .", Johnston Papers, Box 3.
[94] Account of Estate of the late John Johnston, Schoolcraft Papers, Reel 67.
[95] Gilman, "Last Days, " in Bolus, ed., *People and Pelts*, p. 104.
[96] Clayton, *Fur Trade*. p. 216.
[97] James Schoolcraft to Henry Schoolcraft, October 3,

1836, Schoolcraft Papers, Reel 26.
98 Ibid.
99 Henry Schoolcraft to James Schoolcraft, October 9, 1836, Schoolcraft Papers, Reel 26.
100 William McMurray to Henry Schoolcraft, November 11, 1836, Schoolcraft Papers, Reel 26.
101 James Schoolcraft to Henry Schoolcraft, October 3, 1826, Schoolcraft Papers, Reel 26.
102 Henry Schoolcraft to James Schoolcraft, November 2, 1836, Schoolcraft Papers, Reel 26.
103 Ibid.
104 James Schoolcraft to Henry Schoolcraft, November 24,1836, Schoolcraft Papers, Reel 26.

Chapter Thirteen

1 A detailed account of events leading to statehood appears in *Michigan History,* March/April 1985 and January/February,1987.
2 Henry Schoolcraft to Jane Schoolcraft, January 15, 1836, Schoolcraft Papers, Reel 24.
3 Henry Schoolcraft to Jane Schoolcraft, May 20, 1836, Schoolcraft Papers, Reel 24.
4 Henry Schoolcraft to Jane Schoolcraft, March 18, 1836, Schoolcraft Papers, Reel 24.
5 William McMurray to Henry Schoolcraft, September 8, 1835, Schoolcraft Papers, Reel 23.
6 Jane Schoolcraft to Henry Schoolcraft, November 24, 1835, Schoolcraft Papers, Reel 7.
7 Schoolcraft, *Memoirs,* p. 536.
8 Jane Schoolcraft to Henry Schoolcraft, March 15, 1836, Schoolcraft Papers, Reel 7.
9 Ibid.
10 Henry Schoolcraft to Jane Schoolcraft, April 10, 1836, Schoolcraft Papers, Reel 24.
11 Henry Schoolcraft to Jane Schoolcraft, April 24, 1836, Schoolcraft Papers, Reel 24.
12 Henry Schoolcraft to Jane Schoolcraft, November 16, 1835, Schoolcraft Papers, Reel 23.
13 Jane Schoolcraft to Henry Schoolcraft, May 10, 1836,

Schoolcraft Papers, Reel 7.
14 Schoolcraft, *Memoirs,* p. 543.
15 William McMurray to Henry Schoolcraft, January 10, 1837; February 13, 1837; March 14, 1837; Schoolcraft Papers, Reel 26.
16 William McMurray to Jane Schoolcraft, March 14, 1837, Schoolcraft Papers, Reel 26.
17 Henry Schoolcraft to George Johnston, December 8, 1836, Johnston Papers, Box 3.
18 Henry Schoolcraft to George Johnston, May 22, 1837, Johnston Papers, Box 3.
19 William McMurray to Jane Schoolcraft, March 14, 1837, Schoolcraft Papers, Reel 26.
20 George Johnston to Henry Schoolcraft, March 14, 1837, Schoolcraft Papers, Reel 26.
21 George Johnston to Henry Schoolcraft, March 14, 1837, Schoolcraft Papers, Reel 26.
22 W. A. Bacon to George Johnston, December 13, 1837, Johnston Papers, Box 3.
23 William Johnston to George Johnston, February 9, 1838, Johnston Papers, Box 3.
24 Ibid.
25 Louisa Johnston to George Johnston, December 2, 1836, Johnston Papers, Box 3.
26 William Johnston to George Johnston, March 27, 1837, Johnston Papers, Box 3.
27 William Johnston to Jane Schoolcraft, March 15, 1837, Schoolcraft Papers, Reel 26.
28 Statement of Henry Schoolcraft, April 21, 1838, Schoolcraft Papers, Reel 8.
29 Schoolcraft, *Memoirs,* p. 555.
30 William Johnston to Jane Schoolcraft, March 15, 1837, Schoolcraft Papers, Reel 26.
31 Schoolcraft, *Memoirs,* p. 586.
32 William Johnston to Henry Schoolcraft, May 25, 1837, Schoolcraft Papers, Reel 26.
33 William Johnston to Jane Schoolcraft, March 15, 1837, Schoolcraft Papers, Reel 26.
34 William Johnston to Henry Schoolcraft, May 12, 1837, Schoolcraft Papers, Reel 26.
35 "A Descendent of Waubojeeg, Genealogical Record," *Family Trails,* Vol.2, No.4, 1969-70.

[36] John Johnston Genealogy, Chart in Bayliss Public Library.
[37] James Schoolcraft to Henry Schoolcraft, April 7, 1836, Schoolcraft Papers, Reel 24.
[38] James Schoolcraft to Henry Schoolcraft, July 5, 1836, Schoolcraft Papers, Reel 25.
[39] Anne M. Schoolcraft to Jane Schoolcraft, March 14, 1837, Schoolcraft Papers, Reel 26.
[40] James Schoolcraft to Henry Schoolcraft, June 28, 1837, Schoolcraft Papers, Reel 26.
[41] John Hulbert to Henry Schoolcraft, July 3, 1837, Schoolcraft Papers, Reel 26.
[42] Anna Maria Schoolcraft to Jane Schoolcraft, July 24, 1837, Schoolcraft Papers, Reel 26.
[43] James Schoolcraft to Henry and Jane Schoolcraft, August 11, 1837, Schoolcraft Papers, Reel 27.
[44] James Schoolcraft to Henry and Jane Schoolcraft, August 11, 1837, Schoolcraft Papers, Reel 26.
[45] James Schoolcraft to Henry Schoolcraft, August 7, 1837 and August 11, 1837, Schoolcraft Papers, Reel 27.
[46] James Schoolcraft to Henry Schoolcraft, September 29, 1837, Schoolcraft Papers, Reel 27.
[47] James Schoolcraft to Henry Schoolcraft, September 29, 1837, Schoolcraft Papers, Reel 27.
[48] William McMurray to Jane Schoolcraft, undated, Schoolcraft Papers, Reel 24.
[49] William McMurray to Henry Schoolcraft, June 24, 1837, Schoolcraft Papers, Reel 26.
[50] Ibid.
[51] William McMurray to Henry Schoolcraft, June 15, 1837, Schoolcraft Papers, Reel 26.
[52] Jameson, *Winter Studies*, Vol. I, p. 240.
[53] Ibid., p. 241.
[54] Ibid., Vol. II, p. 126.
[55] Ibid., p. 160.
[56] Ibid., p. 148.
[57] Ibid., pp. 224-225.
[58] Family tradition holds that the Johnston children also addressed their mother by this name, or as Wenona, but in their letters they referred to her only as "Mama." In fact, no Indian words at all appear in their correspondence.

Notes to Pages 285-291   399

59 Jameson, *Winter Studies*, p. 228.
60 Ibid., p. 234.
61 Ibid., p. 265.
62 Anna Jameson to Jane Schoolcraft, August 20, 1837, Schoolcraft Papers, Reel 27.
63 Newton, *Sault Ste. Marie*, p. 160.
64 List of Agency Employees, September 30, 1838, Schoolcraft Papers, Reel 8.
65 William McMurray to Jane Schoolcraft, November 18, 1837, Schoolcraft Papers, Reel 27.
66 William McMurray to Jane Schoolcraft, November 10, 1837, Schoolcraft Papers, Reel 27.
67 William McMurray to Jane Schoolcraft, January 8, 1838, Schoolcraft Papers, Reel 28 and March 3, 1838, Schoolcraft Papers, Reel 29.
68 William McMurray to Jane Schoolcraft, January 31, 1838, Schoolcraft Papers, Reel 28.
69 William McMurray to Jane Schoolcraft, March 3, 1838, Schoolcraft Papers, Reel 29.
70 William McMurray to Henry Schoolcraft, January 10, 1837, Schoolcraft Papers, Reel 26.
71 William McMurray to Jane Schoolcraft, March 3, 1838, Schoolcraft Papers, Reel 29.
72 William McMurray to Jane Schoolcraft, April 27, 1838, Schoolcraft Papers, Reel 29.
73 William McMurray to Henry Schoolcraft, June 6, 1838, Schoolcraft Papers, Reel 29.
74 William McMurray to Henry Schoolcraft, July 27, 1838, Schoolcraft Papers, Reel 29.
75 Ibid.
76 William McMurray to Henry Schoolcraft, August 13, 1838, Schoolcraft Papers, Reel 29.
77 Schoolcraft, *Memoirs*, pp. 556-559.
78 Ibid., pp. 576-583.
79 Henry Schoolcraft to Commissioner of Indian Affairs, October 9, 1838, Schoolcraft Papers, Reel 8.
80 Henry Schoolcraft to Jane Schoolcraft, November 13, 1837, Schoolcraft Papers, Reel 27.
81 Jane Schoolcraft to Henry Schoolcraft, November 20, 1837, Schoolcraft Papers, Reel 27.
82 Ibid.
83 Jane Schoolcraft to George Johnston, November 18,

1837 [misdated 1839], Johnston Papers, Box 3.
84 William McMurray to Jane Schoolcraft, January 21, 1838, Schoolcraft Papers, Reel 28.
85 Henry Schoolcraft to Jane Schoolcraft, January 22, 1838, Schoolcraft Papers, Reel 28.
86 Jane Schoolcraft to Henry Schoolcraft, January 15, 1838, Schoolcraft Papers, Reel 8.
87 Ibid.
88 George Johnston to George Johnston, March 14, 1838, Johnston Papers, Box 3.
89 George Johnston to George Johnston, June 18, 1838 and June 24, 1838, Johnston Papers, Box 3.
90 Schoolcraft, *Memoirs,* p. 600.
91 Ibid., p. 619-626.
92 Ibid., pp. 631-632.
93 Jane Schoolcraft to Mrs. General Patterson, January 26, 1839, Schoolcraft Papers, Reel 8.
94 Henry Schoolcraft to Jane Schoolcraft, May 27, 1839, Schoolcraft Papers, Reel 9.
95 Jane Schoolcraft to Janee Schoolcraft, January 28, 1839, Schoolcraft Papers, Reel 29.
96 Charlotte McMurray to Jane Schoolcraft, February 28, 1839, Schoolcraft Papers, Reel 29.
97 William McMurray to Henry Schoolcraft, September 12, 1838, Schoolcraft Papers, Reel 29.
98 Charlotte McMurray to Jane Schoolcraft, February 28, 1839, Schoolcraft Papers, Reel 29.
99 William McMurray to Henry Schoolcraft, September 12, 1838, Schoolcraft Papers, Reel 29.
100 William McMurray to Henry Schoolcraft, February 25, 1839, Schoolcraft Papers, Reel 29.
101 William McMurray to Jane Schoolcraft, December 8, 1837, Schoolcraft Papers, Reel 27.
102 William McMurray to Henry Schoolcraft, February 27, 1839, Schoolcraft Papers, Reel 29.
103 Ibid.
104 William McMurray to Henry Schoolcraft, March 23, 1840, Schoolcraft Papers, Reel 30.
105 Ibid.
106 Henry Kearney to Henry Schoolcraft, September 27, 1837, Schoolcraft Papers, Reel 27.

Notes to Pages 296-300 401

107 Account of the Estate of the late John Johnston, Schoolcraft Papers, Reel 27.
108 William McMurray to George Johnston, March 23, 1840, Johnston Papers, Box 3.

Chapter Fourteen

1 Rintala, *Douglas Houghton*, pp. 23-26, 30-33.
2 Ibid., pp. 66, 71.
3 Louis Agassiz, *Lake Superior*, Boston, 1850, p. 31.
4 Schoolcraft, *Memoirs,* p. 648.
5 James Schoolcraft to George Johnston, July 6, 1839, Johnston Papers, Box 3.
6 George Johnston to Henry Schoolcraft, March 2, 1839, Schoolcraft Papers, Reel 29.
7 Department of War to George Johnston, November 23, 1837, Johnston Papers, Box 3.
8 Statement in Johnston Collection, Bayliss Public Library.
9 Bill from C. Mills, Johnston Papers, Box 3.
10 William McMurray to George Johnston, May 5, 1837, Johnston Papers, Box 3.
11 William McMurray to George Johnston, June 2, 1838, Johnston Papers, Box 3.
12 [Washington A.] Bacon to George Johnston, June 18, 1838, Johnston Papers, Box 3.
13 Bacon to Henry Schoolcraft, August 15, 1838, Schoolcraft Papers, Reel 29.
14 Bacon to George Johnston, December 16, 1838, Johnston Papers, Box 3.
15 Jane Schoolcraft to Henry Schoolcraft, July 18, 1839, Schoolcraft Papers, Reel 30.
16 Mrs. T. D. Gilbert, "Memories," p. 632.
17 James Schoolcraft to George Johnston, July 6, 1839, Johnston Papers, Box 3.
18 Agreement of July 1, 1839, Johnston Papers, Box 3.
19 John Hulbert to George Johnston, February 11, 1840, Johnston Papers, Box 3.
20 List of Agency Employees, September 30, 1838, Schoolcraft Papers, Reel 8.
21 Accounts in Schoolcraft Papers, Reel 31.

[22] Henry Schoolcraft to James Schoolcraft, October 2, 1838, Schoolcraft Papers, Reel 29.
[23] William Johnston to Henry Schoolcraft, May 25, 1837, Schoolcraft Papers Reel 26.
[24] Henry Schoolcraft to Commissioner of Indian Affairs, October 9, 1838, Schoolcraft Papers, Reel 8.
[25] James Schoolcraft to Henry Schoolcraft, March 6, 1839, Schoolcraft Papers, Reel 29.
[26] Jane Schoolcraft to Henry Schoolcraft, July 11, 1839, Schoolcraft Papers, Reel 30.
[27] Wolcott Marsh to Henry Schoolcraft, May 25, 1839, Schoolcraft Papers, Reel 29.
[28] Janee Schoolcraft to Henry Schoolcraft, December 2, 1839, Schoolcraft Papers, Reel 30.
[29] Bills from Misses Guild, July 1840 and from Wolcott Marsh, August 3, 1840, Schoolcraft Papers, Reel 9.
[30] Accounts in Schoolcraft Papers, Reel 31.
[31] James Schoolcraft to George Johnston, March 5, 1840, Johnston Papers, Box 3.
[32] William Johnston to James Schoolcraft, May 19, 1840, Schoolcraft Papers, Reel 31.
[33] Ibid.
[34] James Schoolcraft to George Johnston, May 28, 1840, Johnston Papers, Box 3.
[35] Duane Doty to Henry Schoolcraft, May 27, 1840, Schoolcraft Papers, Reel 31.
[36] James Schoolcraft to George Johnston, March 5, 1840, Johnston Papers, Box 3.
[37] James Schoolcraft to George Johnston, May 28, 1840, Johnston Papers, Box 3.
[38] Document headed "To Mrs. Jane Johnston Schoolcraft," Schoolcraft Papers, Reel 9.
[39] Lucius Lyon to President Martin Van Buren, June 3, 1840, Schoolcraft Papers, Reel 31.
[40] R.D. Turner to His Excellency, Martin Van Buren, June 8, 1840, Schoolcraft Papers, Reel 31.
[41] Henry Schoolcraft to Jane Schoolcraft, June 9, 1840, Schoolcraft Papers, Reel 31.
[42] James Schoolcraft to George Johnston, August 12, 1840, Johnston Papers, Box 3.
[43] Janee Schoolcraft to Henry Schoolcraft, April 2, 1840, Schoolcraft Papers, Reel 30.

44 Henry Schoolcraft to Jane Schoolcraft, July 6, 1840, Schoolcraft Papers, Reel 31.
45 Henry Schoolcraft to Jane Schoolcraft, July 17, 1840, Schoolcraft Papers, Reel 31.
46 Jane Schoolcraft to Henry Schoolcraft, June 17, 1840, Schoolcraft Papers, Reel 31.
47 Henry Schoolcraft to Jane Schoolcraft, July 17, 1840, Schoolcraft Papers, Reel 31.
48 Jane Schoolcraft to Henry Schoolcraft, July 2, 1840, Schoolcraft Papers, Reel 31.
49 Jane Schoolcraft to Henry Schoolcraft, July 13, 1840, Schoolcraft Papers, Reel 31.
50 Ibid.
51 Jane Schoolcraft to Henry Schoolcraft, July 2, 1840, Schoolcraft Papers, Reel 31.
52 Jane Schoolcraft to Henry Schoolcraft, June 8, 1840, Schoolcraft Papers, Reel 31.
53 Jane Schoolcraft to Henry Schoolcraft, June 27, 1840, Schoolcraft Papers, Reel 31.
54 Jane Schoolcraft to Henry Schoolcraft, June 16, 1840, Schoolcraft Papers, Reel 31.
55 William Johnston to George Johnston, June 19, 1840, Johnston Papers, Box 3.
56 Henry Schoolcraft to George Johnston, August 31, 1840, Johnston Papers, Box 3.
57 The Johnston Family.
58 John Hulbert to George Johnston, June 2, 1841, Johnston Papers, Box 4.
59 George Johnston to Sherman Hall, June 21, 1841, Johnston Papers, Box 4.
60 William McMurray to George Johnston, September 18, 1841, Johnston Papers, Box 4.
61 William McMurray to George Johnston, September 18, 1841, Johnston Papers, Box 4; William McMurray to Henry Schoolcraft, August 31, 1841, Schoolcraft Papers, Reel 32.
62 Henry Schoolcraft to Jane Schoolcraft, July 17, 1839, Schoolcraft Papers, Reel 30.
63 Charlotte McMurray to Jane Schoolcraft, November 7, 1839, Schoolcraft Papers, Reel 30.
64 William McMurray to Henry Schoolcraft, June 10,

1840, Schoolcraft Papers, Reel 31.
65 Ibid.
66 William McMurray to George Johnston, September 18, 1841, Johnston Papers, Box 4.
67 Jane Schoolcraft to Henry Schoolcraft, May 3, 1841, Schoolcraft Papers, Reel 32.
68 Schoolcraft, *Memoirs,* P. 703.
69 William McMurray to Henry Schoolcraft, August 11, 1841, Schoolcraft Papers, Reel 32.
70 William McMurray to Henry Schoolcraft, March 30, 1840, Schoolcraft Papers, Reel 30.
71 James Schoolcraft to Henry Schoolcraft June 30, 1841, Schoolcraft Papers, Reel 32.
72 James Schoolcraft to George Johnston, July 7, 1841, Johnston Papers, Box 4.
73 Jane Schoolcraft to George Johnston, June 26, 1841, Johnston Papers, Box 4.
74 Jane Schoolcraft to Henry Schoolcraft, July 1, 1841, Schoolcraft Papers, Reel 32.
75 Jane Schoolcraft to Henry Schoolcraft, July 10, 1841, Schoolcraft Papers, Reel 32.
76 Anna Maria Schoolcraft to Jane Schoolcraft, November 15, 1841, Schoolcraft Papers, Reel 32.
77 Charlotte McMurray to Jane Schoolcraft, September 1, 1841, Schoolcraft Papers, Reel 32.
78 William McMurray to Henry Schoolcraft, March 22, 1842, Schoolcraft Papers, Reel 32.
79 Henry Schoolcraft to Jane Schoolcraft, May 8, 1842, Schoolcraft Papers, Reel 32.
80 Charlotte McMurray to Jane Schoolcraft, April 4, 1842, Schoolcraft Papers, Reel 32.
81 Henry Schoolcraft to Janee Schoolcraft, June 16, 1842, Schoolcraft Papers, Reel 32.
82 Henry Schoolcraft to Jane Schoolcraft, May 8, 1842, Schoolcraft Papers, Reel 32.
83 William McMurray to Henry Schoolcraft, July 22, 1842, Schoolcraft Papers, Reel 32.
84 Henry Schoolcraft to Janee Schoolcraft, June 16, 1842, Schoolcraft Papers, Reel 32.
85 Ibid.
86 William McMurray to Henry Schoolcraft, July 22, 1842, Schoolcraft Papers, Reel 32.

[87] Handwritten copy in Schoolcraft Papers, printed in *Michigan History,* Volume 30, Number 2, April-June 1946.

Chapter Fifteen

[1] George Johnston to Robert Stuart, September 10, 1841, Johnston Papers, Box 4.
[2] Robert Stuart to George Johnston, September 9, 1841, Johnston Papers, Box 4.
[3] War Department to George Johnston, October 8, 1841, Johnston Papers, Box 4.
[4] George Johnston to Henry Schoolcraft, July 24, 1841, Schoolcraft Papers, Reel 32.
[5] George Johnston to John Hulbert, August 10, 1841, Johnston Papers, Box 4.
[6] John Hulbert to George Johnston, August 13, 1841, Johnston Papers, Box 4.
[7] William Johnston to George Johnston, September 14, 1839, Johnston Papers, Box 3.
[8] John Hulbert to Henry Schoolcraft, August 27, 1841, Schoolcraft Papers, Reel 32.
[9] John Hulbert to George Johnston, November 9, 1843, Johnston Papers, Box 4.
[10] Charles A. Stewart to Henry Schoolcraft, September 7, 1843, Schoolcraft Papers, Reel 33.
[11] James Schoolcraft to Henry Schoolcraft, October 4, 1843, Schoolcraft Papers, Reel 33.
[12] Statement of July 1, 1844, Schoolcraft Papers, Reel 67.
[13] The Johnston Family.
[14] George Johnston to sister-in-law Hannah [Rice?], n.d., Johnston Papers, Box 4.
[15] James Schoolcraft to George Johnston, December 18, 1841, Johnston Papers, Box 4.
[16] James Schoolcraft to Henry Schoolcraft, February 12, 1841, Schoolcraft Papers, Reel 32.
[17] Anna Maria Schoolcraft to Jane Schoolcraft, November 15, 1841, Schoolcraft Papers, Reel 32.
[18] James Schoolcraft to Henry Schoolcraft, February 1, 1842, Schoolcraft Papers, Reel 32.
[19] Anna Maria Schoolcraft to Jane Schoolcraft, November 15, 1841, Schoolcraft Papers, Reel 32.

[20] James Schoolcraft to Henry Schoolcraft, February 28, 1843, Schoolcraft Papers, Reel 33.
[21] James Schoolcraft to Henry Schoolcraft, April 15, 1842, Schoolcraft Papers, Reel 32.
[22] James Schoolcraft to George Johnston, August 28, 1842, Johnston Papers, Box 5.
[23] William McMurray to Henry Schoolcraft, January 6, 1843, Schoolcraft Papers, Reel 33.
[24] James Schoolcraft to Henry Schoolcraft, February 28, 1843, Schoolcraft Papers, Reel 33.
[25] Bayliss, *River of Destiny*, p. 102.
[26] Quoted in Bayliss, *River of Destiny*, p. 103.
[27] James Schoolcraft to George Johnston, March 8, 1844, Johnston Papers, Box 4.
[28] Ralph D. Williams, *The Honorable Peter White*, Cleveland, The Penton Publishing Company, 1907, p. 113. Hereafter Williams, *Peter White*; Fowle, *Sault Ste. Marie*, pp. 406-410.
[29] Williams, *Peter White*, p. 85.
[30] William McMurray to Henry Schoolcraft, January 6, 1843, Schoolcraft Papers, Reel 33.
[31] James Schoolcraft to George Johnston, November 28, 1843, Johnston Papers, Box 4; James Schoolcraft to Henry Schoolcraft, December 31, 1843, Schoolcraft Papers, Reel 33.
[32] There is some difference of opinion about the date of Susan Johnston's birth. Some sources say 1772, but in light of other evidence that is probably five years too early. Her father, Waub-o-jeeg, died in 1793 at the age of 46. That places his birth at 1747. His most famous military exploit, the battle of St. Croix River, is dated at 1770; age 23 would have been about right for him to take command there. It was known that he postponed marriage until his late twenties. As Oshaw-guscody-way-quay was the daughter of his second marriage, and he had two sons by the first, she could not have been born as early as 1772. She was said to have been 14 or 15 when she married John Johnston in 1792, a customary marriage age for Indian girls. It is unlikely, in fact, that she would still have been single if she were already 20 years old when he met her. This comparative evidence thus places her birth date at 1777 at the earliest, and her age at death at 66.

33 James Schoolcraft to George Johnston, March 8, 1844, Johnston Papers, Box 4.
34 James Schoolcraft to George Johnston, November 25, 1844, Johnston Papers, Box 4.
35 Seltzer, *Flint*.
36 William McMurray to Henry Schoolcraft, January 6, 1843, Schoolcraft Papers, Reel 33.
37 Ibid.
38 James Schoolcraft to George Johnston, November 25, 1844, Johnston Papers, Box 4.
39 James Schoolcraft to Henry Schoolcraft, October 4, 1843, Schoolcraft Papers, Reel 33.
40 Henry Schoolcraft to William McMurray, April 5, 1842, Schoolcaft Papers, Reel 32.
41 William McMurray to Henry Schoolcraft, March 22, 1842, Schoolcraft Papers, Reel 32.
42 James Schoolcraft to Henry Schoolcraft, February 28, 1843, Schoolcraft Papers, Reel 33.
43 James Schoolcraft to Henry Schoolcraft, April 15, 1842, Schoolcraft Papers, Reel 32.
44 Henry Kearney to George Johnston, April 17, 1843, Johnston Papers, Box 4.
45 William McMurray to Henry Schoolcraft, May 12, 1843, Schoolcraft Papers, Reel 33.
46 James Schoolcraft to Henry Schoolcraft, July 26, 1843, Schoolcraft Papers, Reel 33.
47 James Schoolcraft to Henry Schoolcraft, November 9, 1843, Schoolcraft Papers, Reel 33.
48 Henry Kearney to Henry Schoolcraft, April 12, 1844, Schoolcraft Papers, Reel 34.
49 William McMurray to Henry Schoolcraft, May 31, 1844, Schoolcraft Papers, Reel 34.
50 William McMurray to Henry Schoolcraft, July 3, 1844, Schoolcraft Papers, Reel 34.
51 Henry Schoolcraft to Henry Kearney, September 6, 1844, Schoolcraft Papers, Reel 34.
52 James Schoolcraft to George Johnston, November 25, 1844, Johnston Papers, Box 4.
53 James Schoolcraft to George Johnston, January 1, 1845, Johnston Papers, Box 4.
54 James Schoolcraft to George Johnston, November 25, 1844, Johnston Papers, Box 4.

[55] James Schoolcraft to George Johnston, March 8, 1844, Johnston Papers, Box 4.
[56] George Johnston to Henry Schoolcraft, August 30, 1844, Schoolcraft Papers, Reel 34.
[57] George Johnston to George Johnston, June 24, 1838, Johnston Papers, Box 3.
[58] Mrs. Thomas D. Gilbert, "Memories."
[59] George Johnston to Henry Schoolcraft, August 30, 1844, Schoolcraft Papers, Reel 34.
[60] Affidavit of Eliza Johnston, July 17, 1844 and Receipt signed by Eliza Johnston, July 18, 1844, Schoolcraft Papers, Reel 10.
[61] William Johnston to Henry Schoolcraft, August 20, 1844, Schoolcraft Papers, Reel 34.
[62] William Johnston to Henry Schoolcraft, August 20, 1844, Schoolcraft Papers, Reel 34.
[63] William Johnston to Henry Schoolcraft, March 2, 1845, Schoolcraft Papers, Reel 10.
[64] The Johnston Family.
[65] Agreements dated August 11, 1845 and August 25, 1845, Johnston Papers, Box 4.
[66] James Schoolcraft to George Johnston, July 8, 1845, Johnston Papers, Box 4.
[67] James Schoolcraft to George Johnston, October 28, 1845, Johnston Papers, Box 4.
[68] James Schoolcraft to Henry Schoolcraft, October 9, 1845, Schoolcraft Papers, Reel 11. N.B. "This," or the east side of Keweenaw (Ance) Bay never became a copper location.
[69] James Schoolcraft to George Johnston, October 28, 1845, Johnston Papers, Box 4.
[70] James Schoolcraft to George Johnston, May 27, 1846, Johnston Papers, Box 4.
[71] Andrew Talcott to George Johnston, June 22, 1846, Johnston Papers, Box 5.
[72] George Johnston to Samuel Hastings, June 19, 1846, Johnston Papers, Box 5.
[73] Letter to Lewis Cass, December 30, 1845, Letterbook, Johnston Papers.
[74] Anna Maria Schoolcraft to Henry Schoolcraft, July 27, 1846, Schoolcraft Papers, Reel 35.
[75] Williams, *Peter White*, p. 103; Gilbert, *John Tanner*, pp. 199-200.

76 Anna Maria Schoolcraft to Henry Schoolcraft, July 27, 1846, Schoolcraft Papers, Reel 35.
77 Ibid.; John Hulbert to Henry Schoolcraft, September 14, 1846, Schoolcraft Papers, Reel 35.
78 Gilbert, *John Tanner,* p. 199.
79 Ibid., p. 198; Bayliss, *River of Destiny,* p. 96.
80 R. Jones to Henry Schoolcraft, July 13, 1848, Johnston Papers, Box 5; Bayliss, *River of Destiny,* pp. 98-100.
81 Williams, *Peter White,* p. 106.
82 Gilbert, *John Tanner,* p. 201.
83 Janee Schoolcraft to Henry Schoolcraft, July 16, 1846, Schoolcraft Papers, Reel 35.
84 Anna Maria Schoolcraft to Henry Schoolcraft, July 27, 1846, Schoolcraft Papers, Reel 35.
85 John Hulbert to Henry Schoolcraft, September 14, 1846, Schoolcraft Papers, Reel 35.
86 William McMurray to Henry Schoolcraft, October 10, 1846, Schoolcraft Papers, Reel 35.
87 John Hulbert to Henry Schoolcraft, October 10, 1846, Schoolcraft Papers, Reel 35.
88 Clipping in Schoolcraft Papers, Reel 66.
89 Henry Schoolcraft to Mr. Croswell, July 13, 1846, Schoolcraft Papers, Reel 35.
90 William McMurray to Henry Schoolcraft, January 15, 1844, Schoolcraft Papers, Reel 33.
91 William McMurray to George Johnston, August 27, 1846, Johnston Papers, Box 5.
92 Ibid.
93 Henry Kearney to George Johnston, November 30, 1846, Johnston Papers, Box 5.
94 William McMurray to George Johnston, March 11, 1848, Johnston Papers, Box 5.
95 William McMurray to George Johnston, October 29, 1849, Johnston Papers, Box 6.

Chapter Sixteen

1 John Johnston Schoolcraft to George Johnston, July 3, 1842, Johnston Papers, Box 4.

[2] William McMurray to George Johnston, August 28, 1846, Johnston Papers, Box 5, September 18, 1850, Box 6; Janee Schoolcraft to Henry Schoolcraft, August 14, 1851, Schoolcraft Papers, Reel 11.
[3] William McMurray to George Johnston, December 11, 1846, Johnston Papers, Box 5.
[4] Osborn, *Schoolcraft*, p. 541.
[5] John Johnston Schoolcraft to George Johnston, November 12, 1847, Johnston Papers, Box 5.
[6] John Johnston Schoolcraft to George Johnston, April 17, 1848, May 15, 1848 and September 10, 1848, Johnston Papers, Box 5.
[7] Osborn, *Schoolcraft*, p. 541.
[8] John Johnston Schoolcraft to George Johnston, May 25, 1850, Johnston Papers, Box 6.
[9] John Johnston Schoolcraft to George Johnston, June 27, 1849 and May 25, 1850, Johnston Papers, Box 6.
[10] John Johnston Schoolcraft to George Johnston, August 10, 1849, Johnston Papers, Box 6.
[11] John Johnston Schoolcraft to George Johnston, October 12, 1849, Johnston Papers, Box 6.
[12] William McMurray to George Johnston, November 17, 1846, October 18, 1847, Johnston Papers, Box 5.
[13] Anna Maria Schoolcraft to George Johnston, June 8, 1850, Johnston Papers, Box 6.
[14] Anna Maria Schoolcraft to George Johnston, September 23, 1850, Johnston Papers, Box 6.
[15] William McMurray to George Johnston, September 18, 1850, Johnston Papers, Box 6.
[16] William McMurray to George Johnston, October 24, 1850, Johnston Papers, Box 6.
[17] Typewritten copy of obituary notice in the *Detroit Free Press*, in Johnston Collection, Bayliss Public Library.
[18] Oliver Taylor to George Johnston, September 17, 1852, Johnston Papers, Box 6.
[19] Oliver Taylor to George Johnston, August 5, 1854, Johnston Papers, Box 7.
[20] Letter to Richard R. Lansing, October 31, 1846, Letterbook.
[21] The Johnston Family.
[22] Letter to Messrs. Grant and Barton, July 1847, Letterbook.

23 L.Y. Birchard to George Johnston, April 14, 1842, December 25, 1842 and September 19, 1843, Johnston Papers, Box 4.
24 Letter to Joseph Stacy, November 2, 1846, Letterbook.
25 Letter to A. Randall, January 23, 1847, Letterbook.
26 Letter to Joseph Stacy, November 2, 1846, Letterbook.
27 Letter to Hon. George Moffatt, December 12, 1847, Letterbook.
28 Letter to Truman Smith, July 19, 1851, Letterbook.
29 Edward Clarke to George Johnston, December 19, 1847, Johnston Papers, Box 5.
30 George Johnston to Edward Clarke, August 1, 1848, Johnston Papers, Box 5.
31 Edward Clarke to George Johnston, August 3, 1848, Johnston Papers, Box 5.
32 Letter to James Fenier, August 11, 1850, Letterbook.
33 George Johnston to Truman Smith, July 29, 1851, Johnston Papers, Box 6; George Johnston to Truman Smith, January 26, 1854-April 13, 1854, Johnston Papers, Box 7.
34 Truman Smith to George Johnston, May 27, 1854, Johnston Papers, Box 7.
35 Letter to Lewis Cass, June 24, 1847, Letterbook.
36 Ramsay Crooks to George Johnston, February 19, 1849, Johnston Papers, Box 6.
37 Letter to Col. S.S. Bliss, May 10, 1849, Letterbook.
38 Henry Gilbert to George Johnston, April 6, 1854, Johnston Papers, Box 7.
39 Henry Gilbert to George Johnston, March 23, 1854, Johnston Papers, Box 7.
40 George Johnston Journal of 1854, Johnston Papers, Box 10.
41 Henry C. Gilbert to George W. Manypenny, September 8, 1855, Johnston Papers, Box 7.
42 George Johnston to George Manypenny, October 1, 1855, Letterbook.
43 Henry Gilbert to George Manypenny, September 8, 1855, Johnston Papers, Box 7.
44 Letter to Rev. Joseph Forsyth, May 31, 1857, Letterbook.
45 Letter to O'Meara, September 19, 1852, Letterbook.
46 Letter to C.B. Adams, May 24, 1855, Letterbook.

47 Letter to H.L. Stephens, October 9, 1855, Letterbook.
48 Ibid.
49 Letter to Lewis Cass, April 10, 1856, Letterbook.
50 Letter to C.B. Adams, June, 1856, Letterbook.
51 George Johnston to Dear Sister [probably Mary Johnston's sister], October 28, 1857, Johnston Papers, Box 7.
52 Ernest R. Rankin, "Lake Superior—1854,"*Inland Seas*, Winter 1963, p. 312. Hereafter Rankin, "Lake Superior."
53 Alice B. Clapp, "George Johnston, Indian Interpreter," *Michigan History*, Vol. XXIII, Autumn, 1939, p. 360.
54 Samuel Whitney to George Johnston, June 14, 1853, Johnston Papers, Box 6; December 25, 1855, May 5, 1856, Box 7, Johnston Papers; Mary Johnston to Sister, April 22, 1858, Johnston Papers, Box 6.
55 Advertisement card in Johnston Collection, Bayliss Public Library.
56 Seltzer, *Flint.*
57 Stated on a trading license for 1840 in Johnston Papers, Box 8.
58 John Johnston Schoolcraft to George Johnston, September 8, 1849, Johnston Papers, Box 6.
59 William McMurray to George Johnston, November 27, 1850, Johnston Papers, Box 6. $30 amount in Oliver Taylor to George Johnston, February 14, 1854, Johnston Papers, Box 7.
60 William McMurray to George Johnston, May 22, 1851, Johnston Papers, Box 6.
61 William McMurray to George Johnston, May 5, 1853, Johnston Papers, Box 6.
62 William McMurray to George Johnston, August 5, 1852, Johnston Papers, Box 6.
63 Anna Maria Schoolcraft to George Johnston, September 23, 1850, Johnston Papers, Box 6.
64 William McMurray to George Johnston, July 31, 1851, Johnston Papers, Box 6.
65 William McMurray to George Johnston, August 20, 1851, Johnston Papers, Box 6.
66 William McMurray to George Johnston, August 29, 1851, Johnston Papers, Box 6.
67 William McMurray to George Johnston, November 12, 1851, Johnston Papers, Box 6.

[68] Henry Schoolcraft to George Johnston, June 30, 1847, Johnston Papers, Box 5.
[69] William McMurray to George Johnston, August 27, 1846, Johnston Papers, Box 5.
[70] Decree of Court, August 23, 1848, Johnston Papers, Box 5.
[71] William McMurray to George Johnston, May 22, 1851 and July 31, 1851, Johnston Papers, Box 6.
[72] Oliver Taylor to George Johnston, October 7, 1852, Johnston Papers, Box 6.
[73] Oliver Taylor to George Johnston, February 14, 1854, Johnston Papers, Box 7.
[74] Letter to Henry Schoolcraft, July 18, 1851, Letterbook.
[75] Henry Schoolcraft to George Johnston, July 25, 1851, Johnston Papers, Box 6.
[76] Henry Schoolcraft to George Johnston, April 9, 1852, Johnston Papers, Box 6.
[77] Draft of affidavit of claim, dated September 1851, Johnston Papers, Box 7.
[78] Letter to Henry Schoolcraft, May 9, 1853, Letterbook.
[79] Samuel Whitney to George Johnston, n.d., but filed with 1855 correspondence, Johnston Papers, Box 7.
[80] George Johnston to F.A. Smith, January 25, 1858, Bingham Family Papers, Michigan Historical Collections.
[81] Bayliss, *River of Destiny*, pp. 103-105.
[82] Report of George Johnston to Charles Harvey, July 2, 1853, Johnston Papers, Box 6.
[83] Ernest H. Rankin, "Canalside Superintendent," *Inland Seas*, Summer, 1965, pp. 108-111.
[84] Bayliss, *River of Destiny*, p. 105.
[85] Rankin, "Canalside Superintendent," pp. 112-113.
[86] Chippewa County Population, typescript in Bayliss Public Library.

Epilogue

[1] Letter to Ramsay Crooks, November 14, 1858, Letterbook.
[2] The Johnston Family; Letter to Anthony Dudgen, October 9, 1858, Letterbook; Letter to Ramsay Crooks, November 14, Letterbook.

3 Statement by John E. Floyd, January 26, 1861, Johnston Papers, Box 8.
4 Letterbook, *passim.*
5 Letter to Senator Zachariah Chandler, February 5, 1859, Letterbook.
6 Clapp, "George Johnston," p. 365.
7 William McMurray to George Johnston, February 16, 1859, Johnston Papers, Box 8.
8 Letter to Lewis Cass, June 21, 1847, Letterbook.
9 John Johnston Genealogical Chart, drawn by Fred Rodiger and Charles Lawrence, September 20, 1951, in Bayliss Public Library.
10 Clapp, "George Johnston," p. 355.
11 H. Trowbridge to George Johnston, February 25, 1857, Johnston Papers, Box 7.
12 Mary Johnston to Sister, April 22, 1858, Johnston Papers, Box 6.
13 Gilbert, *Memories*, p. 632.
14 Benjamin Johnston to Dear Aunt, November 1, 1858, Johnston Papers, Box 7.
15 Osborn, *Schoolcraft*, p. 546.
16 Correspondence in Huntington Library, Pasadena, California.
17 Last Will and Testament of Henry Rowe Schoolcraft, March 8, 1850, Schoolcraft Papers in Lake Superior State University Library.
18 Osborn, *Schoolcraft*, p. 551.
19 Genealogical chart titled, "Ancestors, Descendents, and Collaterals of John Johnston and O-Shaw-Gus-Co-Day-Way-Quay," compiled by Leslie Cobb Warren and Elizabeth W. Stoutamire, 1981, in private family collection. Hereafter referred to as Family Genealogy.
20 John Johnston Schoolcraft to George Johnston, February 15, 1851, Johnston Papers, Box 6.
21 Osborn, *Schoolcraft*, pp. 547-548 and John Johnston Genealogical Chart.
22 Unidentified newspaper clipping, March 29, 1929, in Johnston Biography File, Burton Historical Collections, Detroit Public Library.
23 The Johnston Family.
24 Maclean, "An Irish Apostle," pp. 58, 63.
25 Ibid., p. 60.

26 Ibid., pp. 63, 65.
27 William McMurray to George Johnston, February 16, 1859, Johnston Papers, Box 8.
28 Family Genealogy.
29 William McMurray to George Johnston, October 22, 1856, Johnston Papers, Box 7.
30 John Johnston Genealogy; William McMurray to George Johnston, October 4, 1854, Johnston Papers, Box 7.
31 William McMurray to George Johnston, October 4, 1854, Johnston Papers, Box 7.
32 Family Genealogy.
33 Family Genealogy.
34 The Johnston Family.
35 Seltzer, *Flint.*
36 A descendent of Waub-o-jeeg.
37 Seltzer, *Flint.*
38 John Johnston Genealogical Chart.
39 Evalyn Schoolcraft to My Dear Mother, October 18, 1848, Charles Wheeler Private Collection.
40 Evalyn Schoolcraft to George Johnston, June 6, 1855, Johnston Papers, Box 7.
41 Unidentified newspaper clipping in the Charles Wheeler Private Collection.
42 Letter from Charles B. Wheeler to author, June 1, 1980.
43 George Johnston to Dear Sister [Mary's sister], October 28, 1857, Johnston Papers, Box 7.
44 William McMurray to George Johnston, October 22, 1856, Johnston Papers, Box 7.
45 Series of letters from Howard Schoolcraft to his sisters, October 2, 1859 to June 10, 1866, Charles Wheeler Private Collection.
46 E. B. Smith to Mrs. W. K. Allen, February 10, 1867, in Charles Wheeler Private Collection.
47 Unidentified newspaper obituary of Evalyn S. Allen, Charles Wheeler Private Collection.
48 Letters from Eben P. Dorr in Charles Wheeler Private Collection.
49 Typewritten burial list in Bayliss Public Library.
50 The Johnston Family.
51 John Johnston Genealogical Chart and Family Record,

handwritten document in Johnston Family Papers, Michigan Historical Collections, Bentley Historical Library.

BIBLIOGRAPHY

Primary Sources

Agassiz, Louis, Lake Superior, Boston, Gould, Kendall and Lincoln, 1850.

Askin, John, Papers, Burton Historical Collection, Detroit Public Library, also publishied by Detroit Library Commission, 1928

Bigsby, John J., The Shoe and Canoe, London, Chapman and Hall, 1850.

Bingham Family Papers, Michigan Historical Collections, Bentley Historical Library, The University of Michigan, Ann Arbor.

Cass, Lewis, Papers, Bayliss Public Library, Sault Ste. Marie.

Cox, Ross, The Columbia River, Norman, University of Oklahoma Press, 1957.

Department of Finance, War of 1812 Losses, RG 19 E5 A, Volume 3757, Public Archives of Canada.

Doty, James Duane, "Journal," Wisconsin Historical Collections, Volume 13.

Gates, Charles M., ed., Five Fur Traders of the Northwest, St. Paul, University of Minnesota Press, 1933.

Gilbert, Mrs. Angie Bingham, "The Story of John Tanner," Michigan Pioneer and Historical Collections, Volume 38.

Gilbert, Mrs. Thomas D., "Memories of the 'Soo'," Michigan Pioneer and Historical Collections, Volume 30.

Headline, Clarissa and Milton N. Gallup, "The Diary of an Early Fur Trader," Inland Seas, Winter 1962, Fall 1962, and Winter 1963.

Henry, Alexander, Travels and Adventures in Canada and the Indian Territories Between the Years 1760 and 1776, Chicago, The Lakeside Press, 1921.

Hudson's Bay Company Papers, M1, Reel 5, Public Archives of Canada.
James, Edwin, ed., A Narrative of the Captivity and Adventures of John Tanner, Minneapolis, Ross and Haines, 1956.

Jameson, Anna Brownell Murphy, Winter Studies and Summer Rambles in Canada, New York, Wiley and Putnam, 1839, Volumes 1 and 2.

Johnston Biography File, Burton Historical Collection, Detroit Public Library.

Johnston Collection, Bayliss Public Library, Sault Ste. Marie.

Johnston, George, Letterbook, Michigan Historical Collections, Bentley Historical Library, The University of Michigan.

Johnston, George, Papers, Burton Historical Collections, Detroit Public Library.

Johnston, George, "Reminiscences by George Johnston of Sault Ste. Marie, Michigan Pioneer and Historical Collections, Volume 12.

Johnston Family Papers, Michigan Historical Collections, Bentley Historical Library, The University of Michigan.

Johnston, John, Genealogy Chart drawn by Fred Rodiger and Charles Laerence, September 10, 1951, in Bayliss Public Library, Sault Ste. Marie.

Johnston, John, Memorial to Rt. Hon. The Lords Commissioners of His Majesty's Treasury, Michigan Pioneer and Historical Collections, Volume 25.

Johnston, Lewis S., Memorial of January 20, 1820 in Michigan Pioneer and Historical Collections, Volume 23.

Johnston, William, "Letters of 1833," Michigan Pioneer and Historical Collections, Volume 37.

Mackenzie, Alexander, Voyages from Montreal, Toronto, The Radisson Society of Canada, 1927.

Mason, Philip P., ed., The Literary Voyager or Muzzeniegun, East Lansing, Michigan State University Press, 1962.

Masson Collection, MG 19 C1, Public Archives of Canada.

Masson, L.R., Le Bourgeois de la Compagnie du Nord-Oest, New York, Antiquarian Press, 1960.

McElroy, Robert and Thomas Riggs, eds. The Unfortified Boundary, The Diary of Joseph Delafield, New York, Privately Printed, 1943.

Bibliography 419

McKenney, Thomas L., Sketches of a Tour to the Lakes, Minneapolis, Ross and Haines, 1959.

Minutes of the Proceedings of the Beaver Club, 1807-1827, MG 19 B3, Public Archives of Canada.

North West Company Letterbook, 1798-1802, typewritten copy, MG 19 B1, V1-3, Public Archives of Canada.

Osborn, Chase S., Papers, Lake Superior State University Library, Sault Ste. Marie.

Perrault, Jean Baptiste, "Narrative of the Travels and Adventures of a Merchant Voyageur in the Savage Territories of Northern America," Michigan Pioneer and Historical Collections, Volume 37.

Perrot, Nicolas, "Memoir," in Emma Helen Blair, The Indian Tribes of the Upper Mississippi Valley and Region of the Great Lakes, Cleveland, Arthur H. Clarke Company, 1911.

Robertson, Colin, Diary, 1814-1817, Hudson's Bay Company Papers, M-18, Reel 4, Public Archives of Canada.

Russell, Alfred, Brief in Louise Pauline de Repentigny and Others vs. The United States of America, Detroit 1864.

Schoolcraft, Henry R., "Memoir of John Johnston," Michigan Pioneer and Historical Collections, Volume 36, 1908.

Schoolcraft, Henry R., Narrative Journal of Travels Through the Northwest Regions of the United States, Albany, E. and E. Hosford, 1821.

Schoolcraft, Henry R., Papers, Lake Superior State University Library, Sault Ste. Marie.

Schoolcraft, Henry R., Papers, Library of Congress, on microfilm.

Schoolcraft, Henry R. and Mary Howard, Papers, Huntington Library, Pasadena.

Schoolcraft, Henry R., Personal Memoir of a Residence of Thirty Years with the Indian Tribes on the American Frontier, Philadelphia, Lippincott, Grambo and Company, 1851.

Sibley, Solomon, Papers, Burton Historical Collection, Detroit Public Library.

Smith, Emerson, Papers, Michigan Historical Collections, Bentley Historical Library, The University of Michigan, Ann Arbor.

Territorial Papers of the United States, Volume LI, Michigan, 1820-1829.

Thwaites, Reuben Gold, ed., The Jesuit Relations and Allied Documents, Cleveland, The Burrows Company, 1899.

Trowbridge, Charles C. Journal in Ralph H. Brown, ed., "With Cass in the Northwest in 1820," Minnesota History, Volume XXIII.

Twenty-second Congress, First Session, Report on the State of the Fur Trade, February 8, 1832, Senate Document 90.

Twenty-fourth Congress, First Session, House of Representatives, Document number 47.

"United States v. Louise Pauline de Repentigny et. al," United States Supreme Court Reports, 18 Law ed., Book 18, The Lawyers Cooperative Publishing Company, 1901.

Wallace, W. Stewart, ed., Documents Relating to the North West Company, Toronto, The Champlain Society, 1934.

War of 1812, "Copies of Papers on File in the Dominion Archives Relating to the War of 1812," Michigan Pioneer and Historical Collections, Volume 15.

Warren, Leslie Cobb and Elizabeth W. Stoutamire, Genealogical Chart titled "Ancestors, Descen-dents, and Collaterals of John Johnston and O-Shaw-Gus-Co-Day-Way-Quay," 1981, in private family collection.

Warren, Leslie, Private Collection.

Wheeler, Charles, Private Collection.

Woodbridge, William, Papers, Burton Historical Collection, Detroit Public Library.

Bald, F. Clever, Michigan in Four Centuries, New York, Harper and Row, 1961.

Bayliss, Joseph and Estelle, Historic St. Joseph Island, Cedar Rapids, The Torch Press, 1938.

Bayliss, Joseph and Estelle, River of Destiny, Detroit, Wayne University Press, 1955.

Bemis, Samuel Flagg, Jay's Treaty, New Haven, Yale University Press, 1962.

Bradish, Alvah, Memoir of Douglass Houghton, Detroit, Raynor and Taylor, 1889.

Burpee, Lawrence J., "The Beaver Club," Canadian Historical Association, Annual Report, Ottawa, 1924.

Campbell, Marjorie Wilkins, McGillivray, Lord of the North West, Toronto, Clarke Irwin and Company, 1962.

Campbell, Marjorie Wilkins, The North West Company, New York, St. Martin's Press, 1957.

Capp, Edward H., The Story of Baw-a-ting, Sault Ste. Marie, Canada, 1904.

Chapman, Charles W., "The Historical Johnston Family of the Soo," Michigan Pioneer and Historical Collections, Volume 32.

Clapp, Alice B., "George Johnston, Indian Interpreter," Michigan History, Volume 23, Autumn 1939.

Clayton, James L., "The Growth and Economic Significance of the American Fur Trade, 1790-1890," Minnesota History, Volume 40, Winter 1966.

Cook, Samuel F., Drummond Island, Lansing, R. Smith Printing Company, 1896.

Cumming, John, "A Puritan Among the Chippewas," Michigan History, Volume 51, Fall 1967.

Davidson, Gordon T., The North West Company, New York, Russell and Russell, 1918.

"A Descendent of Waubojeeg, Genealogical Record," Family Trails, Volume 2, Number 4, 1969-70.

Dictionary of National Biography, Oxford University Press, Volume 17.

Fowle, Otto, Sault Ste. Marie and Its Great Waterway, New York, G.P. Putnam's and Sons, 1925.

Gilman, Rhoda R., "Last Days of the Upper Mississippi Fur Trade," in Malvina Bolus, ed., People and Pelts, Winnipeg, Pegus Publishers, 1972.

Havighurst, Walter, ed., The Great Lakes Reader, New York, The Macmillan Company, 1966.

Havighurst, Walter, Three Flags at the Straits, Englewood Cliffs, Prentice-Hall, 1966.

Innis, Harold A., The Fur Trade in Canada, Toronto, University of Toronto Press, 1956.

Innis, Harold A., Peter Pond, Toronto, Irwin and Gordon, 1930.

Johnson, Ida Amanda, The Michigan Fur Trade, Lansing, Michigan Historical Commission, 1919.

Jury, Elsie McLeod, "U.S.S. Tigress-H.M.S. Confiance, 1813-1831," Inland Seas, Spring 1972.

Kellogg, Louise P., The French Regime in Wisconsin and the Northwest, Madison, State Historical Society of Wisconsin, 1925.

Killaly, Charlotte E.J., History of John Johnston of Sault Ste. Marie, Michigan, typescript in Johnston Collection, Bayliss Public Library, Sault Ste. Marie.

Landon, Fred, Lake Huron, Indianapolis, Bobbs Merrill, 1944.

Lavender, David, The Fist in the Wilderness, Garden City, Doubleday and Company, 1964.

Loudan, Jack, In Search of Water, Belfast, William Mullan and Son, 1940.

McKay, Douglas, The Honourable Company, Toronto, McClelland and Stuart, 1949.

Maclean, Hugh D., "An Irish Apostle and Archdeacon in Canada," Journal of the Canadian Church Historical Society, Volume XV, September 1973.

"The Quest for Statehood," Michigan History, March/April 1985-January/February 1987.

Morse, Eric W., Canoe Routes of the Voyageurs, St. Paul, Minnesota Historical Society and Toronto, The Quetico Foundation, 1962.

Neill, Edward D., History of the Ojibways, Minneapolis, Ross and Haines, 1957.

Newton, Stanley, The Story of Sault Ste. Marie and Chippewa County, Sault Ste. Marie, The Sault News Printing Company, 1923.

Nute, Grace Lee, Caesars of the Wilderness, New York, D. Appleton Century, 1943.

Nute, Grace Lee, Lake Superior, Indianapolis, Bobbs Merrill, 1944.

Nute, Grace Lee, The Voyageur, New York, D. Appleton and Company, 1931.

Osborn, Chase S. and Stellanova, Schoolcraft, Longfellow, Hiawatha, Lancaster, Pennsylvania, Jacques Cattell Press, 1942.

Rankin, Ernest R., "Canalside Superintendent," Inland Seas, Summer 1965.

Rankin, Ernest R., "Lake Superior—1854," Inland Seas, Winter 1963.

Rintala, Edsel K., Douglass Houghton, Detroit, Wayne University Press, 1954.

Sault Daily Star, The, June 18, 1970.

Seltzer, Donna J., Flint Genealogical Quarterly, April 1959, Volume 1, Number 2, typescript in Emerson Smith Papers, Michigan Historical Collections, Bentley Historical Library, The University of Michigan.

Steere, Joseph H., "A Sketch of John Tanner, Known as the 'White Indian'," Michigan Pioneer and Historical Collections, Volume 22.

Strain, R.W.M., Belfast and Its Charitable Society, 1961.

Warren, William W., History of the Ojibway Nation, Minneapolis, Ross and Haines, 1957.

Washburn, Wilcomb E., "Symbol, Utility and Aesthetics in the Indian Fur Trade," Minnesota History, Volume 40.

Williams, Ralph D., The Honorable Peter White, Cleveland, The Penton Publishing Company, 1907.

Index

A

Abbott, Samuel, 139, 302
Adams, John, 60
Adams, John Quincy, 232
Agate Harbor, 330
Agnew, John, 220
Aitken, John, 189
Albany, 10, 57
Alcoholism, 216
Algic Society, 288
Algonquin (schooner), 322
Allegheny River, 150
Allen, Lieutenant James, 213, 233, 234, 235
Allen, William Ketcham, 358
Allouez, Father Claude, 37, 56
Amable, Pierre, 165
American Fur Company, 91, 92, 118, 128, 129, 137, 142, 176, 210, 224, 249, 269, 270, 280
American Revolution, 99
Amherstberg, 173—174
Antrim County (Ireland), 2, 3, 54
Apostle Islands, 33, 53
Arctic Ocean, 65
Ariel, 106
Ashmun, Judge Samuel, 189, 332
Askin, John, Jr., 80, 97, 102
Assiniboia (modern Winnipeg), 120, 121, 122
Assiniboine River, 122
Astor, John Jacob, 91—92, 96, 118, 119, 126, 128, 131, 202, 249, 269
Athabasca (sailing vessel), 94
Audrain, Francis, 184, 206, 237, 260
Audrain, Mrs., 229
Azores, 9

B

Bacon, Washington A. (school), 279, 298—299
Baltimore (steamer), 351
Barclay, Captain Anthony, 105, 170, 171
Barthe, Jean Baptiste, 54
Bathurst, Lord (Colonial Secretary), 116, 130—131, 135
Battle of Lake Erie, 108
Battle of Seven Oaks, 123
Ba-we-ting, 33, 35
Bay Mills, 354
Beaver Club, 77, 117—118, 127
Beaver trapping, 20
Belfast, 2, 5, 65, 83
Belfast Corporation, 6
Belfast Newsletter, 6
Bell, Judge, 107
Belmont, August, 350
Bethune, Mr., 216
Black Hawk War, 234, 235
Bliss, Colonel S. S., 342
Biddle, John, 163, 164, 302
Bingham, Rev. Abel, 218, 220, 221, 226, 227, 331—332, 345
Bingham, Angie, 244, 327, 332
Birchard, L. Y., 340
Board of Claims at York, 135—136
Bois Brule River, 45
Boucher, François, 123
Boutwell, Rev. William, 231, 234, 250—251
Boyd, Colonel George, 129, 141, 197, 237
Boyd, Lieutenant, 12
Boyd, William, 225
Brady, Fort, 163, 171, 177, 192, 194, 206, 248, 323, 332, 350, 353
Brady, Colonel Hugh, 154, 177
Brant, Captain, 154
British Bible and Foreign Missionary Society, 85
British Landing, 101, 111
Brock, Major General Isaac (Lieutenant Governor of Upper Canada), 96, 97, 98, 102, 105
Brooks, John W., 350
Brown, General Jacob, 139—140

Browning, Mr., 236
Bruce Mines, 341
Brule River, 43, 69
Buffalo, New York, 76
Buffalo, Chief, 308
Buffalo - pemmican prairies, 93, 95
Burbeck, Lieutenant Henry, 63
Burgoyne, General John, 11
Bush River, 3, 54
Butler, General William O., 332
Butte des Morts, 196
Butterfield, Isaac, 210, 220

C

Cadotte, Jean Baptiste, 54, 58, 59, 60
Cadotte, Michel, Jr., 97, 102, 189
Caledonia (schooner), 98, 100, 106
Calhoun, John C., 143, 152, 153, 178, 304, 337
Cameron, Duncan, 121, 122
Campbell, James B., 329
Campbell, John (U. S. Indian Agent at Prairie du Chien), 80
Campbell, Nancy, 80, 110
Ca-mu-dwa, 43
Canada, Bishop of, 85
Canada Jurisdiction Act, 120
Carp River, 69
Cass Farm, 278, 280, 318
Cass Lake, 234
Cass, Lewis, 129, 143, 144, 145—146, 147, 148, 149, 152—153, 163, 182, 184, 189, 191, 196, 203, 206, 224, 225, 236, 252, 265, 342, 344
Champlain, Lake, 11
Chapman, Bela, 189
Charitable Society of Belfast, 6
Charleton, Captain Edward, 29—30
Chase, Alexander, 144
Chase, Salmon P., 144, 166
Chequamegon Bay, 33, 35, 37, 41, 45, 189
Chicago Cab Company, 357
Chippewa (ship), 106
Chippewa County, 206; naming of, 226
Chippewa Indians, 148, 235, 263, 266, 267, 298
Chippewa River, 40, 103, 233
Chipewyan, Fort, 74
Chocolate River, 267
Chovart, Médard, 37, 56
Churchill River, 59
Clara (ship), 1, 8, 9

Clark, William, 96
Clarke, General Sir Alfred, 14
Clarke, Edward, 341
Clarke, Captain N. S., 177
Clay, Henry, 232, 321
Clay, Robert, 233
Clinton, DeWitt, 152
Cockburn Island (originally Grand Manitoulin Island), 170
Coe, Rev. Mr. and Mrs., 197, 201
Colbert (Minister of Finance to Louis XIV), 56
Colborne, Sir John, 231
Coldwell, James, 165
Cole, H. L., 253
Coleraine (Ireland), 3
Collins, Captain, 8 ,9
Colville, Andrew, 87
Colville, Jean Wedderburn, 86
Company of Adventurers of England Trading into Hudson's Bay, 57, 87
Contemplation Island, 75
Convention of 1836, 275
Cooper, James Fennimore, 11
Copper Rock Company, 330
Cork County (Ireland), 83
Corning, Erastus, 350
Cornwall (Canada), 130, 134
Craige, estate of, 3, 83, 131—132, 135
Crawford, Hartley T., 302, 303, 304, 307
Crawford, Redford, 80, 97
Croghan, Lieutenant Colonel George, 180—109, 111, 112
Crooks, Ramsey, 128, 249, 250, 264—265, 294, 334, 342
Crosby, Ebenezer, 105
Custom of Paris, 58
Cutler, Major Enos, 177, 210; Colonel, 261

D

Dablon, Father Claude, 55, 56
Dakota Sioux, 35, 40, 41, 42, 44, 45, 46, 97
Daumont, François, 55
Davenport, Ambrose, 289
Davenport, Susan, 281
David, David, 76, 103, 115, 127, 128, 129, 135, 142, 261, 262
David, Lazarus, 76
Dearborn, Fort (Chicago), 102
Dearborn, Captain Greenleaf, 184
Dease, Frank, 80
de Bonne, Louis (Lieurde Miselle), 58, 59, 165, 348

Default, Joseph, 253
Delafield, Major Joseph, 170, 171, 172, 225
Denis, Louis (Sieur de la Ronde), 321
de Repentigny, Louis-Gaspard, 165, 166, 348
Derry, Archdeacon of, 75
Descharme, Mme., 229
Detour, 80, 197
Detour Passage, 170
Detroit, 42, 54, 76, 102, 108, 112, 144, 149, 196, 224, 233, 262, 276
Detroit (British flagship), 105, 106
Detroit, Church at, 228
Detroit River, 93
Devonshire, Marquis of, 9
Dickenson, Senator, 333
Dickson, Robert, 97
Dillon's Hotel, 77
Donnegal, Earl of, 2, 5, 6, 8
Dorchester, Lord, 7, 13, 14, 15, 16
Dorr, Eben Pearson, 359
Dorr, George H., 359
Doty, James Duane, 144, 163—164, 302
Douglas, Fort, 121, 122, 123, 223
Douglass, Captain David B., 144, 149, 152
Dousman, Michael, 100—101
Down County (Ireland), 2
Doyle, William, 164
Dromere, Bishop of, 255, 259
Drummond, Fort, 119, 157
Drummond, Governor Sir Gordon, 122, 170
Drummond Island, 119, 133, 145, 170, 173, 197, 267, 350
Dublin, 83
Durham, Captain Josiah, 98
Durham, Otis, 102

E

Eagle Harbour Company, 330
Echo Lake, 350
Edward, Fort (of lake George), 11
England, Bank of, 125
English Colonies in North America, 14
Erie, Lake, 93
Erie Islands, Lake, 106
Erie, Pennsylvania, 105, 107
Ermatinger, Charles Oakes, 123, 124, 162, 164—165, 224, 243
Ewing, Claire, 51

F

Fairbanks Company (Vermont), 350

False Detour Passage, 170
Ferry, Rev. William, 217, 227
Fletcher, Mr. (Johnston's attorney), 214, 215
Follavoine, 103
Fond du Lac, 68, 103, 184, 342
Fond du Lac, Treaty of, 263
Forsyth, Major Robert A., 144
Fox River, 149, 196, 233
Foxes, 35, 36, 44, 45, 46, 47
Franchere, Gabriel, 249
Franklin, Benjamin, 60
Frank's Hotel, 13
French-Indian War, 13
French River, 23, 28, 83, 93, 103, 108
Frobisher, Joseph, 24, 73, 77
Fur trade: operating structure, 25; outposts of, 34; restrictions of, 63; details of, 67; changes of, 118—120, 126, 137, 249; decline of, 206

G

Gale, Mr., 255
Gamble, Clarke, 283, 287—288
Garvey's, Mr. (school), 279
George, Fort (later Fort Holmes), 112
George, Lake, 171
Georgian Bay, 28, 76, 93, 103, 126
Ghent, 112
Ghent, Treaty of, 115, 139, 169
Giant's Causeway, 3
Gilbert, Henry, 342, 343
Gibralter, Fort, 121, 122
Gitchy Gansinay, 298
Glencoe, Massacre of, 2
Goose Island, 100
Gore, Lieutenant Governor Francis, 126—127, 130
Governor's Island, 1
Grand Island, 35, 44—45, 68
Grand Rapids, 280
Grand River, 267
Grand River Valley, 264
Grand Traverse Bay, 298, 299, 311, 317, 330, 341
Grant, Cuthbert, 122, 123
Gray, A. B., 329
Great Slave Lake, 74
Green Bay (La Baye), 23, 55, 149, 196, 233, 267
Greenville, Treaty of, 145
Groseilliers, Sieur des, 37
Guild's, Mrs. (school), 292, 301
Gulf Stream, 9

H

Hall, James, 2, 6
Hall, Sherman, 307—308
Hanks, Lieutenant Porter, 100, 101, 102—103
Harper (publishing), 241
Harris, L. A., 356
Harrison, William Henry, 107, 108, 310
Harvey, Charles T., 350, 351
Hasting, Samuel, 330
Head, Lieutenant-Governor Sir Francis, 283
Henry, Alexander, 59
Henry Clay (steamboat), 196
Herring, Elbert, 253
Hibernia (sloop), 10
Hill, Samuel, 10
Historical Society of Michigan, 288
Hoffman, Charles Fenno, 338, 355
Holiday, John, 104, 110, 136, 137, 140, 142, 264
Holiday, William, 194, 219
Holland, Mr., 330
Holmes (soldier), 212, 213
Holmes, Major Andrew Hunter, 109, 110, 112, 113, 114, 265
Hotley, John, 209
Houghton, Douglass, 233, 234, 236, 297
Howard, Benjamin, 355
Hudson's Bay, 56—57, 87
Hudson's Bay Company, 68, 85, 86, 87, 121, 125, 198, 205, 217, 225
Hudson River, 10
Hulbert, Edwin, 348
Hulbert, John, 194, 198, 206, 207, 211, 213, 220, 230, 238, 245, 248, 256, 264, 281, 299, 307, 318, 327, 332, 333
Hulbert, Maria, 248, 333
Hunter (British ship), 106
Huron Indians, 21
Huron, Lake, 23, 28, 29, 83, 93

I

Illinois (steamer), 351
Independence (steamboat), 322
Indians: acquiring of firearms, 21; trade with, 34, 44, 53, 57, 66, 67, 119, 167; ceremonies with, 56; relation with whites, 70; as allies, 100—101, 108, 141; treaties with, 147—148; foreign relations, 180; cessions from, 262
Indian Agency, 141—142, 177, 205, 206, 237
Inverness County (Ireland), 73
Invincible (sailing vessel), 94
Ireland, 15, 82
Iroquois, 21, 35, 37, 110
Irving, Washington, 126
Itasca, Lake, 235, 241

J

Jackson, Andrew, 205, 232, 275
James, Dr. Edwin, 202, 208, 213, 214, 220, 225, 226
Jameson, Anna Brownell (Wasa-ge-won-qua) 283, 284, 285, 286; "Winter Studies and Summer Rambles...," 294
Jameson, Robert, 326
Jay, John, 60, 63
Jay's Treaty, 63—64, 93, 99, 129
Jefferson, Thomas, 95
Jesuits (the Society of Jesus), 37
John Jacob Astor (schooner), 249
John Johnston and Company, 128
Johnson, John (Commissioner of Indian Affairs in N. America), 16, 104
Johnson, Sir William (Indian Commissioner for New York), 16, 42—43, 48
Johnston, Anna Maria (daughter) (O-mis-ka-hug-o-way), 110, 133, 178, 194, 207—208, 230, 236—237, 244—246, 248, 257—258, 259, 270, 281—282, 289, 300, 301, 306, 311, 312, 318, 320, 322, 323, 330, 333, 334, 338, 339, 347, 348, 357
Johnston, Anna Maria (John McDovall's daughter) (Miss Molly), 323, 359
Johnston, Archibald Winfield (John McDovall's son), 359
Johnston, Benjamin Saurin (George's son), 307, 344, 354—355, 358
Johnston, Charles (William's son), 357
Johnston, Charlotte (daughter) (O-gen-a bug-o-quay), 75, 110, 130, 133, 143, 171, 191—192, 197, 207, 208, 218, 227, 231—232, 242, 244, 246, 247, 258—259, 270, 282—283, 284, 286, 287, 293—295, 308—309, 313, 314, 323, 334, 338, 345, 346, 356
Johnston, Charlotte, 3; death of, 4
Johnston, Charlotte Jane (John McDovall's son), 359

Johnston, Eliza (daughter) (Wah-ba-mung-o-quay), 75, 110, 130, 133, 143, 171, 179, 191, 197, 207, 236, 241, 244, 245—246, 263, 270, 278, 327—328, 333, 334, 339, 345, 348, 356
Johnston, Eliza (Kearney) (sister), 3, 132—133, 254, 326, 335, 327
Johnston, Eliza Ann Jane (George's daughter), 340, 355
Johnston, Eliza Susan (John McDovall's daughter), 359
Johnston, Elizabeth (mother), 82
Johnston Family Historical Society, 359
Johnston, George (Kah-mem-tay-ha), 75, 81, 85, 104, 107, 109, 110, 113, 119, 127, 128, 129, 133—134, 136, 139—140, 144, 145, 147, 148, 175—176, 185, 191, 194, 197, 201, 203, 207, 208, 209, 211, 218, 226, 231, 234, 236, 237—238, 241, 243, 244, 250—251, 252, 253—257, 258—259, 264, 278, 285, 298, 299, 303, 307, 308, 317, 318, 327, 329, 330, 334, 335, 337, 338, 340—345, 348—349, 350, 351, 353—355
Johnston, George (cousin), 254, 292, 294
Johnston, George Edgerton (Williams's son), 357
Johnston, Henry William (George's son), 186, 279, 299, 307, 308, 354
Johnston, Howard Lewis (John McDovall's son), 359
Johnston, James Lawrence (John McDovall's son), 359
Johnston, James Rice (William's son), 357
Johnston, Jane (daughter) (O-bahm-we-wa-ge-she-ge-quay), 75, 82, 88—89, 111, 112, 130, 133, 143, 144—145; courtship, 157—158; wedding, 159—161, 162;167, 174, 177, 178—180, 183—184, 185, 191, 194—196, 197, 198—201, 208, 214, 215, 216, 218—219, 227, 230, 233, 235—236, 239, 241, 244, 245, 247, 250, 252, 261, 262, 270, 271, 276—277, 284, 289—292—293, 300, 301—302, 305, 306, 308, 311—312; death of, 314—316, 355

Johnston, Jane (Moore) (sister), 3, 82, 132—133, 160, 255, 261, 295—296, 325
Johnston, Jane (William's daughter), 357
Johnston, John: coming to New World, 1; great grandfather, 2; birth of, 3; schooling, 4; leaving for New World, 8; New World reunion with brother, 10; travels, 11, 12, 13, 26, 27; memoirs, 12; future plans, 13, 49; poetry of, 15; stay at Michilimackinac, 29; journey across Superior, 33; deserting of, 34; rebuilding camp, 35; arrival at La Pointe, 39; meeting of Ma-mong-e-se-da, 40; trading of, 43, 198; meeting of Perrault, 43; meeting of Waub-o-geeg, 44, 48; marriage proposal, 49; return to claim bride, 50, 51; early marriage, 52; set up house, 53; set up business, 54; settling down, 60, 61; work ethic, 65, 69; operations of, 68, 76; relations with Indians, 69, 181; medical aid to Indians, 71; building log cabin, 72; admission to Beaver Club, 77; submitting manuscript, 78; teaching his children, 81; voyage to Ireland, 82—83; job offers, 84, 88, 120; voyage back to U. S., 88—89; "An Account of Lake Superior," 78; established near Fort St. Joseph, 96; with invasion fleet, 98—100; on Mackinac, 102; to Montreal, 103, 126—127; worried about Lewis, 104—105; Civil Magistrate and Justice of the Peace, 104—105, 121, 124; at Mackinac, 110—111; return to Sault, 112—113; rebuilding, 114; letter to Lewis, 117; as Astor's agent, 118; building on Drummond, 119; talk with Selkirk, 123; to Fort William, 124; argument with McGillivray, 127; excluded from fur trade, 127—128; writes to Cass, 129; to Mackinac, 130; to Ireland, 131; sale of Craige, 132—133; help for William, 134; claim for reimbursement, 135—136; semi-retired, 137; trying to keep peace, 139—140; host to Schoolcraft, 154; dinner party, 156—157; Jane's wedding, 162; reaffirming

own vows, 162; land grant, 163—165; continued trade, 167; relation with Schoolcraft, 172—173; relation with sons, 175—176; relation with grandchildren, 177; McKenney's description, 191; relation with McKenney, 192; rheumatism, 194; losing grandson, 195; business affairs, 201—202; death of, 202; burial, 203; estate and will, 206, 210, 227, 265, 269—272, 298, 353
Johnston, John McDouall (son) (Wau-be-guon), 126, 133, 179, 208, 232, 237, 244, 260, 270, 278, 323, 334, 343, 345, 348, 359
Johnston, John McDouall Jr. (John McDouall's son), 359
Johnston, Justine Picquette (John McDouall's wife), 323, 359
Johnston, Lewis Saurin (son), 75, 81, 85, 104—105, 107—108, 117, 119, 133—134, 173—174, 288
Johnston, Louis Saurin (William's son), 357
Johnston, Louisa Maria (George's daughter), 176, 208, 258, 259, 279, 299, 308, 311, 338, 354
Johnston, Louisa Raymond (Way-se-ge-mon-aqua) (George's first wife), 176, 188, 231, 298
Johnston, Margaret Angelic (George's granddaughter), 354
Johnston, Maria (Williams daughter), 357
Johnston, Marian Louisa (William's daughter), 357
Johnston, Mary Louisa (George's granddaughter), 354
Johnston, Mary Rice (George's second wife), 299, 319, 344—345, 353, 354
Johnston, Nancy (aunt), 3, 4, 7, 254, 259, 296
Johnston, Samuel Abbot (George's son), 329, 355
Johnston, Susan (William's wife), 357
Johnston, William (son) (Mien-gum), 104, 110, 130, 134—135, 194, 207, 209, 210, 211, 229—230, 238, 240, 244, 259, 266—267, 270, 271, 276, 278, 280, 281, 287, 289, 300, 302, 303, 304, 318, 328—329, 334, 345, 357
Johnston, William: grandfather, 2, 5; father, 3; brother, 3, 7; meeting with and death of, 10
Johnston, William, Jr (William's son), 357
Johnston, William Meddaugh (John McDovall's son), 359
Jonquiere, Marquis de la, 57
Joques, Father Isaac, 54
Joy, James, 350

K

Kaministiquia, Fort (see Fort William), 95, 96
Kaministiquia River (River of Difficult Entrance), 23, 94, 95, 124, 172
Kearney, Henry, 83, 130, 132—133, 254, 255, 256, 259, 295, 324, 325, 334, 335
Kearsley, Jonathan, 163, 164
Keweenaw Peninsula, 297
Kilgobbin, 132
Killary, Hamilton Hartley, 357
Kingsbury, Major Julius, 332
Kingsbury, Captain James W., 333
Kingston, 93

L

Labadie, Monsieur, 13
Lac Cedar Rouge (renamed Cass Lake), 149
Lac Court Oreille, 103, 189
Lac du Flambeau, 103, 184, 185, 189
Lac la Pluie, 66, 94, 95, 120
Lachine, 19, 25, 76, 93
Laird, Reverend R. M., 162
Langlade, Charles, 42
Langlade, Charles, Jr., 97, 102
L'Anse Keweenaw, 35, 44—45, 68, 103, 104, 110, 342
Lansing, Richard R., 330
La Pointe Island (Madeline), 33, 35, 45, 48, 53, 68, 103, 186, 188, 189, 208, 234, 235, 249, 253, 342, 354
La Pointe du Saint Esprit, 37, 38
Lapraire, 12
L' Arbre Croche, 104, 222
Laughing Whitefish River, 69
La Vase River, 28
Lawrence (American Flagship), 106, 107
Leathes, house of (of Bury St. Edmonds, Suffolk), 2
Le Blanc, Francois, 23
Le Bourgeois, de la Compagnie du Nord-Oest (L. R. Masson), 78

Le Clair (Johnston's chief canoeman), 140—141
Leech Lake, 239
Le Gardeur, Louis (Sieur de Repentigny), 42, 57, 58, 59
Le Grand Portage, 23, 24, 65, 66, 68, 73, 93, 94, 95, 96
Lewis' Hotel, 10
Lewis, Meriweather, 96
Lindsay, Reverend, 9
Lindsay, Mrs., 9—10
London, 85
Liverpool, Lord, 8
Louis XIV, King of France, 55, 56, 58, 59
Louisiana Purchase, 95
Lycrum, 288

M

MacDonnell, Miles, 120, 121
Mackay, Aeneas, 144
Mackenzie, Alexander, 74, 86, 127
Mackenzie River, 74
Mackinac, Fort, 63, 64, 94, 99, 100, 108, 110, 112, 114, 117, 118, 128, 130, 157, 170, 224
Mackinac, Straits of, 29, 38
Mackinac Island, 31, 63, 68, 76, 79, 91, 96, 103, 110, 129, 130, 141, 143, 149, 164, 196, 197, 213, 214, 217, 235, 240, 249, 262, 268, 276, 280, 284, 299, 311, 329, 349
"Mackinaw coat," 97
Mackintosh (Hudson Bay Co. trader), 184
Macomb, General Alexander, 140—141, 178
Madeline Island, 35
Maddock, Mr., 326, 334
Madison, James, 91
Maitland, Sir Peregrine, 135
Ma-mong-e-se-da, 40, 41, 42, 43, 48, 52
Manitoba, 66
Manitoulin Islands, 28, 119, 170, 285, 298
Marquette, Father Jacques, 37—38
Marsh, Wolcott (school), 301
Mason, Stevens T., 288, 297
Mattawa River, 28
Mauvais River, 189
McBean (Hudson Bay Co. trader), 184
McCartney, George, 2, 7, 8
McDouall, John, 194

McDouall, Lieutenant-Colonel Robert, 111, 112, 114, 117, 130
McGill, James, 23
McGillivray, Duncan, 78, 86
McGillivray, Simon, 225
McGillivray, William, 65, 74, 87, 92, 95, 118, 121, 123, 124, 126—127, 225
McLoughlin, Dr. John, 223, 224
McKenney, Thomas L., 184—185, 186, 189, 191—192, 196, 220, 221
McKenney, William, 286
McCoskry, Bishop Samuel A., 287
McKenzie, Kenneth, 124
McKenzie, Roderick (Rory), 74, 77, 78, 95
McLean, General John, 210
McLoughlin, John, 83, 124
McMurray, Amilia Baxter (William's second wife), 356
McMurray, Charlotte Elizabeth Jane (Charlotte's daughter), 334, 357
McMurray, Elizabeth Hamilton (Charlotte's daughter-in-law), 357
McMurray, James Saurin (Charlotte's son), 309, 357
McMurray, John Henry (Charlotte's son), 287, 294, 357
McMurray, Elizabeth Wittaker (Charlotte's daughter-in-law), 357
McMurray, Juanita (Charlotte's granddaughter), 357
McMurray, William, 231, 242—244, 247, 257, 258, 271, 278, 282—283, 286, 287, 288, 291, 294—295, 296, 298, 308, 309, 310, 318, 323, 324, 325—326, 327, 334, 335, 338, 343, 345, 346, 347, 348, 356
McMurray, William Strachan (Charlotte's son), 258, 294, 346, 356
McNaughton, Edmund, 5, 85
McNaughton, Francis, 5
McNeil, John, 131—132, 259, 295, 325
McNight, Sheldon, 322
McTavish, Frobisher (company) (later: McTavish, McGillivrays), 74, 92
McTavish, Simon, 24, 73, 74, 86, 87, 92
McNeil, Elizabeth (Johnston), 3, 4
Me-da-we (the sacred medicine), 36
Ménard, Father René, 37

Merrill, Mr. and Mrs., 240
Merryweather, Algernon, 342
Métis (half-breed), 120, 122, 123, 223
Menominee Indians, 97
Mexican War, 332
Michigan Territory, 143
Michigan, Lake, 23, 24
Michigan, Bank of, 261
Michigan Central Railroad, 350
Michigan Steamboat Company, 261
Michilimackinac, 13, 23, 29, 53, 54, 57, 64, 79, 97, 109; county of, 205; 249
Michilimackinac Company, 24, 92
Mink (schooner), 109
Mis-kwa-bun-o-kwa (Red Sky of the Morning), 223
Mississagi Strait, 170
Mississippi River, 23, 24, 44, 91, 149, 234—235
Missouri River, 96
Mitchell, Dr. David, 119, 136
Mitchell, William, 209, 238
Mills, C., 209—210, 238
Mon-ing-win-a-kaun-ing (place of the golden-breasted woodpecker), 35
Montcalm, Marquis de, 42
Montreal, 12, 15, 20, 23, 51, 64, 73, 81, 83, 85, 93, 103, 108, 114—115, 121, 137
Montreal, Bank of, 76, 129
Montreal Board of Trade, 76
Montreal Mining Company, 341
Montreal River, 69
Moore, John, 82, 83
Morgan, Youngs, 142
Munro, Doctor, 104
Murray, Governor General James, 59

N

Nancy (schooner), 103, 117, 136
Nattawasaga River, 93, 117, 135
Neebish Rapids, 350
Net-no-kwa, 222
New York Bay, 1
New York Express, 333—334
Niagara (ship), 106
Niagara, Fort, 42
Niagara portage, 93
Nicolas, Father Louis, 55
Nipigon River, 23
Nipissing, Lake, 28
Noble, Authur, 165
Nolin, Jean Baptiste, 54, 139, 163, 164—165

Non-Importation Act, 92
North Channel, 29, 108
North River, 1
North Dakota, 66
North West Company, 24, 25, 54, 65, 66, 67, 68, 73—74, 76, 85, 86, 87, 88, 91, 92, 93, 95, 96, 103, 108—109, 110, 118, 120, 122, 123, 125—126, 156, 172, 198, 205, 225, 231, 265
Northwest Ordinance of 1787, 275

O

Oakes, Charles, 189
Ohio River, 60
Ojibway Indians, 21, 23, 29, 33, 35, 36, 37, 40, 41, 42, 44, 45, 46, 47, 48, 50, 68, 97, 148, 193, 231, 235
Ojibway Nation, history of the, 135
O'Meara, Reverend, 298, 343
Onontio, 23, 42
Ontario, 120
Ontario, Lake, 93, 120
Ontonagon River, 36, 69, 148, 234
Ontonagan Rock, 148, 155, 185
Orange, Fort, 57
Ord, James, 286, 289
Oshaw-guscody-way-quay (Susan): Johnston's meeting of and marriage proposal, 49; 51; naming as Susan, 52; set up house, 53; relations with others, 71; as hostess, 73; authority, 104, 115; to Lake Superior, 110; hostess, 145; trying to keep peace, 147; reaffirmed vows, 162; sugar camp, 171; McKenney's description, 191; articles, 193; caring for Jane, 197; care for John, 201, 202; grieving of, 206; carrying on business, 207; care-taker, 208; 229; building church, 231; 233, 244, 245—246, 248, 255, 258, 261, 263, 264, 266, 268, 270, 271, 276, 278, 285, 287, 293, 298, 311, 315, 318, 322, 327, 346, 347, 348, 353
O'Sullivan's Coffee House, 12
Oswego, 57
Ottawa Indians, 21, 23, 29, 97, 235, 263, 267, 298
Ottawa River, 23, 28, 83, 93, 103, 108
Otter (sailing vessel), 94

P

Panic of 1837, 269, 318
Paris, Treaty of, 24, 59, 60, 63, 94, 115, 118, 165, 169, 172, 235
Parkins', Mr. (school in Chambly), 134
Parsons', Mr. and Mrs. (school), 313
Parsons, Usher, 107
Paul, James, 329
Peel, Robert, 135
Pembina, Fort, 122, 223
Pemmican (preserved buffalo meat), 66, 121, 122
Penetanguishene, 173, 256
Perrault, Jean Baptiste, 43, 211
Perrot, Nicholas, 55
Perry, Oliver Hazard, 105, 106—107, 108
Philadelphia, 60
Philipeaux, Ile, 94, 172
Picquette, Jeanette, 231
Pictured Rocks, 148
Pierce, Captain Benjamin K., 130
Pigeon River, 41, 95, 94, 172
Pitcher, Dr. Zina, 184, 202, 208—209, 282, 291, 331
Plains of Abraham, 14, 42
Point Iroquois, 233
Pointe aux Pins, 94, 140
Pontiac (Ottowa Chieftan), 42
Porcupine (ship), 106
Port Rush, Ireland (surveyor of), 3
Porter, Reverend Dr. Jeremiah, 230, 251, 281
Pothier, Toussaint, 96, 97, 265
Prairie du Chien, 149, 180, 182, 197, 233
Prairie du Chien, Treaty of, 185
Prevost, H. M. S. Lady, 104, 106
Prevost, Sir George, 104—105, 115, 117, 130
Prince Edward Island, 86
Proctor, Major General Henry, 105, 106
Put-in-Bay, 106, 107

Q

Quebec, 13, 58, 85, 120
Queen Charlotte (ship), 106

R

Radisson, Pierre, 37, 56
Rainy Lake, 225
Raymbault, Father Charles, 54
Red Jacket (American schooner), 170
Red River, 66, 87, 120, 122, 223

Riley, William, 146
Riverside Cemetery, 323
Roberts, Captain Charles, 96—97, 98, 100—101, 102, 111
Robertson, Colin, 121
Rocky Mountains, 65
Root, Lieutenant, 321
Round Hall School, 292
Royal Isle, 94
Rupert's Land, 87, 121
Rush-Bagot Agreement, 171

S

Sadlers, Water Street home of, 10
St. Anthony's Falls, 234
St. Clair, Lake, 93
St. Croix Falls, Battle of, 44
St. Croix River, 40, 45, 235
St. Ignace, 38
St. Jean, Quebec (Richelieu River), 12
St. John's Churchyard, 314
St. Joseph Channel, 350
St. Joseph, Fort, 63, 79, 80, 97—98, 170
St. Joseph Island, 63, 96, 100, 108—109, 116, 119, 136, 170, 265, 350
St. Joseph River, 135
St. Lawrence River, 12, 20, 21, 22, 37, 55, 93, 120, 169
St. Louis River, 94, 149, 172, 234
St. Lusson, Sieur de, 55, 56, 58
St. Martin's Bay, 101
St. Mary's Canal, 321
St. Mary's Falls, 33, 54, 72, 87
St. Mary's Falls Ship Canal Company, 350
St. Mary's River, 23, 29, 33, 53; trade route, 63, 93; canal, 93; portage of, 113, 148, 205; 335
St. Peter's, 235
Ste. Anne Church (Mackinac Island), 25
Ste. Marie du Sault, Mission of, 57
Sandwich (modern Windsor), 130, 175
Santo Domingo, 10
Saratoga, 11
Saskatchewan River, 59, 66
Sassaba, 146, 147, 154
Sault de Ste. Marie, le, 33, 35, 44, 53, 54, 55, 59, 64, 65, 68, 75, 76, 79, 93—94, 96, 103, 107, 109, 112, 114, 129, 136, 137, 139, 143, 145, 150, 153, 163, 164,

165, 170, 171, 184, 191, 194, 203, 205, 206, 210, 227, 249, 276, 285, 297, 340, 349, 351, 353, 359
Sault Canal: plan for, 321—323; 348, 349—351, 353
Sault Ste. Marie, Treaty of, 147
Saulteur Indians, 54
Saurin, William (cousin), 83—84, 85, 131, 325
Saurin, William (uncle) (Vicar of Belfast), 75
Sauvanne Portage, 149
Sayer, John, 54
Schoolcraft, Abraham, 211
Schoolcraft, Helen Maria Evalyn (Anna Maria's daughter), 300, 323, 339, 357, 358, 359
Schoolcraft, Henry Rowe: 144, 148, 149; family, early life and education, 150; travels on Ohio and Mississippi Rivers, 151; "A View of the Lead Mines of Missouri," 151; visit with James Monroe, 151; "Narrative Journal of Travels....," 152; travels in Miami, Wabash and Illinois River valleys, 153; correspondence with Adams, Jefferson and Madison, 153; appointment as Indian Agent, 153; new house, 155; learning about Indians, 155—156; courtship of Jane, 157; 159—161; wedding, 162, 167; Justice of Peace, 163—164; relation with Johnston, 172—173; 174, 177—178; "Travels in the...Mississippi Valley," 178; 179—180; study of Indians, 181; 182—189; "Mussiniegum," 192—194; 196—197, 198—201; Chief Justice, 206; 208, 210—217, 218, 219—221, 225—226, 227—230, 232—233, 234, 235—236, 237, 238, 240—241, 247, 250—251, 252, 255, 256, 257, 259, 260, 261, 262, 263, 264, 267, 268, 270; fight with James, 272; 275, 276, 277—278, 280, 287, 288—289, 291, 292—293, 298, 299, 300, 301—306, 308, 309—310, 314—315, 317, 318, 324, 328, 329, 332, 333—334, 338, 347, 348, 355
Schoolcraft, Howard (Anna Maria's son), 320, 339, 358—359

Schoolcraft, James Lawrence (Henry's brother), 180, 198, 206, 209, 211—216, 229, 230, 232, 234, 236, 238, 244—248, 257, 258, 260, 264, 270—271, 273, 281—282, 289, 298, 300, 301, 306, 311, 318, 319, 320, 321, 322, 323—324, 326, 327, 328, 329—330, 331
Schoolcraft, Jane Susan Anne (Jane's daughter), 198, 208, 218, 230, 238, 240, 262, 278, 292, 293, 301, 304, 311, 337, 338, 355
Schoolcraft, John Johnston (Jane's son), 208, 218, 240, 262, 270, 278, 292, 301, 304, 311, 337, 338, 355
Schoolcraft, Maria Eliza (Henry's sister), 180, 198
Schoolcraft, Mary Howard (Henry's second wife), 337, 338, 355
Schoolcraft, Minnie (Anna Marie's daughter), 333, 339, 357, 359
Schoolcraft, William Henry (Jane's son), 176—177, 178, 194
Scorpion (ship), 106, 112
Scott, General Winfield, 196
Second Seminole War, 298
Selkirk, Thomas Douglas Earl of, 86—87, 88, 95, 120, 121—122, 123—124, 125, 223
Semple, Robert, 121, 122, 123
Shearman, Francis (Henry's nephew), 289
Shingabawossin (Image Stone) (known as The Orator), 147, 154, 155, 184—185
Sibley, Henry, 207
Sibley, Judge Solomon, 207, 214, 215
Sillery, Battle of, 59, 165
Simcoe, Lake, 93
Sinclair, Captain Arthur, 108—109, 114, 265, 266
Sivereight, Mr., 156
Slacke, Agnes, 165
Smith, Truman (senator), 341
Smith & Driggs (company), 321
Somers (ship), 106
Sophy (Schoolcraft's maid), 219—221
South West Company, 92, 96, 97, 118
Spenser, Sheriff, 121
Strachan, Archdeacon John, 231, 282

Stuart, (Judge), 213
Stuart, Robert, 5
Stuart, Robert (American Fur Co.), 187, 210, 214, 217, 230, 311, 317
Stuart, Mrs. (Robert), 241
Stewart, Adam, 130, 140, 141
Sugar Island, 111, 113, 170, 171, 172, 263
Superior, Lake, 33, 51, 79, 94, 118, 140, 234, 249, 298
Superior (steamer), 153

T
Talcott, Andrew, 329, 330
Talon (Intendent of New France), 56
Tanner, Edward, 223, 224
Tanner, John, 222, 223—226, 331, 332, 333
Tanner, Martha, 226, 332
Taylor, Oliver, 338, 339, 348, 358
Taylor's, Mr. (school in Lowville), 208, 237
Tchehachoff, Captain, 251
Tehquamenon River, 69
Thessalon River, 341
Thunder Bay, 95, 124, 267
Ticonderoga, 11
Ticonderoga, Fort, 99
Tigris (ship) (later Confidance), 106, 112, 170
Tilden, Lieutenant Bryant P., 332, 333
Tilden, Mrs. Bryant P., 333
Todd, Andrew, 13, 15, 16, 27, 31
Todd, Issac, 13, 23
Todd, McGill (company), 13, 19, 24, 31, 43, 51, 76
Toledo War, 275
Torrey, Joseph, 261
Treaty of 1820, 154, 163
Treaty of 1836, 268, 270, 280, 298, 318, 329
Trinity Church, 10
Tripp (ship), 106
Trois Rivieres, 22, 37, 56, 58
Trowbridge, Charles C., 144, 145, 344—345, 355
Two Hearted River, 69
Turner, R. D., 303

U
Ulster, 53
United States Bank, 232

V
Van Buren, Martin, 232, 303
Varennes, 17
Vermillion, Lake, 142

W
Wabasha, 41, 44
Waishkey (The First Born), 110, 112, 155, 267, 285, 287; death of, 322
War of 1812, 99, 105, 142, 164, 169, 268
Warren, Lyman, 189
Washington, George, 10
Watson, Brook, 8
Waub-o-jeeg (White Fisher), 41, 43, 44, 45, 46, 47, 48, 49, 51, 52, 79, 316, 344
Wawashkamo Golf Course, 111
Wayne, Fort, 102
Webster-Ashburton Treaty, 171, 172
Weeks, Aaron, 321
Westcott, Lieutenant George Clinton, 333
Wessiment, James, 162
Wexford County (Ireland), 82, 83
Wheaton, Doctor Walter V., 154
White Crow, Chief, 308
White Park, Reverend Robert Sturrock's Adademy of, 4
Whiting, J. T., 322
Whitefish Bay, 125, 126
Whitney, Samuel, 344, 349
Wilkins, Fort, 340
Wilkins, Judge Ross, 166
William, Fort, 95, 96, 108, 123, 124, 125, 126, 140, 172, 224
Wilmont, 135
Winnebago Indians, 97
Winnipeg, Lake, 23, 87, 121, 122
Wisconsin River, 149
Wolf's Army, 76
Wolfe, General, 42
Wolcott, Dr. Alexander, Jr., 144
Woodbridge, William, 163, 164
Woods, Lake of the, 94, 169, 172, 225
Woodworth's Steamboat Hotel, 332
Woolsey, Melancthon, 233

Y
Yonge Street portage, 93
York (modern Toronto), 76, 93, 126, 177
York Factory, 121

F
Marjorie Cahn Brazer
Harps Upon the Willows

DATE DUE	BORROWER'S NAME

HARPS UPON THE WILLOWS

M. C. BRAZER